Praise for bestselling author Alisa Valdes-Rodriguez and

THE DIRTY GIRLS SOCIAL CLUB

"The feel of a night out with the girls . . . charming . . . undeniably fun."

—*Miami Herald*

"A compulsive beach read . . . smart, brassy, and messy enough to make you pause mid-sunscreen-slathering."

—*Entertainment Weekly*

"This lively debut novel . . . reads like the Hispanic version of *Waiting to Exhale*."

—*New York*

"Laugh-out-loud read . . . with no-holds-barred humor."

—*Dallas Morning News*

"As a guilty pleasure it ranks somewhere between Valrhona chocolate and Jimmy Choo shoes—I simply could not put it down."

—Whitney Otto, bestselling author of *How to Make an American Quilt*

"Wonderful writing, delicious humor, biting sarcasm, and impressive intelligence."

—*Detroit Free Press*

"Alisa Valdes-Rodriguez's writing style is raunchy yet refined . . . but in the end, it's the complex, finely drawn characters who make the book work."

—*Rocky Mountain News*

"Funny, touching, and exhilarating. A winner!"

—Jennifer Crusie, bestselling author of *Bet Me*

MORE . . .

MAKE HIM LOOK GOOD

"Valdes-Rodriguez delivers the raunchy packed-with-attitude tale that her fans expect."

—Booklist

"As Helen Fielding fashioned chick lit with *Bridget Jones's Diary*, Valdes-Rodriguez does the same with chica lit."

—New York Daily News

"Real fun."

—Entertainment Weekly

"A good time between hardcovers."

—New York Daily News

"Skillfully and lovingly illustrates the diversity of Latino culture."

—Library Journal

"Our refreshingly imperfect and insecure heroine, Milan, shines."

—Publishers Weekly

"Entertaining . . . crowd-pleaser."

—Kirkus Reviews

"Start reading it, and it's hard to stop."

—The Ohio Record Courier

"An unabashed glitzfest."

—Arizona Republic

"Scandalous . . . [with] blatant sex appeal."

—The Sunday Oklahoman

"Top-notch look at human nature at its best—and worst."

—Romantic Times

"Valdes-Rodriguez really shines."

—Sunday Journal (Albuquerque, NM)

"Pure escapist fun."

—*Calgary Herald*

"An entertaining and vivid romp."

—*Gazette* (Montreal, Quebec, Canada)

"Through its colorful narrators, *Make Him Look Good* looks at what lies underneath Miami's beautiful shell."

—*Boston Globe*

PLAYING WITH BOYS

"A funny, guilty pleasure of a novel."

—*Publishers Weekly*

"As Marcella, Alexis, and Olivia grapple with men and their careers, they really don't seem all that different from Bridget Jones herself."

—*Miami Herald*

"Valdes-Rodriguez brings savvy, and sometimes savage humor, to chick lit."

—*New York Daily News*

"Once again, without resorting to didacticism, her novel becomes a subtle vehicle for demonstrating the rich diversity of Latina culture."

—*Library Journal*

"The three amigas—a television actress, a single mother, and a manager of musicians—each has her own distinct lifestyle, quirks, and notions of romance, yet each manages to help her friends find balance, along with loads of good times."

—*Sacramento Bee*

"Entertaining."   —*Entertainment Weekly*

"Humor abounds in Valdes-Rodriguez's new novel…women of all ethnicities will identify with the real-life trials of this novel's three friends."

—*Romantic Times*

The Dirty Girls Social Club

Alisa Valdes-Rodriguez

St. Martin's Paperbacks

THE DIRTY GIRLS SOCIAL CLUB

Copyright © 2003 by Alisa Valdes-Rodriguez.
Excerpt from *Dirty Girls on Top* copyright © 2008 by Alisa Valdes-Rodriguez.

All rights reserved. No part of this book may be used or reproduced in any manner whatsoever without written permission except in the case of brief quotations embodied in critical articles or reviews. For information address St. Martin's Press, 175 Fifth Avenue, New York, NY 10010.

Library of Congress Catalog Card Number: 2003041355

ISBN: 0-312-98924-5
EAN: 978-0-312-98924-8

Printed in the United States of America

St. Martin's Griffin trade paperback edition / May 2004
St. Martin's Paperbacks edition / March 2008

St. Martin's Paperbacks are published by St. Martin's Press, 175 Fifth Avenue, New York, NY 10010.

10 9 8 7 6 5 4 3 2 1

For Jeanette Beltran, the original sucia,
in memory of her mother, Aurea Beltran

acknowledgments

Thanks to Alexander Patrick Rodriguez, human angel, living muse, peanut butter honey boy, for guiding Mommy to where she needed to be and reminding her that a life without giggles and geeps is a life without meaning; to Patrick Jason Rodriguez for making me get off my butt and write, for changing diapers while I typed, for believing in my vision and ability far beyond the point at which most rational people would have caught the next bus out of town; to Nelson P. Valdes for filling my childhood home with books and ideas, for listening to my writing since I was nine years old and always responding, no matter how rudimentary the letters, with a serious, approving nod and heartfelt words of encouragement; to Leslie Daniels for believing in my voice, for agenting waaaay beyond the call of duty, for doubling as editor and psychologist, and for fighting with a dancer's grace and actor's guts to have the dirty girls heard loud and clear—all the while climbing into a reinforced crib to nurse the wee one; to Elizabeth Beier, the third in our lactating power trio, for embracing this book with a cheerleader's enthusiasm and a philosopher's edit; and to all of the wonderful, energetic souls at St. Martin's Press who had faith in an unknown.

lauren

TWICE A YEAR, every year, the *sucias* show up. Me, Elizabeth, Sara, Rebecca, Usnavys, and Amber. We can be anywhere in the world—and, being *sucias*, we travel a lot—but we get on a plane, train, whatever, and get back to Boston for a night of food, drink (my specialty), *chisme y charla*. (That's gossip and chat, y'all.)

We've done this for six years, ever since we graduated from Boston University and promised each other to meet twice a year, every year, for the *rest of our lives*. Yeah, it's a big commitment. But you know how melodramatic college girls can get. And, hey, so far we've *done* it, you know? *So* far, most of us have not missed a single meeting of the *Buena Sucia Social Club*. And that, my friends, is because we *sucias* are responsible and committed, which is way more than I can say for most of the men I've known and Ed the bigheaded Texican in particular.

I'll get to *that* in a minute.

I'm here waiting for them now, slouched in an orange plastic window booth seat at El Caballito restaurant, a Jamaica Plain dive that serves Puerto Rican food but calls it "Cuban" in hopes of attracting a more upscale clientele. It hasn't worked. The only other customers tonight are three young *tigres* with fade haircuts, baggy jeans, plaid Hilfiger shirts, gold hoops flashing on their earlobes. They speak slangy Spanish and keep checking their beepers. I try not to stare, but they catch my eyes a couple of times. I look away, examine my newly French-manicured acrylic nail tips. My hands fascinate me because they look so feminine and *together*. With one finger I trace the outline of a cartoon map of Cuba printed on the paper placemat. I linger briefly on the dot representing Havana, try to picture my dad as a schoolboy with shorts and a tiny gold watch, looking north across the sea to his future.

When I finally look up, one of the young men stares me down. What's his problem? Doesn't he know how gross I am? I turn my eyes toward the cars inching through the snow on Centre Street. The flakes twinkle in the yellow glow of headlights. Another dreary Boston evening. I hate November. Got dark at about four this afternoon, been spitting ice ever since. As if the wood paneling on the walls and the old buzzing refrigerator in the corner of the small restaurant weren't depressing enough, my sighing keeps fogging up the window. It's hot in here. Humid, too. The air smells of cheap men's cologne and fried pork. Someone in the kitchen sings off-key to a popular salsa song while dishes crash and clang. I strain to understand the lyrics, hoping they'll match the peppy rhythm and lift me out of my funk. When I realize they're about a love gone so wrong the guy wants to kill his lover or himself, I stop trying. Like I need to be *reminded*.

I chug my warm bottle of Presidente beer, burp silently. I'm so tired I can feel my pulse in my eyeballs. They sting under dry contact lenses every time I blink. I didn't sleep last night, or the night before, and I was too tired to take the contacts out. I forgot to feed the cat, too. Oops. She's fat; she'll survive. It's Ed, of course. The thought of him makes my heart seize up and my forehead get lumpy. You can tell what stage I'm at in my doomed relationships by the state of my fingernails. Good nails: bad relationship, keeping up appearances. Ugly nails: happy Lauren letting herself go. You can also tell by how fat I am. When happy, I keep food down and stay around a size ten. When sad, I vomit like a Roman emperor and shrink to a six.

My lavender size eight Bebe pants, wool and low on the hips, are baggy tonight. If I move in my seat I can feel the space in them, rubbing. Ed, the bigheaded Texican, is a speechwriter (read: professional liar) for the mayor of New York. He is also my long-distance fiancé. According to his voicemail at work (I busted into it, I cannot tell a lie) he appears to be messing around with a chick named Lola. I joke not. *Lola*.

What is *that*? And where's that waitress? I need another beer.

I'll tell you what it is. It's the universe demonstrating once more how much it *hates* me. I'm serious. I've had a crappy life, crappy childhood, crappy everything you can think of, and now, even though I've made something not crappy of my professional life, all the aforementioned *crap* keeps coming back in the form of smarmy, good-looking dudes who treat me like, you guessed it, *crap*. I don't pick them, exactly. They *find* me, with that whacked radar they share. *Attention, attention, ahead, to the right, tragic chick at the bar, sort of pretty, downing gin and tonics, weeping to self, just stuck finger down throat in bathroom—screw her. Over. Yes, screw her over.*

As a result, I'm the kind of woman who will search a man's wallet and pockets and kick his ass if he does me wrong. I would stop this unacceptable behavior except I almost always find evidence of his wrongdoing—a receipt from the dinner he had at the dimly-lit Italian bistro when he said he was watching the Cowboys with his buddies, a scrap of napkin from a deli with the cashier's phone number scrawled in the bubbly blue letters of uneducated, easy women. He always does something sneaky, no matter who he is. It comes with the territory of loving the unlovable disaster of me.

Yes, I have a therapist. No, it hasn't helped.

There's no way a therapist can solve the crisis of chronic, mother-sanctioned infidelity among Latin men. It's not just a stereotype. I wish. Know what my Cuban grandma in Union City says when I tell her my man is cheating? "*Bueno*, fight harder for him, *mi vida*." How's a therapist gonna help me with *that*? Your man cheats, these traditional women who are supposed to be, like, your allies—they blame *you*. "Well," *abuelita* asks in raspy, heavily accented English, sucking on her Virginia Slims, "have you gained weight? Do you make sure you look good when you see him, or do you show up in those blue jeans? How's your hair? Not short again, I hope. Are you fat again?"

My therapist, a non-Latina with elegant scarves, thinks my problems stem from stuff like my dad's "narcissistically self-absorbed personality disorder," her diagnosis for the way he relates everything in life to himself, Fidel Castro, and Cuba. She's never been to Miami. If she had, she'd understand that all Cuban exiles older than forty-five do the same thing *Papi* does. To the exiles, there is no country more fascinating and important than Cuba, a Caribbean island with a population of eleven million. That's about two million less than live in New York City. Cuba is also the mecca to which all older exiles still seem to think they will return "once that son of a bitch Castro falls." Mass delusion, I tell you. When your family lives a lie that big, living with men who lie is easy. When I explain it all to my therapist, she suggests I give myself a "Cubadectomy" and get on with my American life. Not a bad idea, really. But like the children of most Cuban exiles I know, I can't figure out how. Cuba is the oozing recurrent tumor we inherit from our fathers.

Right now, I think maybe a fling with one of the prettyboy gangsters across the room might do the trick. Look how they eat with their fingers, the garlicky oil dripping from the shrimp into their sexy goatees. That's *passion*, an emotion Ed the stiff chuckler couldn't recognize to save his life. I could do one of them for revenge, you know? Either that, or I could eat cheese fries and donuts, get bulemic until the whites of my eyes turn the red of a heartache. Or I could go to my small apartment and slurp too many homemade screwdrivers, hide under my white goosedown comforter and cry while that intense Mexican singer Ana Gabriel—the one with the Chinese mom?—wails on my Bose about the love she has for her guitar.

I *need* a night with my *sucias*, y'all. Where are those girls?

Tonight is special, too, because this (drumroll, please) is the tenth anniversary of the very first time the *sucias* got together. We were all freshman journalism and communications students at Boston University, drunk off peach and blueberry girly beer (hey, at least it wasn't Zima) bought with our fake drivers' licenses, playing pool at that dark, smoky Gillians club where everyone used to go, dancing to a throbbing Suzanne Vega "Luka" remix until the bouncers threw us out on our sorry and naive *culitos*. We clicked that night. Or *cliqued*, rather. Oh, and puked. Almost forgot that part.

Our Reporting 101 professor with the dyed-black comb-over told us it was the first time so many Latinas had enrolled in the communications program at once. He bared filmy yellow fangs as he said it, a "smile," but trembled in his too-tight tweed blazer. We scared him, and people like him, as all things "minority" will—especially in Boston. (I might get to *that* in a minute.) Anyway, our collective power of intimidation in this increasingly Spanglish, Goya-beanified town was enough to make us instant and permanent best friends. Still is.

A lot of you probably don't speak Spanish, and so don't know what the hell a "*sucia*" is. That's okay. No, really. Some of us *sucias* can't speak Spanish, either—but don't tell my editors at the *Boston Gazette*, where I am increasingly certain I was hired only to be a red-hot-'n'-spicy clichéd chili pepper-ish cross between Charo and Lois Lane, and where, thank God, they still haven't figured out what a fraud I am.

I'm a pretty good journalist. I'm just not a good Latina, at least not the way they expect. This afternoon an editor stopped by my desk and asked me where she might go to buy Mexican jumping beans for her son's birthday party. Even if I *were* a Mexican-American (and here's a hint: I want to wax Frida Kahlo's furry caterpillar unibrow and I'm thoroughly uninterested in anything with the words "boxer" and "East L.A." in it) I wouldn't have known something that stupid.

You might have imagined by now—thanks to TV and

Hollywood—that a *sucia* is something beautiful and curvy and foreign, something really super Latina, you know, like the mysterious name of a tortured-looking, bloody-haired Catholic saint, or a treasured recipe from a short, fat, wrinkled old *abuelita* who works erotic magic with *chocolate* and all her secret herbs and spices while the mariachis wail, Salma Hayek flutters castanets, and Antonio Banderas romps a white snarfling horse through the cactus with, like, I don't know what, a winged *pig* or some crap in his embroidered knapsack, and all of it directed by Gregory Nava and produced by Edward James Olmos. Get freaking *over* it, lames. It's, like, so *not*.

Sucia means "dirty girl." Usnavys came up with it. "*Buena sucia*" is actually pretty offensive to most Spanish-speaking people, akin to "big smelly 'ho." So *Buena Sucia Social Club* is, how do you say, *irreverent*. Right? And *obnoxious*. It's a pun, too, see, taken from the name of those old-as-dirt Cuban musicians who record with Ry Cooder and star in German documentaries, who every non-Latino I know thinks I am genetically predisposed to *like*. (I'm not.) We're clever and, like, hip when it comes to pop culture, we *sucias*. Okay, fine. Maybe it's *stupid*. Maybe *we're* stupid. But *we* think it's funny, okay? Well, Rebecca doesn't, but *she's* about as funny as Hitler's hemorrhoids. (You didn't hear that from me.)

I check my Movado watch, a gift from three boyfriends ago. The watch has a blank face, like mine when the man who gave it to me told me he was going back to his ex. Ed thinks I shouldn't wear it anymore, says it upsets him. But I'm, like, Dude, if *you* bought me anything halfway decent I'd throw it *out*. It's a nice watch. Reliable. Predictable. Not like Ed. I'm still early, according to it. I don't need to get so nervous, then. All I need is another beer to calm my nerves. Where's that waitress?

They'll be here in a few minutes. I'm always early. It's the reporter training—come late, lose the story. Lose the story, risk having some envious and mediocre white guy in the newsroom accuse you of not deserving your job. *She's*

Latina, all she has to do is shake her butt and she gets what she wants around here. One of them actually said that once, loud, so I could hear. He was in charge of compiling the TV listings, and hadn't written an original sentence in about fifty-seven years. He was sure his fate was due to affirmative action, especially after the editor in chief of the paper had me and four other "minorities" (read: coloreds) stand up during a company briefing in the auditorium, just so he could say, "Take a good look at the faces of the future of the *Gazette*." I think he felt quite politically correct at that moment, as all those blue and green eyes turned to me in—what was it?—in horror.

Here's how my job interview went: *You're a Latina? How . . . neat. You must speak Spanish, then?* When you've got $15.32 in your bank account and student loans coming due in a month, what do you say to a question like that, even when the answer is *no*? Do you say, "Hey, I noticed your last name is Gadreau, you must speak French then?" Nah. You play along. I wanted that gig so bad I would have tried speaking Mandarin. With a name like Lauren Fernández, they figured Spanish was part of the package. But that's the American disease as I see it: rampant, illogical stereotyping. We would not be America without it.

I admit I didn't tell them I was half white trash, born and raised in New Orleans. My mom's people are bayou swamp monsters with oil under their fingernails and a rusty olive-green washing machine in front of the double-wide, the kind of people you see on *Cops,* where the guy is skinny as a week-dead kitten, covered with swastika tattoos and crying because the police blew up his meth lab.

Those are my people. Them, and New Jersey Cubans with shiny white shoes.

Because of all of this and more that I won't bore you with right now, I have molded myself into a chronic overachiever, and have focused my entire existence on a singular goal: succeed at life—meaning work, friends, and family—in spite of it all. Wherever possible, I dress as though I sprang from a completely different and much more normal set of circumstances. Nothing thrills me more than when people who don't know me assume I'm from a typical, moneyed Cuban family in Miami.

Sometimes I think I've made it to the other side, where well-balanced people without "issues" live; but then a big-headed Texican like Ed comes along and I'm paralyzed yet again with the realization that no matter how perfect I make myself, I'll never be as important as a Harley beer bong to my mom; no matter how much I sock away in my 401(k) or how many writing prizes I bring home, I'll never be near as important to my dad as pre-1959 Cuba, where the sky was bluer and tomatoes tasted better. Men like Ed find me, because they smell the hidden truth of Lauren on the wind: I hate myself because no one else has ever bothered to love me.

I ask again: What the heck kind of therapist can help someone like me?

I sat in the editorial offices during that interview in my navy blue discount Barami suit and three-year-old pumps with a hole in the sole, and told them what they wanted to hear: Sí, sí, *I will be your spicy Carmen Miranda. I will dance the* lambada *in your dismal gray broadsheet.* But what I *thought* was: *Just* hire *me. I'll learn Spanish later.*

FIRST WEEK ON the job an editor strolled past my desk and said in the deliberate, too-loud English they would all come to use on me, "I'm so glad you're here representing your people." I wanted to ask him just who he thought my people were, but I already knew the answer. My people, as far as his people are concerned, are stereotypes: brown of face and hair, uniformly poor and uneducated, swarming across the border from "down there" countries with all their belongings in plastic grocery bags.

I need another beer. Bad.

"*Oye,*" I call to the waitress. "*Traeme otra.*" She leans into her big hip and pushes the long black hair out of her pretty eyes. "*Como?*" she asks, looking confused. She was watching a Mexican soap opera on a small TV behind the counter and looks annoyed to be bothered with, you know, *work*. I have to repeat the request for another drink because my accent is so thick. Still confused. Crud. I finally hold the empty beer bottle upside down and lift my eyebrows. Sign language of a poseur. She nods, chews her cud, and moseys to the back for another *cerveza*. I learned Spanish later, all right, on the job. But the Puerto Rican waitress can tell I'm a fraud.

I watch the street again, and wait for a familiar *suciamobile*. You can tell a lot about a neighborhood by the cars in it, right? It's an even mix around here these days. You got your short, crummy Honda and Toyota lowriders with the FEAR THIS decals and "peeing Calvins" in the back window, scraping along the gutters with ice all up in the engines (please, someone tell me why Puerto Ricans think Japanese lowriders are a good idea in *New England*) and you got your newish Volvo sedans transporting some mom to the pharmacy for meds while her ADD triplets rip chunks of hair from their scalps.

I MYSELF DON'T *have* a car. I could afford one, okay, so don't laugh. I'm past the fabled six-figure mark, thanks to that little national writing prize. But I got used to the city's public transit system when I was a student, and I like the rumble of it in my life. Plus, in my position, it's cool to get out and listen to the way people really talk.

I write a new weekly Lifestyles section column mercifully called "My Life," created originally by Chuck Spring as *"Mi Vida Loca,"* a way, he told me, "to connect to the Latina people or whatever."

It's supposed to be confessional, my column, a (Latina) diary with "punch." Would I rather run to the woods in stained coveralls and live like Annie Dillard, examining the brutal life of—what lives in the woods? Ants?—*ants* when I see Chuck Spring, bounding toward me with that "golly-gee" look on his face, dressed for another meeting of his Harvard Final Club, where square-jawed men drink martinis and throw change at strippers? Yes. Do I need this job too much to flee or complain? Double yes, with a cherry on top. So I make the best of it.

It's not that I'm not appreciated at the *Gazette*. Chuck and the other editors value my "diversity," as long as I think like they do, write like they do, and agree with them on everything. Far as I can tell, *Gazette* newsroom diversity means hiring "team players," compliant as beaten dogs yet different enough in skin tone, last name, or national origin to be shut out of the little silly things, like promotion. It means sending the only black guy in the news department to Haiti to cover "unrest," even though there's a white woman reporter who sits ten feet from him and happens to be fluent in Haitian Creole; it also means labeling said woman an ungrateful, vitriolic banshee if she complains. I don't want to talk about it right now. Ow, ow, headache in my eye.

Right now, me want beer. Ooga ooga.

It's getting a little harder to take public transit because the *Gazette* recently put up billboards all over town with my huge red-brown curly hair and grinning freckled face on them, accompanied by the idiotic words "Lauren Fernández: Her Casa Is Your Casa, Boston." This happened, of course, right after all those new census stories came out about how Hispanics are the "biggest minority" in the nation now. Before everyone published *that* oxymoron on the front page, the mainstream media could not have given a Chihuahua *chalupa* about Hispanics. I couldn't get Chuck Spring interested in any stories about Hispanics to save my life. Now that Hispanics are big business, that's *all* he wants me to write about.

Money talks, see. Hispanics are no longer seen as a foreign unwashed menace taking over the public schools with that dirty little language of theirs; we are a domestic *market*. To be *marketed to*. Thus, me. My column. And my billboards. Greed makes people do crazy things. Craziest thing of all is the way the promotions department had my face *darkened* in the picture so I looked more like what they probably think a Latina is *supposed* to look like. You know, *brown.* First day those ads popped up next to Route 93 and in the T stations the *sucias* started calling. "Hey, Cubana, when did you get Chicana on us?" Answer: When I became useful to the *Gazette,* apparently.

In honor of Usnavys having christened us, we allowed her to choose the venue for tonight's anniversary celebration dinner. In keeping with her general need to return to the 'hood and prove she has made something bigger and better with her life than anyone there ever can or will, she picked El Caballito. A gray-haired Cuban guy with a warm smile owns it, and I swear he looks exactly—exactly, girl—like *Papi.* That means he's five-six, so pale you can see the blue veins in his bowed legs, balding, and with a nose that reminds you of that *Sesame Street* Count Muppet. Every time I see that dude I get the sinking feeling I'm the product of centuries of enthusiastic tropical inbreeding.

Anyway, Usnavys—not a small girl by any stretch of the imagination—also likes El Caballito because each order comes with—no lie—*four* album-sized plastic plates. You get your meat or fish on one. You get your mountain of white rice on another. You get your soupy black or red beans on a third. And a plate of greasy fried plantains, either "*maduros,*" which are ripe, squishy, and sweet as candy, or "*tostones,*" which are green, fried in slices then smashed flat, fried again, and tossed in garlic.

Refried plantains, if you will.

That's how we had to explain them to Amber, anyway, because she thinks all Latinas are just like *her.* She thinks we all eat the same dishes *she* grew up eating in Oceanside, California. She thinks all Latinas give a rat's rear about *menudo,* a soup they *voluntarily* make with tripe, a line of little Mexican ladies rinsing corpse poop out of the pig intestines in the kitchen sink. Uh, no. Sorry. Not for me. She honestly thinks California-style Mexican food is universal among Latinas and so the only bananas she'd ever seen before coming to Boston were the ones her mom got at the Albertson's and chopped over her corn flakes before taking her to marching band practice in the minivan.

She should know better by now, but I honestly can't tell if she really gets it yet. She's still always up in my face with all that dated, 1970s Chicano movement, "brown and proud," West Coast *Que viva la raza* jive. And when she's not up in *my* face, she's up in Rebecca's face. Rebecca is her cause. Amber's a trip. You'll see.

Sometimes you get a fifth plate at El Caballito, too, filled with something we Caribbean Latinos call "salad," a couple slices of avocado, raw onion, and tomato; to this you add salt, vinegar, and oil. There's a reason, my friends, that all the Puerto Rican ladies you see on the street are wide as a damn bus. There's a reason the Cubans down in Union City argue about politics while those sausage fingers jab the air. Cubans and Puerto Ricans don't dig salad much, but they love anything *fried*, especially meat that once oinked. The people on those islands, isolated, you would think, for tens of thousands of years, seem to believe *puerco* makes you strong and healthy. I went to Cuba a while back, to meet my relatives, and they slaughtered a scrawny little sad-eyed yard pig for me, and I was, like, *ick*, and they were, all, what's wrong with you, don't you eat *meat*? *You're going to die de flaquita!*

Papi always says he can't get used to the American idea of salad as something full of "leaves" and "complicated as hell." He still boils up a can of condensed milk for breakfast, too, and eats the sickly sweet paste with a spoon, in spite of a mouth full of caries. With my mom's people, y'all, it's bakinineggs (all one word and never one without the other) with white bread, coke (soda or drug, don't matter none), and a menthol cigarette garnish. Fine, okay. I'll stop talking about *Papi* now. My therapist would be proud of me. *Cubadectomy.*

And me? I don't know where the *hell* I came from. *I'll* take a good Caesar salad any day. And I eat bagels for breakfast, with a schmear of salmon cream cheese. Oh, and I am what you'd call a Starbucks *addict*. I think they put cocaine *and* ecstasy in their drinks, which is fine with me, and even though the whole deal with them being too good to use "small, medium, and large" like everyone else annoyed me for a while, I'm *over* it. If I don't get my venti nonfat caramel macchiato every morning—yeah, I said *venti*, so what?—I'm useless. But *don't* tell my editors. They expect me to be like those frisky Latina lawyers having orgasms while they shampoo their hair in court on the network TV ads. They expect me to reach up and pick mangoes out of the fruit basket I must wear on my head whenever I'm not in the newsroom talking about, you know, Mexican *jumping* beans. A Latina breakfast of mango and papaya—heyyyyy macarena, a'ight!

In reality, we *sucias* are all professionals. We're not meek maids. Or cha-cha hookers. We're not silent little women praying to the Virgin of Guadalupe with lace *mantillas* on our heads. We're not even like those downtrodden chicks in the novels of those old-school Chicana writers, you know the ones; they wait tables and watch old Mexican movies in decrepit downtown theaters where whiskery drunks piss on the seats; they drive beat-up cars and clean toilets with their fingernails coated in Ajax; their Wal-Mart polyester pants smell like tamales and they always, *always* feel sad because some idiot in a plaid cowboy shirt is drunk again and singing José Alfredo Jiménez songs down at the local crumbling adobe cantina instead of coming home and fixing the broken lightbulb that swings on the naked wire and making passionate *amor* to her like a real *hombre*.

Orale.

Usnavys: Vice President for Public Affairs for the United Way of Massachusetts Bay. Sara: wife of corporate attorney Roberto Asís, stay-at-home mom to twin five-year-old boys, upstanding member of the Brookline Jewish community (yes, we Latinas come in "Jew," too—shame on *you* for being surprised), and one of the best interior designers and party-throwers I've ever known. Elizabeth: co-host for a network morning show in Boston, current finalist for a prestigious national news co-anchor position, former runway model, born-again Christian (former Catholic), and a national spokeswoman for the Christ for Kids organization.

Rebecca: owner and founder of *Ella,* now the most popular Hispanic woman's magazine on the national market. And Amber: a *rock en Español* singer and guitarist waiting for her big break.

Then there's *moi.* At twenty-eight, I'm the youngest (and only Hispanic) columnist the paper has ever had, but I don't want to brag or anything. Eddie Olmos might as well just take a big old crap in his East L.A. outhouse, you know what I'm sayin'? The chicks be here, Eddie, so move your tired old zoot suit *over.*

OH, SWEET JESUS. I should have known Usnavys would pull a stunt like this. Look at her. She just slid up to the curb out front in her silver BMW sedan (leased), driving super slow with Vivaldi or something like that blasting out of the slightly open windows so all those poor women with all those kids and shopping bags from the 99-cent store hunching away from the wind and snow at the bus stop could stare at her. Now she's opening the door, slowly, stabbing a little black umbrella out into the air so she won't get her precious hair wet. She's on her cell phone. Wait, take two: She's on her *itsy-bitsy* cell phone. It gets smaller every time I see her. Or maybe she gets bigger, I can't tell. Girl loves her food.

I doubt she's even talking to anyone, just wants it stuck on her ear so everyone around here can go, oh, wow, look at that! What a rich Puerto Rican! And how would they know she was a Puerto Rican? That's easy. Because she's shouting in Puerto Rican Spanish (yes, there's a difference) to someone, real or imagined, your guess is as good as mine, on the other end of the line.

But that's not the worst part. She's got a fur coat on. *That's* the worst part. A big, thick, long, white fur coat. Knowing Usnavys, I would bet the Neiman Marcus tag is still attached inside so she can take it back tomorrow and get all that money back on her poor abused credit card. And that precious hair? It's ironed flat as a Dutch cracker, twisted up like she just stepped off the set of some telenovela, the heroine, only she's too dark to ever get cast in that kind of role. Don't tell her she's dark, though. Even though her daddy was a Dominican, ebony as an olive in a Greek salad, her mother has from day one insisted that Usnavys is light, and forbids her from dating "*monos*." (Read: monkeys.) If her African ancestors had been shipped to New Orleans instead of Santo Domingo and San Juan, she'd be black in the U.S., not even high yellow, but we won't get into that right now. As an American "Latina," she's . . . white? Go figure.

In case you were wondering about her *name*, you say it like this: Ooos-NAH-vees. She was born in Puerto Rico, and her mom had this idea that she wanted to take her daughter away from the island once and for all and make a better life for them in "America" (which, I assume, she didn't believe she was already living in when she was living in Puerto Rico, an American territory since 1918). She wanted her daughter to be American, in the *Leave It to Beaver* sense, because then maybe she'd have a chance, you know, a chance at a good man and a good life. So she wanted to name her baby something patriotic. On slow afternoons (there's no other type in Puerto Rico, okay?) Usnavys's mother used to go to the docks and watch American ships come and go on their way to bombing the hell out of the island of Viequez, amazed that the gringo sailor boys used brooms and mops on deck without shame. That, she thought, was freedom. Men with mops. So that's where she got the idea for the great name for her daughter—from the side of the ships. U.S. *Navy*, girl. I am *not* joking. That's what Usnavys is named after. You can ask her yourself. Now and then she tries to front like the name comes from a distant relative way back, you know, that it's Taino or something. But we all know the friendly, naked, peace-loving Taino Indians were wiped out by the Spaniards. Usnavys was named after an aircraft carrier.

Now she's taking her Tiffany key chain out, aiming the lock button at the car, triggering the little alarm whistle. It peeps three times, as if to announce: *Bo-RI-cua!* A couple of neighborhood *tigres* walk by in their Timberland boots and puffy parkas and stare at her long enough to turn their heads right around on their thick necks. She drinks in the attention, plays it up like a star. Always *was* like that. And, look. I don't begrudge her any of it. (Remind me never to use "begrudge" in any of my columns.) She's the only one of us from Boston, and the girl grew up in messed-up stereotype come true, in the red-brick projects, on welfare. She watched her older brother—the only father figure she ever had after her real dad split when she was four years old—get shot in the neck as he walked her home from school. He died in her nine-year-old arms. In spite of all that, she had a brain under that tightly tugged, truly tortured Afro. A *brain*. So smart, Usnavys, it scares you. She graduated at the top of her public high school class, got a scholarship to Boston University, where we were dorm mates. She graduated cum laude at B.U., and went on to get a master's degree from Harvard, also on a scholarship. Now she supports her mom; she bought the woman a condo in Mayagüez, and gave her a credit card all her own. All that after growing up poor, dark, and Puerto Rican in New England, speaking Spanglish. Tell me she doesn't deserve to gloat a little! The woman is my hero. I like to tease her about all the materialism, but that's just because I love her so much. She knows it's funny. She laughs at herself, too.

"Sucia!" I call as she walks in the door. She looks over at me and gives a distracted smile and keeps chattering on the phone. Oh, excuse *me*. All the Dominican women working the deep-fry vats behind the front counter look over at her with their tired horse eyes, and slip a little lower in their despair. The owner looks up from the Spanish-language newspaper he's reading behind the cash register. His eyes run up and down Usnavys, and his eyebrows rise up, like *What is this marvelous creature that has stumbled in from the cold?* She holds one leather-gloved hand up to me, as if stopping traffic, and I notice the tiny Fendi handbag dangling from her arm. She has this choreographed, I think, for full effect. As she tiptoes toward me, I notice she's wearing sharp little Blahnik pumps—in this snow! And I don't mean sharp as in

"fashionable," I mean sharp as in "could poke your eyes out." Not that I would know a Blahnik pump from a gas pump, but she told me all about them on the phone yesterday. *They're winter white with gold stripes.* These couldn't be any others. I listen as well as I can to her end of the conversation and marvel that she can fit her big girl feet into those little dainty shoes. It reminds me of those ballerina elephants leaping across the screen in *Fantasia.*

Earlier, when I said I didn't speak any Spanish during my job interview I was exaggerating a little. I picked up a bit, mostly when my dad was pissed off or in pain. The good news is he was pissed off pretty much every day, so I got plenty of Spanish lessons, and with my mom cheating on him every other weekend until he finally dumped her, there was plenty of pain to go around too. We mostly spoke English at home before Mom left, because my mom wasn't willing to learn my dad's language any more than she was willing to say "no" the first time my brother asked her to buy him pot. Later, when Mom was in prison already and my brother was grown up and gone, Dad and I spoke English because it was just easier and he wasn't angry as much anymore. Now that I'm, like, Miss Berlitz the Token Hispanic in the name of employability, *Papi* and I speak *only* Spanish. Oh, Jesus. I'm talking about him again, aren't I? Forgive me. He raised me to think he was the most important thing in the world, with Cuba a close second; and as with any religion, the faith is hard to shake, even when you secretly doubt its validity.

I wonder if they give anesthesia for Cubadectomies? Anesthesia other than beer, I mean.

From the sounds of it, Usnavys is ordering one of her assistants to schedule a very important press conference for next month, and she's rattling off the details of what needs to be supplied, counting them off on her meticulous, chubby fingers. Usnavys has so far hired only Latinas for the assistant jobs under her, including ones less qualified than other applicants. I tell her this is not legal. She laughs and says the white boys do it all the time and she's just making up for past injustices. "My goal," she says, pointing directly in my face, "is to get it to the point that *they* need affirmative action to work for *us*. Got it?"

"Whew!" she says, finally hanging up and slipping out of her coat in a crafty way that tells me she has, indeed, left the price tag inside and doesn't want anyone to notice. Beneath the coat she's wearing yet another elegant pantsuit, this time in a pretty pale green wool. I'm amazed she can find these things in her size, which I'm guessing has fluctuated between an eighteen and a twenty-four for the past five years.

Don't let this fool you, though. She's *gorgeous*. Her face is delicate, with the kind of nose other women pay lots of money to achieve, and big, expressive brown eyes she likes to hide with green contact lenses. She gets her brows waxed at a salon near the projects every three or four days (she swears the hoochie girls working there are the only ones who get it right) and her makeup is always perfect, a fact I attribute to her constant, uncontrollable impulse to pull out her Bobbi Brown compact in public so everyone *knows* that a Puerto Rican has arrived, y'all. She eats with the grace and appetite of a woodland deer; you'd think she lived on grass, she's that hungry all the time. She calls herself "the fat girl" in front of the rest of us, and laughs about it. We don't soothe her with lies to the contrary. Her upper arm is bigger around than Rebecca's thigh.

Maybe it's because she's always been heavy, and is now at her heaviest, but she's also the most outgoing of us. We used to go clubbing, ending up at some cheesy all-night pancake place afterward, and by the end of the night, or rather by the time the sun came up, Usnavys would have managed to make everyone in the room friends with everyone else. I saw her do this with a collection of silent, bucktoothed chess players from Wentworth Institute of Technology and a pack of pretty sorority girls from Brandeis. She had everyone singing songs and telling jokes and playing charades. That's why she practically runs the public affairs department at the biggest nonprofit agency in the state. You've never met a friendlier, smarter, more organized, and more sincerely kind— and materialistic, yes—woman than Usnavys Rivera.

Usnavys has no problem getting men, either. Of all of us, she seems to attract the most men. She's aloof with them, and that makes them love her more. They follow her, call her all the time, beg her to marry them, threaten to kill themselves if she doesn't reciprocate their affections. We're not talking shady characters, either. We're talking doctors and lawyers and international spies. Yes, spies. She dates no fewer than three men at a time, but not in a sleazy way. She doesn't sleep with most of them. She uses them for backup, plays one off the other. Usnavys's men trail her like pound puppies. Does she want them, though? No. All she wants is Juan. Juan Vásquez, even if she won't admit it in public.

I got nothing against Juan, either. I *like* the guy.

But the *sucias*? I can't say they feel the same way. Some *sucias* think Juan, with his congested old Volkswagen Rabbit, doesn't make enough money to do right by a woman like Usnavys. Juan heads a small nonprofit agency in Mattapan that mainly helps rehabilitate and employ drug-addicted Latino men. He has an amazing success rate, as many articles in my own newspaper have documented. So *what* that he doesn't make much money? I know deep inside Usnavys feels the same way, but she's got what you might call "issues" about money, as you might have guessed from looking at the long white fur coat and the BMW. Juan, who's actually really good-looking—for a short man—could care less about all that. The one time I met the guy was at a black-tie fund-raiser for the Democratic candidate for mayor of Boston; he showed up in a faded black T-shirt with a tuxedo silkscreened in white on it, black jeans, and ripped, snow-stained, red high-top sneakers, with a seven-hundred-pound Che Guevara biography under his arm. Usnavys, in her sparkly gown and jewels, pretended she didn't know him, even though she had spent the night at his place the weekend before. She ended up leaving with a floppy, damp-faced Argentine doctor she met at the cheese and pâté table. Juan had only come to see Usnavys; he wanted to show her he supported the candidate she raved about all the time. She didn't even return his initial enthusiastic wave. When he finally approached and said hello, head hanging down like a whipped dog, she pretended she didn't remember who he was, and then introduced her ugly pâté man as "*Doctor* Hiram Gardél," shooting Juan the iciest stare this side of Greenland before prancing off on the *medico*'s squishy arm. It's the dance they do, Usnavys and Juan, and have been doing since college.

Rebecca comes next, driving cautiously in her brand-new burgundy Jeep Grand Cherokee. All the spaces on the curb are now taken. I watch her circle the restaurant three times before she pulls into the discount grocery store parking lot across the street. She does not make nearly the fuss getting out of her car that Usnavys did, though I can see from the nervous way she peers around as she trots through the snow toward us that she's not exactly *comfortable* in this part of town. She smiles, like she always does, but I can see the evil tiger crouching within her, ready to bite.

Rebecca's been here many times, as we all have, and though she has never come out and said she dislikes this neighborhood—and all others like it—any person with a shred of sensitivity would realize it from the strained secondary look she gets at the mention of "El Caballito," as if you just stuck a pile of steaming excrement under her nose and she's too polite to turn away. I say "secondary" because Rebecca always seems to have two facial expressions—the one everyone else sees, and the one I see. Most people who know her think Rebecca is one of the most charming and motivated people in the universe. No one but me seems to notice how much Rebecca hates and fears *everything* around her. Everyone I know thinks she's this wonderful humanitarian. And I admit, no one works a room the way Rebecca does, with her slightly tilted head and her faux concern, and few people I know give away as much money as she does, to battered women's shelters and runaway youth homes, or spend as much time on volunteer activities, like reading to the blind, even with her packed schedule. But the cynic in me thinks she does it out of Catholic guilt and a need to end up in heaven. Sue me. People think Rebecca is this *über*-Latina, a role model who can roll her Rs, but I think she's just a skilled politician, that's all. I grew up surrounded by my mom's people, and I've got antennae for dangerous phonies. Either that, or I'm extraordinarily jealous of her, the way she controls her emotions and wins friends. I'm, like, the opposite of that.

As she runs across the street, shielding her eyes from the snow with a white-gloved hand, her face twists with stress. She'd be pretty if she didn't always look like she was smiling through a mouthful of lime juice. Don't get me wrong: Rebecca likes to have fun as much as the next person—as long as everything has been taken care of and all the rules have been followed and it's perfectly *safe*. Sure, Rebecca Baca (or Becca Baca, as I like to call her—she *hates* that) likes to have fun—in an orderly fashion.

I'm relieved to see she has come alone. Sometimes Brad, her moron of a husband, insists on joining her for our outings. Don't ask me why. We've asked her to stop bringing him to *sucias* gatherings. He still shows up every now and then. He's a tall non-Latino white guy from Bloomfield Hills, Michigan, who has been working on the same doctoral thesis for the past eight years, at Cambridge University in England. I can't remember the exact topic, but it's got something to do with philosophy and stern, dead German authors with bushy eyebrows. Bunch of useless crap if you ask me. He spends a couple of months a year in England, and the rest of the time going to lectures and reading and writing in Boston. Eight *years*.

I hope my therapist will forgive me for mentioning him again, but *Papi* was able to get his bachelor's and Ph.D. in a total of six years, in a language he learned when he was fifteen, all the while working as a night janitor and raising two kids and trying to figure out just why he'd had the misfortune to marry a sociopath in a Marilyn Monroe costume. Why it's taking this Brad joker so long to finish school I do not understand. I've told Rebecca as much, and she just gives me that look, like it's none of my business. Withering stare, you might say. (Remind me never to use the word "withering" in a column.) Why doesn't anyone else notice when she gets that face going? Everyone else, asked to describe Rebecca, would say "nice and sweet." Not me. I'd say, "ice queen." I get the feeling Rebecca tolerates me as if I were a family pet that pees on the floor. She doesn't have the heart to get rid of me, but she wouldn't be devastated if, say, someone "accidentally" left the door open and I got hit by, like, a UPS truck. I think she comes to these meetings of ours mostly to catch up with Sara and Elizabeth. I *know* it's not to see *me*. And God knows it's not to see Amber.

As she enters the restaurant, Rebecca gracefully shakes the snowflakes out of her short, shiny black hair, then smooths it back into place. I don't know how she manages it, but she always looks perfect. One year, she dragged all the *sucias* to a business etiquette seminar at the Ritz-Carlton hotel on Newbury Street, so we could learn what to do with a fish fork and how to scoop our creamy corn chowder *away* from us in the bowl. It's the only time I've really seen her face light up with unbridled joy. She sat in the front row, too, taking notes on everything and nodding furiously. When the speaker, a former debutante from my hometown, running down a list of things a professional woman should avoid if she wants to make it to the top, wrote "hair that falls below the shoulder" in neat black letters on the spotless white marker board, Rebecca turned and shot me a look that said "I told you so." For years she has helpfully suggested that all *sucias* keep their hair short, yet feminine, and, in the worst case, at least wear it up around the office. "No one will take you seriously with all that Thalia nonsense," she told me recently, smiling warm and friendly, as she will when she has something critical to say, lifting my long, curly hair off my shoulders like it was something she found clogging her drain. I *like* my hair. I need all the bouncy size of it to cover up my fat face and round nose. So, like, leave me alone.

Needless to say, *Rebecca's* dark hair is impeccable, stylish, and short without being overly so, the best Newbury Street has to offer. It brings out her big, beautiful brown eyes, accented with only a touch of black mascara and a glow of mauve eye shadow. She always has tiny, perfect earrings, and neatly knotted neck scarves in conservative patterns. She reminds me of that woman Benjamin Bratt married, Talisa Soto. Her. But with short hair. She hates to shop, so she hires a personal shopper named Alberto to do it for her. Rebecca has never to my knowledge worn a skirt that came anywhere above the knee, and all her heels are the sensible things you'd expect to see on Janet Reno. She's only twenty-eight, but Alberto shops for all her clothes at Talbots or Lord & Taylor. Conservative in appearance, austere when it comes to *real* emotions, though the fake emotions she hangs out like laundry for all to see.

To his credit, bizarre Brad has a cute, boyish face and messy short blond hair. He's tall. But he dresses like a freaking hobo. If you saw this dude rattling around on the street, you'd think he was some kind of parolee, down on his luck and sinking lower by the minute. I think he'd have a beard if he were capable, but he's got that weirdo yellow patchwork fuzz instead, like a mutt with the mange. With his round face it makes him look like a teenager, until he smiles and you see the crow's-feet and you realize this loser is going nowhere fast, a tattered hamster slogging on his rusty wheel. He wears round wire-framed glasses that are always sort of smudgy and lopsided, as if he'd sat on them a few times. It shocked us all that this was the guy Rebecca planned to marry. When she introduced him to us the first time, we all sort of scratched our heads and tried to be polite. He attempted to talk to us, but what came out of his mouth was incomprehensible, robotic bull. In a five-minute span, he quoted Kant, Hegel, *and* Nietzsche and, it seems to me, got most of it wrong. (Yes, we *sucias* took a few philosophy courses, too.) I think I corrected him, and he didn't like it much; he got this faraway look in his eyes, stared up at the ceiling, cocked his head to the side, and then stood up and spun around one time before sitting down again. All I could think was, *Telegram to self:* "Dahmer, stop. Jeffrey, stop." When Amber, never one to hide her feelings, said, "What the hell you doing, man? Spinning on your axis?" he said he had an *eye* problem and had to do that every so often to keep his *balance.* "Only one eye works at a time," he said in that electronic voice, "and they switch with no warning." Ohhhh-kaaayyy. I was, like, Becca, girl, I love you like my own sister, or at least as much as a first cousin—okay, maybe a second cousin—but *what* do you see in that guy?

It took a couple more weeks to draw out of her that rotating Brad was Bradford T. Atkins, son of Henry Atkins, a wealthy real estate developer in the Midwest, maker of the kind of strip malls that carry upscale coffee places, juice bars, and video rental chains. Brad, it turns out, is the black sheep of the Atkins family, and attended Cambridge only because his old man built a library for the school when the son couldn't get in on smarts. The old man's estate is estimated to be worth a little more than a billion dollars, and Brad is slated to inherit one-third of that when the geezer croaks, which should be any day now because dear Henry is pushing ninety. Meanwhile, Brad, who says he despises material goods and believes we should "kill all the capitalists," is happily living off a trust fund allowance that gives him about $60,000 a year just for breathing with an open mouth. That's not as much as it used to be, Rebecca told me. Brad got $200,000 a year before he married her. The old man and his wife both believe they can punish Brad out of marrying an "immigrant" by slowly cutting him off. So Brad, weirdo that he is, comes to our gatherings and sits a few feet away from the rest of us, listening with that gaping rich-boy maw to our conversation as if he were Jane Goodall and we were the goddamned gorillas, taking notes. Notes, *chica.* We fascinate him, apparently, especially when we speak Spanish. I think that's why he watches Elizabeth the hardest. Soon as that freak hears Spanish, his face gets all red and flushed and he looks like he's hiding a hard-on. Total certified *weirdo.* We're waiting for Rebecca to snap out of it, but with more than $333 million staring you in the face, it could be mighty hard.

After college, Rebecca worked as a magazine editor for *Seventeen,* and two years ago launched her own monthly magazine, *Ella,* which quickly became the top-selling magazine for Latinas in their twenties and thirties. She's starting to make a lot of money all on her own, and doesn't need Brad's. I would bring it up with her, but Rebecca has always been a very reserved person, a woman who prides herself in self-restraint, a calm and calculating person who I have never seen either lose her temper or dance. She comes from an established family in Albuquerque—you know, that ridiculous-sounding New Mexican city you only hear about on Bugs Bunny?—and they're the kind of people who have lived in the Southwest since before the pilgrims landed at Plymouth Rock, Mexicans—er, Spaniards—who did not come to this country, but were *overtaken* by it. When she speaks Spanish, it's antiquated and awkward, as if someone broke out Chaucer's English in the middle of a frat party. Elizabeth and Sara get a kick out of it. Rebecca's family is actually from northern New Mexico, and those people just kind of froze in time up there, speaking that old mother tongue and wearing lace on their heads.

She insists on being called "Spanish," too. God forbid you call her a *Mexican*. She swears she can trace the family tree back to royalty in Spain. Now, I'm no anthropologist, but I do know what a Pueblo Indian looks like. And Rebecca Baca, with her high cheekbones and flat little butt, fits the description. If any of us *sucias* were to be chosen to play a "Latina" in an Edward James Olmos production, it would be *this* chick, okay? And it doesn't matter how many times Amber comes at her with that Mexica Movement "we are Indians, not Hispanics or Latinos" mumbo jumbo about Aztlán and the indigenous holy war against the *pinche* gringos, Rebecca ain't buying it. "I'm Spanish," she'll say, calmly, patiently, with that sweet smile, "just the same way you have people in this country who are German and Italian, I'm Spanish. I respect very much who you are and what you believe, and I support everything you're doing. But trying to recruit me to your Mexican cause makes as much sense as going after the Korean who owns the market." Don't try to ask her about the straight black hair and the brown skin and the nose that looks like it came out of an R. C. Gorman painting, though. She'll wrinkle said dainty hook nose, as she does when people curse or raise their voices, and say with a smile and a mock exasperated sigh, "Moorish, Lauren. We have some Moorish blood in us." And that, my friends, is that.

Rebecca walks in a straight line to the table without moving her hips. Usnavys tumbles up to give her one of those bear hugs that knocks your wind out. "*Sucia!*" Usnavys cries. Rebecca gives a pained smile and doesn't answer with the usual reflected "*sucia*" cry. Rather, she pats Usnavys gingerly on the back, as if the very pudge and jiggle she finds there is offensive, and says, "Hello, Navi, hello, Lauren. How are you both?" Usnavys doesn't notice the dis. I do. I always do. Usnavys sees the best in people. I see the worst, I guess. Rebecca hasn't used the term "*sucia*" since college, even though she still comes to our gatherings. She thinks it's immature. It makes me feel even more like a loser than I usually do, because I *love* saying "*sucia*" and that must mean I'm about as immature as people come, so, like, *whatever*, dude.

Rebecca hangs a red peacoat on a wall hook, wrinkling her nose at the brown smudge on the wall. I notice again that she's a tiny woman, barely five feet tall, with the delicate wrists of a cat. I daresay she's anorexic, in a fashionable David E. Kelley series kind of way. She wears a dark gray wool pantsuit, with understated but clearly expensive silver jewelry. Or is it platinum? Her tiny earrings have tinier rubies embedded in them. I'm amazed they make bracelets so small. She never eats more than a bowl of soup or white rice when we get together, and usually only half of that, and never drinks. Not that I'm big, really, but I *would* be if I didn't stick my finger down my throat every now and then. Skinny does not begin to capture the essence of Rebecca. She's wiry, muscular, delicate, and fierce, all at once. And, you know, for all our female talk about how awful we supposedly think it is to be skinny like that, the truth is I'm as conditioned as anyone else, and I'm envious. Mad envious. Rebecca is everything I'm *not*: diplomatic, evenhanded, publicly nonjudgmental (who knows what she thinks to herself), rich, dedicated to a good diet and exercise plan, generous with time and funds, and good at numbers. I think mostly about myself. I bounce checks. Maybe I *am* jealous of her. Probably. Men never get sick of Rebecca and decide they need space.

Mostly, I wish I had a mom like Rebecca's. La Doña Baca never calls *her* daughter from jail, asking for bail money, like mine did. Rebecca's mother, at graduation, was *there*, and not just there, but there *in a nice suit* and smelling of Red Door perfume, with a bouquet of flowers for her daughter, and genuine tears in her eyes. "I'm proud of you," I remember she told Rebecca. Me? I stood to the side and scanned the crowd for my dad, who had found another unsuspecting victim to talk to about Cuba B.C. (before Castro) for the rest of the afternoon. Playing once again the role of the fascinating foreigner, he all but forgot about me. Mama wasn't there; she'd said she was coming. When I called her later, she answered the phone in Houma (she moved back in with my granny last year) with a sleepy voice and apologized. "I forgot, sweetheart," she said. I could hear crickets over the phone. "But I guess it's official now, you got your degree and I bet you think you're better than me now."

In my quiet moments, when no one's looking, I wish I could switch families and pasts with Rebecca—only I'd never marry Brad.

No wonder that cute British computer software mogul thought Rebecca's idea to start a magazine was so good he cut her a check for two million dollars to start it up. What's that? You thought maybe her little orbiting millionaire-to-be husband was footing the bill? Uh, no. I don't *think* so. I asked her about that, too. Turns out Brad had asked his parents for the money, and even asked for a loan, but when he told them what it was for, they'd answered by saying, "Bradford, dear, these people don't—how shall I put it?—enjoy *literature*. You might as well throw your money away." *These people?* I don't know how Rebecca can stand it. But then, Rebecca probably doesn't think she's one of "these people" anyway. She's Spanish, remember? She art dethended from Thpaniard kingth and queenth.

We sit and wait for the others to arrive, drink strong Cuban coffee from small polystyrene cups. Usnavys orders a couple of appetizers, fried, of course. Rebecca opens her Coach briefcase and extracts a couple of copies of the latest issue of her magazine, with Jennifer Lopez wearing a business suit on the cover. It's a beautiful publication. She asks me again when I'm going to write for her, and I explain, again, that I am property of the *Gazette* plantation. "Massa don't let me write for no uddu peoples, Miss Sca'let," I say. She smiles tightly and shrugs. Usnavys tries to smooth the moment over and suggests we take bets on which *sucia* will show up next, but it's pointless, because we all agree: the next *sucia* through the door will be Sara, with Amber in tow. Elizabeth is always late to evening functions, mostly because it's the middle of the night for her. She has to get up at three in the morning to get ready for the morning show, and by the time evening rolls around she's usually balled up under the covers, sound asleep. For the *sucias* she makes an exception.

Sara shows up next, skidding down the now-icy street a million miles an hour in her shiny metallic green Land Rover. She's always in a rush, this one. You got as many things going on as she does, you'd probably always be in a rush, too. Just because she's a stay-at-home mother does not make Sara less busy than we are. You hear her schedule, and between the driving around of Seth and Jonah, volunteer work, and continuing education classes at Harvard Extension (wine-tasting, sushi preparation, interior design) she's got a packed life.

Her driving, all that skidding and screeching, is also in keeping with the way Sara moves her body through space. Sara, for all her charm and beauty, is clumsy. I have never known one woman to land so many times in the emergency room. Her mother once told me Sarita had been like this "since she got boobs." And now that she has two young sons, forget it. The woman is covered head to toe with scrapes and cuts, meted out, she says, by miniature fingernails and a variety of expensive, non-battery-powered, highly educational wooden toys. Clumsy, lovely, loud, and charming. And usually quite punctual in spite of all this. Our Sara.

Amber's airplane must have been delayed. I'm looking forward to hearing the story; with Sara, a story is not just a story. She has the gift of storytelling, something all our professors noticed at B.U. Everyone thought she should have been the one to go into newspapers or magazines, her stories were so amazingly written. Only problem was half the stuff in them wasn't *true*. Big no-no in journalism. Sara exaggerates. Okay, fine, she lies. That better? She's Cuban. What did they expect? We like to exaggerate, the fish getting bigger with each new telling of the story. She weaves a tale with drama and tension, infuses it with mystery and intrigue, even if all she's talking about is buying new drapes for her upstairs study. For this reason, she'd never last in a news job, and she knows it; I think that's why she stays home, but what do I know?

She parks—next to Rebecca's ride in the grocery store parking lot—and steps out of the Range Rover. Amber jumps down from the passenger's side looking like Marilyn Manson's dream girl. What a *freak*. Every six months, one of us foots the bill for Amber's plane ticket back here from Los Angeles, and the *sucias* with the cars pick her up at Logan. Amber can't afford it herself, see. We tease her about it, and she says, "Just wait, soon you'll be standing in line for my autograph." She doesn't laugh when she says it, because ever since she discovered the "Mexica Movement" Amber has lost any sense of humor she used to have. The Mexica Movement, for those who don't know, consists of Mexicans and Mexican-Americans who insist on being called Native Americans, and specifically Aztecs, instead of Hispanics or Latinos. Anyway, Sara's laughing and talking, slicing her hands through the air for punctuation. She's still talking, loud as always, when they get to our table for hugs and *sucia* cries. The two could not look more different if they tried. It almost, almost, makes me laugh.

Sara Behar-Asís is dressed like Martha Stewart, her idol. That's how she always dresses. You'd think she'd want to lounge around that big house of hers in sweats or something, but I swear to you she can't function if she isn't *coordinated*.

Gets catatonic or something. Even in college Sara lived for coordination, and her family—former Cuban rum barons—gave her a clothing allowance greater than my dad's yearly professor's income. Blew my mind, I'll tell you that. I always scooped up her leftovers and hand-me-downs, and I still get the occasional spare cashmere sweater.

She's perfectly put together tonight, of course, coordinated down to the blush on her rosy cheeks, but probably thinks she looks very casual. Dabs of concealer mask a couple of gashes under one eye, handiwork, she says when Rebecca asks, of her kids' latest adventure with their new junior golf club set. She looks like the perfect, calculatedly casual, colossally klutzy Liz Claiborne–issue suburban mom. She wears beige wool slacks, a white turtleneck covered by a thick cable-knit sweater in the palest of yellows—a color she would no doubt refer to as something like "lemon wash." I can't tell for sure, but I think I see a spot of red scabby skin peeking up over the sweater's collar, the last healing bit of evidence from our ill-fated New Hampshire ski trip last month with our men. While Roberto and Ed slalomed along the black diamond trails, chuckling and back-slapping as their type of filled-with-crap male will, I hunkered down at the side of various blue trails and stared in horror from behind my goggles as an overly ambitious Sara flung her pink-parka-wrapped body like a wet rag over moguls and into frozen pine trees. She even plowed through a family of five at one point, taking down the smallest child in a chorus of parental shrieking. She's not what you'd call the outdoorsy type. After she slid down half a mountain on her throat and face, skis splayed in the air like the antennae on an old television, I gathered her up and we retreated to the lodge for hot chocolate and watched competitive aerobics on ESPN for the rest of the afternoon. Tonight, she wears stylish hiking boots that have never been hiking and, if she's lucky, never will—just like her SUV should never go off-roads unless someone else is driving—and a black leather jacket. Her naturally blond hair with the salon highlights might as well be Martha's, too. Same cut, same color, same *vibe*. She is white, a fact that would no doubt shock my editors, but which would not shock anyone from Latin America or Miami, where white Cubans still ban other shades of people from their social organizations.

In spite of her lack of grace, it's hard not to be envious of Sara. She's married to Roberto, her high school sweetheart, a polite, tall, white Jewish Cuban lawyer from Miami whose parents have known her parents since they were all back on the island; she has two beautiful children who just started kindergarten at the most expensive day school in the area— basically she has it all. Great guy, great house, great family, great twins, great car, great hair. No need to work for money. Her ski trips come for free, not like mine, which cost me. Ed makes a lot more than I do, but does he pay for anything? Heck, no. Fifty-fifty, he says with that wink. That's the only way to know our love is true, he says. Roberto would go into cardiac arrest if Sara ever wanted to pay for anything herself. He buys her presents all the time, too. Just because he loves her. Been with her since they were in high school, and he still does these things. A Range Rover with a big white bow on the hood, just because he loves her. A diamond tennis bracelet hidden at the bottom of a box of kosher chocolates, just because he loves her. A newly remodeled bathroom, decorator everything, just because he loves her. And his head is not enormous and deformed, either, like some heads we know. As a matter of fact, Roberto has a very nicely shaped head, which goes nicely with his nicely shaped everything else. He's yummy handsome, that Roberto, in a taller–Paul Reiser sort of way. I think every *sucia* has had Roberto fantasies. We all want Roberto, and because he's taken, we all want a guy exactly *like* Roberto, only problem is he appears to be the only one out there. A guy who's faithful, dependable, rich, handsome, kind, funny, and who has known you since you were a goofy girl covered with pimples, accidentally falling into the canal behind your parents' mansion and he jumps in with all those muscles to save you from yourself. Together, shivering on the grass, you watch his velvet yarmulke float toward the sea and you think—this is it, he's the one. A wonderful guy who continues to save you from yourself for the rest of your life.

Must be nice.

We *sucias* are happy for Sara, *por supuesto*, but we hate her at the same time because our lives are not nearly that neat and perfect. I think she could make a decent living as an interior designer, provided she left the vases and pottery and such to someone with less butter on their fingers, and I've told her so. She has expressed interest in pursuing a career once the boys are old enough not to "need me at home," but she seems to be in no hurry. Give her a couple old curtains and a junkyard and she'll come up with something fabulous. Not cool, not interesting, not great, but *fabulous*. We used to joke that she should have been a gay guy.

Now, Amber. Ugh. I don't know where to *begin* with *this* girl. When I first met her, in freshman media writing, she was a little *pocha* from So Cal, a coffee-skinned, pretty girl with an unnaturally flat tummy. She plucked her eyebrows completely off, and drew them back in as thin arching lines. (*"Pocha,"* for the uninitiated, refers to the kind of Mexican-American who speaks no Spanish and breaks into a sweat if she eats anything hotter than Old El Paso mild salsa.)

Back then, Amber wore her dark, shimmering hair long, with heavy bangs curled under, and she wore the kind of baggy girl clothes and fake gold "dolphin" earrings that probably seemed normal where she grew up but that seemed a little 'hood-ratty to us. She had grown up in a coastal town near San Diego, a town full of clean-cut U.S. Marines, where pretty much everyone had a Spanish surname and a Camaro with a worn-out Bon Jovi cassette in the tape deck. She was only vaguely aware of being a Hispanic when she got to B.U., and didn't think much about it until she met Saul (pronounced Sah-OOL), a longhaired, emaciated rock guitarist from Monterrey, Mexico. He was a Berklee College of Music student who told her he thought she looked just like an image of the Virgin of Guadalupe he saw in a dream, dropping to his knees in reverence in the middle of the B.U. quad in a snowstorm. She thought that was cool, and thought

Saul, with his pasty skin, yards of tattoos, and constant reefer rolling, was just weird enough to freak her Republican parents out for a while. He gave her all kinds of books on Chicanos and the Mexican immigrant struggle in the United States and started dragging her to these "movement" meetings and concerts. And that was the end of Amber as we knew her.

Amber plays awesome guitar, flute, and piano, and always had an incredible voice. She has tried for the past six years to get a record deal, but it never quite works out. She invariably calls us (collect) for pep talks when she gets rejections, and we always oblige. We may question her fashion sense, or her ethnic identity, but none of us has ever doubted for a minute that Amber was phenomenally talented.

Amber actually attended B.U. on a classical music scholarship and took communications classes just in case she couldn't become the next Mariah Carey, her original goal. She could always play the guitar, better than Saul did, in fact, thanks to her uncle giving her lessons at his auto body shop in Escondido, California. Her full-blown Chicana awakening happened when she boarded a crusty old green VW bus with Saul, and trekked across Mexico and the southwestern U.S. one summer on the "Free Chiapas" tour with his band. She came back having exchanged all "ch"s with "x" and all "x"s with "ch." Like Chicana was now Xicana, "just like the Aztecs spelled it," she said. Don't ask me how the pre-Columbian Aztecs had access to the Roman alphabet, but according to Amber and her Mexica friends, they did. Mexicans were now "Mechicans" too. She still painted her eyebrows in, but now they looked more like angry upward slashes than surprised arches. She began to collect eagle feathers, ankle bells, and gold shields, and spoke almost nothing but Spanish, a language she never before spoke much beyond the words she heard growing up: *m'ija, albondigas, churro, cerveza*, make *mimis, abuelo, sopa*, and *chingón.*

She had this new CD collection, too, full of screaming homely Latingirls like Julieta Venegas and that man-looking chick from Aterciopelados. At *sucias* gatherings back then, she screamed along with songs by a heavy-metal group called Puya, until she lost her voice. Amber dropped her last name that year, too. Quintanilla. She said she didn't want people in the recording industry associating her with Selena. (You know, dead Selena, murdered Tejano singer Selena, holy, practically sainted Selena?) That was because, she said, "My music is harder than that, tougher than that. Selena was a *wuss.*" What kind of sacrilege is *that*?

And now? Now she's living in Los Angeles with another *rock en Español* guy from Mexico. Apparently, they had an Aztec wedding ceremony last year, but did not exchange rings (Eurocentric symbols of ownership, she says), did not invite any *sucias* (we weren't enlightened enough yet, she said, and she didn't want our "mocking energy" to ruin things), and did not register the marriage with the government (false governments mean nothing to us, she says). This dude calls himself "Gato" and he's the son of a corrupt Mexican government official. (That's redundant, isn't it?) Amber plays in a rock band of her own, singing mostly in Spanish and increasingly in Nahuatl, and, she says, negotiating with a few labels about that record deal she's been chasing for a few years now. She records her own albums and sells them from fold-up card tables in nightclubs. Her hair is still long, but now it's *black. Black* black, witchcraft black, all twisted up in these Medusa things that look like a cross between braids and dreadlocks, with strands of colored yarn woven in here and there. I don't think she's brushed it in a year. Her lipstick is this dark, gothic purple that almost matches her hair, and her eyes are rimmed in black liquid eyeliner. She's had her nose, eyebrow, tongue, belly button, and nipple pierced, and her clothes are usually black, like her hair. She's not *ugly* or anything, mind you. She's just Amber. She's pretty, always was. And she's got these abs to die for because she only eats raw food, "the way our ancestors did," she says, and because she runs a million miles a week with Gato up in the Hollywood Hills. Come to think of it, wasn't it the Aztecs who ripped people's beating hearts from their chests and took big old bites? That's raw, for ya. But in the magical American Mexica movement of the new millennium, the Aztecs are now, like, pacifist vegans, not bloodthirsty conquerors. The Mexica version of the Aztecs, to me, sounds a lot like Ralph Nader in a loincloth.

Tonight she's wearing a tight black jacket with fake feathers around the wrists and neck, like something Lenny Kravitz might spit up. She's got a tight black crop shirt under that, even though it's the middle of winter, so we can all see her damn rippling abs. Her pants are giving Rebecca a heart attack because they're covered with colorful drawings of the Virgin of Guadalupe in a bikini. She has platform boots that lace up the front. Looking at her next to Sara is almost as shocking as that time the real Martha Stewart presented an award on MTV with Busta Rhymes.

We all move to a bigger table, and start chatting as *sucias* will. We don't order yet, and everyone but Usnavys waits to start on appetizers until Elizabeth arrives. That means we wait another half hour. Then here she comes. I'm distracted by the rest of Sara's story, which has to do with a bad deal on fabric for the guest room at her house, but seems as thrilling as a good mystery novel, so I don't see when Elizabeth pulls up in her white Toyota Tacoma with the massive cross hanging from the rearview mirror and those little metal fish stuck to the back grate.

I find it hilarious; here's this woman, so tall and thin and beautiful that she earned a living as a runway model during college, and she drives a freakin' pickup? *By choice?* Maybe it's because I'm from the Deep South, where pickups are reserved for a certain kind of Kool-Aid-drinking, bra-needing man named Bubba. She says it's comfortable, handles well in the snow, and is just right for carting stuff around. It's true: Elizabeth is always taking boxes of donated clothes and canned food from her church—a mammoth, shiny space-cube in the suburbs—to the city's homeless shelters. She volunteers her truck every summer to the Christians for Kids summer camp in Maine, hauling inflatable rafts and archery equipment. At the end of summer, she piles the truck bed high with bales of hay, and children on top of that, for a slow drive to the creek. Whee.

Maybe it's because she grew up poor in Colombia and doesn't understand the nuances of American culture the way the rest of us *sucias* do. Elizabeth Cruz thinks trucks are *cool*.

One time I asked her how she ever expected to get a man driving a thing like that, and she shrugged. For a woman who loves kids as much as she does, Elizabeth seems in no rush to find a father for some of her own. She's been single *forever*. Never even had a serious relationship that I know of. She goes on dates now and then, but never seems to stick to one guy more than a month. We try, we *sucias*, to set her up with whatever halfway good man we know and don't want ourselves. But it never works out. And it's not because no one is interested, okay? Just today Jovan Childs, my favorite dreadlocked flirting buddy at the paper, asked me—again— if I would hook him up with her. "I can't believe you," he whined. "You're friends with Elizabeth Cruz and you won't give a guy a break and introduce him. What's wrong, you want me all to yourself?" I blew Jovan a kiss and didn't tell him the truth: that I like Elizabeth too much to wish his brilliant, womanizing self on her—though I'm just self-loathing enough to think he might be an interesting prospect for *me* if things with Ed end badly, which I'm sure they will.

Anyway, Elizabeth says her tepid romantic life is because most men think she's supposed to be a docile imbecile. They think this because she's so intimidating in her beauty. "Great beauty can be a great handicap," she said once, at one of our *sucia* dinners, without a hint of vanity. We all just stared at her. Amber laughed out loud. "I'm serious," Elizabeth said. "I recognize beauty opens certain doors, but it also keeps some doors locked. Given a choice, I'm not sure I would want to look like this." Usnavys said, "Don't worry, Liz, it won't last forever."

Of all the *sucias* Elizabeth is by far the most fine. Her limbs are long and lean, even though she eats everything she wants, and her face peacefully symmetrical. She doesn't talk much, but when she does, you can count on her saying something deep and unexpected.

Elizabeth is also the *sucia* with the best chance of ever stealing Roberto away from Sara, something she would never do because she's Christian, a very nice person, *and* Sara's best friend. On those occasions when we assemble for a meal, ski trip, or yawny Boston Pops concert on the Esplanade, Roberto always asks about Elizabeth, and no other *sucia*. He gets that *look* in his eye, too, when he asks. He also stares at her like *that*, even in front of Sara. He did it *at their wedding* even. We all just stood there watching him watch Liz while Sara danced with her father. We looked at each other and wanted to kick his ass. Liz seemed embarrassed, and avoided him at every turn. I've mentioned it to Sara, and she says, "What do you want, perfection? Elizabeth is gorgeous, he's a man. He can look, but if he touches, and he won't, he's a dead man."

I can't imagine trusting a man that much. Again: Must be nice.

Elizabeth also has a hard time because she's a black Latina. Black as in African. She won't tell you this, but I know it's true: Black American guys love the way she looks, and more than one has commented on her resemblance to Destiny's Child lead singer Beyoncé Knowles, in part because of the dyed blond hair and in part because of the perfect body. Tonight, she's wearing comfortable-looking blue jeans, duck boots, a thick brown wool sweater, and one of those Patagonia-type parkas, in forest green—very bland if you ask me. Her hair hangs down long and straightened, and she has no makeup on and *still* looks better than the rest of us *combined*. It's those teeth, those incredible white teeth, and that golden brown skin, and those large, liquid eyes. She's a hell of a dancer, too, especially when you throw on a *cumbia* or a *vallenato*. Girl digs her some Carlos Vives.

Non-Latino black guys don't understand her background. I can't tell you how many times a black American guy has accused me of lying when I told them my beautiful "black" friend was a Latina. "She doesn't *look* Latina," they say.

"She looks like a sister." Says who? I ask. They don't know what to answer. You can't make people travel or understand history, and I'm tired of trying. White American guys come at Elizabeth with all this baggage most of the time, and have a hard time wrapping their minds around the fact that she's Latina and *looks like that*, too. And most Latinos, sadly, would prefer to date a butt-ugly illiterate white girl from South Boston, bucktoothed, retarded, and pigeon-toed, than a super-fine, virtuous black Latina with an amazing career.

This is true of all Latinos I know, no matter what color they themselves happen to be. They want a light girl. You can see it in our soap operas and magazines. All of the women are blond. No lie. I mean, if Hollywood pretends we all look like Penélope Cruz and JLo, the Latin media pretends we all look like a Swedish exchange student or Pamela Anderson.

Either way, everyone ignores the black Latinas.

It's like black Latinas, deep dark Latinas, don't even *exist*, you know, even though nearly *half* the nation of Colombia is black, and same with Costa Rica, Peru, and Cuba. There are more blacks in Latin America than in the United States, but no one here seems to know that. Now and then a black character will pop up on a Univision or Telemundo series, and she's invariably wearing a turban and a long white skirt, pushing a broom around and concocting some witchcraft revenge on her kindhearted blue-eyed master; the evil Aunt Jemima, in other words. Or Sambo. Just last week I saw a telenovela with a black male character and the dude actually had a bone through his nose and danced around a big old bonfire, ululating. Most of that Latin soap garbage is made in Mexico, Brazil, or Venezuela, where they have yet to experience any kind of civil rights movement for people of color, but it gets watched all over the Spanish-speaking United States. Nobody in the American media is commenting on it, either. They probably don't have a clue it's going down, or if they do they're probably too scared of seeming critical of those neato Latinos to even try. Anyway, I've tried to bring it up with Elizabeth, but she brushes me off.

"That's not it," she says with that placid look of hers and

that sheepish, magnetic smile. (She's got the whitest teeth I've ever seen—did I mention that already? I guess I did. That's because my own are a spectacular yellow.) Then politely, with her almost imperceptible hint of a Spanish accent, she'll say something like: "I'm seek (sick) oaf (of) the way jew (you) relate everything to skeen (skin) color, Lauren. It's so . . . American. In Colombia, nobody cares." I find that very hard to believe. Plus, she's here now, and America cares. And she has yet to find a man.

SO HERE WE are. The *sucias* of Boston University, gorgeous and brilliant, talented and crazy, every color of the rainbow, a few different religions. We hug, we gossip, in Spanish, English, and every conceivable mix of the two, we order our twenty-one—yes, twenty-one, four for five of us, one for Rebecca—plates of food, our beers, and Materva sodas, and then we get down to the business of catching up.

We talk about that first night out with the *sucias*, after the bouncers at Gillians dumped us on the curb.

"Remember how cold it was?" Sara asks, sipping on her ginger ale. Why does she look green? Is she ill, or am I drunk?

"Ooosh." Usnavys waves her hand in front of her. "It was freezing!"

I remember. There's this way the night air just sort of stands chilled and still in Boston after all the clubs have closed and even the T has stopped trundling through Kenmore Square. Dead, frozen, salty air. Like tonight.

"We were crazy," Elizabeth adds, shaking her head and leaning forward. "Completely crazy."

Oh, yeah. Only the youngest, dumbest college students are still out on the street at that hour, puking in gutters to prove they've finally, like, grown *up*. That was us, the *sucias*, sick and laughing and staggering and, we believed, finally free.

"And we *walked*," Amber says. We all laugh, and she retells the story.

Like the young *estúpidas* we were, we *walked* back to the

dorms that night—past the trashy alleys swarming with water rats the size of small dogs, past Fenway Park, along the creepy, butt-smelling Fens. We saw some young Latino guys handing foil balls to some white lawyer-looking guys in nice cars on one corner. We saw a guy with a greasy Afro and a pink pimp hat yelling in Ebonics at some chick. We saw two *men* getting it on in the reeds along the stinky water. It was, like, *Wow*, girl, we finally here, in Boston, in college, in the big city. Without parents, together. We pushed each other and giggled like we'd never die, freezing cold in our tight Rave club clothes—all of us except Rebecca, who looked like she was on her way to catechism class in a wool suit and red headband; she hugged her thin arms close to her body and stared at us like we were crazy. The rest of us had this crazy blue steam coming out of our mouths into the dark cold, but not Becca Baca. I wondered then if she were the devil, with icy communion wine in her veins, and was just loaded enough to ask her. She didn't find it amusing. In fact, she didn't talk to me for two months. Even then, that girl was *uptight*.

We *sucias* were stupid in other ways, too, like always walking around trying to speak Spanish just so people would *know*, you know? Just so they'd know we were Latinas, because with us you can't always tell from looking. Only Sara and Elizabeth got Spanish right all the time, and that's because Sara's from Miami, where (duh) Spanish is, like, the *official language* (*don't* laugh, it truly is a foreign country down there) and Elizabeth is from Colombia, where Spanish, like, *is* the official language. The rest of us stumbled through *El Castellano*, with all the grace of drunk hippos in a glass shop. Nobody knew the difference. Nobody knew that we had no idea what a Latina was supposed to be, that we just let the moniker fall over us and fit in the best we could. The important thing, though, is that *we* were *sucias*, and *sucias* stuck together. We studied together, shopped together, worked out together, complained together, laughed and cried together, grew up together. *Sucias* stuck to their word, too. Still do.

"We've come a long way since then," Usnavys says with a wink. She raises her glass of white wine, pudgy pinky out. "To us."

"To us," we chime in. I guzzle the rest of my beer, burp—prompting another wrinkle in Becca Baca's nose—and signal the waitress for another. I can't remember how many I've had. I guess that's a bad thing. At least I'm not driving. I keep drinking for the next hour, and listen to the stories.

"*Miranos*," I babble in Spanish, convinced, as I get when drinking, that I can do anything, including speak Spanish without butchering the language. "*Que bonitos somos*."

"*Bonitas*," Rebecca corrects me. Is that a triumphant smile? "*Que* bonitas *somos*. We're girls."

"Whatever."

Rebecca shrugs in a way I interpret to mean, "Fine, be an imbecile if you wish."

"Leave her alone," Elizabeth says. "She's doing the best she can."

"It's good you're trying," Usnavys says, her eyes soft with pity. But it's too late. I feel like an idiot. And the words burble up.

"My life sucks," I say. "It's true. I'm stupid. You happy now, Becca *Baca*? I'm an idiot. You're perfect, I'm crap. There, I said it."

"No, no you're not. Stop it, Lauren," Elizabeth says. "You're fine."

Sara puts her hand on Elizabeth's arm and nods. "Yes," she says, "you're fine, Lauren. Cut it out."

Even though I swore I wouldn't do it again, I'm drunk and can't help it. I begin to offer what are probably too many pitiful details of my own life. I can feel Rebecca thinking I shouldn't reveal so much. She gives me that *look*. No one notices, so I feel crazy paranoid again. And pathetic. But I can't help it. There's something in me—beer, mostly—that makes me talk too much.

I tell them the whole thing: that Ed the Head has been distant and evasive, that I think something's going on but can't be sure, that I tried to find out by breaking into his voice mail at work, which happened to have the same password as his ATM card, whose code I remembered from that one time I had to use it to get cab money while he hailed the taxi. I tell them what I found there: a couple of messages from a cute little breathy voice thanking him for dinner and the great time. I tell them I don't know if it's worth it to marry a guy I don't even find physically attractive, who lives in New York and spends more money on just one of his tailored shirts than he did on my last birthday present, a big-headed San Antonio Texican who wears cowboy boots with his Armani suits and tells everyone his name is "Ed Gerry-mile-oh" instead of being honest and saying his name is Eduardo Estéban Jaramillo, former dusty-ass adobe church altar boy.

I tell them I've tried to boost my sagging self-esteem by flirting unhealthily with the slick hip-hoppy Jovan Childs across the newsroom, that it escalated almost to the point of a kiss just the other night when he took me to a Celtics game, that we were so close I could see the wet, yellow rubber bands on his braces. I tell them that even though I have seen Jovan in action with other women—he measures his self-worth by how many ladies he can date at once—I have this crazy hope that I'll cure him of the commitment phobia because he is the most intensely intelligent and talented writer I've ever known and his columns make my heart break in a million pieces every time I read them.

"And I hate basketball, okay?" I say. The tears come, and I stare at my now-greasy map of Cuba. Havana is soggy with oil. Matanzas is covered with a hunk of saucy beef from my *ropa vieja*. Holguín has disappeared beneath a black bean. None of the other *sucias* have left such a mess on their placemats. Of course not. I look at the front of my white sweater and, sure enough, there's a greasy line of tomato sauce between my breasts. I look up at the girls, and start to talk before I even realize I'm talking.

"Jovan can write about a basketball arena and I'm, like, in convulsive tears—he's that good. I think I love him, but he sucks at love. He's beautiful, but, God, how can such a sensitive writer be such an insensitive human being? He sucks. I hate him."

I tell them about my increasing curiosity in the kind of dangerous prettyboy *tigres* that roam the streets of this neighborhood and others. I tell them I think Dominican men are the handsomest on the planet. I tell them of my dream of saving one of them, making him a professional, putting him through college or—something. "At the least I'd like to *do* one of 'em, you know what I mean? Just to see what it's like."

Rebecca breaks her silence, smiling kindly, and says, "Lauren, I hope you don't mind my saying, I respect you a lot. But you've got a real self-destructive streak. You must protect yourself more. You have to stop getting attracted to these gangster types who are only out to hurt you. I don't want to have to go ID your body at City Hospital."

"Just because he's a black American doesn't make Jovan a gangster," I say, pissed. "He's a writer. An amazing writer."

"Not race again," Liz says. "It's always race with you."

"That's so racist," Amber says to Rebecca. "You should examine your hatreds."

"I meant *Ed*," Rebecca says with that tight little smile. "I don't even know Jovan, though I do enjoy his columns. I'm *not* a racist."

"And Ed's not a gangster," I say.

"Oh, please. Miss 'I like blacks but I'd never date one'?" Amber says to Rebecca. "You're not racist?" She laughs, and I'm struck again by the gravelly power of her voice.

Rebecca ignores her, raises a perfectly plucked eyebrow at me, and tilts her head in a way that says, "You sure?" She smirks. I hate when she does that.

"What do you mean? He's not! He's a speechwriter for the mayor of New York!"

Several *sucias* laugh at this defense.

"Oh, Ed's fine," Sara says with a shrug. "He was a doll on the ski trip. A real gentleman. Hold on to him, *cariño*."

"Oh, please, how would you know?" Elizabeth jokes. "I hear you spent the whole day sliding down the hill on your *culito*."

"Be careful, *m'ija*," Usnavys jokes to Elizabeth. "You're almost acting un-Christian. Don't let no one—anyone—catch you."

Elizabeth blinks slowly, annoyed. "Christians can have fun, too."

"It's true," I say of Sara's skiing. "She's an awful skier. I witnessed it. It was seriously sad."

"Please," Amber says. "He's a fake Indian. Don't trust *Indios falsos*."

"Who's a fake Indian?" Usnavys asks.

"Ed," Amber says.

"What in the world is a 'fake Indian'?" Rebecca asks.

"Like you," Amber says. "In denial of your beautiful brown roots."

"Not this again." Rebecca rolls her eyes. She covers her forearms with her hands.

"I think Ed's got some . . . good qualities," chirps Usnavys. Her eyes betray the lie. She drowns her guilt with a swig of wine and looks away from my eyes.

"Name one," Elizabeth demands, pounding the table with her fist, flashing her beautiful grin.

"*Ay, bendito!*" Usnavys cries, staring at Elizabeth in mock surprise, with a hand on her chest. "*Que manera de Cristiana* hits the table like that? *Por Dios*."

"I'm serious," Elizabeth says, ignoring Usnavys. "Name one good quality in Ed. Just one. That's all I want." She pulls her shoulders to her ears, holds her hands out as if waiting for a gift she knows will never come.

Silence. Amused glances all around.

Laughter. *You too-honest bitches*.

"See?" Elizabeth asks. She drops her shoulders, dusts her palms together in a conclusive sort of way. Then, looking at me, she points with a long finger: "You can do better. And should."

"Shut up, you guys!" I cry. "I'm going to marry him. Remember? Look at this ring! It's a nice ring, isn't it?"

Amber rolls her eyes. Elizabeth bites her lip to stifle a laugh. Rebecca looks at her watch. Sara covers her own beautiful engagement/wedding ring set with her right hand and raises her eyebrows in a deliberate, charitable smile. Usnavys gulps, smiles, and says, "Yeah, sure," but shrugs.

"It's a piece of junk," I say. I turn the stone side down and curl my hand into a fist over it. Rebecca looks up from her watch and purses her lips.

"It's fine," Sara offers, moving her ring hand beneath the table. "A ring is a ring."

"He didn't even get me a good ring," I say. I uncurl my hand and examine the rock, again. "It's probably not even a real diamond. It's probably cubic zirconia."

"It's a ring, *nena*," Usnavys says. She holds up her own undecorated ring finger, uses the other hand to point at it. "That's the good thing."

"Rings are symbols of ownership," says Amber, chewing on her short black fingernails, spitting what she gets onto the floor. "Why would you even want one?"

"Oh, please," Rebecca says, fingering her own massively expensive ring set. "Not everyone wants to have a barefoot Mayan wedding they don't even invite their *friends* to."

Amber shoots her a hateful stare. "Aztec."

"He's got a master's in public policy from Columbia," I say. "He's going to run for office himself someday. He kisses babies! He shakes hands. He charmed my uncharmable grandma. He's incredible!"

Sara, in spite of the right hand over her mouth and the sympathetic look in her eyes, laughs. "I'm sorry," she says. "It's just so funny."

"New York has been run by gangsters for a long time," Amber says with a sad look in her eyes. She takes a notebook out of her pocket and starts scribbling.

"I hate when you do that," I tell her. "We're trying to talk and you start writing."

Amber ignores me.

"She's an artist," Usnavys offers. "She creates whenever the muse bites her skinny butt."

"New York couldn't run any other way, I don't think," Sara adds, placing a hand over her belly. "Roberto has a lot of friends in New York, and the mob really does control everything there, even now. The docks and everything, and the bridges. It's an island, so you control the bridges, you control the city."

"All I'm saying is be careful, Lauren," Rebecca concludes, with that pompous smile and one of her skeletal little hands on my robust one. Her manicure looks much better than mine. Until now, I was proud of my manicure. Now I see it is pedestrian, the edges too square, the color not quite right. Rebecca does this to me. "You've got everything going for you. If you put half the energy into your personal life that you put into your writing, you'd be in great shape."

"I second that emotion," says Elizabeth.

"I thought you loved me," I say to them. The room spins like, like, why, like Brad. "I thought you were my *friends*."

"If we weren't, we'd say marry the guy, *que no?*" says Amber, popping up from her creative place with that humorless Aztec priestess look. Fierce. "You need guidance sometimes, because alone you get lost."

Usnavys sees the pain in my eyes, the kind of terrified pain that comes with having someone hold a mirror to your face when you look your worst, and she jumps in. "Hey," she says. "I got something for you guys." She fishes through the pockets of her fur coat and takes out five little boxes wrapped in elegant paisley paper.

"What's this?" Sara asks, sitting forward.

"*Unas cositas,*" Usnavys says, doling them out, one for each of us. I take the small box in my hands, and begin to shake. I don't know why, but I feel like crying.

"*Que esperan, sucias!*" Usnavys says, with a mock critical wave of her hand. "Open them already!"

We begin to remove the skins from the gifts, and find light blue Tiffany boxes underneath. Inside each one is a shiny, heart-shaped pendant, gold, with each of our initials engraved on the front, and one simple word carved into the back: *sucias*. There is no price tag attached; they will not be going back. She'll be paying for this for months. This little thing must have cost ten times what the nicest gift Ed has ever gotten me cost. My trembling escalates up through my legs and torso, into my hands, and finally to my face, and I start to cry.

"*Ay, Dios mío*," Usnavys says with a roll of her eyes. "What a *llorona*!" But she still gets up and comes over and puts her arms around me. "What's the matter, *mujer?* You okay? Tell the *sucias*. That's what we're here for."

I look around the table at these people, these incredible, loving, dedicated people, and I think of Ed, of Jovan, of all the men I've made the mistake of allowing to live in my heart, of how empty every single one of them has made me feel. *Papi*. I shake my head and start to sob.

"It's just," I start, and stop. I look at Rebecca, and even *she* looks sympathetic. "It's so beautiful, so thoughtful. So incredibly incredible. And it's just this—" I hear my little drunken slur inside my head, as if I were somewhere else, watching everything go down. Part of me is embarrassed, but another part of me just can't stop talking, as usual: "It's just this. Why can't there be one single guy out there as committed as all of us?"

I admire those women who buy Christmas presents in July and store them in plastic Tupperware boxes under the bed, alongside the box of wrapping paper (bought when it was on sale the year before) and Scotch tape. My friend Rebecca is one of those people. I wish I had those kinds of organizational skills. Judging from the swarms of bodies I battled at Downtown Crossing this weekend, I'd guess many of you are just like me: procrastinators. Only thirteen more shopping days to go. Have you found what you're looking for? I haven't. But enough about my love life. Let's talk about gifts.
    —from "My Life," by Lauren Fernández

rebecca

M Y SCHEDULE FOLLOWS.
    5:15 A.M. Grapefruit, two glasses of water, and a cup of coffee, black.
    5:40 A.M. Dance France tights and red leotard, red socks and new Ryka sneakers, North Face parka, gloves and scarf. Walk across Copley Square from my apartment on Commonwealth Avenue to the gym for a 6:00 A.M. step aerobics class.
    5:55 A.M. Claim my spot in the front row. Greet the other regulars. Ask about their jobs and families. When they ask about Brad, say everything is fine.

6:50 A.M. Pick up dry cleaning. Put mother's Spanish-language religious birthday card in the mailbox.

7:00 A.M. Buy flowers for the large vase in the dining room, tulips in dark red, to match the wallpaper.

WALKING HOME, I admire the Christmas displays in the shops, the wreaths with red and green plaid bows and twinkling white lights. I take out my Palm Pilot and make a digital note to remember to buy a present for my "little," the girl I mentor through the Big Sister Association. *Shanequa regalito, quizás una cámara digital.*

Shanequa Ulibarri is thirteen, born in Costa Rica, now a Dorchester gang member. She wants to have a baby right away so someone will love her. Her "man" is a twenty-eight-year-old who, she says, wants to knock her up. I got her one of those fake babies, the kind that cry at regular intervals unless you feed, diaper, and love them. I said that if she could make it through one weekend I'd give her my blessing to have a child. She agreed, but the next week told me she had "lost" the baby at a party.

She paints as well as anyone I know. And when I let her use my camera at a concert once, the photos came back artistic and brilliant. She has talent, but doesn't know it because her mother is an illiterate who beats her with extension cords. Her stepfather calls her names I wouldn't use on my worst enemy, and I've seen him stare at her blooming body. I think I'll get her a digital camera to go with the computer I got her last year. Come to think of it, I haven't seen that computer in a long time. I wonder who she sold it to.

7:15 A.M. GO home and begin to prepare for another long day.

I've stapled holiday lights in the two front bay windows of my top-floor apartment, and decorated the firm, full pine tree in the living room. I did these things alone while Brad read Marxist theory in his underwear, sprawled on my antique day bed in the guest room. As he walked past on his way to the kitchen, his privates almost poking out of his drawers, he mumbled, "Religion is for the feebleminded." He was not really speaking to me, as he didn't wait for a reply. He and I haven't spoken of the Christmas tree, or anything really. Talking for us is limited lately to "Here's your mail."

7:45 A.M. I write a detailed list for Consuelo about what needs to be done around the apartment, including scrubbing the bathroom floors and removing the scum from the shower curtains. She can't read. When I have time, I help her with her literacy program homework. Today Brad will have to read her the list. I'm busy.

Brad stares at the ceiling when I talk and mumbles to himself. I can't tell him anything and have him remember it, so I write the list for him as much as for her. Brad's head is always up in the clouds with his "research." I used to admire that about him. I even used to find it sexy, and used to enjoy sitting across from him listening to his ideas. I'd never known someone so proudly intellectual. But lately it irritates me. His ideas are harebrained when you take them apart. I didn't go to an Ivy League school like all his friends, but even I recognize that my husband is a dolt with a large vocabulary.

When I met Brad, I wasn't exactly well read when it came to esoteric philosophy or academic publications. I made it a point to immerse myself in that type of material as a way of showing my love for him. What a mistake. The more I learned, the more I realized he didn't know what he was talking about, the more I recognized that he just stuck words like "paradigm" and "undergird" into his daily speech to impress people. Brad, I have realized, approaches academia the same way his parents approach life: by advertising brand names. With his family, it's designer clothes and cars. With Brad, it's predictable male intellectuals. Now his spouting irritates me. His peppery, papery library smell irritates me. The way he blows his nose all the time in that dirty monogrammed handkerchief irritates me. His hair is messy because he *wants* it that way. His friends all look just like him, and they irritate me, too. Basically, Brad, my husband, the man I am stuck with for life, irritates me.

God help me.

Consuelo is scheduled to come at noon. This time, Brad better be here. Last time, he claims, he forgot and went to the MIT library. Poor Consuelo had to get back on the bus in the cold and go all the way back to Chelsea. I'm surprised she didn't quit. Brad suggested we give her a key. He's suspicious of all men who look like his father, but Consuelo he trusts? He's got to be crazy.

7:50 A.M. I pull the Cherokee onto Commonwealth Avenue before Brad has even rolled off the guest bed that is now officially his nest, full of papers, old food, and dirty socks with holes in them. It has been five months since we slept in the same room. I don't wake him to say good-bye anymore. I prefer it this way. It hurt at first, but now I can read through magazines in my own bed at night without him complaining about how crass pop culture is. I can enjoy my work without him sniffing and snorting about my magazine and my mission. The silence between us does this much, at least. Thank the Lord for that.

8:00 A.M. I head to South Boston to have the jeep washed. Tonight is the monthly dinner of the Minority Business Association, at the Park Plaza Hotel, and it's not acceptable to have a dirty car. Lauren would tell me I'm shallow, but she hates me for some reason. And there are studies about this kind of thing. People make up their minds based almost entirely on nonverbal cues. The shade of your teeth, if your nails are clean, your posture as you wait for the valet. I try not to judge people based on these kinds of cues, but we're animals. That's how God made us, and who are we to challenge His work?

In March, I will be the keynote dinner speaker at the Minority Business Association gathering. This is a great honor. And it's no mistake. I prepared for this in every way, in my presentation of self. I have begun working on my speech, about media images of minorities, and taking control of our images of ourselves. I have a lot to say.

I neglected to say I shower at home. Public facilities are for the public. I am wearing a tasteful suit, nothing too flashy or worth detailing. Work clothes.

8:10 A.M. I wait in the heated lobby of the car wash and watch through the observation window to make sure none of the droopy, embarrassed young men working here scratches my vehicle. A heavyset woman bumps me on her way to the door, and I choke on the protest I would like to issue.

When Brad started to remove himself from my life, I kept quiet too. I think my parents removed themselves from each other the same way, long before I was born. I wonder if they ever had passion for each other at all. I used to wonder if I was adopted, but I resemble them both. Whenever I see that painting of the farmer and his wife, where they frown behind a pitchfork, I think of Mom and Dad in church, side by side, shoulder to shoulder, with me on the other side of my mom. There was no yelling, no crying, little talking in our house. My mom took me aside once or twice and whispered, "Please remember that you don't have to be like me."

That was all the guidance she gave.

8:15 A.M. IN the shiny Cherokee, I steer toward my office. I turn on the stereo and my Toni Braxton CD plays softly. I crank the volume up until I can feel the thrum of bass in my chest, and try to sing along. I tap time on the steering wheel, and move my shoulders until I notice a man in the car next to me smiling my way. I blush and stop. Was he laughing, or flirting? I dare not look again. I turn down the stereo and look the other way. Snow has begun to fall again.

I try to remember music playing in my childhood home, and it seems to me there was only ever quiet opera or Dad's old-time country-western. We were comfortable in our spa-

cious adobe hacienda with the flowers and poplar trees dron-
ing with big-eyed cicadas in the summers. We were successful with our new American cars and conservative clothes
from Dillard's, an old family carrying on an old tradition of
manners and sophistication. There was no discussion of
much of anything, other than the business my mother started
a few years before she met my dad and he took over.

"A man makes the decisions," Dad says, "and a wife
obeys. That's what it says in the Bible, that's what we do in
this house." My father controlled everything, informing
Mom in short, proper Spanish sentences. I have never seen
her without the bitterness of resentment clipping the corners
of her mouth tight together. In college, I realized the Bible
does *not* say a woman must obey a man. That's my father's
interpretation. The northern New Mexico, Hispano interpretation. The Bible says a man and wife ought to respect each
other. That's what *my* God teaches. Poor Mom.

At the next stoplight, I snap open my cell phone and press
the speed-dial for my mother. It's only 6:20 in Albuquerque,
but I know she will have been up for more than an hour already, scrambling eggs with chorizo, heating tortillas on the
open blue flame of the stove, tidying the house, and picking
out Dad's tie. My dad will have left for work by now in his big
silver four-door truck with the Republican bumper stickers.

"Baca residence," she answers, trying to sound cheerful. I
ask how she's doing. She says, "Oh, fine," but there's a sigh
in her voice. "How are you?" she asks. I tell her I'm fine. She
asks about Brad. "Fine, Mom." She asks about the weather. I
answer, and return the question. "It's snowing here, too," she
says. "It's getting to be Christmas. We've started selling out
of *biscochitos* already." I remind her not to eat any. "I know,"
she says. I ask if she's going to dialysis today and she says,
"Yes." "Don't forget your shots," I say.

My mother's lower abdomen is tie-dyed with bruises from
the insulin injections. She pinches up a fresh spot of skin several times a day, jabs the needle into her flesh without flinch-
ing. By day's end, the tiny red drop of blood marking the
entry point will have blossomed into an angry purple flower.

She never complains. Never. "I won't forget, *m'ija*," she says. The light turns green. I tell her I love her, say I'm in traffic and have to go. We hang up.

I turn up the stereo again, and begin to move a little. The traffic is brisk, so no one can focus on me. I want a man who makes me feel the way Toni Braxton sounds. I thought that man was Brad. It wasn't. It has been years since I felt the tingle of lust. I know I shouldn't, but I miss it. The lack of it makes me feel old. I catch myself midthought, make the sign of the cross, and ask the saints on the laminated cards in my glove box to forgive me. I think they will. I approach a yellow light and gun the engine. I blast the stereo even more, and barely get through the intersection before it turns red.

My phone rings. I turn off the stereo and answer without checking the caller ID, thinking it might be Mom again. "Hello?"

"Becca, it's Usnavys."

"Hi, sweetie, how are you?"

"Good. Look, you got a second?"

"Sure."

"Would you be interested in being on an antismoking panel we're putting together with the Department of Public Health?"

I swerve to avoid hitting a Buick that has cut me off. I almost honk. The old man inside flips me his middle finger, as if I were the one in the way.

"Sure, I think so. Look, Navi, I can't really talk now. I'm in the middle of traffic. Can I call you later?"

"Oh, I'm sorry. Call me later. We'll talk. I want to ask you about some other things too, guy things."

"Sure. Bye, hon'."

"Bye."

Guy stuff. It's so easy for her to talk about guy stuff. I watch people like Usnavys, Sara, and Lauren, the way they express themselves, the way they raise their voices, curse, cry, and slam their palms on the table for emphasis. I can't do that. So many things my friends carry over to me about their personal lives could have, I think, been better left alone with them. I don't want to know about their abortions and eating disorders. Their problems make me feel heavy inside. That's why I haven't told them what's happening with Brad. I don't want to weigh them down. And that's why I haven't confronted Brad, either. I don't know how, and I'm not sure how much I really want to learn. Thank God for work.

8:30 A.M. I have timed my commute to the *Ella* offices in the warehouse district of South Boston, just over the bridge from downtown, and depending on traffic it takes between half an hour to an hour. Today was quick, even with the snow. Toni had something to do with that. I love this disc. It was a gift from Amber, believe it or not. She got all of us CDs at the last gathering, each chosen, she said, to balance our karmas. She suggested I find an Ayurvedic restaurant to complete the balance, and explained that this type of restaurant serves food the cook believes the patron needs, vegetarian. I made a note to look into the phenomenon for a future issue of the magazine. Sounded interesting. Amber and I have more in common than you might think at first, especially our eating and exercise habits.

I admire the crisp silver of downtown's buildings against the dingy gray sky. Boston is marvelous, a fresh-aired city of grays and browns, with plenty of red brick to balance it, and flowers and greenery in the summer. In the autumn, clouds slide across the sky in fast-moving sheets. It's not like home, where the clouds are so big and so far you can't imagine touching them. Anything is possible in Boston. I belong here.

I turn off L Street onto the side street next to the renovated warehouse building housing my magazine. Shawn, the parking attendant, waves and smiles as I steer past his booth into the underground parking lot. I slide the Cherokee into my assigned spot near the elevator, exit, check the locks, then head up.

8:45 A.M. I surprise the receptionist, who is talking on the phone in a voice too friendly to be business.

"Good morning, Miss Baca." She smiles, hanging up midsentence and trying to hide the soggy white paper cup of coffee she's nursing. We have a policy against eating or drinking at the front desk.

"Good morning, Renee," I answer.

I'll let the coffee thing go—today. She looks tired. She's a college student, and was probably up late studying. But I'll check again tomorrow. If she's still breaking the rules I will write up a warning. You must be sensitive and compassionate, and most of all kind, but you must set limits and make it clear that you mean business. Women managers walk such a fine line. When you are assertive, you are called a "bitch." When you are demanding, you are called a "bitch." The better the job you do, the more people use that word.

I close the door to my office and take a deep lavender breath. I read once that Nelly Galan, the TV executive, keeps aromatherapy machines in her office, spraying out the scents of success every hour. So I bought one, just in case there's something to the theory. At the very least, my corner office smells fresh. In addition to lavender, this recipe has Roman chamomile and sweet almond oil. My office is filled with light, too, and appointed in a minimalist, modern fashion that has grown on me. My desk is made of glass, and my computer is sleek and black with a large flat-screen monitor. Plants warm it somewhat. And the pictures; I have framed photos of Brad, my friends and family on a shelf behind my chair, where people can see them. I log on to my system with the password I use for all work-related machines: exitos4u. It means successes for you.

I use the extra time to catch up on my E-mails and other correspondence and make sure Dayonara is handling the files properly. I learned the hard way to double-check things after my first assistant botched the filing so badly I had to have an accounting firm come in and sort the mess out. You try to help someone out, give them a chance to get their foot in the door, and it's amazing how some don't realize the opportunity in front of them. Dayonara is doing a very good job, though. We checked her references very carefully.

Everything is always on time, and it's put in the right place. I have never missed a phone call since she started, nor a message, never had an appointment lost.

The *Ella* offices have expanded quickly, and we now occupy more than half the third floor in the renovated warehouse. We're in discussions to take over the entire thing starting early next year. As I walk across the tidy lobby from my office to the conference room, breathing in the scent of the holiday greenery draped along the walls and doorways, my heart swells with pride. I was sent to college to find a husband, if you can believe that, in the 1990s. I learned a lot at college, especially about what was possible for a woman in the world today. My father has never told me how he feels about my business, but my mother has. "You have made my life worthwhile," she told me in a low voice the last time I saw her. "I'm proud of you." She had tears in her eyes, wiped them away as soon as Dad walked in the room.

I built this, I think, looking at the elegantly exposed red brick walls with the framed four-foot blowups of all twenty-four published *Ella* covers hanging on them, and notice with pleasure that the plant people have come and finally delivered the Christmas tree for the main lobby. We've had the top Latina talent grace our covers, from Sofia Vergara to Sandra Cisneros, and, once a year, the top Latino talent for the "men's" issue. This year we got Enrique Iglesias—my dream man—posing with his mother. I went to the photo shoot in New York a couple of months ago, and, come to think of it, I felt lust then. It was the last time. If he'd asked me to come home with him, I might have. Who wouldn't?

We try to avoid just putting models on the cover, because the mission of the magazine, as I created it, is to elevate the image of Hispanic women, to inspire and empower them to be the best they can. All of us have been exposed to too much information telling us the most important thing we can be is sexy or subservient. It's time for a change, and you can tell by how well my magazine has done that Hispanic women are ready to hear it.

I pass the tall, potted plants, the sitting area with its luxurious rose-colored velvet furniture. I admire the Christmas tree, decorated with red and gold glass balls and blinking pink lights. I look at the curved marble of the front desk, the wall of windows with the view of the downtown skyline. I wasn't sure at first when the interior designers came to me with their drawings for this front room. I wanted something more conservative, something Victorian with French country undertones, like my apartment, but they were insistent, telling me people would be expecting a young, feminine yet strong and exciting atmosphere. They were right. I'm glad I finally trusted the designers to go with this look. Sara's the one who convinced me. I do not gravitate toward anything colorful on my own. "Very Latina," Sara assured me when I showed her the plans. "But still very Boston." Renee sits up taller as I pass, and smiles at me. The coffee cup is gone. Good girl.

I make it a point to know everyone's name in the company, even the janitors'. Look people in the eye, shake hands with conviction, and address everyone by their proper name. Treat people respectfully, no matter what job they do, because you never know when you might run into them again.

As I enter the room I am pleased to see all eight of my editors seated around the black conference table, chatting quietly. Seven women, one man. The women wear fashionable, modern suits, and have their hair in neat, stylish cuts. The man, Erik Flores, is swishy, as Usnavys would say, and might as well be a woman. I wonder sometimes if he doesn't buy his clothes in women's boutiques. Today he wears a salmon-colored jacket with a fitted waist, and a lime green turtleneck. He's tall and handsome and a fantastic beauty editor—and completely off-limits to girls.

"Good morning," I say to them.

"Good morning," they answer. A few begin to shuffle papers around in front of them.

"How were your weekends?" I ask as I settle in at the head of the table.

"Still feeling mine," says Tracy, our notoriously party-hearty arts editor, with a dramatic groan and fingers to her temples. Everyone laughs.

"Get some more coffee," I say with a grin.

"Any more and I'll burst a vessel, *chica*," she says, tilting her *Ella* mug toward me. It is stained brown inside from months of overuse. "Third one of the day already."

"That stuff'll kill ya," says Yvette, my photo editor. I agree, but say nothing and smile.

We have had a very low turnover, by magazine standards. I want people to have positive associations with my magazine, and with me, from the plant lady to the freelancer to the long-time subscriber to the woman who picks us up for the first time at the doctor's office.

My personalities editor, Lucy, gets up from her spot and moves so that she sits next to me. She looks as if she's been crying, puffy and red around the eyes even though she tries to look happy. Her usually neat and plucked eyebrows are a mess. She hangs her head as if to hide them. It's not unusual for my employees to come to my office in order to spill out their personal problems, and I indulge them. I know, from last week's episode, that Lucy's boyfriend left her for a much, much older woman. Lucy is twenty-six, and the woman her man found is fifty-four. I can't even imagine her pain. Down the road, not too soon, I'd like to assign a feature on older Latinas and younger men. I'll wait until she's healed a bit, even though I don't think it's appropriate for my employees to tell me about their crazy mothers and abusive boyfriends, or whatever. I think it is even less appropriate to castigate a person in pain. Good manners, George Bush senior once said, sometimes mean having bad manners just so those with bad manners in your presence won't feel bad. So I listen.

"You okay, sweetie?" I ask Lucy softly. I put a hand on her shoulder and squeeze, lightly. She thinks I'm a good friend. She smiles up at me and nods. "I'm glad," I say, then take my seat.

Though it's only early December, we are scrambling for one last story for our Valentine's issue. A story fell through, and we ship next week. I like all of the ideas my editors put forward today except for one. The new fashion editor (our last one left to spend time with her new baby) has proposed a racy spread on sexy lingerie, with the top Latina models from the Ford agency posing on a Miami beach. She spent the better part of her career so far working at the Spanish-language version of *Cosmopolitan*, a magazine full of crass language, lascivious ideas, and photos that border on pornography.

"That's an interesting idea, Carmen," I say, leaning forward with my hands open on the table. My fingernails are of a conservative feminine length; filed into neat ovals, with the palest pink nail polish, almost white. My wedding ring is the only jewelry I wear on my fingers today. Never close your hands together in a business setting, especially if you are about to reject someone's ideas; you want to appear open, and body language has as much to do with someone's perception of you and your message as your words. I smile, and note that Carmen has scooted back in her seat, arms crossed protectively. I don't want her to be afraid. I just want her to *think* more like an *Ella* editor, and I tell her so. I continue: "Valentine's Day is certainly a time when many women want to look sexy. But we need to keep in mind that some of our readers are teenage girls. I don't want us giving them the wrong message, okay?"

"Oh, please," Tracy says, rolling her bloodshot eyes. "Girls start having sex in fifth grade now, Rebecca. They get periods when they're *nine*. It's not like we'll corrupt anyone. You listened to pop radio lately?"

I smile. I actually respect Tracy more than anyone in the room, because she has the guts to speak her mind. I need people like that in this organization, because I know I don't always have the best ideas.

"That's probably true," I say to Tracy, thinking of Shanequa, who told me she's been sexually active for four years. "But I don't want to be part of the problem."

"Fine," Tracy says. "I respect that. But you know what we're up against out there. It'd be stupid to come off prude in this market. Especially at Valentine's Day."

Carmen's eyes flash with admiration, and amazement.

Tracy's right, of course.

"Okay," I say. "How about we try to come up with something less sexual and more celebratory of love in general, but still sexy. Okay?"

Tracy shrugs, Carmen nods.

"Does anyone have any other suggestions?" I ask.

"Naked men," Tracy deadpans. "Men in g-strings."

"Oooh," Erik answers, reveling in his swishiness once again. "I *like* that."

Everyone laughs.

"Any *real* suggestions?" I ask.

"We could do something sexy, but not revealing," Carmen suggests, with a quake to her voice. "Let people know you don't have to take it all off to get your Valentine's attention."

"That's good," I say, pointing my pen in her direction. "I like it."

"Nah," Tracy jokes. "Take it all off. Get the *men* to take it all off, for once."

"How about," I say, ignoring Tracy now, "we do a red and pink spread? Carmen, why don't you contact the top Hispano designers in New York, L.A., and Miami, and have them come up with their best red and pink outfits for different kinds of Valentine's dates, like a date for a couple married thirty years, all the way to a date for a couple in high school. And you can still use the Ford models if you like, for some of the shots. But I'd like to see real people, too. Attractive people, but real. Maybe contact the acting agencies about finding older people, and a big variety of people."

"That's a really good idea, Rebecca," Lucy says. She always compliments me.

"What do you think, Carmen?" I ask.

"I like it," she says. "Sounds fine. Sorry for the other idea. It was stupid. It's an adjustment, coming here."

"Oh, please, don't apologize," I say. "It was a fine idea. We hired you because we *like* the way you think. This is still your idea, just with an *Ella* twist."

Carmen's posture softens and she smiles.

"I still like the naked boy idea," Erik says.

"You *would, nena*," Tracy says with a hoarse laugh.

I check my watch. "It's about that time," I say. "Anything else before we get out of here?"

Erik raises his hand confidently. I swear his nails are buffed shiny. I suppress a giggle. He has that smug look on his face that I can't stand. I'm bad, I know. He's a wonderful editor, very reliable, always on time with deadlines. But he's a diva. I get the sense that if he could, he'd take over the magazine and throw me out. Until I asked him to stop, he used to place himself at the head of the conference-room table. I point to him. "Yes?"

He folds his hands in a prissy way in front of him and cocks his head to the side with a girlish smile. "Rebecca," he says, drawing out the A. "I couldn't help but notice you were mentioned in the new issue of *Forbes* magazine as one of the hot young entrepreneurs to watch in the next ten years. I wanted to congratulate you on that." He pauses for emphasis, purses his lips, and everyone claps. "I was also wondering if we might include a small item on it in the magazine, with a photograph of you."

I laugh and shake my head as if the honor were no big deal.

"Thank you, Erik. That's nice. But, no. I'm not going to take the blame for this mess by myself."

"Blame?" he asks.

"It's a team screwup around here," I joke. I gather my papers from the table to signal the meeting has come to an end. Hubris has ruined many a good business.

WHEN I GET back to my office, my assistant hands me a thick Italian pottery mug of unsweetened herbal tea infused with Echinacea extract. She reminds me that I have a lunch appointment with the director of advertising sales and a representative from a major cosmetics company. They have already agreed upon a tentative long-term contract, and simply want me to approve it before they sign on the dotted line. I've looked over the details with our lawyer and find it agreeable.

At my desk, I sip the tea and look over proofs for the next issue. I had read that this blend helped boost the immune system, and I believe it. I haven't been sick in more than a year, since I started drinking it. It helps, too, that I have cut out meat and dairy, sugar, caffeine, and fat.

After a while, I take a break and look out the window. The sun is peeking through the clouds, melting the roof snow. It drips down my window in sensuously twisting streaks. I look at the wedding picture on the shelf. We married in Our Lady of the Sacred Heart in Albuquerque, a warm adobe building in the oldest part of town, a humble yet strong church where my family has sought spiritual guidance for more than three generations. Everyone from my side was there, my parents, my brother and sisters, my aunts and uncles, my grandparents, all my cousins and nieces and nephews, the family from Truchas and Chimayó. On Brad's side there were just a few people, his sister the filmmaker, who has become a good friend, and three of his friends from school.

His parents were nowhere to be found.

He told me they had prior obligations they couldn't change. It wasn't until we were already married that he told me the truth: His parents did not approve of me because they were under the mistaken notion that I was an *immigrant*. You have no idea how much that hurt me. My family has been in this country since before Brad's family got to Ellis Island. But they have the nerve to call me an immigrant! It's precisely that sort of prejudice I want to battle through my charitable works, getting my name and face out there as a new philanthropist, alongside the Rockefellers and the Pughs.

We look happy in that picture. I lift it off the shelf and hold it in my hand. It's lighter than I remembered. I try to recall the happiness of the woman in the wedding dress, but it's gone. I don't remember what it felt like. In the photo, Brad smiles. He so rarely does that. I remember he told me he loved the church, my family, and the way we covered all of the cars with paper flowers for the post-wedding procession around old town. He loved the posole and enchiladas and the wedding cake made by that great Santa Fe chef. He said so. I felt it, didn't I? We had a wonderful, passionate honeymoon in Bali.

What happened? Where did that man go?

I close the door to my office and dial my home number. Brad doesn't answer right away, so I assume he is still sleeping and dial again. He sleeps all the time lately. It's one of the symptoms of depression, I know that much. This time, he answers.

"It's me," I say.

"Oh, hi." He sounds disappointed. Cold.

"I just wanted to remind you to be home when Consuelo comes by today. You forgot last time."

"That it?" It is not, but I don't know how to bring these things up.

"Yes," I say.

"Okay."

We hang up, and my heart sinks. My skin feels too thin. I get a chill, even though the temperature in the office is always seventy-four degrees.

I wait five minutes, stare at the inky red marks I've made on the proofs, and try to will down the dark feelings welling up in my chest. I don't want my heart to beat this fast, I don't want this adrenaline rush. I breathe deeply. I dial home again.

"Hello?"

"Brad."

"Hey." He sniffles and blows his nose.

I don't know what to say. For some reason I think about how when someone in my family growing up got a cold, there was no babying them the way I've seen in other families. Brad expects to be babied when he's sick. We weren't what you'd call *demonstrative*. I never baby him.

I want to ask Brad if he remembers what we felt like on our wedding day. But I can't.

"Listen," I say, turning toward the large windows that look down over the bustling street. I clear my throat.

"I'll *be* here," he says. "Don't worry."

"What?" My heart flutters.

"When Consuelo comes."

"Oh. No, that's not—"

Silence. A long, awkward silence.

"Rebecca?" he finally asks. "You still there?"

"Yes."

"What do you want? I have reading to do."

"Nothing, I guess."

"Well I gotta go then."

"No, wait."

"Yeah?"

"What's going on?" I ask.

"What do you mean?"

"With . . . us." This is so hard.

"Nothing." His tone of voice is mocking.

"Please," I say.

"Please what?"

"Tell me what's going on."

"I told you. *Nada.*"

"Can we make a time to talk about this face-to-face?" I twirl a pen in my fingers and turn toward my desk calendar.

He laughs. "Oh, you mean like an *appointment*?"

"What is so funny?" I ask. My face feels hot and tight. I look at the clock on the wall; I have half an hour before I have to head to the advertising department to get Kelly for the lunch meeting.

"Oh, God," he says with a laugh. "*You're* so funny. You don't know how funny you are. That's what's so funny."

"How?"

"Never mind. Bye-bye."

"No, tell me."

He sighs. "You really want to know? I'll tell you. I didn't set out to marry some status-quo wanna-be white girl. Happy? It's—it's like you've become my worst nightmare."

His worst nightmare? I am dumbfounded. "I have to go," I say. I fight the urge to drop the phone even though it seems to burn my hand. "Just be there when Consuelo comes. Don't forget again."

"Oh, right. Consuelo! That's another thing. How in the world can you exploit a woman like that?"

"Like *what*?"

"Hispanic."

"Oh, God. I have to go now."

"Fine. But would you tell your realtor friend to quit calling here all day long? I'm sick of talking to her. I hate her."

"She can't call *here*. You said you'd help."

"I don't *want* a brownstone. I don't *need* it. I *hate* people like that. You're not who you used to be."

Blood has filled my ears and I can hear my heart beating. "So," I whisper, turning my back to the closed door of my office, "who did you think I was, then?"

"Earthy."

"Earthy?"

"That's right. Earthy. Earth mother."

"I'm hanging up now, Brad."

"Fine. Bye."

I don't hang up. Neither does he. We listen to each other breathe for a few seconds and I try not to cry.

Finally, I say, "Why are you doing this?"

"Good-bye, Rebecca."

Click. He hangs up.

Earthy?

I look at the other snapshots, some early ones of us. I look giddy and flushed in the photos. We didn't know each other much then, but I remember being excited about his money. I'll be honest. That was the big draw, that and his light hair and handsome face. There's a picture where he's resting his head on my shoulder, bending over to do it because he's so tall, and I see something now I never saw before. He looks like he's praying.

I have never met his parents. His sister took step classes with me and we shopped for clothes together on Newbury

Street and went to the Isabella Stewart Gardner Museum one afternoon with Au Bon Pain sandwiches in our handbags. I expected the parents would want to get to know me, too. How was I to know they would despise me so much they would start to restrict Brad's cash flow? It made no sense. I tried for months to make contact with them, to win them over, with letters and gifts. My father even called to invite them to spend a weekend at our ranch near Truchas, so they could see that we have been in New Mexico for generations, that we're not immigrants. He called and told me the mother had told him she had no interest in going to "Mexico." Was it possible for people with that much money to be so ignorant?

Brad curled his hands into fists when I told him about the exchange with his parents, and told me it was useless; he reminded me that for all their money, his parents had never bought a computer for the house, and didn't have a single book in their mansion that he himself had not put there. Not even a coffee table book, or a cookbook. No books at all.

"They are idiots, Rebecca," he said.

I used to tell him not to say such things about his parents. I was raised to respect my elders. But he may have had a point. I mean, I called and left a message for them, explaining that *New* Mexico was a state, and that I came from a long line of successful politicians and businessmen there, that we were descended from Spanish royalty from the Andalusia region, near France, where everyone is white. They did not respond. Now, it looks like Brad may get written out of the will altogether. That's what his sister tells me.

I used to deny accusations of gold-digging when my friends brought it up, but I have to be honest with myself now; if Brad were not the son of a billionaire, I would never have married him. I close my eyes and focus. I do not think I love him anymore, if I ever did.

10:00 A.M. ON my way to get Kelly for our meeting, I walk past my assistant. She stops me, and holds out a pink message slip.

"Andre Cartier," she says, raising one eyebrow. I doubt she meant to raise it, but it happened. I'm not sure what she means with the eyebrow, but it almost seems like she thinks I've got something going on with Andre, or else she herself thinks he's attractive. People have very little control over their facial muscles, which betray our inner thoughts all the time unless we master them. They're called "microexpressions." World-class liars and politicians don't have them. Bill Clinton never had them, for instance. He had a face that did whatever he wanted. My mother never has microexpressions, either, and I inherited that gift from her. No matter how bad I feel, no matter what negative thought crosses my mind, I am not the kind of person who other people ask, "What's wrong?" I smile serenely and lift the message from her hand.

Andre is a software mogul from England who relocated his company to Cambridge, Massachusetts, several years ago. And he's the reason my magazine exists.

When my family couldn't come up with the funds, and when Brad's family refused to help me, when I was just about ready to let my dream of *Ella* magazine die, Andre was there. He listened to me describe my idea at a Minority Business Association dinner (much like the one I'm going to tonight) where we had the good fortune of being seated next to each other. He did not tell me who he was or what he did, just listened to me talk about my idea for my business. He's a good listener.

I thought he was handsome, well-bred, and charming with that British accent and understated tuxedo, even though he *was* black. Not that I am racist, but I was raised a certain way. I have nothing against black people—I mean, Elizabeth is one of my closest friends—but I wouldn't feel comfortable dating someone outside of my own race. My mother made it clear when she told me repeatedly, "Date a black man, and you will break my heart." That's why this whole business with Brad's parents is so shocking. They don't understand where I come from, who I am, or what I believe in.

Andre has a nice, honest, open face. After listening to me

go on about *Ella* for nearly an hour, he reached under the table, pulled out a briefcase, opened it, and took out a checkbook and an expensive pen. "How do you spell your name?" he asked. I thought he was joking, or that he was going to give me a small investment, because I had just finished telling him I would need a cool two million dollars to do the first issue right. He smiled secretly and continued filling out the check. Then he handed me his business card. I recognized the company name from the business pages of the *Wall Street Journal*. Under his name, it said President/CEO. When he handed me the check for an even two million, I almost had a heart attack. I tried to refuse it, but he insisted. "It's a good investment for me," he said. I couldn't tell if he was joking, but I came to learn he was not. Andre's company is worth more than 365 million, and it's growing.

I read the pink memo as I walk down the hall toward advertising.

Says he'll see you at the MBA dinner tonight, hopes you'll finally dance.

. . . It's a new year, and already the planners of this year's Saint Patrick's Day parade in South Boston have once again announced they intend to ban gays and lesbians from the festivities. Don't they realize this practically guarantees the media will focus on gays and lesbians who wish to be included? If the goal of the parade is to celebrate Irish heritage in Boston, rather than bigotry, organizers might take a lesson from the armed forces: Don't ask, don't tell. Otherwise, they ensure that homosexuality and the Saint Patrick's Day parade are inexorably linked in our civic memory.

—from "My Life," by Lauren Fernández

elizabeth

I PROBABLY SHOULDN'T have, but after seeing Lauren at the last *sucias* gathering, and after reading her sensitive column on the parade, I called and invited her to dinner, just the two of us, with the idea of telling her, finally, how I feel about her.

We went to the Elephant Walk in Brookline for Cambodian and French food, and spoke in the civilized, careful cadences we always use with each other. She wore a blue wool hat and jeans, carried a backpack as if she were still in college. Her eyes sparkled. Her lips shone. Ed, Jovan, problems, pain. She talked and talked. Drank and drank. I

listened and choked on the words held prisoner in my throat.
I almost told her, almost. Almost told her I could rescue her
from all that, love her eternally, without condition, hold her
until the doubting rose from her skin like steam, until all that
would be left is the gigantic, striding beauty of her. But
didn't. Couldn't. The risk would be too huge, losing her.
Facing her polite rejection. I couldn't bear it. Coward in my
own skin.

Selwyn senses something, I think. When I mention my
friends, she is usually passive. But when I mention Lauren,
Selwyn stiffens, a wolf whose fur rises along her neck.
Something is there, she senses it, in the woods, lurking,
threatening. Her nostrils open. I have told Selwyn of my past
loves, but never of this one, the longest-gnawing love I've
known, the one that makes me weep. What wolf Selwyn
senses is my love for Lauren, this never-diminishing, ever-
pulsating thing that—what is the word, gloms?—gloms on to
my corpuscles, making the blood thick and useless every time
I see her, pushes at me, tilts me toward the moon, howling.

I called her later that night, to thank her for a lovely dinner.
She seemed sleepy and puzzled and I said nothing of what I
felt. I paused with my secret, her scent in my nose, listened to
her breathing and tried to think of a way to say it, this thing
I've fought for a decade. "Hello? Liz, you there?" she asked.
"Yes," I mumbled, mouth full of ghost blood. "You okay?"
she wanted to know. "Of course," I'd said. "Just wanted to say
we should do it again soon." "Sure," she said, a longer word
than usual, with a question in it, maybe too an answer. Curiosity in her voice, listening to the coded message in deliberate
silence. "Well, good-bye, then," I said, rushing to run away,
again. "Good night." "Take care, Liz," she said. "Love ya."

The fluttering up of a million inner pigeons. The dying
inside of hope. Love ya. Love? Love, in the straight woman
way, where you may walk arm in arm while shopping for a
dress, may kiss on the cheek, may even, as she once did in
college, craftily grab a woman you love and stuff a condom
into her bra before she heads out on a date with a man she
has agreed to see mostly for show, love that means many

nearly sexual moments, but where you may never open your mouth against hers to receive her tongue sweet and soft, where you may never slide your knee up between her legs, gentle and with eyes wide open.

I'm back to normal now. Or nearly so. Back to Selwyn. Thoughts of Selwyn all day long. I have removed Lauren from my heart. Again. She'd never understand the strangling of it all, the way she gets in there and pushes until I have to bite my pillow to stifle the thoughts, the way I love her. Straight women never do, entirely. After the last "curious" one used me for her experiment and left me sucking for air, beached on the loneliest of shores when she returned to her man with a "Thanks, it's been fun," I've stopped trying.

Selwyn is reading tonight, poems of love. For me.

Without my makeup and with this scarf on my head I don't think anyone can recognize me. I waited in the truck on the darkened street a few blocks from the bar after she got out, for about fifteen minutes, then I slipped in after she had started reading, walked down the darkened, narrow flight of stairs into the basement bar and took an anonymous seat in the back of the room. I keep my sunglasses on, even though it's late at night and the bar is dimly lit. I don't want to be bothered. Not here. Not while Selwyn Womyngold is reading. I don't need to be spotted here, either, not on a Wednesday night. Womyn's Night. But I wouldn't want to be anywhere else.

It is the first week of a new year. Perhaps it is time to become a new woman. I don't know. I don't know if I have that kind of courage.

Rising from the sea, your body, wet-salt, sun, air / Mermaid womyn, seashell skin, rolling in the sand of my heaving, leaving your handprints as you go . . .

She reads on, and I get goose bumps. This strong, stout woman from Oregon is like a poem herself. Her soul is as green as the pine trees she writes about. You can see it there, her soul, every time she pauses in her recitation and looks out at us, her audience, drinking in every perfect, delicious word. Tonight, her cropped, spiky hair is purple. It changes with her mood. Last week it was platinum white as she gave us a poem about growing old; she is only twenty-four years old, so this was a great exercise in empathy. This week it is the color of love, for she is reading love poems.

I shouldn't say reading, I know that's not the right word. I came to this country when I was seventeen years old, for college, and though I studied English in Colombia and am fluent, sometimes I still have trouble finding the right words to say what I mean. I mean, I have trouble finding them in English *and* in Spanish. After ten years of bilingual life, I don't know where all my words have gone. I reach for them, feel them floating just there, in the periphery of my consciousness, and then they fall away, recede into the ether again. That's why I love poetry. If the right word is missing, you can create the same intention with another, follow the tentacle through to the other some way. Wormholes of the spirit.

I have not told any of my old college friends that I want to write poetry. That I *write* poetry. Amber might understand the need for poetry in the world. Maybe Lauren, too. The others would appreciate the creativity, I suppose. What they wouldn't understand is the part that keeps me from telling any of the *sucias* about my poems. I don't think they'd understand the feelings they'd find there. I know they wouldn't. When we get together, when I see Lauren and the passion in her eyes, I want to tell them. I want to take a knife and open my chest and remove my heart and hold it out to them on the palm of my hand so they can finally see how differently it beats. How oddly. How, what do you say? How *queer*. Queerly. But it took me until I was twenty-five, just three years ago, to even see it myself, or to even acknowledge it. And it was mine. I can't imagine any of the *sucias* would appreciate the lopsided beat of the thing, the offness of it, the strangely patterned, entirely foreign seashell skin of it. Selwyn understands that part of me, because she shares it herself. And here it comes, rumbling from her mouth in words she captured from the cosmos just for me.

I used to see you, shadow girl, hunched girl, talking to your demons in the corner/ I used to sing you in my sleep, breathe you in my slow alone deathness/ and then I stepped into your wave, felt below the water, found you there, found you there/ Darkgirl, longgirl, found you there, waiting for me, Spanish words dripping from your mouth like honey, dripping down and down, good and good.

She wouldn't make a good impression on them. I'm sure of that. She is bulky, and she wears plaid flannel shirts and loose-fitting men's work pants. Her hair is short, and that might please Rebecca, but she only puts earrings in one ear, and then there are at least five of them, hard silver hoops. That would not please any of them. That would send them running for the nearest door. They're like that. They wouldn't be able to see past their own misplaced instincts in order to appreciate Selwyn's eyes. Dark brown, on-fire eyes. Lit up with humor. Lit up with life. She wouldn't make a good impression. Not on them. But she did on me. She did on me. She did. On me. On me, she was almost Lauren.

I started coming here with the intention of one day reading one of my *own* poems. But to do that I would have to emerge from these shadows, swim to the surface, stand bare and dripping in front of all of Boston, rip my heart out for millions of strangers to see and bite. No. People know who I am here. They know me. They think they know me. They eat eggs and drink coffee and stare at their televisions and see my face behind all that makeup. They send their children to the bus stop and rustle their newspapers while I read them the news of the day with my perky smile. They send me Christmas cards and thousands of letters with all sorts of unsolicited advice. They tell me to grow my hair, to cut my hair, to gain weight, to lose weight, to speak more clearly, to be proud of my accent, to change my name, to revel in my Spanish surname. They tell me to go back to Africa, they call me a hundred ugly names. They ask me to marry them and offer to bring their mothers to the studio to meet me. They send postcards with neatly drawn people dangling from neatly drawn nooses. They ask me who I think will win the Super Bowl. They ask me to give shout outs to their baby daddies. They all think they know me.

None of them do. No one does. Not even Selwyn. She tries. She reads about Colombia, studies the history of Colombia, she buys *vallenato* CDs and tries to learn to dance. She started subscribing to trade magazines like the *American Journalism Review* so we might have more to talk about on Sunday afternoons. But there's this thing about me, the rhythm of my childhood, the garden of flavors I like to eat, and the bright, brave colors I wish they painted houses in this town, the warm, floral ways I think a city street should smell in the summer, things about me she will always find exotic and unknowable. I am from the warm and humid coastal town of Barranquilla, and though the place was cruel to a single mother who was a doctor in spite of her color and sex—and cruel as well to her tall, skinny daughter—that is how I think the world should be. Moist. Green. Alive with music and flavor. I am never more at home than when I am in Colombia, for even with all of her violence and infections I do desperately love her.

Selwyn grew up short and thick and American, with liberal parents who loved her no matter what, and knew from kindergarten that she would love women. I grew up tall and narrow with a mother who did not talk about these types of things, and though I knew I felt something particular and pink for girls and not for boys, I did not know loving women was an option until I got to college and learned the word for it. Lesbian. Such a clumsy, ugly word, buzzy and not at all like the way it feels to be one.

In Colombia, we don't have a word for it at all. We have a word for men who love men, and it is "woman." Men are not thought of as gay unless they are "on the bottom" where I come from, and almost every man has had sex with another man at least once. Women are not thought to be sexual in Colombia. Sexual women are bad in Colombia. In the popular lore, I mean. And even when they are called whores, everyone knows they are getting paid and do not enjoy it. Women are mothers in Colombia, and cooks. They are virgins or whores and there is nothing else, nothing in between, nothing. That's why my mother never wanted me to go back.

She stayed there, but she always told me she wanted me to live free, in a nation where my sex and skin would not cause outpourings of hatred. In America, my mother taught me, women are at the very least human beings. And now, here in Boston, I am a woman and a celebrity. My mother is very proud. She asks me to send her videotapes of every newscast. We talk on the phone every Sunday, and I fly to see her whenever I can. She knows nothing of my feelings for women, and I want to keep it this way. This is why I hide in the back of the room, listening to Selwyn's words. This, and the fact that I don't know how the producers of the national network evening news show who have been courting me for months would react if they knew. And I want that job. So much. A national news anchor. Me. This is why I cannot emerge from the penumbras and *sombras* and stand up and cry my description: lesbian! It would kill my mother, maybe kill my career, and I might lose the *sucias*, my anchor in this city for a decade.

In particular, I would lose my best friend, Sara, that quirky, loudmouthed woman from Miami who makes me laugh harder than anyone I have ever met. I don't find Sara attractive. I never have, and I never will, not in that way anyway. But I can't tell her what I am. She does not seem to like gay people, and she has told all of us this fact once or twice—a hundred hundred times that I can remember she has told jokes at the expense of people like me. How, you wonder, can I have Sara for a friend, even with her dislike of people like me? And I will tell you this: Sara and I have a history, a long friendship of shared coffee and tea and dreams, her humor is my humor, her family like my own, her children like my sons. I do not think it wise to fight prejudice with prejudice, so I cannot hate my best friend for being ignorant. I prefer to hide from her hatred and bask in her laughter. I cannot come out. I would lose Sara. I might even lose my job.

The first woman I ever loved was Shelly Meyers, in the fifth grade. I lived to watch her walk. I never told her. Didn't know I could, didn't know how. Didn't know. I have always favored the same type of woman. The second woman I ever loved was Lauren Fernández. Shelly and Lauren are both fair, with dark, crazy hair spilling everywhere and those big, angry eyes. They are both powerful in the hips and legs, with a confident bounce to their strides. Selwyn is like that too. Sometimes, I imagine she is Lauren. She does not know this, and she must never know this. It would send her over the edge. Selwyn is like that, fragile. She may look tough, but she's not. She's emotionally fragile the way only true artists can be. I call her paperglass, ready to break with a strong wind. She calls me seaweed. These are the names we whisper to each other in the dark, where no one can hear. Paperglass and seaweed.

Seaweed flows over me, under me, into me / I taste seaweed on my tongue when I least expect it, I taste seaweed in my moments of bright bursting light / Paperglass light in a thousand shades of yes.

She continues, and then she stops. The audience claps and whistles and a few groupies rush the stage and try to touch her hand. I am not jealous. They are students of hers. I know Selwyn, and she's not the type to cheat. She is the first one who told me that joke: *What does a lesbian bring to a second date? A U-Haul.* We have been together for almost a year, sneaking around like teenagers, me taking curly routes to her home in Needham, her waiting and listening to me on her cell phone until I can tell her my neighbors across the street have closed their shades so then she can run around the corner and slide into my neat white Beacon Hill townhouse door. It is Selwyn I thought of when I bought the comforter with the plaid flannel duvet, Selwyn I think of when I stop in the deli section of the market and buy potato salad, something I never used to eat, Selwyn I think of when I water the plants she insisted I put everywhere in my home for balance and serenity and oxygen. It is Selwyn, always Selwyn, standing in the center of every decision I make these days with her muscular legs and narrow hands.

We would live together by now, but I can't admit it, what I am. She is patient, Selwyn. She does not pressure me. She says it takes a long time for a green tree to grow tough bark. She is gentle and generous and does not call me at work unless I page her first. She is careful and does not look at me the wrong way in public. These are the inside-out ways Selwyn must show her love for me now. These are the hoops I make her jump through. These are the injuries I carve into her character each and every day, yet she comes back and back, always back, asking for more. This is the way of it for Elizabeth Cruz and Selwyn Womyngold. This is what love looks like from my perch on the razor's edge.

The jazz trio takes over. Selwyn signs a few autographs, smiles for a few photos, and then glances my way. She gives the signal—a scratch to her left eyebrow—that means it's time to meet back at the truck. I watch her go first, walking as she does in the body of a panther, wait a slow hard minute, then slither my way along the back wall to the stairs that lead out into the cold night. I walk down Massachusetts Avenue and around the corner, and feel like all the oddball nighttime Central Square eyes are on me. But they aren't, of course. In my scarf and dark glasses and big long trench coat, I am just another eccentric in one of the world's most densely populated eccentric places. I have parked a few blocks down, on a side street near the Women's Center, the place I first heard Selwyn read. I walk, and am vaguely aware of the sound of footsteps behind me. There are many people here, so it's nothing new.

When I get to the truck, the street is empty. Selwyn leans on a light post next to the truck, and watches me come. She smiles, paperglass pantherwoman. Beautiful like that. I smile back. I want to rush her, grab her in my hands and knead her like bread dough, devour her. I want to kiss her. So much. I look around, and see no one. Her poetry got me tonight, made me feel alive. Invincible. I decide to let go, for just a moment, to leap from the ledge and see what happens. I run toward her, grab her quickly, and plant a kiss on her lips. She is surprised. Shocked. Not uncomfortable at all, because she has never been the one with a problem. If she had her way, we would stroll through malls together holding hands, ignoring the horrified mothers and fathers who rush their children to the side and away, away from us. We would make out at the movies like normal people.

"What was that for?" she asks, rubbing my shoulder.

"For being you. For being mine."

I feel like a girl again, giggly and silly and ready to dance in the street. But it's too cold here in Cambridge, in Boston, isn't it? Too very cold in your very bones. Selwyn pulls me close to her, and kisses me again, warm, soft, mine, woman. But before we are through, I hear the voice. Not mine. Not Selwyn's. But familiar.

"Liz Cruz?"

I stop, release Selwyn, and spin toward the direction of the voice. It's Eileen O'Donnell, gossip columnist for the *Boston Herald,* and a frequent guest on the morning show where I am a co-anchor.

"I thought that was you," she says with a smile too big for her small, pointy head. "Listen, I was just at the reading, got a tip about Selwyn Womyngold—that is your name, isn't it? Womyn with a 'y'? It was really good, Selwyn, the performance. Really . . . touching." Her words come in ugly white puffs of steam from her mouth; she has been running and the cold air makes her cough.

"Eileen," I say. I beg. I plead at her with my eyes.

"It's good to see you, Liz. How have you been?"

I don't answer.

"Where might I find one of your books, Selwyn?" she asks. Selwyn wolfgirl stares at her with all the love of a trained fighter.

"I have to be honest with you kids," Eileen continues. "I was here last week, too. And I followed you to Needham. You have a nice house out there, Sel. You make a pretty good living for a poet. A twenty-four-year-old poet fresh out of Wellesley. I saw on the Internet you teach over at Simmons College. That an all-girl school or something?"

"Fuck off," Selwyn seethes.

"Now that doesn't sound like a poem to me. What is it, haiku?"

Selwyn takes the truck keys from my hand and opens the passenger side door. She pushes me into the truck. "Let's go." I am numb, cold, hard, terrified of what Eileen is going to do. Selwyn lets herself into the driver's seat, and guns the truck out of there. We drive most of the way to her house in silence. "Don't worry about it," she says, finally, making a sad attempt to appear cheerful. I look at her, and see tears in her eyes. "Please, Elizabeth," she says. I can see the little girl she used to be. "You have to let it go."

I nod. She leads me into the house, makes me a cup of hot chocolate, brings me my long nightgown with the Snoopy decal, and my fuzzy slippers. She gives me a massage and sings to me, American lullabies with words so sad I can't imagine why anyone would want to sing them to a child, and she strokes my hair. Then she puts me in bed, tucks me in like a mother, with a gentle kiss to the forehead.

"You get some sleep, *mío amore*," she says, her Spanish mangled as always. "I have some writing to do yet."

I nod, and close my eyes. But I can't sleep because I know Selwyn isn't the only one with some writing to do yet tonight.

Somewhere in her oniony devil den, Eileen O'Donnell is writing too.

. . . Only four shopping days 'til Christmas, and I'm pleased to report I finally got most of my shopping done last night. But there's one friend I can't find anything for. We all know someone like that, don't we? It's almost a cliché—the woman who has everything, including the perfect man. But in my pal Sara's case, it's 100 percent true. I'm thinking a Chia Pet or one of those massive "massage toys" from the Sharper Image, but she's probably got plenty of both already.

—from "My Life," by Lauren Fernández

sara

COÑO. I COULD hardly sleep last night, *chica*. And it's not because of the sex, which I'm sure Roberto thought was great. I was so sick. He had no clue. I did the usual thing I do, the moaning and the faces, the ridiculous lingerie, all the while willing the vomit down. I pulled a full Meg Ryan in the end, and Roberto, as always, loved it—until he was done. Then he decided I'd acted like a *puta* and gave me "the speech," which goes something like this: *You're a Cuban woman, a decent woman. You aren't an American whore. It's fine that you enjoy yourself, but why do you have to act like that? You're the mother of my sons. Where's your pride?*

He has said this sort of thing since we first did it, when I was sixteen. I like sex, liked it from the first time. I'm not shy. And Roberto's the only one I've ever been with, but he's convinced there must have been others, because I like it so much. "No woman is born loving sex the way you do," he says. "Someone taught you this filth. When I find out who it was, you better tell him to hide." I try to tell him it's just chemistry, that I love his body, his smell, the whole package. But he is suspicious. *Que cosa más grande.* He is forever accusing me of cheating on him, even though I am *completamente* faithful.

Fíjate, chica. If you're born in this country, you might think Roberto is about eighty years old because of the way he acts. He's not. He's my age, twenty-eight. He is like most men raised in Latin America—or Miami—which is to say he thinks women come in two flavors: pure and dirty. Pure women are sexless and you marry them and pump them full of babies and they are not supposed to like sex. Dirty girls love sex and you seek them out for pleasure. So a wife who is too sexual, too pretty in public, too demanding in bed— these are all thought of as bad things to men like Roberto. At first it got to me, his criticism, but then I got to B.U. and Elizabeth convinced me to take some feminist theory classes with her and we realized it was all bull.

Like me, Roberto has spent a lot of years in the United States, and he knows at some level how ridiculous this is. We've discussed it. I've shown him diagrams about the female body and explained to him that all women are wired the same and have the same kind of sexual response, that even his mother has a clitoris and it's wired just like a penis—all the stuff I learned in college, that *Mami* never bothered to teach me. He slapped me for that one and stormed out of the house for a few hours. It was so funny, that look on his face as he imagined his mother having an orgasm, it was worth it.

He finally admitted that it was natural for a woman to like sex, "But it shouldn't be as much as a man likes it," he insisted. "Only women who are psychologically messed up love sex as much as you do." *Oye, chica.* Can you believe it?

I'm working on that. He'll come around.

But lately, with the pregnancy, I don't like sex so much. I just do it to keep up appearances. After we finished and Roberto started to snore in the bed next to me, I had to keep running down the hall to the other bathroom, to throw up. I didn't want Roberto to hear me and figure out what's going on, know what I mean? I don't want him to know yet.

I've got two boys, twins, five years old and running all over the place with heavy boy feet and a thousand questions a minute. What is this? How does this work? Why? Why? Why? You'd think they were the trained reporters, not me. They say boys and girls are the same unless you make them different, and I don't think that's true at all. My boys were all boy from the beginning, looking for dirty things to stuff in their pockets, gurgling over their toy trucks, scampering around the house in those sneakers that squeak like parrots on the hardwood floors.

I want a little girl. When I was shopping for linens for the downstairs bathroom a few days ago, I couldn't help but notice the little girl clothes and toys in the department stores. I'm tired of tiny jeans and race cars. I'm ready for velvet dresses and baby dolls.

Don't misunderstand me. I love my boys. They are my *world, chica.* My entire day revolves around them, taking them to school, picking them up, taking them to music classes and swimming lessons at the health club, combing the cowlicks out of their hair before we go to temple, washing their bodies in the bath at night, reading their bedtime stories, comforting them when they wake with scary dreams, singing Cuban bedtime songs, and telling them about Miami and how much I miss it.

I remember when Jonah was three years old I told him about Miami, always talking about Miami, and he finally said, "*Mami,* I want to go to your-ami, too." He breaks my heart, that one. He's more sensitive than Sethy, who, I'm sorry to say, takes after his father.

You try not to pick favorites, and with twin curly-headed boys that no one but Roberto and I can tell apart, you try even harder to treat them exactly the same. But you find a favorite one anyway, without wanting to. My Ami. What a sweetheart, that one. You could just eat him up with those big green eyes.

No, *te lo juro chica,* I would be happy to have nothing in my life but these two gorgeous, energetic little men. But a girl would *complete* me, you know what I mean? A girl would make the family a real family at last. She would be someone I could shop with, someone I could take to concerts on the Esplanade in the summer and she wouldn't spend the whole time looking for a tree to climb so she could spit on people walking below. Boys embarrass you with their misbehavior.

We've been trying, but I want to wait to tell Roberto about the pregnancy until our anniversary in March, when we go on our yearly trip to Buenos Aires. I want it to be special. He's noticed that I'm gaining weight, even though it's just one or two pounds. He keeps telling me to eat less. He always tells me to eat less. And I always ignore him. Ha.

He'll be happy, too. He always complains that our house is too big. We live in a six-bedroom, three-bath, Tudor-style home near the Chestnut Hill Reservoir, on two acres of land with our own little patch of forest. I grew up in a house bigger than this on Palm Island, with marble floors, a swimming pool, dozens of palm trees, and a gated entrance. But there were four kids, and lots of parties, parties for everything you could think of, with the people *Mami* and *Papi* knew in Cuba drinking *mojitos* and eating little sandwiches with butter and pimentos, acting like they never left the island. Our house in Miami never felt empty, because it never *was*.

This place feels empty, because Roberto doesn't have any real friends in Boston, only acquaintances, and he doesn't like it when I have my friends over. He always thinks we've been talking about him if we laugh. Of course, we're never talking about him at all, but it got too hard to explain. He gave me a bloody lip after the *sucias* left the house last time, and I've just decided it isn't worth it to try to bring friends here anymore. I love to give parties, the planning and execution of them. But I love not bleeding even more than that.

All Roberto's friends are in Miami. Our marriage would probably be different there. Violence in the home is rare in Cuban Miami, because everyone's always visiting. Someone is always watching your back. My own parents would have hit each other—and me—a lot more if there weren't always friends and relatives around, sampling our pantry. We're a passionate family, and a little yelling, name-calling, and hitting never killed anyone. It goes with family. I just wish we lived somewhere else. Roberto's rage is getting scary. We're alone here. He's got a good job.

I want to fill this house up with little feet. Little girl feet, clicking around in their patent leather Mary Janes. I am two and a half months along. I told Dr. Fisk I don't want to know the sex until the baby is born, but I already know it's a girl. I've had such morning sickness, day and night. I don't know why they call it morning sickness, every woman I know who got it had it worse at night. That's how my mother was with me, but not with my brothers. It's a girl. I sense it. If I am wrong, I'll keep trying until my daughter comes along.

I know Roberto wants a baby because he's been talking about having a corner of the backyard leveled and cleared so we can put in a toddler gym again. He thinks we'll have another boy, but that's just the way he is, *sabes*. I don't even pay attention to it anymore. It's not worth fighting about certain things with Roberto. It really isn't. *Te lo juro, chica.*

He swore he'd get help after the last time we fought really badly, in the hotel in New Hampshire after the day of skiing, when he fractured my collarbone. He was convinced I'd spent the afternoon in the lodge so I could get it on with the teenager who served me and Lauren hot chocolate. "I saw the way you looked at him," he said. It was completely crazy. I didn't even remember what that boy looked like. Roberto thought the red marks on my neck were from that guy sucking on me in the bathroom, and so he planted his foot on my chest until the bone snapped. I told Lauren I'd fractured it skiing, and she believed me, thank God.

I'm not blameless. Sometimes I get angry and hit him, too. He's a lot bigger than I am, but I can get *loca*, believe me. That last time, he'd done the usual thing and shoved me and called me ugly names in front of the boys and told me to pack my things; he has never come right out and hit me in front of them, you know, like *slugged* me. He does that, and worse, only when we are alone. That's something I don't understand. Society always blames the man in physical marriages. But my mom used to belt my dad, and I regret to say I inherited that tendency. Sometimes, when he hits me, poor Roberto is only defending himself. I don't expect outsiders to "get" it. That's why no one knows. We are usually very happy, and that's what counts.

He's usually a great father and provider to his boys, that is the main reason I have stayed. He has a good sense of humor, and even though most people would find this strange, he's gentle most of the time, and thoughtful. He noticed I was sad last week, and came home with a bag full of chenille pillows from Crate & Barrel that I mentioned I liked as we raced past the store on our way to a movie. I didn't even think he was paying attention when I told him I liked the pillows, but he was. He does that kind of thing all the time. I have conservative beliefs about family and marriage, and I honestly feel the good with us still far outweighs the bad. He always feels terrible after he loses control, and does the nicest things to make up for it. How do you think I got the Land Rover?

I know he doesn't mean to do it, that it's just the way he was raised. His dad was (still is) a drinker, and when he was drunk he lost his temper. Poor Roberto used to get beaten, I mean really beaten, *chica,* with tire irons, things like that, until his bones broke and he had to tell the doctors he fell off his bike. I'm the only one who knows about it. Not even my parents know, and they've known his parents for years.

It's not like we're some welfare family where the guy is slopping around in his undershirt beating up on the little wifey, right? *Por favor*. He has never left a long-lasting mark on my body anywhere people can see it—I stayed in for a few days after the bloody lip. Oh, and there was the time he left finger impressions on my arm when he thought I was flirting with one of our gardeners (I wasn't, of course) and that went away in about an hour. I slugged him one time, and the skin under his eye turned purple for a week. He told people he got hit with a racquetball.

Roberto and I love each other. We know how our relationship works. Is it ideal? No. But it's love. Love is never ideal. If I can control my own temper, I think he'll get his in check too. It's as much my fault as his. He can change. I know he can. You think that sounds like a stupid woman talking. I don't care. He's my soul mate and my best friend. I can't remember my life being empty of Roberto. Like a brother, he's always been there. Our dysfunction, if that's what you want to call it, runs deep.

Roberto's grandparents and mine ran a rum company together in Cuba, and both our families originally came from Austria and Germany many generations ago. Our parents stayed in touch once everybody fled to Miami in 1961. I pulled his curly brown hair at his fifth birthday party, and we wrestled all over the yard at his bar mitzvah. We've had the kind of rough physical contact you have with a sibling for as long as I know. At my *quinceañera* (I was one of the first Jewish girls in Miami to have one) he threw me in the pool at the hotel, in my beautiful silk dress. I grabbed his ankle and yanked him in, too. We dunked each other for ten minutes, and finally shared our first kiss, floating in the water while my *Mami* screamed from the shore.

I haven't told the *sucias* about the really rough stuff. I've told Elizabeth, my best friend, about our fights and the occasional slap, but that's it. I can't tell the rest of them. Knowing the *sucias* they'd call the police immediately and have him thrown in jail. They think everything is abuse, every man evil. The *sucias* would want me to leave him, but they all have careers. After eight years of being a housewife, the thought of being alone terrifies me. What would I do for money if I were alone with two—*ay, chica,* I mean *three*—kids to raise? I have no real job experience, and I'm accustomed to a certain kind of lifestyle that requires adequate funds, money of a quantity I could never earn on my own.

My parents aren't rich anymore, no matter what it looks like. They still have the house on Palm Island, and the ten-year-old Mercedes. But that's *all* they have now, except credit cards and each other. When my mother called me last week, it was to ask for a loan. Their neighbors don't know anything about it, but my father had to file for bankruptcy five years ago.

My grandparents, God rest their souls, owned whole hillside towns in Cuba. They brought a lot of money to Miami and tried to start a few new businesses: Laundromats, pharmacies, restaurants, radio stations, one or two with *Papi* in charge. But my dad is better at throwing parties than running businesses. Same with *Mami*, who is still very beautiful. And now, with *Papi*'s father dead almost ten years, there hasn't been anyone to run things.

Mami still gets new clothes every week, a habit she developed when she was a tiny, spoiled girl with starched dresses, growing up on Quinta Avenida in Miramar. She never learned to pace her spending, and why should she have? I love *Papi*, but *chico*, he's never been the smartest bulb on the string. He puts bank statements in a file without bothering to open them. Last time he came to visit, I was saddened to see he was still crumpling his ATM receipts and tossing them in the nearest trash can.

When I turned sixteen and asked for a convertible, *Papi* bought me a new white Mustang. *Mami* took me shopping for my prom dress on Rodeo Drive in Beverly Hills. I didn't know it then, but now I realize they were slowly going broke the whole time. They would hire fifteen people to work serving drinks at parties in our huge backyard, and I'd weave through the adult legs to the shore of the canal and throw nickels and dimes into the water. Not pennies. Our family vacations lasted a full month. There were cruises, jazz festivals in Europe. We went to Rio de Janeiro for Carnival one year, and the Cannes Film Festival another, with some other families from my school. *Mami* took us shopping in the spring in New York City and in the fall in Buenos Aires, for shoes and handbags.

Neither of my parents went to college. They moved to Miami when they were about eighteen and had to hit the ground running. Like many of their friends, they never bothered to learn English. There were enough Cubans around, it wasn't necessary. All of them thought (and still think) they would go back one day, as soon as the Marines arrive and overthrow that *hijo de puta*. (We are forbidden from saying the name Castro in my parents' house.)

Even with bankruptcy, they're *still* throwing parties for their friends, and offering anyone who drops in a full meal and a bottle of fine wine, prepared by a live-in cook they can't afford. They still keep the thermostat on the air conditioner set at sixty degrees, which is really cold; all the richest Cubans always sit around the house in sweaters and fuzzy slippers, just to show how rich they are. I tell them to turn it off and use fans, or to get little window unit air conditioners for the rooms they use the most, but they won't hear of it. That's *insulting* to my parents, who want uninvited guests (Cubans drop in whenever, wherever, as Shakira sings) to freeze. That's the way my parents are, and they don't know how to be any different. They are too embarrassed to be any different. They asked for a loan because they had run up such a huge bill taking too many guests out on that old leaky yacht. I told Mom to sell the yacht, and she started to call me those names she calls people when she's not happy with them: *Buena cuero, cochina, estúpida, imbécil, sinvergüenza.*

Roberto knows all of this. He gave them the loan, but made sure I understood that if it wasn't repaid, I would be the one to suffer the consequences. He knows the situation I'm in. I won't inherit a dime. This gives him even more power over me than he had before. Now he can threaten to throw me out, too. And he does, all the time. His favorite thing is to grab a suitcase and start throwing my things in it and lock me out of the house while the boys cry for *Mami* and scratch at the glass on the front door.

Roberto is downstairs already, talking to Vilma about something. Sharon, our Swiss nanny who lives in the guest house out back and studies for correspondence courses in her free time, took the boys to school this morning because I was too sick, so they've already gone. Good old Vilma. When my parents couldn't afford to keep her in the house on Palm Island anymore, she moved up here to work for us. She has never known any family other than mine. She's almost sixty years old, and like a mother to me. We offered her the guest house, of course, but she says she prefers to be in the small back bedroom off the kitchen. All she has in there is her old television—she won't let me buy her a new one, and won't let me hook her up to cable even though it wouldn't cost anything extra—her Bible on the bedside table, a rosary she hung on the wall, a few postcards from her daughter in El Salvador, and a few changes of simple clothes folded in the dresser. She'll be happy for us, too, when the time comes for our daughter to be born. She doesn't care that we're Jewish, she loves us. I think she already knows about the pregnancy; she's the one who takes out the bathroom trash, and there haven't been Tampax for months now. Vilma is observant. Lately she tells me not to strain myself and she's started trying to get me to drink that paste she says is good for pregnant women, with cornstarch, water, and cinnamon. The smell of it sends me reeling.

Oye, I can hear Roberto's booming voice going on and on about something he saw in the newspaper while Vilma runs the water. People say I'm loud, but they should meet my husband. I'm serious. You think Cubans are loud? Try Cuban Jews. *Te lo juro.* I didn't realize how loud we were until I came to Boston for college and had a hard time hearing people who were talking to me. The whole city seemed like it was going around whispering all the time in the snow and ice. It was crazy to me. Miami is loud, hot, and wet. My house growing up was even louder. I've never known life any other way.

I have to wait until this latest wave of nausea subsides before I go downstairs to breakfast with my husband. I sit

down on the chaise lounge chair in the corner of the master
bath by the sunken Jacuzzi and try to focus on the latest issue of *Ella*. I try to keep my mind off the way the room has
started to spin. I've tried everything, even wearing those
"sea bands" on my wrists, but nothing helps. I'm a little surprised Roberto hasn't noticed I'm not feeling well. He
seems occupied with this big case he's on. It's probably going to drag on until March, he says. The stress is killing him.
I hope he wins. If he loses, *ay, chica*.

I try to read an article about adding romance to one's love
life. I'm not sure what's happened to *our* love life, honestly.
No enthusiasm, you know what I'm saying? Roberto used to
be able to keep going for an hour or more when we were
younger, but it's gotten fast and faster with us, until now it's
like we might as well be doing it alone or something, because it's so automatic and functional, trying to make this
baby. I'd like more romance, some candles and smooth music. The article in *Ella* suggests a few tricks involving love
notes and red rose petals. Roberto would laugh if I tried any
of them.

Another pregnancy probably won't spice things up in that
department. Roberto is already disappointed in the weight I
gained with the last pregnancy—five permanent pounds for
each boy, and now this new weight. He lets me know his lack
of desire is related to my size so often that now I won't do it
unless I can keep a T-shirt over me so he can think of Salma
Hayek. I wasn't big to begin with, though, and my doctor
says my weight is fine. I am five-foot-five and weigh 145
pounds. Dr. Fisk says this is actually a perfect weight for my
size. I tell her Roberto would like to see me drop a few
pounds, and she frowns. She asked about the bruises on my
back once, and I told her that I'd fallen on the ice. She
looked at me for a long time behind her eyeglasses and
asked if there were human hands on the ice. I didn't answer
and she didn't push.

I stare at the same photograph of Benjamin Bratt with
that scraggly goatee in the "men" section of *Ella* and wait to
feel better. Why is everybody always talking about how

handsome this guy is? I don't see it. Me, I prefer Russell
Crowe, a real man, a tough guy. Benjamin Bratt looks like
he'd snap in two if you hugged him too tight. I get up, but
then I have to sit back down. I feel like I've been riding my
sons' Sit 'n Spin. I've had to learn to act, *chica,* with this
pregnancy. Maybe I should just tell everyone and get it over
with. It's so hard to seem like I feel fine with the boys, to
hold them and carry them around the way five-year-olds
like, to ferry them around on my back, neighing like a *ca-
ballo.* I get so tired at times I feel like I'm going to die.
When you have nausea like this all the time, you can't think
straight.

I'm scared out of my mind, *chica.* I'm remembering labor and delivery and it isn't pretty. I had the twins naturally
and they sliced an episiotomy in me that I thought would kill
me; the pain of that thing healing all red and raw down there
was worse than the labor itself. I swore I'd never do that
again, and now here I am, with no way out. I manage to get
up and go to my closet and open the floral storage box I have
set aside for all my pregnancy things. I've also got some
books in there: *What to Expect When You're Expecting*; *Diet
for a Fit Pregnancy*; *Funding Your Kid's College 101*; *Best
Jewish Baby Names*; things like that. I never threw them out,
just in case there would be more. The sea bands are in here,
too, though I should just throw the useless things away.

Roberto won't find all this because there are so many
dainty boxes in here, and he's not the kind of man to take
much interest in things with flowered paper on them. He's the
kind of man who leaves his clothes on the floor wherever he
has removed them, knowing someone else will pick them up.

I undress and examine my belly in the mirrors all around
the large bathroom; it's essentially the same size as always. I
didn't really "show" with the boys until the fourth or fifth
month—and that was with twins. I watch what I eat. But
Roberto's right. I could stand to exercise. I'm a little soft, especially my upper arms. I don't like exercise, though. It
makes me feel sick. I honestly feel better when I don't exercise. Now that I'm pregnant, though, I think I'll have to start

working out. It's good for the baby. That's what all the books say. And I'm not sure the marriage can stand for me to gain another permanent five pounds. He has come close to strangling me for wearing the wrong thing. He can get that stupid. There's no telling what Roberto might do.

I step into the shower and stand in the middle, letting all five heads strike me. I wonder if I'll have to stop showering in here now that I'm pregnant. We didn't have this shower with the other pregnancy. It's new. The whole bathroom is remodeled. That was my payment for the time he got mad about the scratch on the side of the Land Rover. I don't know where the scratch came from. I took the boys to see a movie at the Chestnut Hill cinema, and when we came back out, it was there. Roberto was very mad. It's a nice bathroom.

These side jets are pretty strong, intended to help massage tension out of your muscles. I don't want to hurt the baby. I'll have to use another shower, I guess. I'll ask Dr. Fisk. I put a hand over my lower belly and finish the shower, then get out and get dressed in the khaki pants and oversized white button-down shirt I picked out last night, fix my hair and makeup, tie a pink sweater around my shoulders, and head downstairs.

Roberto is still here, with his dark green eyes and shiny brown hair, handsome in his dark blue suit and white shirt and yellow tie, reading the newspaper. He has good taste in clothes all on his own, and rejects my offers to pick things out for him. He wants to do it himself, and that's understandable. Would you want someone else dressing you? I wouldn't. Vilma is wearing her powder blue work uniform embroidered with the name we chose for our house, "Windowmere." Her white hair is pulled back in a tight bun and held in place with a hairnet. She's busy wiping down the counters, and shows no sign of emotion or thought on her face. She tried to intervene during one of Roberto's tantrums, right after she first got here, but I had a talk with her afterward and asked her to please just stay out of it and concentrate on her work. My counters gleam.

"Buenos días, mi amor," Roberto says, standing up to greet

me and planting a kiss on my cheek. He is tall, my husband, taller than any other Cuban I've ever met, topping six-three. When we're home, we always speak in Spanish. Vilma doesn't speak English. Actually, she speaks more than she lets on, just like my dad, but she doesn't use it unless she absolutely has to. She likes people to think she doesn't speak English. She learns a lot about people that way.

"Buenos días, señora," Vilma says with a light bow of her head. I don't know when she started calling me that, exactly. "Ma'am." It feels weird, and I've asked her before to call me Sarita, like she used to when I was a little girl. I love when she does that. But she says it's not fitting. So you can see who's in charge around here—and it isn't me or Roberto.

Amber and Lauren give me a hard time about Vilma, accuse me of having a slave. It's a joke, right, but they do it anyway. I'm the only one of the *sucias* with a live-in maid, but that's the way we do it in Miami, and it's the way I like it. Vilma would be lost without us. Her daughter in El Salvador comes to visit now and then, but they don't seem very close. Vilma loves us like her own family. The *sucias* don't understand that, especially the ones that grew up poor. They think I'm running a plantation. They didn't grow up with Vilma, and they don't know that she's *la que manda* in our house.

"Buenos días," I say, going out of my way to appear cheerful and healthy and normal.

"What are you so happy about?" Roberto asks as he sits back down. I sit across from him in the breakfast nook and shrug. I hope he can't hear my thoughts. They're so loud.

"Nothing, just happy today."

"Better not be another man," he jokes with a finger wag. Or half jokes. "I know how certain kinds of women get when laborers come to fix things in the house. You keep an eye on this one, Vilma, *oíste?*"

Vilma remains silent and brings the silver tray with little cups of Cuban coffee. I reach for one of the cups, but she stops me. "That one is for the señor," she explains. I like my coffee sweet. Roberto likes his straight. Vilma makes it just the way we like it.

Roberto rolls up the newspaper he's been reading and taps it on the table and sucks his lower lip. He looks at Vilma, and she looks at him, and I know there's something going on they aren't telling me. You don't live in this house with these two and not learn how to read them.

"The usual?" Vilma asks me in Spanish.

"Sí, gracias," I say. She waddles to the stove to prepare my fried egg with cheese and Cuban toast. Vilma's legs are swollen, as usual. I've tried to get her to go to a doctor. She has diabetes and arthritis, but she says she doesn't want to be trouble. We can't put Vilma on our family health insurance, but we always pay for whatever she needs. I'm going to drag her to the doctor myself, before they have to amputate her foot or something. While the egg cooks, she pours a glass of fresh-squeezed orange juice and brings it to me. The acidic thought of it makes me sick. She stands at my side with her arms crossed and waits for me to drink it.

"I'm glad you're in a good mood," Roberto says. He looks at Vilma, and she whistles low and shakes her head to herself, a gesture I have seen many times that usually means something bad is about to happen.

"Why is that?" I ask. "Something going on?"

Roberto unfurls the newspaper, and smooths it out on top of the table, then pounds it with his fist. He is scowling. It's the *Boston Herald*, the tabloid. I try to get him to read the *Gazette* instead, but he says he likes the *Herald* better because it's easier to read. He turns the paper toward me, and jabs his finger down on a headline.

"Read this," he says. Then he lifts the finger and wags it in my face. "But don't take it out on me. I told you that woman was weird, but you never listen to me."

Vilma scoops the egg onto a plate, adds the toast, a few mango slices, and a parsley garnish. Vilma knows the value of good presentation. I've borrowed a few ideas from her over the years, that's for sure. The breakfast looks delicious, but she holds off on handing it to me because of the newspaper in front of me. I look at the headline and have to read it three times before it makes sense to me.

LEZ CRUZ? POPULAR MORNING ANCHOR LIKES GIRLS.

"Oh, get rid of this," I say, sliding it back to him. "I've told you a million times this is the worst newspaper; you can't believe anything you read in it. Remember that time they said your friend Jack was getting kickbacks from local contractors? It was a lie, right? So is this. Poor Elizabeth."

Roberto takes the paper and turns the page. He points out a grainy, dark photograph of what appears to be my best friend Elizabeth—kissing a woman. Suddenly, I'm not feeling so happy anymore. How could Elizabeth be a lesbian? She has been my best friend for ten years, and the possibility never even occurred to me.

"She dates men," I remind Roberto. "We've set her up with some of your friends, for crying out loud."

"That was years ago," Roberto says. "Think about it, Sara. When's the last time you saw her with a man?"

It's true. It has been years. I ask her about it, and she always says she's seeing a guy but that it's nothing serious. She always tells me she's too busy, or her hours are too weird, or men are too intimidated by her for anything to ever work out. Why would she lie to me like that? Every time there's a problem with anything in my life, she's the one I call. I've even told her about Roberto roughing me up a couple of times, and she, true to her word, never told a soul. She's been my co-conspirator in life. If she is a lesbian, if it's true, then I will feel as betrayed as I would if I'd found Roberto cheating on me. Or worse. Yes, worse.

"She's disgusting," Roberto says, slapping the back of his hand against the paper. "This picture! I can't believe they would print such a picture in a family newspaper."

"It can't be true," I say. "She would have told me."

"She knows we don't approve of homosexuality. She'd never tell you."

"We? You. I don't care. She's my best friend."

"She was. Not anymore."

"Don't you think you're being a little extreme?"

"I'm protecting my family."

Oh, God. I think of all the times I've said homophobic

things to Elizabeth, all the times I've pointed out gay or lesbian couples to her at the movies or the mall and laughed.
That must have been hard on her. So why didn't she tell me?
Does she think I'm so close-minded I would reject her completely? Does she think so little of me?

"A total, complete waste of a beautiful woman," Roberto
says, examining the photo again, up close. Then, lifting one
eyebrow suggestively, he adds, "She just never met the right
man."

Vilma grabs the newspaper, clicks her tongue at Roberto,
and places my breakfast in front of me. "Why do you want
to upset her right now?" she asks in Spanish. "Let her eat
her breakfast." Then, to me she says, "Eat. You need your
strength."

"Whose side are you on, Vilma?" he asks. Then, looking
at me and the egg, he says, "You don't need to eat all that.
You're getting too fat. I told you already."

Vilma resumes her counter wiping, and I pick at the egg.

"It can't be true," I say. "If it were true I would have
known a long time ago. I've known Liz for ten years. That
paper is so sleazy. They doctor pictures. They must have
something against her."

Roberto shrugs and holds the newspaper out in front of
him. He begins to read it in his booming voice, with his
slight Spanish accent. *"I Spy caught up with the lovely and
talented WRUT morning anchor Elizabeth Cruz last night, at
a poetry reading at Davios bar in Central Square. For those
of you not in the know, Davios on Wednesday night is for
'womyn' only. Liz, who is up for a prime anchor slot at a national network, was there the week before, too, and both
times left with celebrated butch lesbian poet Selwyn Womyngold. You don't have to be a rocket scientist to know that this
anchor has her boat docked near the isle of Lesbos."*

"Oh, God. That's the stupidest thing I've ever heard," I
say. "Listen to that writing, would you? It's horrible. How
can you trust someone who writes that badly?"

*"The Colombian beauty queen and former model has
been fingered as one of the most eligible single women in*

Beantown by Boston *magazine for the past three years, since her appearance on the WRUT morning program spiked station ratings and catapulted the show to the number one spot. It was the first time any station in Boston had hired an anchor with an accent, a risky move that proved profitable because Liz was so darn peppy and cute everybody seemed to find her exotic pronunciation and looks exciting. Question is, now that we know the willowy Latina is playing for the other team, will Bostonians still love lovely Liz? Or maybe we should call her Lovely Lez?"*

I listen to the rest of the article, all written as poorly as the first part, and feel sick.

"They must have something out for her," I say.

"I don't know, this picture looks pretty real."

"They must be trying to ruin her for some reason."

"I don't think so."

"I'll call her. Vilma, please hand me the phone."

"No, you won't," Roberto says, pointing his finger in my face. "I don't want you talking to her anymore, you understand?" Vilma leaves the room with a loud sigh.

"Why not?"

He gives me that look, the same look he gives me when he thinks I'm screwing the ticket boy at the opera or the elderly lawyer seated next to me at a "Holiday" (read: Christmas) banquet for Roberto's firm.

"Oh, please," I say. "What is wrong with you? You think I want to sleep with my best friend? Are you crazy?"

"I'm not the one with the problem," he says. "You know that. *You're* the one with the problem. Normal women, *decent* women, don't have that kind of problem, and you know what I'm talking about. Your clitoris and all of that."

"I don't believe this. You think I'm going to get it on with Elizabeth now? Is that what you're trying to say to me?"

"You said it, not me."

"Just because *you've* wanted her for years, don't accuse me of the same thing. You're sick in the head. Sick and twisted."

"Who, her? She's black, Sara. I don't like black women."

"Come on. Admit it. I see the way you look at her. You think I don't see it?"

"What are you talking about? I don't look at her. I never look at anyone but you." He laughs.

"Whatever, Roberto."

"I don't want you talking to her. And I don't want her here anymore, no more Sunday lunches. Got it?"

"For crying out loud, Roberto, she might not even be a lesbian, you know that? She's probably straight. Even if she *is* a lesbian, who cares? Does it really matter?"

"You'd like to find out, too, wouldn't you? Yeah, I bet you would."

"What?"

He moves in close, grabs me behind the neck, and shakes me lightly. "No calls. No visits. No . . . clitoris."

"What on earth are you talking about?"

"You know what I'm talking about." He squeezes my flesh until it hurts. I shrug out of his grasp.

"You just want to fight," I say. "Calm down. I don't feel like fighting right now."

"No, I don't. Think about it, she never has a boyfriend, right? I've seen her stare at you before. I bet you even knew about it already, didn't you? Best friends in college, huh? What else did you girls do?"

"Oh, shut up."

"I'm serious. I've seen her staring at you like a man. I told you that once, remember? I bet you liked it."

"God, Roberto. Shut up. You're losing your mind."

"You knew."

"No, I did *not*. I don't want to hear it."

"Hey, hey. Don't speak that way to me," he says, chest puffed out, his voice reverberating against the tile floor even louder than normal. "I'm just warning you. I don't want you hanging out with her anymore. She's a pervert. I don't want to see her in this house again. And I better not find out you knew about this before, you understand? I don't want to find out I married a pervert."

"She's Elizabeth, Roberto. My maid of honor. My best

friend. Our sons love her like an aunt. Why would you care so much who she sleeps with? My God."

"My sons love no lesbians."

"You don't even know if this garbage is true!"

He taps his watch. "I have to go to work. I don't want to come home and find out you've talked to her on the phone. No calls. Understand?"

I pick the newspaper up from where he has dropped it and look at the picture again. It doesn't look fixed. And that's her truck in the background.

"No," I say, dropping my head to the table. I try to hold down the urge to vomit. "I don't. I don't understand at all."

So I noticed the gym was packed today, where it wasn't packed last week. My cycle class must have had thirty new people in it, all with the same New Year's resolution: to lose weight. The instructor reminded us all that most of the new participants would drop out in two weeks, or by month's end at the latest. She said it's that way every year. That's so sad! I don't want to be one of the ones who gives up, and I don't want any of you to give up either. So I called my friend Amber, the most persistent person I know. She's been hoping for a record deal for almost ten years now, and still thinks it will happen. Her advice? "Believe in yourself, especially when no one else does."

—from "My Life," by Lauren Fernández

amber

GATO WANTS ME to go down in the mosh pit. Dude, he's out of his mind! The last time I did that I ended up with a bruised rib and some Ecstasy chick puked all over me. I'm fine right here, sitting up on the edge of the stage, watching.

They wanted us to play here New Year's Eve, and we agreed at first but then we got a better gig offer in Hollywood and blew this club off like a-holes. It was worth it, though, because we got a good review in the *LA Weekly* for the Hollywood deal, with a photo of me screaming into the microphone. We're making up for flaking on this club by doing the next three weekends here, up until the end of the month and the real New Year. New Year's Eve. What a joke. Gato and I had reservations about celebrating that holiday at all, because it's only New Year's Eve on the gringo calendar. I called my friends in Boston on New Year's Eve. They all still get together to do something called "First Night," where you walk around in the cold and look at ice sculptures of clowns on the Boston Common. I caught them at Government Center, on those Stalinesque outdoor stairs, staring into the sky over the harbor, waiting for fireworks. I reminded them they were celebrating a false New Year, told them the pre-Hispanic new year in the Americas isn't until February. I could almost hear them rolling their eyes, all except Elizabeth, who listens, and Lauren, who's angry enough about everything in general to humor me. Rebecca didn't want to talk to me, of course. Too close to home for her. So I asked Usnavys to give her the list of names to think about. So many of us, gone. Zapotecs, Mixtecs, Otomies, Tarascans, Olmecs. A whole continent disappeared, except for those few of us who remain, and now all the world trying to call us Latinos so this hemisphere's bloody history will disappear for good, so we'll seem like foreigners even though we're the only ones who can truly stake a claim to these lands. What's up with that?

I'm buzzing. The club has black walls and red lighting. It's one of the leading *rock en Español* clubs in Long Beach, which is the most important city in the international Spanish-language rock movement, believe it or not. Our leading magazines are based here, our major critics.

Gato's band, *Nieve Negra*, or Black Snow, just finished their set and now the DJ is spinning some Manu Chao and all these beautiful brown faces that a minute ago were staring up at my Gato swirl around and around like messed-up wheels on a Mayan calendar. Did you know the Mayans created the perfect system for telling time, that it's more perfect even than the calendar the *pinche* gringos force us all to use?

That's right. And my people invented the zero. Mexica people have excelled in the arts and sciences since before the Europeans were pulling their women by the hair into caves. *Qué padre, no?* I think about this for a minute while I watch the dancers, and decide I'll write a song about it. I take the notebook out of my pocket. *I got me a theory see / Must be a big fat conspiracy / 'Cuz it don't seem all right to me / For Mexica to decorate a Christmas tree / Why add a day to February / When the Maya understood time perfectly / You'd rather be wrong than brown, whitey / It's leap year genocide / Leap year genocide.*

I make it a goal to have the song completed by the gig we have here at the end of February. It will be the perfect debut.

"I'm going," Gato says, "I'm descending into the pit." His dark brown eyes glow with intensity. He liberates his long hair from the rubber band, and leans over so it cascades down his legs. He shakes his head, then flips his hair back and jumps up. He is an Indian prince, dark, powerful, and proud. He's ready to take on the universe. He's pumped, man. His set was incredible. He had the slide show tonight, and I did the projector from the back of the room. It went perfectly. We used the pictures we took in Chiapas last summer, black and white portraits of people involved in the struggle, the beautiful Mexica faces of our people. We used pictures Gato took of the janitors from that L.A. strike, too, and we mixed them all up so that people would understand what we were trying to point out. Los Angeles isn't America. It's Mexica. It's time to wage *Xochiyaoyotl* on the oppressors, once and for all, brothers and sisters. We were here for tens of thousands of years before all those Europeans came. Spanish is as foreign to our genes as English. The kids in the crowd roared, man. They dug it. They get it. Every time they look in the mirror, they get it.

My parents don't, but lots of other people do.

My band, AMBER, is up next. This is the first time Gato has opened for *me*. I'm not sure how he feels about it. He didn't reply when I asked if he was okay with it, just like he didn't say anything when the manager called from Club

Azteca after getting both our demos (we like to send them together). The manager said he thought mine was a lot stronger. I told Gato he'd said it was "slightly" stronger, to soften the blow. Gato hugged me and told me he was proud of me, but I don't know if he really meant it. It's hard to tell with Gato. He's still doing battle with all the demons that come with growing up male in Mexico. I shouldn't even bring it up, because he's as much of a feminist as I am. Did you know the Mexica of the Anahuac had coed universities thousands of years before the Europeans? It's true. The Spaniards were the ones who imposed the *machista* culture. Gato knows that, but his parents are part of the elite in Mexico City, so he grew up with the ranches and horses and his dad has a big black mustache. The stuff you grow up with is hard to shake. I think Gato has freed himself, but sometimes I'm not certain.

With me, it's that my mom, for all her sexist posturing, for all the times she says "You know how men are" or "You know how us girls are," was the one who lorded it over our family. She couched everything in sweet language, but she controlled my dad from the first day they met. In public, she expects him to do the talking, but in private she tells him what to say. They'd never admit it if you asked them, but it's the truth. She still does it. And he still loves it.

Sunday, I was visiting them and they were sitting in front of the TV—or as my mom says, the TEEvee—on that weird love seat thing they bought that has the table built in right between the seats. My mom got bored with the football game. "Honey," she said to Dad, all sugar, "don't you *want* to change the channel?"

The usual routine is that he would say yes and ask her what she wants to watch, or just hand over the remote. He knows a question from my mom is an *order*. But he was feeling a little frustrated—or, as my mom says, "fust-rated"—because he woke up wanting to go for a ride on his mountain bike but got guilted into watching football because my mom thinks that's what "real men" do. She asked him, over breakfast, what he wanted to do that day, and when he said, "Ride my bike," she gave him that "sweet" look and said, "But the football game is on, I know you *love* to watch football." He shrugged, scared to stand up to her, and she kept at it. "I could make some little smokies. You want a beer? Don't you *want* to watch the football game?"

He gave up pretty quickly, sat down in that contraption, and flipped the TEEvee on with a sigh. It was a gorgeous day, too. I felt so sorry for him, man. So maybe just to spite her, when she asked about changing the channel, he said no, for the first time I can remember. Didn't say it loud, but he *said* it. She didn't know how to handle it, so she did what made sense to her. She glared at him with all the rancor in the world, then snatched the remote out of his hand. "Who listens to you anyway?" she asked, smiling as if it were a joke. It wasn't. I knew it, and she knew it. And most of all, *he* knew it.

She switched the tube to the shop at home network, where they were selling ugly jewelry, and her face lit up. "Oooh, look, honey. It's tanzanite. We love tanzanite." He didn't move, or breathe, or anything. Just grunted slightly. Then, looking at me, Mom said, "Isn't it just so beautiful?" I said no, but she ignored me. "It's so beautiful. Tanzanite goes good with everything you want to wear. Honey, wouldn't you like me to get one?" Dad handed her the phone. She placed an order, with his credit card. Then she hung up, smiled at me, and said, "You know how us girls are. We love to shop."

"No," I said, "I don't know how us girls are. I don't love to shop."

She ignored me.

Dad ignored me.

It's easier that way.

THE GUYS FROM my band are here already, hoisting the drums, amps, and microphone stands into place on the darkened stage. I'm nervous. DJs are starting to play my music on some stations in San Diego and Tijuana, and lots of kids in the movement are buying my CDs, which we produce ourselves. I got a postcard from a fan in McAllen, Texas, last week, who said she heard my music on a station out of Reynosa, Mexico. What a trip. It's growing, my thing, so fast I almost don't know what to do. People in the movement know my name. Last year at this time I was lucky if fourteen people showed up for my gig. Tonight they had to turn people away. That should tell you something. There's a real hunger out there. You have no idea how happy I feel when I look out at this sea of brown and see mostly girls in the pit. Women. It makes up for every time some *cabrón* has asked me if I'm a groupie. It makes up for all those record executives who've sent back my demo saying they didn't think there was really a market for the kind of *Mexicoytl* I channel out of the universe. Angry, strong, female rock in Spanish and Nahuatl. The last one who called asked me if I'd be willing to tone it down and do it more pop. "Like a Latina Britney," he said. He wanted to team me with Latin pop producer Rudy Perez. That's when I hung up on him.

I'll do it myself if I have to, sell it on the streets. The execs don't understand that you don't make music to make money, not if you really mean it. If you really mean it, you make music to balance the energies of the universe. You harness the voice and the power and you unleash it. You don't control it. You let it control *you*.

Gato dives into the swirling mass of glistening bodies. They swallow him up with a roar and then there he is, riding their shoulders and hands over the top. They rip his shirt off and spit on him. They love him. The spitting thing started in Argentina. If they love you in Argentina, they spit on you, at least in the rock world. Now the Mexicans are doing it. Everyone is watching, even that creepy midlife crisis sipping an umbrella drink at the bar. He looks like he fell out of Spago. What's he doing *here*?

I study him and try to figure out his story, a bad habit of mine. Maybe his wife ran off with the pool boy tonight, and he came to the first bar he found. Maybe he's looking to buy the club and turn it into a Hooters. He seems amused, as that type of man will. Maybe he's a drunk. Men like that make me uncomfortable. They remind me of Ed, Lauren's fiancé. They seem like the kinds of guys who come home, roll up their sleeves, and screw the maid.

Gato spreads his arms like Jesus and they lift him high. He's feeling it. We smoked a little reefer a few minutes ago, and Gato's flying. I smile. Gato's deep. Gato's got it. He'll probably get a record deal before I do. We're both after the same Holy Grail, you know? He's suggested once or twice that we team up, which I found offensive. I don't need his help. I know he's trying to be nice. But I want the control of my art. I guess you could say I'm an egomaniac that way. I don't want to share the stage with anybody. I got too much to say for that.

I walk across the creaky floorboards of the stage and through the dented black metal door that leads to the little dressing room. A cockroach scurries into a crack in the wall next to the mirror. I rub gel into my braids to get them to stand out more, and retouch the purple lipstick and black liquid eyeliner. For performances I go extra heavy on the makeup, the lights on the stage will wash you out. I want them to see me.

I have ten minutes until we're supposed to start. I'm trying something new tonight with the clothes: a black rubber bodysuit, with a diamond shape cut out of the abs area. My friend Lalo drew Mexica symbols all over it. Tonight I'll be singing part of a song in Nahuatl, the language of the Aztecs. Gato and I have been taking Nahuatl lessons from a shaman named Curly out in La Puente. He's planning a naming ceremony for me at the Whittier Narrows next month, and I can't wait to have my real name at last.

I go back to the stage and make sure everybody's standing where they need to be. These guys give nothing but respect. At first they didn't know what to make of me, my being a "girl," but then they heard my music and decided I was okay. After they played in my band for more than a year, they decided I was better than okay, that I was really good. Now they treat me like one of the guys, and that's fine.

Brian, my drummer, is the short, powerful dude with the green skullcap and the feathered boa. He came to L.A. from Philadelphia to study law and dropped out to be a rocker. Sebastian, the tall skinny one with the shaved head, is my keyboardist and programmer. He's from Spain and actually used to play with a famous band in Madrid before he joined my group. My bassist Marcos comes from Argentina; he's the quiet one who looks like an accountant, saves all his pent-up craziness for when we play. The backup guitarist is a girl from Whittier I heard play at a festival at Cal State L.A. She had no idea how good she really was, and still doesn't. Somebody must have beat up on that girl bad, way back. There's Ravel, a Dominican guy who plays percussion and pan flutes and sings backup. He's an incredible musician and so cheerful all the time it makes you want to hurl.

We're all in place, and the lights go out. The crowd roars. A small blue light comes on, and we start the first song, a churning, angry thing I wrote with a mix of hip-hop, metal, and traditional Peruvian sounds. The fans go crazy. The spotlight shines on me and I lose myself to the trance. The adrenaline flows through me. I forget who I am or where, and *become* the music. I transcend time and space and I howl. They say my voice is rough, gravelly, and harsh, like Janis Joplin. There hasn't really been a Mexica singing like that yet, at least not on record. Alejandra Guzmán's voice comes close, but her music has too much girly pop in it. Mine is sharper and more painful, more mad crazy.

After the first song, I grab the postcards and address the crowd in Spanish: *"Chingazos! Chingazos!"* They go crazy. "Listen to me, *chingazos*. Did you see Shakira lately?" Everyone boos. "That's right. She's a *pinche* disgrace. Blond hair. She's a disgrace to La Raza and La Causa. She might as well be Paulina Rubio!" Everyone cheers. I throw the postcards out and they float down into the sea of brown hands. "They're addressed to her manager, *hijos de puta!* We're telling them we don't want this kind of representation. We're telling Shakira she's a traitor!" More cheers. Then they start to chant. *"Que Shaki se joda, que Shaki se joda, que Shaki se joda.*" Fists raised in the air, teeth bared like animals. I let them go on for a little while, then I hold my hand up to silence them. "Your job is to get out there and educate people, Raza. There's too much self-hatred going on, too much wishing we were like the white man." Cheers. "Love yourself. Love your brown Aztec self, Raza!" More cheers. *"Que viva la raza, raza!"* Screams and hysteria. Then, in English, I say: "Love your big, bad, beautiful brown self, *chingones!*" It's the lead in to a new song, and we begin to play. The mosh pit churns, and I float away in the magic of it. I'm gone.

When I finish the set, everyone is sweaty and crazy. They chant for an encore. I'm wasted, drained by the cosmos. I can't do another one. I bow and start to pack up. The DJ puts some Jaguares on, quick, and everyone starts to bob and dance. A few people get past the bouncers and storm the stage in search of autographs, or just to touch my hand. I make contact with my fans for fifteen minutes, then turn my back to the crowd and pack up my guitar. As I start to break down the microphone and other sound equipment, I feel a hand on my shoulder. I turn and see the older man in the dark coat I noticed at the bar earlier.

"Amber? How you doing? Joel Benítez," he says with what sounds like a New York accent, all business, holding his thick hand out to shake mine. I wipe my hands uselessly on my rubber pants and shake his, feeling filthy and sweaty. He searches my eyes in a way that makes me uncomfortable and holds the hand longer than is customary, turning it over to inspect my short, messy green fingernails.

"Magic Marker," I say. "I paint my nails with Magic Marker." It's a stupid thing to say, but I'm overcome with nervousness.

"I was wondering," he says. "I couldn't tell from back there. Very creative."

I recognize his name. Joel Benítez is the director of artists and repertoire for Wagner Records' new Latin division. In other words, he's the guy with the juice, the one who signs artists. On a whim, I sent him a demo CD a few months ago. I never heard anything, so didn't think much of it. It's unusual to hear back from a big-time guy like that unless you have an agent, and I don't. I had an agent before, and didn't like the way he tried to get me to change my hair and sound. I tried for a while to find another agent who might understand my music, but I was unsuccessful. I don't even have a manager, for the same reason. I'm a control freak. Anyway, I never expected Joel Benítez would show up here in his suit and tie.

"Sounded good," he says. He lifts one corner of his mouth and his eyes gleam. "Really good, actually."

"You liked it?"

He smiles. I can smell his strong cologne. It reminds me of the stuff my grandpa wears. Plumber's cologne. Gato doesn't wear cologne, just woodsy patchouli oil.

"Can you come by our offices next week, say Monday morning?" he asks, point-blank. He looks bored, considering.

"Monday morning?" I stall.

"That's the second of February," he says—the Mexica New Year. Coincidence? "In the morning. Unless that's too early—for a musician." He laughs. I laugh like a hyena. My hand zooms up to my hair and starts to fiddle with it.

"Ten okay?" He's looking away now, watching the people in the club, confident.

"Ten's fine. That's good. Ten." I hear terror in the staccato rushing of my voice.

He takes a silver business card holder out of an inside pocket of his coat and flips it open with one hand, slides a single card out with his thumb, graceful and practiced. Snap, the case shuts. I pluck the card from his fingertips. "The address is right there," he says, still looking away. "Tell the receptionist you're there to see me."

I think to ask him what he wants to talk about, but he has already turned away from me and weaves through the dancing bodies toward the door. He walks like a man with power. I watch him go and once he's gone keep staring into the dark until I feel another hand on my shoulder, Gato.

"You ready?" he asks. He's still missing his shirt, and his

exposed skin is covered with angry scratches and welts from the pit.

"Yeah, sure." I shake myself and remember I still have to pay the guys in the band. "I have to get the money from Lou," I say, referring to the club manager.

"I already did that. Here." He pulls out a check from the club owner. It's more than I expected, a couple thousand more. I grab the check and my jaw drops. I smile at Gato. He tells me the owner was so impressed with the turnout that he wanted to make sure I'd come back. *Cool.*

I look at Gato's face to see if he noticed me talking to Joel Benítez. I don't think so. I don't want to tell him. Not here. I never wanted to be the first one to get a deal, in the same way you love your children so much you hope you're the one who dies first.

I pay my band in cash. We shake hands and then Gato and I head out the back door and climb into my Honda Civic. My mom gave it to me last year, after she bought a new Accord for herself. It's a nice car, almost too nice. Too clean and too normal, like my family. I had Lalo draw ancient Mexica symbols all over it. On the hood is a big drawing of Ozomatli, the Aztec monkey king of song and dance. I've got bumper stickers all over the back, I think it's important to educate people about the truth every chance you get. One says MEXICA: WE DIDN'T COME TO AMERICA, AMERICA CAME TO US. There's FEMINIST MAJORITY; EVOLVE, DAMNIT; and the NICE TRY, WHITE MAN. The one I get the most comments on is my big magnetic Darwin fish eating the little puny Jesus fish. I get a few crazies trying to run me off the road sometimes for that one. Nothing makes me sadder than seeing Raza with those little magnetic fish all over their cars, like Elizabeth. They have no clue. Jesus is a white man's religion.

The drive back to our two-room apartment above a watch repair shop on Silver Lake Boulevard takes a long time, like all commutes in Los Angeles—more than an hour. The smokestacks of the oil refineries along the shore in Long Beach turn the horizon an unnatural orange, flames lapping at the sky everywhere you look. I apologize out loud to

Mother Earth for the sins of my fellow man. There aren't many people on the road at this hour. Gato and I don't talk much. Performances take so much out of us, we like to just hold hands and listen to the ringing in our ears.

The police choppers are out in full force tonight. We see three before we get to our exit. I think of my brother Peter, an officer with the beleaguered LAPD. He's so lost. He came to one concert of mine in West Hollywood. He didn't say much. He shook Gato's hand, and he patted me on the back, but he never came back. I haven't talked to him since. We don't have anything to say to each other. It's been like that since we were little. Peter liked to burn ants under a magnifying glass and I liked to run out after rainstorms and rescue the worms stranded on the sidewalk.

When the janitors were striking, Gato and I used to go support them every night. We'd set up our equipment and play right there in downtown Los Angeles, next to the Museum of Contemporary Art. One time, the police came to break up our gathering—we were playing without a public permit—and who do you think was the guy who showed up with the notice to vacate? My brother. It was deep. We just sort of stared at each other for a good long minute and then I went on my way. He's a Republican, too, if you can believe that. He likes to make fun of Mexicans, just like our dad. So many Mexican jokes. Pete thinks we should shut the border with Mexico and shoot "illegals" on sight.

I pull the car into the parking lot behind our building and take the notebook out of my pocket. I open the car door for light, pin the notebook to the steering wheel and write, ignoring the chime alerting me that I've left my keys in the ignition. *Two children, me and you / From the same seed we are us two / I saved worms while you burned ants / Now you wear policeman's pants / Young we used to share a room / Now you'd point your gun in my face and go boom / Just because I know where we're from / An ancient land, an Indian land / And you, Brother Officer, don't understand / The immigrants you hate have American roots / They're original here, and so are you.*

Gato carries my guitar up the stairs for me. Once we've locked the door behind us and I've started to make hot tea—a ritual designed to save our voices—we finally speak again.

"You played *un* set *increíble, mujerón*," Gato says, coming up behind me at the sink. He lifts my hair and his mouth is warm and soft on the back of my neck. *"Tu eres la mujer más increíble que yo he conocido en mi vida, sabes."* He presses up against me and I can tell that he has more than compliments on his mind. I turn to pull him to me. I wrap my arms around him and lead him gently toward the bedroom. There's something about playing a really good set, getting all that energy out there, that cleanses my spirit and leaves me humming with life force.

"Forget tea," I say.

"Yeah, forget tea."

Our bedroom is a paradise. We have a king-sized futon on the floor, covered with beautiful pillows from all over the world. We have candles and incense everywhere, and the walls are draped with blankets from Mexico. We can't paint the walls because it's a rental, so we've covered every inch with sensuous fabric, even the ceiling. Gato calls it our "womb." We undress and look at each other.

He is gentle with me, tender, open, loving. Most men have so many issues they don't know how to keep their image of you as a *friend* and *human being* once you've got your clothes off. They say ugly things. Gato is the first man I have known who smiles while making love. There's no difference from the smiles he gives when you're having a meal and telling jokes together. He's the first man I've known who really and truly makes love to me. Our bodies become one. It's a peaceful sort of passion, a low smoldering fire. When Gato and I make love I feel the spirits of our ancestors rise up from Aztlán and shake the earth.

We climax together. We always climax together. Gato studies yoga. He's able to control his body in ways that amaze me. "I listen to your body," he tells me, "I hear its chords and melodies. I feel it as if it were my own. There's a way you tense, I can tell."

Afterward, Gato gets up to turn off the teakettle, which has been whistling for a while now. He prepares the tea, with honey and lemon, in the dark brown clay mugs we bought from a Navajo man in Flagstaff when Gato had a gig at the university. I sit up on the bed and cradle the cup in my hands, more exhausted and happy than I have ever been. My muscles are sore. Maybe Gato will rub me with that elixir of marijuana stems.

"So," he says, sipping tea, smiling, "that was Joel Benítez, wasn't it?"

I can't believe he knows, that he knew this whole time and didn't say anything. I feel so guilty I can't speak. I nod, wondering why he waited.

"What did he tell you?" I see pain in Gato's eyes, even though he tries to conceal it.

I look at him. I blush. I don't know what to say. I look down at the comforter, then into my cup.

"That's great," Gato says, leaning over to kiss me softly. I look up at him. He runs a finger softly across my cheek. "Your joy is my joy. Truly." I detect nothing in his face or voice to indicate he might be threatened or upset. But his eyes. It's there. Envy.

"I'm sorry," I say. "I wanted it to be you. I'm so, so sorry."

He shrugs and smiles, but his eyes look sad. "For what, *mi amor?* I'm so happy for you."

I feel his arms around me again, and realize how lucky I am. Lauren spent so much time complaining about men last time the *sucias* got together, I almost started to believe her. She said even the ones who seem nice and wonderful really aren't. She's wrong. Gato is perfect. He's one of the few men I know capable of moving beyond his *machista* upbringing.

He is happy for me, he says, and I am pretty sure he means it.

I was as stunned as the rest of this city to hear of the suicide of Dwight Reardon, a longtime Gazette Metro columnist and occasional mentor. Those of us who knew Dwight knew the good—his booming laugh, his seemingly cynical take on local politics that was really a mask for a huge, compassionate heart, his plainspoken encouragement of young reporters— and the bad, namely that he had for years suffered from Seasonal Affective Disorder. He'd come in on gloomy days with a frown, complaining of a headache, telling anyone who'd come close to his desk how depressed he felt. On particularly dreary days, he'd miss deadline. Our mistake was not taking his words and symptoms seriously enough. Seasonal Affective Disorder is a form of depression brought on by a change in seasons, believed to be related to decreased exposure to sunlight as the days grow shorter with cold weather. Those of us who work in Boston know it's not unusual to get to the office in the dark of morning, only to leave in the dark of late afternoon. As January drags darkly on, I encourage any of you who think you might suffer from SAD to get help. I wish I'd had the good sense to help Dwight. I miss him. This town is a drearier place without his words.

—from "My Life" by Lauren Fernández

lauren

T HE *BOSTON GAZETTE* building looks like a really big, ugly public school, built sometime in the sixties and perpetually patrolled by beefy lunch ladies in hair nets. Red bricks, green glass windows, lawns that would like to seem inviting, except for the KEEP OFF THE GRASS signs. Enough said.

One side of the mammoth structure is lined with a fleet of bright orange trucks. The back of the building is the loading dock where union guys sit around reading the *Herald,* even though they work for the *Gazette.* In this town, the newspapers represent the pervasive class conflicts. The union guys like the *Herald* as a workingman's paper, a tabloid full of big pictures and none of that multicultural nonsense. They come to work with the *Herald* folded under their tubular arms and leave the papers lying around for us reporters to see as we come scurrying by out of the wind and snow.

The only *Gazette* writer the loading dock guys like now that Dwight is gone is Mack O'Malley. The paper used to run O'Malley's right-wing screeds on things like why women shouldn't work and why we should do away with affirmative action, until a *McCall's* magazine fact-checker figured out he made up most of the people and facts in his columns. I wasn't surprised. My first week on the job, his old buddy, sports columnist Will Harrigan, took me aside and in a scotch-smeared voice grumbled, "Kid, I'll give you three bits of advice on working here. One, O'Malley makes all his shit up. Two, Dwyer [editor in chief] is a mental vegetable. Three, don't wear your skirts so short 'cuz you're makin' me sweat."

After much posturing, O'Malley was fired, but went on to make even more money writing about the same crap for a New York City tabloid where accuracy has never been an issue. Last I checked, he had his own talk show on a cable news network, too.

Inside, the *Gazette* building is dreary. Long echoing hallways with gray tile floors and twitching fluorescent lights. There has not been fresh air in this building for several decades, not since the anti-busing group from Southie came red-faced and surly to throw a Molotov cocktail through the front window. When the presses shudder to life in the early evening, the entire building shakes. On the desks of those who sit beneath air vents are small piles of black ashlike substance. They will tell you this is dust. But everyone knows it's ink.

Only the offices of the editors have windows. They are the only ones. Over in my department, the Features wing, there are no windows and never will be. Our light comes from long white bulbs, exposed like femurs. The carpet was once blueberry, but has faded to a foamy jeans color. I'm not quite sure how.

In spite of all this, I love my desk. I have draped it in Mexican rugs and Santeria beads just to scare everyone. It's like a gigantic wedding cake stuck in the middle of the newsroom I share with about forty other reporters and copy editors. It makes them nervous, I like to think, jealous and terrified. La Virgen de Guadalupe stands at attention on top of my computer terminal, with the brass handles of a broken clock poking out of her navel. In my drawer, I keep a bottle of "Boss Be Fixed" oil I found at a botanica in Chelsea for two bucks when I did a hard-sell feature on the Palo Mayombe religion before I got my column. Took me weeks to get my editor to agree to that one. *Palo who? Is that like Voodoo? If it's Satan worship our readers won't understand. We're in a very patriotic, very Christian swing here. We'll get cancellations. There's a nice march for a couple of saints over in the North End somewhere, that's ethnic, why don't you go cover that? You should be able to understand some Italian, right? Here's twenty bucks. Bring me back some biscotti, almond.*

I pasted two dried red beans to my phone receiver, along with a Barbie doll with a crew cut and war paint on her face. Onto the huge partition that separates me from the rowdy, farting guys in the Sports section, I have tacked the requisite phony-baloney photos of me and Ed. Next to the photos is a list of all the Latino business leaders in the Boston area, men (yes, all men) who had, until I started working at the *Gazette*, concentrated their efforts only in the extraordinarily weak and biased local Spanish media, convinced that the *Gazette* did not care what they were up to. They were right.

But now that I'm here, the *Gazette* has to pretend. And so do I.

Because of this grand charade I call a career, I am bracing myself for the meeting I'm about to have with my nervous twit of an editor, Chuck Spring. I will try to convince him to approve a column on feuding between Dominicans and Puerto Ricans.

It has been less than one minute since I pressed the buttons to call my Message Pending onto the screen. I'd seen the words "Come In." That's what Chuck writes when he wants to talk to you about a story idea. Or at least that's what he writes to me, and to Iris, the other female Lifestyles columnist. When he writes to Jake or Bob, he sends them somewhat chummier words. This is because Jake is male, graduated from Harvard, Chuck's alma mater, and is a member of the same Final Club. For those unfamiliar with Final Clubs, I'll tell you they were deemed illegal by the university because they refuse to admit women. In some cases, they don't even let women in the front door of their buildings unless they're discreetly hidden inside a large cake. Nonetheless, Final Clubs continue to meet, albeit several blocks away from university grounds in order to avoid scrutiny. Chuck continues to wear his secret pink button-down shirt with the secret striped tie on those days when he has a secret Final Club meeting after work. They all wear that outfit. Gang colors.

Chuck is seen by his peers at the *Gazette* as a man with the intellect of a newborn hamster. But he is well connected, so no one who values his or her career complains about him. He is the godson of the publisher. He is from an old New England family of the type that goes to The Vineyard to experience diversity once Nantucket has gotten dull. Far as I can tell, from my couple of years talking to him, that's all just a fancy way of saying the man is inbred. He's got pictures on his desk of his family and they all look just like him, including his wife. Square heads, beady eyes, hair of a color that is not quite a color, skinny bodies in button-downs and cardigans. He once assigned me, without a hint of humor, to write about Mexican migrant workers he'd seen stooped in tobacco fields on his way to the Berkshires—yes, there are tobacco fields in Central Massachusetts. "I want you to get in there, Fernández, live the life with them. Find out what moves them, what makes them tick. Find out what songs they sing around the campfire at night." I daresay he expected those grizzled men from Zacatecas would hold hands after a long day of backbreaking labor and sing "Kumbaya," just like he used to as a promising well-bred lad at the local Episcopal summer camp.

When I get to his office, Chuck is leaning back in his chair with his feet on the desk and the phone stuck on his ear. His argyle socks don't match because he is colorblind. His penny loafers have pennies in them. He is laughing in a way that is nervous and nerdy, because this is how he always laughs, like he is six years old and has just slipped something slimy into his friend's milk carton. Snort snort snort. Hee hee hee.

I concentrate on a rack of compact discs by the door. Boston Pops appears more than once. Chuck once told me, in all seriousness, that Keith Lockhart, the conductor of the Boston Pops, was the most famous celebrity in town. I smiled and nodded because to remind him of all the athletes and pop musicians seemed a waste of time. He wouldn't have understood. When Kurt Cobain stuffed a rifle in his mouth and went bang, Chuck asked someone who that guy was only after he saw an article in the *Washington Post*. Every time a new intern comes, Chuck tries to rope them into doing a story that doesn't exist, about a group of young women called LUGs, which, Chuck swears, stands for Lesbians Until Graduation; it's an idea that makes Chuck's undies wet, and so he can't quite give up on the story, which he saw in *Details* magazine once and so believes to be true, even though every reporter who has ever gone after it for him has come back with the same news: no such thing as LUGs.

It wasn't until Keith Lockhart (who, incidentally, somewhat resembles Chuck Spring and his wife) dressed in leather pants on the cover for his too-late Latin album that Chuck found out who Ricky Martin was. Now he goes around, years too late, singing "Livin' la Vida Loca," only he can't say "*vida*" and he can't say "*loca*," so he ends up singing "Livin' Evita Loqua."

Chuck has stopped laughing and now he is saying "uh-huh" a million times in a row, and nodding furiously, even though no one can see him but me, and I am trying hard not to. He's not an appetizing sight.

I turn around, unsure whether to stay or to go, and take a few paces back from the door. I examine the fax machine outside. I greet the secretary. I suck my upper lip. I whistle.

I glance over at the table where the co-op students from Emerson College and Northeastern University sit. They are supposed to be sorting mail and taking transcriptions, but mostly it appears that they are making long-distance personal phone calls on the unlimited *Gazette* dime. The one with the pierced nose and long skirt shouts at the phone and says the same thing over and over. Then she motions for me to come over. I oblige, because there is nothing else to do. Chuck, meanwhile, has begun snort-laughing again. His legs are bouncy as little rubber bands.

"You're Nicole Garcia, right?" the co-op asks me.

"No, I'm Lauren Fernández," I say. It is the millionth time someone in the building has mistaken me for the only other Hispanic female to work here, an obese, middle-aged food writer who comes in only at night to scribble about broccoli rabe and walnuts, leaving a trail of gourmet potato chip crumbs to the parking lot when she leaves.

"Sorry," the co-op says, blushing. "But you speak Spanish, right?" she asks.

I nod, but feel guilty. It's not *exactly* a lie, is it?

I take the receiver and when I put my ear to it all I can hear are the outside sounds of cars honking.

"*Boston Gazette*," I bark.

"Us, *jes*, to Lauren Fernández *por* please."

"*Yo soy* Lauren," I say, letting him know he's found the

woman he seeks. *Tenth grade, Mr. James, Spanish 2, first floor, Benjamin Franklin School, Carrollton Street, near the crescent turn to Saint Charles.* Yo soy, tu eres, él es, ella es, nosotros somos, ellos son. *Walking to Burger King after school with Benji and Sandi for french fries, taking the streetcar to the Esprit outlet, spending all our baby-sitting money on plastic purses and canvas shoes. Walking down to Jax and getting fudge, looking out at the river, flirting with the Creole boys in the rugby shirts because they were hotties.* Yo soy, tu eres, él es . . . *What was that other one? Vosotros? Do people use that word anymore?*

The person on the other end starts to scream at me in fast Spanish. I can't catch much, but I get the impression they didn't like a column I did about sexist behavior at the Puerto Rican Day Parade.

"Write a letter to the editor," I say.

I look around, and there's Chuck. He has hung up his phone and is annoyed that I am not sitting in the hard wooden chair across from his desk, awaiting his sage advice on all things journalistic.

He flutters in his khaki pants and suspenders to the doorway to his office. Suspenders, ladies and gentlemen. He makes a jerky, nervous motion to let me know I should not be on the phone at the co-op desk.

"Be right there," I sing out, smiling. I apologize to the caller and hang up.

I return the phone to the astonished co-ops, and move toward Chuck, who greets me by stuffing his busy hands deep in his pockets, bouncing on the balls of his feet. "What the heck were you doing over there? Talking to Castro?"

I should laugh, but I don't. I used to try to laugh at Chuck's jokes, but it always sounded so forced that he would just look sort of hurt. Finally, I stopped trying, partly because it wasn't worth the eye wrinkles.

"Have a seat," he says. The glass coffee table between my seat and the expansive desk is littered with fashion magazines. A copy of the *New York Times* sits in one corner, the

Washington Post on the other. This is the second-rate newspaper editor's secret to trend coverage: read other papers and magazines and if they're saying it's hot, it's hot. And you must use that exact word, "hot."

I notice that underneath a stack of papers on Chuck's desk is a *Playboy* magazine. Actually, several copies. Several *Playboy*s. Damp and wavy on the sides like they've been dipped in . . . I don't want to know.

"Uh, Chuck," I say, staring. Pointing. He gets even more nervous than before, laughs, and stirs things around on the desk with his frantic hands.

"Oh, that. Just left over from Bob's story on that big hulking wrestler from Framingham who was in *Playboy*. That's nothing. The others, those are from Jake's story on Nancy Sinatra that time in *Playboy*. You know. Just leftovers. I was curious after reading the story, er, I mean, do you think those pictures are real? A lady her age? I mean, my God. She's probably older than my wife!"

I cross one leg over the other, and think about all of the buttery things in the windows of the Kenneth Cole store. I lace my fingers together and notice my nail tips have grown out and look cheesy and chipped. Note to self: Make manicure appointment. I take a deep breath and lift myself higher in the chair, try to look natural.

"So, how are you? You happy?" he asks. It's not so much a question as an instruction. I better be happy. Everyone in Chuck's world is happy. Smile through the indigestion of life, sweeties, drink champagne and drive a foreign car.

Chuck nods and says that's good. We stare at each other for a moment with nothing to say. I do believe he hates me. Then he puts his loafered feet back up on the desktop and plants his hands behind his head. Despite the creases at the edges of his eyes, he still looks fresh out of a tennis club somewhere.

"I need to ask you about something," he says. It is the usual prelude to the psycho-spiritual flogging I am regularly subjected to here. My neck starts to hurt. Then my head. Then my left eye.

He continues, "I've been getting a lot of letters and calls about that last column you did, the one on your musician friend and the Indians and genocide and all that . . . stuff."

"And?"

"I want to talk to you as a friend here, not as your editor." Uh-oh.

"You're a good writer, a strong writer. That's why you're here."

"But . . . ?"

"But sometimes I think your opinions are a little too strong and they get in the way of whatever point you're trying to prove."

"Oh."

"I don't think what happened in New England or Mexico was exactly *genocide*. The Holocaust in Germany was genocide. Lots of the Indians died because they hadn't been exposed to white man's diseases before. It wasn't intentional."

I think about answering, but decide against it. Smile, smile, smile.

"You put people on the defensive by attacking them all the time. You come across too opinionated."

"I'm a columnist. I'm supposed to be opinionated."

"Sure, but you undermine your arguments by coming out so . . . combative."

I'm Cuban trailer trash. What do you want from me?

"I understand. It won't happen again."

"Everyone just thinks you're too angry. They feel like you're preaching all the time."

"Okay, well thanks for telling me," I say with a forced smile. "I'll keep that in mind." *New shoes. New comforter. Breathe.*

"It's a good idea to run your ideas past a few people before you pursue them, so you don't write anything daffy again. We were talking in the morning meeting about it, and most of the editors think it's a good idea for you to focus more on your life and less on politics and history and that sort of thing. No one wants to see you self-destruct here."

That sort of thing? I nod. "Point taken. I appreciate it."

"Good. You know, the columns you write that people like the best are those 'hey girlfriend' kind of things." He actually tries to snap his finger in front of his face like a character from a black sitcom on the WB.

"Anything else?"

"Just a couple things. You okay with all this? You look upset."

"I'm fine. No, really. I am."

"We on the same page?"

"Absolutely."

"Good. Say, have you met that new editor, over in Health/Science?"

I nod. I know who he means. That *black* editor, that's what he means. Black female editor. He assumes we'll have much in common.

"Have you seen the car she drives?" he asks in a conspiratorial whisper. He actually puts one hand to the side of his mouth, the way they do when whispering in cartoons.

I have, indeed, seen her car. It's a green Mercedes. She also dresses well and sometimes wears hats. She's from Atlanta.

"How do you think a woman like that can afford a car like that?" he hisses. Chuck senses something in my body language or facial expression, perhaps, and retracts, somewhat. "I'm not saying, I mean, you know, those people have just as much right as anyone else to buy as nice a car as they want . . ."

"Of course," I say.

Chuck changes the subject.

"So tell me about this Dominico thing," he says. He flips through a *Vanity Fair* magazine as he speaks. The rest of his body language tells me already that he's not interested. He is interested in breast implants, sex scandals, and, well, that's about it.

"Well, here's the deal," I begin. I place one hand on each of the armrests, and it's a conscious gesture because my inclination in all of these meetings is to curl up in a ball and hide. I explain the issue. "Puerto Ricans and Dominicans have a lot in common. They're both from Caribbean, Spanish-speaking lands, they have similar cuisine, a lot of the same values. But there's this Balkan-like hatred one group has for the other."

"They're from the same kind of country. Why do they hate each other?"

I pause. Do I dare correct him? Must. Do. It. "Puerto Rico's not a country." I smile, try not to seem "combative" or "daffy."

He rolls his eyes and nods fast, as if he can't be bothered right now with petty details, flips faster through the magazine. "You know what I mean. You're getting into that political territory again. We don't want that."

"I know, I know, but that's a big part of the reason they hate each other. They're both here in Boston in huge numbers, fighting in many cases for the same low-paying jobs, living in the same neighborhoods. Because they're American by birth, Puerto Ricans get government assistance, Dominicans don't. Dominicans have legal immigration issues, Puerto Ricans don't."

He looks up, confused. "Why wouldn't Puerto Ricans have immigration issues?"

"Are you serious?" I ask.

"This is what I'm talking about, Fernández. You just get on these weird tangents that only make sense to *you*."

"Because they're American by *birth,* Chuck. Puerto Rico is a United States territory." They don't teach that at Harvard?

"So they can just come here? That's not true, is it?" He looks unsteady, nauseated.

"They're born here. They don't *come* anywhere. That's what territory means. They're as American as you are, except we don't let them vote in presidential elections unless they live on the mainland."

"Oh. Really? That can't be right."

"It's true." *Don't sigh, Lauren, don't roll your eyes. Smile, sister, smile.*

He shrugs as if he still doesn't quite believe me, and says, "Go on. But I'll tell you right now I still think it's not personal enough. I want people in your column, flesh and blood people that real people can relate to."

"Okay. So Dominicans have their stereotypes about Puerto Ricans, like that they're lazy or the women are too independent, and vice versa. Puerto Ricans have their stereotypes that Dominicans are all drug dealers or overly macho."

Chuck is nodding furiously in his discombobulated way, waiting for me to finish. I wonder to myself what it would be like to someday have an editor who actually would not, upon seeing me, begin to whistle the jingle from the Chi-Chi's restaurant commercial.

I do my best to explain it all.

Chuck makes the "just smelled a fart and I'm a toddler" face. This is too complicated for him. He doesn't like the idea. "I don't think to the average reader there's any difference between Dominicos or Porta Ricans. If they don't get what you're saying in the first graph, Lauren, they're not going to read on. This is a *newspaper*, not a textbook. Give them real girls with real problems. This is Lifestyles, not Metro."

"Puerto Ricans and Dominicans will get it," I say. "If you care. If this paper cares." *Why did you say that? Bad Lauren, combative Lauren. Slap, slap.*

"Don't start with *that* again. We already talked about this. Your column should be fun, light, accessible. It's meant as a syncopated counterbalance to all the dreary stuff in the rest of the paper. No politics. Okay?"

"Sure, okay."

A co-op peeks her head in the door and tells Chuck that his wife is on line four. In one gesture he lifts the phone, presses line four, and continues talking to me, waving one hand about as if conducting a symphony. "Something light, something fun. You know, 'you go girl,' *sassy*. Entertaining. Hi, honey?"

He swivels his chair until his back is to me. And with that, I am dismissed.

. . . Consider today's column a shout-out to all the lazy boyfriends out there, girlfriends. Guys, you've got less than a month to get your girl something perfect for Valentine's Day; and please, don't do flowers or chocolate—again. While you're out there shopping, here's a little something to think about. Saint Valentine was a Roman priest who, in spite of a decree from Emperor Claudius II to refrain from allowing soldiers to marry, continued to conduct weddings. Ah, the power of love! And as a reminder to all you ladies who might, upon receiving a box of dimestore chocolates from a dashing Casanova, consider doing the deed: Valentine was sainted for standing up for the glory of commitment.

Don't give it up unless he plans to stick around.

—from "My Life," by Lauren Fernández

usnavys

L AST YEAR, JUAN took me to San Diego for Valentine's Day. We got to visit Amber in Los Angeles and see that bleak little hole where she lives with that freaky Mexican rat man, but that was the only highlight of the trip. I hinted then that I expected him to take me somewhere better next time, so this year he arranged a European trip. He said he wanted to take me to Rome, the birthplace of Valentine's Day. We leave today.

When I pick Juan up at his apartment, he looks shocked to see all the bags I'm taking. That's how small he thinks. It makes me crazy, *ay, m'ija*. I'm serious. I'm only bringing two large apparel cases—Vuitton—one small suitcase for handbags, gloves, scarves, and shoes, a makeup box, a carry-on, my travel purse, a Kate Spade tote with plenty of room for my bottled water, magazines, CDs, and snacks. "We're only going for a long weekend," he says. "Do you have to bring all *that*?"

Yes, I wanted to say, but a long weekend *in Rome*. It's supposed to be a Valentine's gift, but it was too expensive, he says, to actually go to Rome on Valentine's Day. Plus, he wants to be around for the rehab center's Valentine's dance. So we're celebrating in early January. Tacky, no? But that's how it always is with Juan. I just rolled my eyes under my Oliver Peoples sunglasses and didn't say anything because I told myself (and Lauren) that I'd be nice to Juan this time. Lauren reminded me that Juan saved his pennies for a long time to get this for me, and I should appreciate it, as she said, on a percentage scale. The percentage of Juan's income it takes to get us to Rome for four days is big. I get it. I get it. I get it that he's *broke*. Just kidding! God, you take everything too serious sometimes, *m'ija*. If I really *cared* how much money Juan made I wouldn't be here at all. To be honest with you, I love this man. I love him more than I've ever loved anyone in all my life. That's what's so scary.

I don't even want to *tell* you what Juan brought. One small green plastic suitcase, Samsonite, with a big gash in the side. I was mortified. *Mortified*. He wanted to pick me up in his loud Volkswagen Rabbit, the one without heat, with the crusty windshield wiper blades that smear everything up and paper coffee cups all over the floor. I was, like, uh-uh, no way. I may *act* ghetto, but I ain't *that* ghetto.

I picked *him* up in my BMW, which didn't really seem right to me, under the circumstances. But I'm being nice, re-member? And he was there, waiting outside on the street with that sad little luggage and his hair parted in the middle and those JCPenney shoes he thinks are "nice." Oh. My. God.

Juan's good-looking until he *tries* to look good, if that makes sense. His hair, when he leaves it alone, curls up and looks attractive in a mad scientist way. His beard looks attractive if he lets it go for a couple of days. He almost looks like his hero, Che Guevara. His black-framed glasses—which I picked out for him, thank you very much—make him look smart and interesting. But when he thinks he *has* to make an effort to look presentable, it screws everything up for him. He slicks his hair down like a third grade boy, shaves his beard so you can see his weak chin. And all those cuts he gets from the razor? The *nene* never did learn to shave. He wears contact lenses that irritate his eyes so he ends up looking like he's been crying or drinking all day. He wears polyester "slacks" he thinks look nice instead of the jeans and sweatshirts he's comfortable in. I'm not telling you anything I haven't already told him. But does he listen? No. But don't get me wrong. I think he's incredibly handsome, *m'ija.* He rocks my boat. I just wish he had more money. Is that a crime?

When he called and told me we had the choice to fly Boston to Rome through London's Heathrow Airport or through Dublin Airport in Ireland, I picked London, of course. The Irish have no sophistication, *m'ija,* you know that. You've been to Southie. I wish there was a direct flight from Boston to Rome, but there's not. We probably could have gotten a direct flight from New York, and that would have been so much easier, but I didn't bring it up. Juan doesn't really think about practical things. He's always obsessing about work, trying to come up with a new way to make his programs run better. Sometimes you actually have to shake him to get him to hear you talking.

So here we are, on the last leg of the trip, from London to Rome. I've been on planes for the last twelve hours. That's twelve, *m'ija,* with a one and a two. Twelve hours of trying to get comfortable in these little seats because Juan couldn't get first class for us. Twelve hours of my feet falling asleep in these pointy red St. Johns; I've got a wide foot, but I can't bear to wear wide shoes, especially not in red. Twelve hours without a real bathroom or a real meal. Twelve hours listening to case stories about the men Juan helps at his rehab center. David, who was strung out for nearly twenty years but who now holds down a job at Wendy's and has been sober for a full year. Luis, whose house caught fire from him smoking crack in bed and nearly burned to death, who is now a sanitation department worker and got clean and found a nice girlfriend. On and on. There are lots of happy endings. He likes those the best. But there are sad ones, too. I don't mind listening to the stories. I know I always say I wanted to leave the 'hood, and I did. I wouldn't go back there for all the riches in the world.

I *admire* what Juan does. He has a degree in civil engineering from Northeastern and could have done any number of other things to bolster his social standing, but he made the hard choice to forgo a higher standard of living in order to give back to *nuestra comunidad.* He's explained all that to me, and I understand it. It's the same with me. I've had offers from for-profit firms to do the same kind of work I do at the United Way, believe me. They pay almost double what I make now. But I'm probably more like Juan than anyone realizes; I need to feel like the work I'm doing matters. But I still earn more than four times what that boy makes. It's sad, girl.

I fill him in on all this media nonsense about Elizabeth being a lesbian. She's worried she won't get the big national job because Rupert Mandrake, head of the network's parent company, is some big "family values"—meaning lesbian-hating—crusader. People are so stupid. I called her and told her I didn't care. I don't. It doesn't matter to me who my *sucias* sleep with, as long as they treat my girls right. I asked her if that little-boys-don't-cry–looking poet of hers was good to her. She said yes, and I said that was all that mattered. She thanked me and started to sob and said that Sara won't talk to her.

"That's so stupid," Juan says. "Sara's a bitch."

"They were best friends. It's weird."

"Makes you wonder if they weren't more than best friends once, doesn't it?" Juan asks. I hadn't thought of that.

"*Seriously* doubt it. Sara's really conservative."

Elizabeth said Lauren was being supportive, and so was Amber. She hadn't talked to Rebecca yet, but I'm sure she won't be mean, even if she doesn't approve, because she's not rude to anyone. She ran a story in *Ella* once about lesbian Latinas.

Lauren is the rudest of all of us. Even I'm getting sick of the way that girl drinks too much and lectures everyone all the time like we don't know our own history. It's the gringa in her, I think, that makes her like that, a big know-it-all that gives you a headache just being around her. Juan and I talk about life and art and politics and our families and everything else in the world. That's the best thing about us, the way we talk. If he were a woman, he'd be my best friend. I might even let myself cry in front of him, if he were a girl.

We finally land in Rome. It's just turned morning. I'm so tired all I want is to take a cab to a cushy hotel, get a little room service, and fall asleep. Juan has other plans. He has decided to rent a car and try to drive us around Rome *himself*. He has never *been* to Rome, *m'ija*. He acts surprised when he sees that the steering wheel on our sad little green Fiat is on the *right*. Dang, the cars here are small! Plus, he hasn't slept in a day, his contact lenses have irritated his eyes so much they look like someone poured battery acid in them. He forgot to bring saline solution and doesn't want to take his lenses off and put his glasses on because they're the only contact lenses he brought. Sad as hell.

I don't have to tell you that Rome is one of the biggest cities in Europe and, as we soon find out, not only has different traffic laws than we do in the United States, but is also entangled in dozens of massive reconstruction projects at many of its historic locations. We sit in unmoving traffic more aggressive and horrible than any I've ever seen, with people gesticulating at one another from their little motor scooters and taxicabs. All they seem to do is shout here and wave their big hairy arms. Even the women have hairy arms. Haven't they heard of hot wax? Hello? It gives me the worst headache I've ever had, a pinching right *here* in the front. It even seems like the shopkeepers and workers on the street *enjoy* screaming in their horrible little language as loud as they can, just to annoy me. They sound like they're speaking retarded Spanish. I thought Puerto Rico was loud. It's nothing compared to Rome.

It takes us three hours just to find the neighborhood where our hotel is supposed to be, because Juan keeps taking wrong turns and thinking he can understand enough Italian to get directions from people who have no idea what he's saying to them. He's too proud to admit he doesn't know what he's doing, *m'ija.* And I'm still being too nice to criticize him. I'm serious. We finally find the place, thanks to some Romans who speak this singsongy Spanish, but once we do, I start to wish we were back in the traffic again.

I'm expecting something else. I know I shouldn't complain, but I'm accustomed to a certain level of comfort. I know the trip was free for me, and Juan is trying to be nice for Valentine's Day—a month early. I didn't even complain that he thought we should go to Rome in *January,* when it's cold and dreary. I've *tried* to be patient and nice with the boy.

But, *m'ija,* I'm not used to the kind of hotel Juan has booked for us. I travel all the time for work, and you know the types of places I have Travis book for me. I mean, Juan should have known from the name alone that this wasn't going to be a very nice place. The "Aberdeen Hotel." Who goes to Rome and stays in the Aberdeen *anything*? I swear. It sounds like something you'd find tucked behind a meat processing plant in Duluth. The view out the front of the building is of the Italian Ministry of Defense. How *romantic,* right, *m'ija?* The hotel is small, it's dingy, smelling like antiseptic and irritable bowels. I'm so tired I don't have the energy to protest. I follow Juan up to our little room with the one battered-looking queen-sized bed, my feet aching.

"No way," I say when I see the bed.

"What?"

"I'm not sleeping with you. You know that. We need a room with two beds. Get us a room with two beds." I sit on the little lumpy chair and give him the guilt face.

Juan's shoulders sag and he rubs his eyes. One of his disposable contact lenses pops out and falls on the floor. He gets on his hands and knees and starts patting the stained, hard carpet with that Mr. Magoo look.

"You'll get a disease if you put that thing back in your eye," I say.

"Fine. Whatever you say." He removes the other contact lens and drops it on the floor, too, then takes his glasses out of his suitcase and puts them on. He takes them off, and rubs the bridge of his nose. He sighs. He has that blurry look he gets when he can't see where he's going. "Can you just wait until tomorrow, Navi? We're both tired. I'm not going to try anything, I promise. Let's just get some rest."

"Two beds." I hold up two fingers.

He leaves me in the room and returns fifteen minutes later with another key. We go to the new room with its two beds. *Twin sized.* I'm not a small woman. Italian twin beds, like everything in Europe, from the clothes to the portions at restaurants to the people themselves, are smaller than the American equivalent. I don't know how I'm supposed to sleep on this thing; it's like a tightrope. I don't say anything because I don't want to make Juan feel any worse than he already does. There's not even a bellhop, so Juan has to go back to the car to get my bags. While he does, I check out the bathroom and the closet. Very bland and functional and not luxurious at all. I won't be able to use my hair dryer and my curling iron because they use some crazy-looking electric outlets in Rome, *m'ija.* There's no hotel-provided dryer either, of course. You know how these hairy Italian women are, they like to drip dry, wild and untamed. I'm going to look like a poodle with electric shock unless Juan figures out a solution. I'm going to look like Buckwheat's sister. I need to have a serious talk with him.

I'm so tired, though. I wait until Juan brings the suitcase with my lingerie in it, remove my silk pajamas, light blue with a matching robe, and change in the awful blue light of the bathroom. Without a word to Juan, I crawl into my squeaky little bed and fall asleep with the chiggers. When I wake up later in the day, I find Juan has already been out scouting around for some food, and has set up a little meal for us on the rickety table. He's brought Italian-style pizza, which is really different from American pizza because it's very flat and doesn't really have much cheese, some cold pasta dishes, and a fresh salad. He bought wine and bottled water, and a few fresh flowers he has put in the smudgy short glass from the bathroom. He's even brought some Italian pastries in a little white box tied up with string like a present.

"Would you like me to serve you?" he asks.

I get up and join him at the table and apologize for being so snippy to him earlier. He says he understands because we're both just tired. "But you better find an adapter for that outlet in the bathroom," I tell him. "I can't go out in public without being able to use my curling iron."

"Fine. Whatever you want."

The food is delicious and I decide I won't demand that he find us a new hotel. I've lived in worse housing than this—for most of my childhood in fact—so I can handle it. I'm not pleased, and I want him to know I'm not pleased, but I'm not going to intentionally try to hurt him, either. That would be rude.

After we eat, we take turns showering and getting dressed. I choose a simple black dress and heels, topping the ensemble with a shawl. I beg him not to make that same mistake with the hair and clothes, and pick out something decent for him to wear from his suitcase. Juan has made plans for us to see a concert tonight at a jazz club in a trendy part of Rome. I insist that this time we take a cab, and he looks uneasy. I know it's probably because he budgeted the whole trip down to the last lira. I tell him I'll pay for the cab, and he reluctantly agrees. We hit the ATM machine next door and find a cab. He says he has a friend who told him the club has salsa dancing upstairs. When we get there we see that it's true. And, guess what? There are tons of Puerto Ricans there! I can't believe it. It's like we never left Boston. We dance most of the night, then cab it back to the dungeon. I've had a good time in spite of myself, and I even allow Juan to be physical with me, though we don't go all the way and I make him give me a foot massage first.

The next day, he's up early again, foraging for an adapter for that stupid outlet, and scrounging for fruit and bread and cheese and coffee for breakfast, which he serves me in bed. I shower and get dressed. I choose a black and white Escada twin set with matching black pants. I add black and white Blahnik flats and a luxurious alpaca wool black Giuliana Teso cape (made in Italy, of course) and my sunglasses. I put on a pair of black leather gloves, and transfer my wallet and cell phone to a smooth leather Furla, in black and white.

Then he lays out the day's itinerary. We're to go to the Forum and see the Colosseum, the Arch of Septimus Severus, the House of Vestals, and all of that sort of thing. Walking. All of it *walking*, girl. *Ay, no, m'ija.*

"I hope you brought some comfortable shoes," he says with a wry smile. "I don't think you should wear *those*." He points a shaking finger at my feet.

I did not bring "comfortable" shoes. Sorry. I don't wear the types of shoes other people refer to as comfortable. Nor do I own a pair of *jeans*. Growing up, my mother taught me that girls didn't wear sneakers or pants, and though I resented it at the time (I wasn't allowed to learn how to ride a bike, either) I have come to feel I must have attractive, ladylike shoes on at all times.

"What's wrong with these?"

"We're *walking*, Navi," he tells me. "They look like torture chambers."

I say nothing. Outside, the sky grows cloudy. I don't change shoes, in spite of his repeated admonishments. He gives up, saying, "Whatever you want. They're your feet."

Of course, he wants to drive again, because he thinks the Forum is too far from the hotel for a cab. I don't say anything. He looks over his little map and does the best he can, and I spend the whole ride holding on to the roof and the door and the dashboard because it feels like at any moment we will be crushed by a crazed Italian driver. He parks at a lot designed for tourists and I notice the price of parking is almost as high as what I figure a taxi would have cost us. I keep my mouth closed. By the time we get out of the car, it has started to sprinkle. Good thing I brought an umbrella, because Lord knows the boy didn't think of anything practical like that himself.

Juan takes his little cheap dusty camera and starts snapping pictures of everything. I follow him around and try to keep up. It's hard for me, but he doesn't seem to notice. He just keeps running back to whatever spot I've chosen to sit down, babbling about the history and the "atmosphere." Then, he says he wants to *climb* the Palatino, this big hill where the wealthy used to build their houses. Climb, girl. I can barely walk, and he wants to climb things. I tell him I'll wait for him down below, near the Arch of Titus.

"Are you sure?" he asks. I look around me. A tour bus full of bluehairs from Nevada has just arrived, yakking in their awful hickish way.

"Oh, I'm sure," I say. The rain is getting heavier. "I'm having a *great* time, Juan. Don't you worry about me. I love all these old buildings and old people."

Juan shakes his head and sighs. "Come on, Navi," he says. "This is such an incredible place. Let's just go up and take a look around. They say the view from the top is fantastic."

"No, thanks."

"Never mind," he says. "I'll stay with you. I don't want you here all alone. Plus, it's raining."

"Oh, *is* it?" I ask, sarcastic. I'm sorry, Lauren, I think. I can't keep that promise I made you, *m'ija.* I'm hungry and wet and tired, and my alpaca cape is starting to smell like a wet dog.

"Maybe we still have time to see the Vatican today," he suggests. I shrug. He holds his hand out for me to help me up, then tries to hug and kiss me, saying something stupid about how romantic Italy can be in the rain. I'm cold. I'm hungry. My feet hurt. I push him away.

We go back to the car in the overpriced lot. Juan asks the

parking attendant how to get to the Vatican in his bad Italian and the man fires off directions so fast my head spins. Juan thanks him, and pulls out into the kamikaze traffic once again.

"Do you know where you're going?" I ask him. I am certain he does *not*.

"Sure," he says, trying to seem cheerful. He raises a fist, like someone who has just said "Onward Ho," and cries, "To the Vatican! To see the pope!"

My stomach growls so loud, he can hear it. He looks at me, then hits himself on the forehead with his palm. "Oh, Navi, I'm sorry," he says, looking at his watch. "It's past lunchtime. I'm all thrown off from the time change. You hungry?" He hardly ever eats, and he's skinny. So of course he forgot *food*. I mean, we're only in *Rome*. Who wants to eat *there*?

I don't say anything. I just glare at him and *hope* he understands how unhappy I am with this whole day. He gulps, and then asks if I'm hungry, again. I hiss at him. "What do *you* think?"

He starts turning at random corners in that flimsy little car, dodging stray dogs and cats and children, trying to find a restaurant. He stops at the first one that appeals to *him*. It's a run-down-looking trattoria in the middle of a nondescript residential block, with sorry-looking old men sitting around inside attached to cigars and watching a soccer match on an old black and white television. Juan manages to park the car nearby, and when we enter, everyone turns to stare. What's the matter, I want to say, haven't you ever seen a lady with taste and style before? God. Juan looks pleased, as if he has just found a hidden treasure.

He asks me what I want and I tell him I don't know because I don't understand the "menu"—a powdery old blackboard with all those stupid Italian words on it. A woman with deep circles around her eyes and a litter of dirty-faced children scampering around pulling on her apron tries to understand what Juan is saying and a few minutes later brings us a couple of plates with something that looks like meat and pasta. I eat it. It's not half bad, actually, but it's no five-star situation. The water glass is greasy, like the one in the "hotel."

"I hope you plan on taking me to a nice restaurant *some-time* on this trip, Juan," I say as we head back to the car. "I mean, this is *Rome*, it's full of classy places. Why do you have to take me to a dump like that?"

Juan looks angry. "Do you ever stop complaining?"

We drive the rest of the way to the Vatican without saying anything to each other. Juan tries to find something on the radio, and decides on this strange Italian disco music that makes my head hurt again with all that electronic beeping and bopping. The air is cold and stale and it's raining hard now. The windshield wipers smudge up the glass with whatever the oily substance is that seems to float in Rome's air. Smudgy and cold and in a horrible car. Juan should feel right at home.

There are lines everywhere in Vatican City. It might as well be Disneyland. We finally get into the main building and start looking at the exquisite artwork. Juan has to spoil the moment by telling me in his lecture voice all about how the Vatican had relationships with the Nazis and supposed Mafia ties. He reminds me of Lauren at times, with all his political preaching. I listen as politely as I can, but think it's rude for him to speak this way in the Vatican itself. We were both raised Catholic, I'm surprised he doesn't have the same awe and reverence for the place that I do. I am too polite to ask him to be quiet, but I am as embarrassed as I've ever been, I can tell you that.

By the time we head back to the hotel, I've just about had it. I love Juan, I do. I think he's a good guy, a smart guy, and a handsome guy. But he doesn't think about others. He has not once asked me what *I'd* like to do. He hasn't tried to take me shopping, or to the kinds of things that I'd like to see. Even though he tries to find a nice restaurant for dinner that night, and offers to buy me some "better shoes" when we pass a sporting goods store (as *if!*) the rest of the trip is just more of the same. He wants to walk everywhere. He doesn't know where he's going half the time. He wants to "get lost" in Roman neighborhoods and eat in more local places like that first dump instead of the nice elegant places. When we finally turn the car in again and board the airplane to Heathrow, I'm relieved. Twelve hours on a plane sounds really good to me. I squish my body into the tiny seat, put on my headset, and ignore Juan when he tries to talk to me.

By the time we land in Boston, he has taken the hint. I'm mad at him. I am disappointed in him and the way he treated me on the trip. When the plane rolls to a stop at the gate, I take my cell phone out of the Kate Spade tote and dial the number for Dr. Gardél, with Juan sitting next to me.

"Hello, Doctor," I say. "How *are* you? Oh, I'm fine. *Thank* you for *asking*. You're so *thoughtful*. Uh-huh . . . uh-huh . . . Well. I've been busy with a project, but some time has opened up for me. The symphony? That would be *marvelous*. You have *such* good taste."

Next to me, Juan buries his face in his hands.

I don't usually use this column to talk about the arts, but I saw a show last night that floored me, and I wanted to tell readers about it. It was the first in a week of performances at the Emmanuel Church for the Boston Early Music Festival, in celebration of Holy Week. The sixteen-piece choir's performances of both early English compositions and early Spanish compositions by Tomas Luis de Victoria gave me hope that we Bostonians, regardless of our differences, might one day celebrate in harmony all those things we have in common, instead of focusing on all those things that separate us . . .

—from "My Life," by Lauren Fernández

amber/cuicatl

W HEN GATO WAKES up he tells me he saw the fifth sun burning brightly in a dream, and that then Jaguar appeared to him and said we should move up my naming ceremony to this weekend, before I meet with Joel Benítez.

We are scheduled to go to Curly's house in La Puente in three weeks for a small, private naming ceremony, but the spirits have told Gato that the ceremony needs to be big and public and immediate. He holds me gently and says, "If you go to that meeting without your real name, you will not meet with all that you should." He has been right about these things before. Gato has dreams that are not dreams. Gato's dreams are conversations with the animal spirits of the Mexica universe.

We rise, take our morning shower together, eat our fruit on the small balcony in the back of the apartment. Then Gato sets about organizing the ceremony, and I retreat indoors. A melody is poking at me from the inside. The contractions have begun. The song is waiting to be born.

While I sit on the floor with my guitar, working out the chord progression, Gato gets on the phone. I vaguely hear him talking in the background. *"Es que es muy urgente, 'mano, urgente urgente que hacemos la ceremonia pronto, pero pronto pronto,"* he says. Mostly I'm just focused on my new song, the one about the Brother Officer. He hangs up, and waits for a lull in my activity before updating me.

"Curly says tomorrow is good," he says. "He had another ceremony, but he will reschedule it. He understands the importance, and he says the Jaguar appeared to him as well. It's meant to be, Amber. You'll see. It's short notice, but I think we can reach everybody."

He gets back on the phone for a couple of hours, calling everyone in our Aztec dance group, organizing a big *danza* for tomorrow afternoon. By the time he is finished I have worked out the skeleton of the song, and have started to hang bits of flesh on it. He takes his headgear and shields out of the closet and begins to polish them for a dance.

In all, thirty of the thirty-six people in the group say they will make it. The location is changed from Curly's house to an open space in Whittier Narrows. There is not enough room at Curly's for a full *danza*, drums and all, and Whittier Narrows is where we usually go anyway. I spend the rest of the day completing my song.

Gato cleans the apartment and buys groceries at the food co-op. When night comes, we make love and listen to the deep green voice of the moon.

Sunday, we all gather in the park at noon. I am dressed in my long embroidered purple dress with its many layers, my gold headdress and moccasins. Gato wears only a loincloth, ankle bells, and his large feathered headdress. The other members of the group are dressed similarly.

Many families are here in their Sunday finest, most from Mexico or Central America, speaking in Spanish. The women waddle in their discount dresses and carry children in their arms or push them in strollers. The men wear white cowboy hats and tight black jeans with large belt buckles and yellow ostrich-skin cowboy boots. A few of them have portable stereos with songs from Los Tigres del Norte or Conjunto Primavera blaring out of them. The baby girls have frilly headbands, and their little ears have been pierced with tiny gold studs. The little boys run and play in slacks and boots. Families ride in pedal boats on the lake, or stroll along the sidewalk eating their *churros* and *tortas*. Young men with bandanas on their shaved heads shake hands elaborately as they watch the girls in their baggy sweatpants and big earrings. I love them all.

Most of them don't seem to know what to make of us in our Mexica ceremonial gear. We are proud Indian princes and princesses, kings and queens. When the beautiful brown people laugh at us it puts in me a sadness and a rage. I try talking to a few of them about what we're doing, who we are. I know how they feel; I used to be like them. That was before I discovered the lies of history. Before I realized I carried in my veins the blood of an ancient and proud people. We're here to honor the past, I tell them, we're here to honor our ancestors who died defending their culture. A few cars drive past and honk in solidarity with us, a few of them raise their fists and shout *"Que Viva La Raza!"*

Most of the time the people seem to understand what I'm saying, especially the younger ones. All of us have photos in our family albums of a great-grandfather who wore braids. Most of us know we are Indians. It's just those uppity Xicanos who work at the *Los Angeles Times* who don't want to acknowledge us. That newspaper has slandered us so many times I've lost count. We went there once, to talk to the highest-ranking Mexica there, a man in his fifties who is a dead ringer for Sitting Bull. He did not want to hear our message. Just like Rebecca. We make them uncomfortable.

We light the sage bundles and place them at the edges of our circle to burn and cleanse the area of evil spirits. The drummers set up their equipment. Everyone assembles without speaking much. We bow our heads in silent prayers. The women gather their shakers, the men hold their shields and shakers. Curly stands in the middle of the circle and addresses us all in Spanish, then English, then Nahuatl. He reminds everyone of the protest this week at the DreamWorks studios, where they're planning a new animated film designed to destroy what is left of our history. He tells us of another protest at Disney studios, this one aimed at Edward James Olmos.

"That *vendido* wants to do a movie about Zapata," Curly says. "We need to show the studio that we don't want that Eurocentric sellout portraying our people anymore! Are you with me?"

We roar.

Finally, he reminds us to write to everyone we can think of to build support for the legislation one of our Mexica sisters has proposed in northern California to have Mexican-Americans recognized by the national government as an indigenous people.

Now Curly says we are here today to dance in honor of me, Amber, and my meeting tomorrow with a record label interested in my music. This is important because if they sign me, he says, then the Mexica message will travel across the earth.

"Please join me in meditating on the success of our Mexica sister, and the success of her music."

One of the group's members, an entertainment lawyer named Frank Villanueva, raises his hand and asks if he may speak. Curly says yes.

"I would like to volunteer my presence at the meeting with the record label," he says. "If Amber will allow me."

"Thank you, brother Frank, for your generosity," Curly says. "Amber? What do you say?"

I look at Gato, and he nods. His eyes are electric. Then I remember, Frank represents some of the top emerging Mexica talent in Hollywood, mostly in film.

"I say yes, and thank you."

"It would be an honor. I am glad you accept," says Frank. "We have all heard your music and I know you will make it. But it makes no sense for a young artist to enter a meeting such as this alone. Evil can be done so easily to a young hungry artist. When is your meeting, and where?" I tell him, and he nods. "I will meet you there."

I stare at the offerings we have piled in the center of our circle, the fruit and the incense, and I focus, I feel the eagle within me spread her wings, rising to the sun. I feel the energy of my sisters and brothers surround me. Curly says he will choose a name for me this day, a Mexica name, to help guide me and lead me to my destiny. The drummers begin.

We dance for three hours, without stopping. Vanessa Torres, who is too pregnant to dance, delivers bottles of water to us. I enter the zone, the same kind of place I reach when I perform in public, the same place I reach when Gato and I run for hours in the hills. I feel the energies of the universe converging inside of me. I lose myself to the spirits. I know that this is how things are meant to be. I have been led here to this point in my life for a reason.

The dancing stops. Curly reenters the circle. He invites me to join him. I kneel before him, and he gives me my name.

Cuicatl.

I will no longer be Amber. I will be Cuicatl. It is a strong name, a name that means "song" or "sing," a name with the power to communicate through music. It is the name I was supposed to have, it is the name of my true destiny. If the Spaniards had not come and slaughtered my people in Aztlán, if they had not taken our villages and towns and burned them to the ground, if they had not filled us with their gunpowder and poisonous foods, I would have been Cuicatl. The most beautiful part of it all is that it's not too late. I still have time to embrace my true self, my Mexica self, my beautiful Mexican self. Cuicatl.

We return home, and my mother has left a message on our answering machine for me to call her back. I do. She's home, and answers the phone.

"Hello?"

"Hi, Mom."

"Oh, Amber! How are you?"

"Fine, Mom, and you?"

"Doing good, *m'ija*. Where have you been?"

"I had a naming ceremony today."

Silence. My mom can say more with her silence than she can with her words. She does not approve of the Mexica movement. She has never said so, but it's obvious. Just like it's obvious she doesn't like the way I do my hair or makeup, or what I've done to the car she gave me. She never comes right out and says it, but she does other things, like send me pictures of women in magazines with a note saying she thinks my hair would look good styled like the hair in the picture.

After enough silence to make me feel uncomfortable, she asks, "Well, did you get the package I sent you?"

"Yes, Mom. I'm sorry I didn't call. I've been busy. Thank you." I want to tell her off, you know? I want to scream at her for never asking about what I do at the ceremonies, for never coming to a single one of my gigs, for never asking me how Gato is doing, for never asking about me. But I don't. I can stage dive in a crowd of rowdy rockers, but I can't risk upsetting my mom. I'm twenty-seven years old and I still can't get up the courage to confront my mother. It's ridiculous.

"You just put your things inside the bags and then use your vacuum cleaner to suck all the air out. It makes everything real flat so you can put it in your closet and not take up so much room."

"I know, Mom. Thanks."

"You can use it for blankets or sweaters, those things." This is her way of asking me to change the way my apartment is decorated.

"Okay, Mom."

"I got them on home shopping. I got some for your grandma, too, and for your Nina. I purchased them using the ultra-convenient E-Z pay plan. You pay everything off in five easy payments."

I can always tell when my mother is quoting the TEEvee.

"That's good, Mom. Thanks."

"So you can have more room." Translation: She doesn't approve of my small apartment.

"It's very nice. How's Dad?"

"He's over at the Rez, donating money to the Indian cause."

This is how my parents describe their latest addiction: casino gambling. She doesn't think this might offend me. She doesn't understand that we *are* Indians. She thinks Mexican, or as she says, "Messican," is a race unto itself. The number of casinos on reservations in San Diego County is growing so fast it makes me sick. My parents used to go once a month, now they go every weekend, maybe even every day. My mom is not a senior citizen yet, but she takes the bus with the senior ladies to the Viejas casino on weekdays because, as she says, it's free and you get a free hamburger.

"I wish you wouldn't put it like that, Mom, it's sick."

Again, silence.

"I saw a real good job in the paper here. It would fit you perfect," she says at last. "I put it in the mail for you. You should get it by tomorrow."

"I don't need a job, Mom."

"I'm just saying, in case."

"Thanks."

"I put it in the mail for you."

"Thanks."

"It pays real good, *m'ija*. Eleven dollars an hour." She is tired of sending me money to help cover the rent, but can't bring herself to say it.

I change the subject. "How's Peter?"

"He's doing real good. He came over last week to help your dad cut down that one tree."

"What tree?"

"That one back up the hill."

"That enormous pine tree?" I ask. I love that tree, and used to spend many hours in it as a kid contemplating the world down below. It must be five hundred years old. I can't believe what I'm hearing. "Why?"

"Your dad worried it was going to fall on the house. You know how he is."

Now I give her the silence.

"Peter's real good. He's doing good—well—at work. It's always good to see him. He's someone I can always count on." And I'm not. That's the point of this one. Of course she's always glad to see him. They're two of a kind.

"I'm glad, Mom."

"I just wanted to call and see if you got the package and tell you about that job. It's for a admin-stratative assistant." An administrative assistant. I can't tell you how many times I've corrected her, but it never sinks in. I know she knows how to say "administrative." Her blood sugar must be low.

"OK, Mom."

"In case you were looking for something."

"I'm not, Mom. I have a meeting tomorrow with a record label."

"Oh, good, *m'ija*. Are you still playing that Messican music?"

"I play rock, Mom."

"Well, that's real good about the meeting. I'll pray for you."

"Thanks."

"You take care."

"You too, Mom. Eat something, okay? Have some juice."

"I love you."

"Love you too."

I hang up, and sigh. Gato looks at me from where he has hunkered down over his keyboard, sympathy in his eyes. He knows phone calls from my mother make me insane. He's writing a new song, a ballad called "Cuicatl." He plays a few bars of it, and it gives me goose bumps. He has no shirt on, just his low-riding ripped-up jeans and his woven hemp sandals. His hair is tied back, and he wears a leather headband. My Mexica prince.

"What would I do without you?" I ask, wrapping my arms around him. He's warm, and solid.

"You'd be fine without me," he says. "You're strong."

I consider his words, and invite him to join me in the meeting at the label. He frowns and shakes his head no. "Why not?" I ask.

"You'll do fine alone," he says.

I make dinner, raw vegetables and sprouted wheat grains, with pineapple for dessert. After Gato and I eat, we make love. He tries my new name again. *"Es perfecto, tu nombre, perfecto perfecto,"* he says. "It suits you." And we fall asleep in the cozy cocoon of our love.

I wake early the next day. I'm too nervous to eat, but Gato forces me to drink some tea. He rubs my shoulders, helps me into the shower. I decide on the tight pants I found at a funky boutique in Venice, with portraits of the Virgin of Guadalupe all over them, the same ones I wore to the *sucias* meeting in Boston, the ones that gave Rebecca seizures. I wear a tight red, cropped sweater and red boots, my black trench coat. I put red twists into my hair, put on my makeup, a few chokers, and dark silver, gothic rings on every finger. Gato says I look good. I ask him what he thinks I need to bring. He says nothing, says that I should just leave all the negotiating to Frank. "The gods are with you on this," he says. "I can feel it."

Gato drives me to Beverly Hills for my meeting with Joel Benítez. Frank will meet me here. Gato drops me in front and asks me to call him on his cell phone from my cell when I'm done. Cell phones are the only luxury item we have invested in, beyond our instruments; in Los Angeles the traffic is so bad you really must have one. Gato says he's going to meditate at a park near the Beverly Center Mall, spend the entire time sending good vibes to me. I kiss him good-bye and walk toward my destiny. As I pass the security guard at the front desk and enter the quiet, expensive-looking elevator (even the elevator here is nice. *Mexicatauhi!*) I almost have to pinch myself. I've never been so nervous in my life.

Frank is already seated in Joel's office when I walk in; he doesn't look like the same person. I have only seen him in his Mexica clothes. Today he wears a conservative blue suit and a paisley power tie. He has the same intense look in his eyes, but to see him like this, legs crossed casually, neatly trimmed goatee, wire glasses, you would never know he was an Aztec dancer. My demo CD pounds out of the stereo. Both men rise to greet me. Joel's assistant, Monica, a tall blonde with a flag of Venezuela on her neck chain, hovers nearby. She's frighteningly thin and wears tight pants and a halter top with a sheer blouse over it.

"Would you like some coffee or tea?" she asks me in Spanish.

"No, thank you."

"Water?"

"Water would be fine."

Monica leaves in a puff of sweet perfume. Joel grins, and paces the room. The office is large and elegantly appointed, with two white leather sofas, oil paintings, and a big window behind Joel's desk. One wall is taken up with a large, shiny black entertainment center and a tremendously sophisticated-looking stereo system. Framed silver and gold records hang on another wall. Small, powerful speakers hang in each corner. The music is loud. We have to shout to be heard. Joel bobs his head to the rhythm of the song, a cumbia reggae mashed up with metal, and a heavy, pulsating bass line that imitates a heartbeat. *Madre Oscura.* Dark Mother. It's one of my favorites.

"So," Joel says, in English. I'm relieved he's not speaking Spanish. I'm fluent now, but I'd rather not have to negotiate in it. "Amber."

"Cuicatl," I correct him.

"Right, Frank told me about that," he says with a wry smile. He brings his fingertips together in front of him. "Kwee—how do you say it?"

"Kwee-cah-tel."

"*Cuicatl.* That will take some getting used to."

Monica returns with my water and a glass of ice. Not a cup, a blue goblet of blown glass with little air bubbles in it, the kind from Mexico.

"Let's get right to the point, Joel," Frank says, all business. "Let's not waste anybody's time here." He signals Joel to turn down the music

I'm shocked by his attitude. In our Mexica gatherings he is always polite, almost meek. "Joel wants to sign you," he tells me. "His label is excited about you. They like your music. You want to get the best deal possible, because you're going to make millions of dollars for this company if you sign with them, right?"

"Right," I say, even though I'm not sure I agree. Joel watches Frank with a mixture of respect and irritation.

"We've been talking for a few minutes already, and I think we'll be able to come to an agreement," Frank adds.

"I'm sure we will," Joel says with a moderately pained look.

"What I've proposed, Cuicatl, is outlined here."

Frank hands me a thick file folder.

"I've given one to Joel as well. It's very basic. This isn't the only label interested in you, and he knows that. I have included market data on the genre and the demand, and some sales figures for similar artists worldwide. What we're asking, under the circumstances, is reasonable. Joel knows that. We want to go with the label that gives us the most support and resources. I've detailed what we'll need as far as an advance, promotions budget, and points for the artist as composer, performer, and producer. I'd like to take a few minutes now for all of us to look over the numbers, and see what we think."

Joel opens his folder, reads for a few minutes, then presses the speakerphone button. He dials a four-number extension, and when a man picks up, begins speaking in nervous Spanish to him. He invites the man to come by right now to review the proposal.

The president of the label, Gustavo Milanes, appears. He is younger than I imagined, tall, with a curly mullet haircut and large eyeglasses. He shakes my hand and tells me he has heard many good things about me. The men adjust a few numbers, argue about others, all in Spanish. An hour passes without me saying a word. Whenever my demo CD ends, Joel Benítez presses his remote and starts it again, until I am sick of hearing myself.

The executives make suggestions that begin to make me queasy: that I use my old name, go a little more pop, lose the nose ring, lighten my hair.

Frank nips it in the bud. "She is perfect the way she is. You must know what you've got here. Have you seen how many kids show up at her shows? There are lines around the block, and this with no promotional money. Do you realize what the demand is for an artist like her? There's no one like her out there. The material is ready to go now, she's recorded six of her own CDs. The label could use a success after the year you've had. It's an easy, risk-free project. You know it and I know it. Let's move forward."

There is more talking in Spanish. My nausea fades.

Finally, Frank says he is happy with the proposal and its amendments. Joel suggests meeting next week to sign the contract. Frank is adamant that we should do it now. "I thought you gentlemen were serious," he says.

Joel says something about needing approval from the financial director of the company. Frank counters that there must have already been discussions and caps set and the offer must fall within what was already approved. "We have other possibilities." He begins to gather his papers. "Let's go, Cuicatl."

Joel and Milanes whisper for a moment. Then Milanes says that he will return shortly with a contract. "It may take an hour or more," he says. Frank says fine. We wait. For a brief moment, I wonder if I can trust Frank. I don't really know him. But he is Mexica. I have no reason to doubt him.

The contract is delivered in two hours. I look at Frank, and he mouths the Nahuatl word for "trust me."

I sign.

Joel signs.

Milanes signs.

"I'd like to hold a press conference next week," Joel says. "To announce the signing. We should aim for an April release.

It's fast but you're ready. We could sell your homemade CDs now, but I want you to shine them up a bit.

"You'll get your first check in six weeks," Joel tells me. His demeanor has changed, and it's clear he, not Frank, is calling the shots now. "For the amount here." He points. "Use that for any remixes or production and for new songs you might want to record."

He points to a number buried in the fine and voluminous print of the contract. I gasp, and Frank laughs. I quickly do the math. It's in the millions. I would have been happy to come away with a hundred thousand.

Joel explains, "It's for living expenses, of course, but primarily to produce your first album, to be delivered by the end of March, with advance promotional copies as soon as possible. Don't spend it all in one place. It sounds like a lot right now, but you have to pay for everything yourself, the studio time, production, engineering, mixing, the musicians. Everything but the promotion, and we'll start that today."

I stare at the number.

"Once you deliver the album on time," Joel says, "you'll get the rest of the money." He points to another number: more millions. I gasp again. Frank's eyes shine and he smiles the ancient powerful smile of our people.

"In addition," Joel continues, "you will earn points adding up to a percentage of each album sold after that, as well as points on the songs played on the radio, as writer, artist, and executive producer. And, of course, any earnings you accrue on your promotional tour, which will be international in scope. We have agreed to pour a lot into promotion, so I imagine you will be known across Latin America, Spain, and the Spanish-speaking U.S., at a minimum. Asia is a possibility for this music. Always is. Foreign rights are another discussion, but Frank will make sure you get the best deal. Right, Frank?"

Frank nods.

Joel says, "Hey, Cuicatl, I know you don't necessarily want to do an English single. But consider it. We're doing more collaboration with Wagner mainstream. Your sound has crossover potential."

"How much will that add?" I ask. I am not wedded to Spanish anymore. One European language versus another, I could care less.

Joel whistles through his teeth.

"It depends on you," Frank says. "But it could be as much as a few million more."

"*Chinga*," I say before I can stop myself.

"*Oye eso*," Joel says, looking at me with humor in his eyes.

Then, because the contract is signed, because I am Cuicatl and protected by the spirit of Ozomatli and Jaguar, and it doesn't matter if I look like a surprised bumpkin, I shout the word out loud, again.

Joel stands up as we leave, and gives me a hug. "Welcome to the Wagner family, Amb—err, Cuicatl," he says. "It should be clear by now that we expect a lot from you."

No kidding.

It's mid-February, usually a hot time for the housing market,
but most of us in this city are nowhere near getting a house.
Why? Because the median home price in Boston is now the
third highest in the United States, according to a new study.
A home here costs about triple what it would cost just about
anywhere else. I wish I could buy a house, but like millions
of others here, I'll remain in a passionate, rented affair with
this overpriced burgh, paying, as I often seem to, way too
high a price for love.

—from "My Life," by Lauren Fernández

lauren

I'M HIDING BEHIND the small cardboard sock dresser in
Ed's living-room closet. I called in sick, hopped the Delta
shuttle to LaGuardia, and took a taxi to Ed's spiffy two-
room apartment on the Upper East Side. Chuck Spring let
me have it again yesterday, for not being "Latina" enough in
my writing, and rather than risk kicking him in the teeth I
decided to take some time off and snoop a tiny bit. I let myself in with my key. He's not expecting a visit from me until
next weekend.

A few minutes ago, I went through his drawers and pockets, looking for evidence. I found a jumbo box of blue con-
doms with six missing, and a butterfly hair clip that didn't

belong to me. Ed's not the condom type; the barrette might be his.

He has just come in the front door, and he's not alone. I peek through a crack in the closet door and see her as she clicks by on her tacky *tacones*, high-heeled sandals made of white plastic. It's freezing out. I suspect she's insane. She also wears a pink jersey miniskirt with white triangles on it, with nude panty hose. I catch a glimpse of her face. She looks as young as she sounded on his voice mail, but darker than I expected. For some reason her little Valley Girl voice didn't sound to me like it would come out of a streetwalker from Juarez, with caked tangerine lipstick and a big, frizzy perm. Her latest message had them scheduled to have dinner here tonight. "I'll cook for you," she'd said, dopey and orgasmic. "At your place."

Sure, I'm a psycho. But justified. I need to cough. Damnit. Hold it, Lauren, hold it. I gulp, squeeze my eyes shut, focus on something else. The urge subsides. I open my eyes just in time to see Ed smack the girl on the rear. Chuckling, he removes his navy blue blazer with the brass anchor buttons, hands it to her. Uh-oh. I'm paralyzed. Will she open the closet? I mouth the words "Please no, please no," mantralike, and it works. She drapes the jacket on a dining chair.

I hear Ed take a surprisingly long piss with the bathroom door open. Lola starts opening cabinets looking for pots and pans. Ed flushes, comes out whistling. He stops in front of the closet and stretches, burps, moves on to the living room. Really, the kitchen and living room are one room, differentiated only by tile to carpet. Ed plops into his leather armchair, the one with all the massage knobs under its skin, turns the television to CNN. He burps again. What a charmer. They speak slow Mexican Spanish while she chops an onion with precision and speed. I try to hear what they're saying, but the raw pipes next to me have begun to clang in my ears. Old building, steam heat. I clear my throat a little, hope no one hears. Soon, I smell oil heating, onions frying with chile powder, pinto beans, and meat cooking. An ad for a Cowboys football game comes on and, predictably, Ed punches up the volume, hops out of his seat, and raises one arm like John Travolta in *Saturday Night Fever.* I've seen the move many times; he pantomimes slamming a football to the ground, his own little touchdown. *"Ahua!"* he cries, shaking his rump. Lola doesn't look up. Ed looks disappointed that she didn't notice his athletic prowess. He shrugs, sits down, chuckles along with a beer commercial featuring men doing stupid things. I lean forward and squint through the crack, see Lola planted in front of the stove, stirring so hard her big, firm butt wobbles. Once, when Ed's mom asked me if I knew how to cook *"m'ijo*'s favorites," I joked with her about making "a mean buttered toast when I'm not working." Frowning, she whispered in Ed's ear, and left the room.

I'm covered with itches and have to pee when Lola finally calls Ed to the table. I hear rustling, scooting chairs, Ed whistling through his front teeth the theme to O'Reilly's talk show. My foot is asleep. I'm suffocating. I hear flatware scraping the plates. He pops the top on a beer. Then another. *"Delicioso,"* Ed says. "You're such a great cook, *así como mi madre, chula."*

Ouch.

If I barge in now, he'll say they're just friends. I must wait.

I stay curled and cramped until Lola has washed the dishes, dried them with a towel, put them away, and rubbed Ed's shoulders as he picks his teeth with his thumb. Finally, I hear the wet slurp of kissing. He lows like a sick bull, she giggles like a chicken. He says she's beautiful. Lola calls him *"guapo,"* which means handsome; now I *know* she's insane.

Ed is many things, but handsome he is not.

Their voices recede to the bedroom. It's amazing how many women want to get with that big ugly Mexican. I could rush in now, kick his ass. But I want him to be guilty as possible. I'll give him another minute or two, any more than that and he will be finished. Stupid closet, smells like a department store. He keeps the suits in the bedroom, the casual clothes here. For Ed, that means khakis, oxfords, cowboy boots, and a Dallas Cowboys cap he refuses to launder out of superstition.

Guapo? Maybe, if you blur your eyes a little. He's *almost* handsome, which is worse than being flat-out ugly because he can trick you into thinking he's good-looking with his good body and wardrobe. He's got that large-ass head, as I think I've mentioned once or twice, covered with old acne craters. His ears have bulbous lobes you don't notice at first, but can't take your eyes off later. His nose is crooked and wide and one of his eyes is lower and runnier than the other, like a St. Bernard abandoned at a truck stop. But he's tall— you *know* that counts for a lot in a man—and has really nice teeth and a pretty smile. His body is almost spectacular from all that squash playing and sushi—but he has a double chin anyway. Don't *ask* me why; I've tried to figure it out, and there's no excuse other than bad genes. He smokes a cigarette occasionally, but you can't tell because he has gum in his briefcase. See? With a guy like Ed, you can choose to see the glass as half empty or half full. It's up to you.

I start to move, stealthy as possible with frozen, aching joints and a strained bladder. A pair of khakis hit me in the head, stiff from starch. I shove them out of the way; he's got about twenty pair, all ironed in a row. He dresses as if he grew up going to country clubs instead of Mexican rodeos. Fridays, Ed "dresses down" and goes out after work for drinks with "the guys" (the white guys) at sports bars on the Upper West Side. He told me they've asked him if he's Cambodian, Pakistani, all sorts of things. They never asked if he was *Mexican*, you know? When he told them, they looked at him like Elvis just went by, naked and riding a goat. He grinned and gave them that cheesy wink with the snap. You *betcha.*

When I first met Ed, he was the information officer for the mayor of Boston; I was a cub reporter covering City Hall. I was stalking a few other guys casually and had lost all faith in men. He was the first Latino I met who could actually tell if the "woman" who just walked into the restaurant was a drag queen. Most of them can't. They see a dude with an Adam's apple, shaved legs, a tight skirt, a long blond wig, red lipstick, and big fake chichis and they're all tripping over themselves, making kissy-lips at her, chanting: *Ay, Mami. Ven aquí preciosa, bella, mujer de mi vida, te amo, te adoro, te quiero para siempre.* Such total freaking *lames.*

Ed was nothing like that. He was the first Latino I'd met who was measured and professional, the first one who didn't complain about oppression and imperialism all the time. He was the first Chicano I'd known who had zero interest in lowriders or big graffiti murals. He played *golf,* chuckled around white people the same way they do. He used the word "absolutely" all the time, each syllable crisp, nodded his head like he cared. He radiated so much grace and pure *power* it put me in a daze. Ed is exactly the kind of stable man I would like to father my children, I thought. He seemed like the type who'd never leave the garden hose out in the sun to rot, the way *Papi* did. An organized gentleman. So *what* that I had zero sexual attraction to the dude. Few married couples I know have good sex.

I creep out of the closet and see those Tupperware containers piled on the counter with yellow masking tape labels on them: Monday, Tuesday, Wednesday, Thursday. Ed's sister Mary comes over on weekends to do his laundry and cook. She's a graphic designer, but does this, like it's her duty. She leaves chicken enchiladas, *menudo,* tamales, pinto beans, and red rice for every meal, and exits without a smile. She had a better job offer in Chicago, but stayed in New York to be near her *hermano.* What is he, *six?* I asked him about it, and he said they were raised poor and traditional by a single mom who was not afraid to use a belt, so he and Mary got really *close.* Mary stares me down, refuses to talk when I try to make conversation, solely because I'm her brother's fiancée. That's plain weird. I'm not sure I want to know *how* close those two got, okay? *Cooks* for him. Washes his dirty Calvin Klein briefs. Irons the gold toes.

I tiptoe to the half-closed bedroom door, stepping over Lola's stained, lemon-yellow bra as I go. It's as cheap and sleazy as her plastic shoes. I can hear the springs on his Ethan Allen sleigh bed. My blood is ice, and I can't breathe right. I stop and listen for a good full minute and try to remember why I love this man.

He proposed New Year's Eve, at a fancy hotel in downtown San Antonio, as his mom cried into her holly-sprigged table napkin. It was a big dinner-dance champagne thing and his whole family was there. He made a big deal out of it, getting down on his knee and giving me that cheap ring with such drama that everyone stopped what they were doing and clapped for him, a bunch of total strangers, all of them with big Texan heads. I was happy for about an hour, while we danced to the bad Huey Lewis cover band, blew on rolled-up paper whistles and got confetti in our hair. Then we went to our room, and consummated the engagement, so to speak. Suddenly he was different. He was rough and started speaking Spanish—something he never does. *"Tu eres mi puta?"* he growled, eyes crazed—are you my whore? *Are you my little whore all opened up like that just for me? Are you my bitch?*

When I asked him about it later, he apologized and said that his first sexual experience had tainted him forever. It occurred in a little town just over the Mexican border, where his uncles took him to a whorehouse to teach him to be a man when he was thirteen. They drank tequila and he went to a Pepto-Bismol pink sewer-smelling room with a pregnant prostitute. When he came out, his uncles gave him pats on the back and a bunch of cash in a shoebox. They piled into Uncle Chuy's Crown Victoria and sang *corridos* all the way back to San Antonio. Like I said, I shoulda known *then*. But I chose to see the glass, well, you know—half full. What I didn't know was it was half full, all right, but half full of *bile*.

Not surprisingly, he pants identical insults all over little miss Lola as I muster the courage to stand in the bedroom doorway. "Are you my slut, my little stupid whore, all opened up there just for me?"

Only she says, *"Sí."*

Sí, Papi, soy tu putita estúpida, dámelo duro papi, dámelo duro, así de duro, chíngame, si quieres, meteme por detrás. Con ganas, mi amor, rómpeme.

His hairy brown ass pumps up and down, khaki chinos accordioned around his knees, the belt buckle clanking. He still wears his starched white shirt and tie. All I see of Lola are little feet with dirty pink toenails, still encased in the cheesy sandals, bouncing around by his ears. *Rómpeme,* she repeats. Break me.

Time moves slowly. I see myself grab the brass bowl where he keeps all his shiny cuff links and tiepins, including the new American flag ones; I hurl it at that big brown moon. It hits him square on. He yelps like the dog he is. I hear Lola scream, but it's far away, a high-pitched echo. I grab other things from his dresser, desk, and shelves. Picture frames, bottles of cologne, books, a computer keyboard, a pair of scissors, a golfing Snoopy paperweight, the phone shaped like a football, everything I can, and send them raining down over these people.

Ed pushes Lola up in front of him like a shield. His face is terrified for a moment, red, sweaty, and ugly. His mouth is open, teeth bared. Snarling. I see *her* perfect little brown body, legs spread wide open as she struggles to gain her balance. She shrieks, breaks free of his grip, and clomps in those stupid shoes to the bathroom. She looks petite, perfect, and scared—and *young.* She can't be more than eighteen. Where would he meet a woman like *that*?

"It's not what you think," Ed says, the fear replaced by a charming grin, hands in front, palms up. He shuffles toward me with khakis like prison chains around his ankles.

"Bastard!" I scream. I attack him with my fists, knees, and feet. "You son of a bitch! How dare you! How could you!"

He grabs my wrists.

"Stop it," he says, "you're bleeding. Let's take care of that cut before you get an infection." He clicks his tongue as if I were a child who'd broken the cookie jar, patronizing.

"Don't touch me," I hiss. "*You're* the infection."

"You're being ridiculous, Lauren. You know I love you. I just had to get it out of my system. That's how we men are. Better now than after the wedding, right?"

"Oh, my God!" I scratch at his eyes, spit in his face. "I hate you!"

He backs away and I see the blue condom dangling sticky on the end of his lost erection. I smell the girl's cheap perfume on his skin, her musky adolescent perspiration. He says, "You know I love you. Calm down. Take a deep breath. Let's talk about this."

"Are you insane? There's a little *girl* in your bathroom."

"Her? Nah. She's nothing to me." He pulls his pants up and shrugs. "You're the one I love."

I stare, jaw on the floor. I almost reply, but think better of it. Instead, I turn to leave.

"Wait, baby," he calls, strolling after me. "What about Valentine's in Tahoe? You still coming? Let's talk about this."

I open the front door.

"The ski trip with my buddies and their girls? I paid a lot of money for that trip! I can't cancel it now!"

I face him one last time.

"Take Lola."

I slam the door, and trip my way down the stairs to the street. I was going to throw the ring at him, but figure I'll pawn it and get something I can use, like a ballpoint pen. I feel like killing myself. I stop at the corner Korean market and buy a bag of Hot Cheetos, a carton of powdered sugar donuts, three chocolate bars, and a can of Pringles, then hail a cab. I eat every last salty, sugary crumb on the way to the airport.

After we reach our cruising altitude, I lock myself in the airplane bathroom and stick my finger down my throat over the puny metal toilet. When I exit, I ask the flight attendant for some chilled white wine. By the time the plane touches down in Boston the sun has begun to set, and I'm feeling pretty bad/good.

I call Usnavys from an airport pay phone, tell her what happened. She tells me her doctor blew her off, too.

"Men suck, *m'ija*," she says.

"Got that right. (Hic.) Menschuckbad."

"You been drinking?"

"(Hic.) Who me? No. What makes you ask that? (Hic.)"

"I'm glad you don't have a car, *m'ija*. I'll pick you up. You shouldn't be alone right now. Let's go have some fun."

USNAVYS TAKES ME to a real 'hood rat bar over near Dudley Square. The projects where she grew up are near here, in the middle of boarded-up buildings and bodegas with yellow awnings. The DJ spins "both" kinds of music, salsa *and* merengue, to appeal to "both" kinds of people: Puerto Rican and Dominican. Usnavys talks. I drink. I talk. She sips red wine.

I'm angry. Sure I am. We both are. Angry and disappointed. We talk about our respective situations and offer advice. Mine to her: Give Juan a chance and quit worrying about the kind of car and shoes he has. Hers to me: Give it some time, wait for a good guy to come along, and make sure he has a lot of money next time.

"Nah," I say, downing my third Long Island Iced Tea. "You know what I'monna do?"

"What?"

I look around this dump, at the Dominican boys with strong faces, short-cropped Afros, full mouths, and baggy designer clothes. It's unnatural the way their hips move when they dance, like metronomes. They lick their lips all the time, in the same way. I spot one much more handsome than all the others. Strong jaw, long eyelashes, full lips, perfect nose, broad shoulders, and a tasteful outfit. He could be a Ralph Lauren model. You know who he looks like? The host of *Soul Train*, the black soap opera star. He has intelligent eyes. Why does that surprise me? I want to hear his story. To taste his salt.

I tip my cup toward him. "Navi," I slur. "I, my dear, am going to go home with that man right there."

"Which one?"

"The cute one in the dark green plaid shirt and the Warner Brothers leather jacket."

She looks at him and shakes her head. "*Ay, m'ija,*" she says, squinting. She waves her hand in front of her nose as if a bad smell just wafted in. "He's not worth it."

"Yes, I am. Tonight."

"*Ay, Dios mío. 'Tas loca,* you know that? *'Tas muy loca, m'ija.*" She puts her hand over the new drink the bartender has just delivered to me. "You've had enough of these. I know you're hurt, *m'ija,* but let's just go home, okay? Let's don't be stupid. I *know* that guy. He's no good."

"Of course he's good. Look at him." I push her hand out of the way and guzzle, wiping my mouth with the back of my hand when I'm finished. "I'm serious. He's beautiful. He looks like a revolutionary, a warrior." He notices me looking, smiles at me. It's like in those cartoons when the little flash pops up off of someone's teeth—*ping!* My heart flops like a broken toad.

"He is a drug dealer, like Rebecca said. Trust your *sucias.* You have to quit being drawn to men like that."

I don't see how in the world there's any similarity between this attractive young Dominican and the uptight *puta*-loving Ed. So I get defensive. "Oh, and I suppose your sleazy doctor is better?"

Below the belt, and it hurts her.

"I'm sorry," I say quickly. "I didn't mean that. It's just I want him. I want him!" I pound a fist on the table. "What Lauren want, Lauren get, waa, waa."

"*Ya, basta,*" she says, taking my drink away. "That's enough."

"He's *hot*, girl. Look at him. He's on *fire.*"

Usnavys makes a face like someone just asked her to eat ground mouse. She fishes in her shiny black handbag for the Bobbi Brown compact. "I don't *think* so, *m'ija.* You can do better. Be patient."

"I don't *want* better. I *had* better, remember? *Better* is screwing a kid in Frederick's of Hollywood crotchless panties right now. *Better* blew you off tonight. Better *ain't* better, you see what I'm getting at here?"

Usnavys powders her nose, her pinky out. She laughs dramatically, checking to make sure someone, anyone, is watching her have a great time, even though she's, like, *not*. I look at the pretty boy again and see two young, bouncy things hitting on him. They have flat chests and ponytails on top of their heads. Teenagers. More teenagers. I have the urge to actually go and beat the crap out of them, until I notice he doesn't seem interested. He keeps looking my way.

I snatch the cup from Usnavys and down the rest of the drink in two swift chugs before she can take it away. Then, just to spite her, I down her wine, too. Feeling invincible, I slide off my barstool and traipse toward him. Usnavys rolls her eyes and doesn't try to stop me. She knows me well enough by now to know there's no point.

He's standing in a group of other young men. They joke around and speak fast, slangy Spanish. Most of them have a gold hoop in each of their ears. I catch a few words here and there. I pretend to be headed somewhere else, but smile at him as I walk by. He says hello in English, or rather "hahlo," and smiles. His friends look at me and shift around uncomfortably. I guess they don't get too many people like me in this place. I'm not wearing what the other females here wear, which is cheesy little clingy minidresses or hot pants and heels. I'm suddenly very self-conscious. I'm wearing baggy wool pants from the Gap, plaid, and a matching brown turtleneck. Oh, and my glasses. Not exactly sexy. And my hair is up in a twist because it was too much work after the day I had to blow it out. My makeup is different from theirs, too. They have dark lips and very little makeup on their eyes. I have light lips and heavier makeup on my eyes.

"Lauren Fernández, her casa is your casa, Boston," the pretty boy says, bouncing up and down on his heels like a happy little boy. Oh, right. The billboards. They recognize me from the stupid billboards. "You more white," he says. "You look more *morena* in the ads." No kidding.

I'm not sure what to do. The friends have all turned their backs to me, I'm not sure why. Pretty boy is staring into my eyes, licking his lips, just like I imagined, his hands crossed over his crotch as he leans against the bar. "You got anumba?" he asks, point-blank. His English is tainted with both a Spanish accent and a street Boston accent. I remember how fat, stupid, and unattractive I am, and turn to see if his question is aimed at some thinner, prettier, better-dressed being. It is not. He is talking to *moi*.

Could it really be that easy? Is that what his world is like? No beating around the bush, no telling me about his degree or investment portfolio. The room twirls. Blood surges to my pelvis. I feel hot and sweaty and fat and ugly and stupid and cheated and sad and curious, all at once. Could a man this handsome really be interested in little old me? I'm already down to a size eight, I'm sure of it, but not yet a six.

"Yes," I say. He takes a pen and a little address book out of his jacket pocket and opens it to "F," for Fernández. I give him the number.

"You so beautiful," he says in his weird English. "You so pretty, baby. I loves you."

Loves me? I look over at Usnavys. She's watching me, shielding her eyes the way someone might while witnessing a nasty car accident. She's curious, but doesn't want to see what happens next.

"What's your name?" I ask.

"Jesus," he says. His friends laugh. Not sure why. Then he says, "Not Jesus. It's Tito. Yeah. Tito Rojas." His friends laugh again. Then, "It's Amaury." No laugh.

"Where are you from?"

"Santo Domingo."

"What do you do?"

"*Limpieza.*"

He's a janitor. That's noble enough.

"So call me," I say. The floor shifts beneath me and I have

to grab his arm to keep from falling. I'm drunk. I point at him and say, "Tonight." I start to walk away, yelling, "Call me tonight. I love you too."

The friends raise their eyebrows and Amaury looks embarrassed. I return to Usnavys and say, "You see? He's *not* a drug dealer, like you said. He's a *janitor. Limpieza.*" I stick my tongue out at her.

"His name Amaury?" she asks, all miss smarty-pants. I nod. "He from Santo Domingo?" I nod again. "He tell you about his *kids*?" I shake my head. I can't tell if she's joking. She is laughing out loud. "*Ay, m'ija.* You have a lot to learn about Latinos."

"What is that supposed to mean?"

"*Na'. Olvídalo.*"

"You don't think *I'm* a Latina? Why, just because I'm light? You think you have to grow up in the projects to be a Latina?"

"No, you are, technically. But you have, like, some serious issues from your white side. You trip me out, girl."

"My Latina side *is* white, remember? We come in all colors?"

"Don't start writing one of your columns at me right now, okay?" She pantomimes a bored yawn. "I'm *not* in the mood. Plus, you know what I mean."

"Shut up."

"*Como quieras, m'ija.*"

I'm not even going to touch that one, not tonight.

"He's going to call me tonight," I brag. "When I get home. I want him. After today, girl, I *deserve* him. Taste him, eat him up, throw him out. That's how *they* do it, so that's how *I'm* doing it from now on."

Usnavys shrugs. "I can't stop you then," she says. "All I'm saying, *m'ija,* is be careful. I mean really careful. I've known his family for a long time. And he ain't never touched no mop in his life, okay, *sucia?* Believe me. *Ese tipo no sirve pa'na'.*"

Rough translation: *That dude ain't good for nothing.*

No good, huh?

Sounds like a perfect match for *me*.

AMAURY CALLS AFTER I get home, just like he said he would. He asks for my address. Against my better judgment, I give it to him.

"I there fifteen minute," he says in crippled English. "You be ready me, baby."

I hang up, sit stunned on my floral Bauer sofa, the one I got at the discount furniture place in the basement of Jordan Marsh. I look at the colorful pile of photo scraps heaped on the center of my glass coffee table. I destroyed them all, every relic of Ed. Us at the outdoor Botero exhibit in Manhattan last year? Rip! Us skiing in New Hampshire? Rip! Ed in a chef's hat, smiling over a pan of burned, dishwashing-liquid-tasting lasagna, his only attempt to cook anything for anyone? Rip, rip. My Ana Gabriel CD wails in the background. I wail along until my geriatric upstairs neighbor pounds his floor.

I ate two pints of ice cream while I tore up the photos, purged, ate some more, drank a couple of beers, purged again, then drank some more. And I cried. Like a moron. I mean, why cry if you're ridding yourself of a dumb ugly Texican like Ed *before* you've actually gotten hitched to him? For the same reason Cuban exiles talk about Cuba all the time. The Cuba they left doesn't exist anymore. You cry because you mourn the dream, not the real place—or person. The loss of the person you thought he was, not the one he is. There is no Santa Claus. There is no Ed in my future, teaching our son to put the hose away.

Fifteen minutes? I dig my crooked toes into the plush blue carpet, make kissy lips at my cat, Fatso, who sleeps in the huge, crescent-shaped window. She ignores me, so I kiss harder. Kiss kiss kiss kiss. Finally, I wake her. She yawns, fangs flashing, and lifts her giant round body. She stretches, tumbles down, wobbles over to me on her dainty little feet. It's my fault she's fat, of course. I'm the one who gives her four cans of Fancy Feast a day. That's how I show my love. She shows hers by rubbing my shins, leaving smeared sheets of white fur as she goes. I scratch behind her ears until she purrs.

"Okay, big girl." I grab her can of salmon-flavored treats from the side table, pop the top; the noise sets her twirling in desperate, mewling circles. Pavlov's cat. I toss a few her way. She pounces as best she can, reflexes slow for a cat, eats them with gusto, purring and chomping all at once. "What have we gotten ourselves into this time?"

I stand, start to topple over, and realize—again—I'm not sober. Still drunk. I hold the white banister, step carefully down to the mid level of my apartment, where the kitchen, dining room, and bathroom are.

This apartment *rocks*. High ceilings, modern. Trendy. At least I've got *that,* even if I'm fat and ugly and fiancé-less.

It's all open and airy with tons of light, artistic. It's the nicest place I've ever lived. Usnavys made me move here, mind you. I thought I couldn't afford it. She was, like, "Stop being so stingy and poor-minded, *m'ija.* You can afford it now. Issues, issues."

She was right. I still haven't really gotten used to having enough money. More than enough. There are, in my memory, too many days of *Papi* giving me my lunch money in a damp wadded ball from his pocket, sighing as he took it out, saying, "We're not made of money, remember that." I always had to ask, too, you know? Every morning. *Papi* forgot things like that. He's a good dad, but a professor. They don't remember most practical things. That's not a stereotype, either. We never had enough money.

Okay, done. I won't talk about *Papi* anymore. Sorry.

So now that I have money, I don't know what to do with it except hoard it for the inevitable famine. This dining-room set? Usnavys made me get it. Same for the bedroom set downstairs. "Don't wait," she said. "Live now."

I hold the wall to balance myself and "walk"—or something noodley and similar—all the way to the bathtub. The cat box is dirty, again. I have to fix that. You can't have a man over to your house with a dirty cat box. The whole apartment probably reeks of her neat little turds, coated in gray litter. I don't notice it anymore. I'm immune. But I want to make a good impression on my drug dealer.

Drug dealer?

Jesus Christ, Lauren. What have you done?

I run the hot water in the tub. It will actually be hot in about three minutes. This is a nice apartment, newly renovated, but like everything else in this overpriced iceberg of a town, it has old pipes. Something's always not right with the apartments in Boston for people in my income bracket. I know, I make more than most people, right, but here's the thing: It costs more to live in Boston than any other city in the country, pretty much, even more than San Francisco. So you end up with six figures on paper, but you're living like a graduate student.

I should go back to New Orleans, where things make sense. Palm trees, humidity, hurricanes, the Neville Brothers, Café Du Monde, crawfish, jazz funerals. I've had nothing but bad luck since I came here. I grab the little red scooper and start shoveling Fatso's poop into the toilet. Plop, plop. I love this cat *too* much, okay? Way too much freaking *effort*, this cat. Does she appreciate it? What do you think? She comes in and rolls around on the bathmat, the first really nice bathmat I've ever had, an expensive purple thing I got at a bed and bath shop on Newbury Street. She leaves hair all over it. I just washed it. It's like I wash this bathmat every two or three days, because of her hair. Just like I have to run the vacuum every two days. Her hair is everywhere. That's one of the reasons I never quite feel like the successful woman people seem to think I am. Successful women have cats, yes, but they're able to keep the fur under control, you know what I mean? They don't walk around in a cat fur fog, like Pigpen with his dirt. I do. I go somewhere, and this cloud of cat fur follows me. The other day, in Bread & Circus, when I was buying food I thought would be healthy for me and might actually turn me around on the bulimia thing, this lady in line starts *sneezing* on me and asks me if I have a cat. I say yes, and she says she can tell by all the hair on my jacket. "You ever thought of using a lint brush?" she asks, sniffing. I'm, like, what the *hell*, lady? You're a complete stranger and you're gonna get up in my face like that?

Fatso rolls on her back and watches me, and as soon as I've scooped everything out, flushed it away, replaced it with fresh litter, and sprayed Lysol over the whole deal, she tiptoes over, steps in, and lays another giant crap.

"Et tu, Brute?" I ask her.

She ignores me.

This is my life. Lysol, cat box, and Ed porking that skinny little *putita*.

"I thought I could at least count on *you*," I say to the cat. I collapse in sobs, again.

Fatso finishes her business, digs around a little halfheartedly, and scrams, back leg shaking litter all over the hallway as she goes. She is not what you'd call a fast-moving cat. The vet keeps telling me to put her on a diet. A diet? For a *cat*? Our relatives in Cuba struggle to get enough calories out of their stupid ration cards, and they want me to put my *cat* on a *diet*? What a world.

Besides, it's up to Fatso, not me, if you believe the law. There's still a law in Massachusetts that makes it illegal to own a cat because those men who hanged all those girls in Salem thought cats were people, sort of. So I guess I don't own Fatso, not legally. She chooses *me* as her *slave*. I should be honored. At least *someone* wants me. I clean up her latest mess and spray the Lysol again. The water is hot now, so I pull the shower curtain (also nice, and dark purple, matches the rug) and lift the shower lever.

I undress and look at myself in the mirror over the sink for a second, my face. I look sick and puffy and tired. I look old and fat and stupid. How am I going to get cleaned up enough in fifteen minutes to impress a guy like Amaury? You've seen the girls he's used to! They dropped out of school in the ninth grade so they can dedicate all their time to things like shaving their legs and putting on lip liner. Why would someone like him be even remotely interested in this sallow-looking freak with the messy hair and glasses? I have a theory: You work in newspapers more than three years and you start to look like a dancing corpse from a Michael Jackson video. Newspapers are *factories* that think they're *offices*. So every evening the whole building trembles as the presses start to roll, and ink sprays out of the vents. There's no natural light anywhere, just this big warehouse where people sit around staring at computers. There is no pastier, greasier, sicklier, sorrier-looking bunch of people than those that work in newspapers.

"You make me sick," I tell myself. "You're so ugly."

Time. Passes. Room. Spins.

I realize I've been standing there making faces at myself for a while and the water from the shower has splattered all over the floor. I'm drunk. Did I tell you that yet? I think so.

How long have I been standing here? I don't know. Is the door buzzer going off? I can't tell, the water's too loud. I don't have a lot of time. What was I doing again? Oh, yeah.

Crying and insulting myself.

I laugh and get in the shower and start the long girl-process of becoming sexable. You *know* what I'm saying, don't pretend you don't. Shave, wash, scrub, shave again, get out, dry off, moisturize, shave that little scraggle you missed at your left ankle and pretend it doesn't hurt when you cut yourself. Smear deodorant everywhere. Spritz fragrance. Stuff yourself into a velvet push-up bra, endure the invasive threadiness of your thong. Find something suggestive in your closet, something you hope doesn't make you look *fat*. Black is your best bet. Leggings and a sweater from the Limited. Don't want to look like you're trying too hard. Put it on. Oh, but you're not done yet. You still have your *head* to deal with. I mean what's outside, not the inside. (That's hopeless.) You put your long hair in a towel to keep it out of the way, use that cream that's supposed to stop wrinkles, even though you are living proof that it's a lie. (Why didn't anyone tell me you start to look old in your mid-twenties?) Then you do the foundation, the blush, the eye foundation, the base shadow, the contour shadow, pluck the brows, fill them in again with black powder, smudge eyeliner, do the mascara like that, with your mouth open. Just try doing mascara with your mouth closed, girl. It won't work. Then your lips. Liner, filler, smack the lips together, blot on tissue. Then powder over the whole royal mess, to *set* it, as they say. Take out the hair, run the brush through it, dry it with the blower for five minutes, then take the big round brush and work it through, piece by little piece, hundreds of pieces in all, to get the curl out, to get it straight and shiny and "natural" looking. I got me some curly Portuguese hair. It's like taking care of a Victory garden on PBS, being a girl.

I examine the finished product in the full-length mirror in the bedroom downstairs and have to admit that in the right light, at the right angle, I don't look half as bad as I seem to think I do. Elizabeth and the other *sucias* are always telling me how pretty I am and that I have to stop thinking so poorly of myself. Maybe it's true, but if you have to put *this* much effort into looking pretty, then you probably actually *aren't*.

Pretty girls probably don't dump all their dirty clothes on the closet floor. I've got suits now, just like my other *sucias*, but I wad them up. I iron them because I think I can't afford the dry cleaners, and it burns the fabric so it's different colors in different places. The suits smell like weird chemicals because you're not *supposed* to iron them. I try to fix it by spraying them with perfume. So imagine all that mess, with the cat hair, and the bulimia. My wedding is off. And *now*, a drug dealer is coming over.

Loser.

I go upstairs, ram the dishes into the dishwasher, wipe up the crumbs on the glass dining table, pick up all the photo scraps and ice cream tubs, dump them in the trash under the sink. There. Done. Ready to be romanced.

No, wait. He's Dominican, right, from the island. So he likes Latin music. I go through my CD collection, pass over the Miles Davis and Missy Elliott, find some merengue. That's what those kind of homie boys like, right? Merengue. Olga Tañón. I put the CD in the stereo and go to the couch and wait. I'm drunk, as I might have mentioned. Forget Ed and his big pockmarked head. I hate him. I pick up the phone and dial his number and when he answers, I hang up. I do it again. Four times. I start to cry again. I call Usnavys and tell her I want to kill Ed. "Can we hire a hit man? Could we actually do that?"

Usnavys's voice groans with sleep interrupted. "Coffee, *m'ija*," she grumbles. "Go drink some coffee. Go to bed. Get some rest, *sucia*. I'll talk to you tomorrow."

"Just shoot him. It's not hard. His head is so big, you can't miss."

She sighs. "Is Amaury there?"

"No."

"Good. He's dangerous. You don't need danger. You need to love yourself more, sweetie."

"That's a great idea! *Amaury* could shoot him."

"Good night, *m'ija*. You go to bed right now, *sucia*. *Sola*. I'll talk to you in the morning. Don't do anything stupid."

Five minutes later, stupidity arrives in a leather jacket.

The buzzer rings. I pull some big knives out of a kitchen drawer and run around like a psycho, planting them in convenient hiding places in every room, under the sofa cushions, between my mattress and box springs, between stacked towels in the linen closet. Just in case. I check my butt in the mirror one more time. I toss my hair. Lights, camera, action! I must be ovulating.

I buzz him in, wait for him to find me here on the second floor. He is wearing the same green and white plaid shirt, leather jacket, and khaki pants with Timberland boots. Though I have degenerated into a scary old woman since my soaring moment of glory in the bar, he looks the same. Better. He looks better. He does not walk, he prowls. He is confident and happy to see me. A real live homeboy.

"*Que lo que*," he says with a laugh. He's singing, bouncing, jazzed. He brushes past me and walks right into my apartment, without waiting to be invited, starts running his fingers over everything, nodding his approval. He even opens my closets, looks in them, singing along to the Olga Tañón song and dancing as he goes.

Fearless.

"What are you doing?" I ask him in my crap Spanish.

"Nothing," he answers in Spanish. It's the first time I've heard him speak the language, and he sounds more educated than I expected he would. Like, most hoodies would say "na" the way Usnavys says it. But he says "*nada*," using both syllables. "Just checking," he says.

"Checking?"

"Yeah," he says in English.

"For what?"

He ignores me and continues his rounds. He finally comes to rest in the upstairs living-room loft, collapsing on the sofa as if he owned the joint. Just kicks his feet up, boots and all, puts his hands over his privates, smiles with the playfulness of a tiger kitten. I've never seen anything like it. There was no greeting, no small talk. Just this.

"Make yourself at home," I say sarcastically in English, cautiously approaching him as the apartment twirls on its axis.

"It's a nice place you got here," he says in Spanish, spreading his arms like a long lost friend. Then, in English, "Come here, baby."

"I don't know," I say.

He laughs, and says, "*Oye ahora.*"

I sit on the living-room floor and say, "Tell me a little about yourself first." This makes him laugh extra hard, a big booming rasp of laughter. I hear a little electronic trilling sound. He tugs the red plastic beeper from his belt, and checks it, licks his lips.

"What you wanna know?" he asks in English. "You know everything already." I know nothing about this dude, okay? In Spanish, he says, "You didn't tell me to call you tonight because you wanted to talk, did you?"

"Do you sell drugs?" I ask.

He purses his lips and looks shocked, in a mocking way.

"Usnavys says you sell drugs. You lied to me about the janitorial thing, right?"

He grabs his belly he's laughing so hard. Freak.

"Oye ahora," he says again. *"Escucha es'o*, man." I have no idea what he's saying.

"I'm serious. I need to know. You sell drugs or what?" I lean back on my hands, trying to look casual and unafraid. I realize, with a sick feeling, that I am probably looking at *him* in exactly the same way all my guilty white liberal colleagues look at me. *Don't hurt me, please, exotic little Latin thing.*

He looks at me, still grinning. In English, he says, "What you care, eh? What matter what I do?"

"I just don't want to get involved with someone who sells drugs."

He shrugs. *"Bueno,"* he says.

"So do you?"

He sits up now, and I realize he's as uncomfortable with me as I am with him. I actually feel sorry for him.

"What, *mamita?"* Fingers drumming together.

"Sell drugs."

"Drugs, no." He leans forward over the coffee table and picks up the Olga Tañón CD case, opens it and takes the booklet out, pretends to be very interested in it. Then, without looking at me, adds, "Drug. One drug. *La cocaina.*" Then he looks at me, and grins.

I should know this is when you ask the drug dealer to leave. You escort him to the door, never talk to him again. There must be some etiquette book over at Rebecca's with the protocol for this situation all mapped out, yeah? You do not go to college, work hard, become a columnist at one of the country's top newspapers, and spend thousands of dollars on therapy just to suddenly start sleeping with a drug dealer.

But you know what? As soon as he says it, I mean, like, as *soon* as he says it, as soon as he confesses, my body *boings*. To be specific, my clitoris sits up and pays attention. My spine tingles, my nipples stand up and salute the push-up bra. I realize, with a sick feeling, that this pretty young gangster *turns me on.*

"I think you better go," I lie. A *sucia* must keep up appearances.

He says something in Spanish, fast, and I don't understand. I ask him to repeat himself, and he does, in English.

"I never touched it." He's looking at me with an honesty I can hardly believe. I have years of interviewing people, and I usually have good radar. I know when someone's lying. He's not.

"You mean the cocaine?" I ask.

"*Sí, claro,*" he says. *Of course.* He shrugs again, looks at the bookshelf next to my computer desk. He continues in Spanish, speaking slowly and simply so I can understand him. "I have never sold it to my own people, either, Lauren. I sell it to lawyers. Gringos. They're the ones who buy it." Then, with a laugh, he adds, "My people can't *afford* it."

I sit next to him on the couch, all tenderness and guidance-counselor cool.

"So why do you do it?" I ask. He surprises me a second time, and gets up. He walks to the bookshelf and scans the titles.

"You like this one?" he asks, pulling out a Spanish-language version of Isabel Allende's *Portrait in Sepia.* I got about thirty pages into it one time, with my Spanish-English dictionary, looking up every third word or so, kept a nice long list on a yellow legal pad of all the words I had to learn. I remember well the first few sentences, because I had to read them for so long to get the meaning of them.

Book closed in his big brown hand, Amaury recites the first two sentences. "*I came into the world one Tuesday in the autumn of 1880, in San Francisco, in the home of my maternal grandparents. While inside that labyrinthine wood house my mother panted and pushed, her valiant heart and desperate bones laboring to open a way out to me, the savage life of the Chinese quarter was seething outside, with its unforgettable aroma of exotic food, its deafening torrent of shouted dialects, its inexhaustible swarms of human bees hurrying back and forth.*"

"You read?" I ask. He laughs again, starts dancing a little to the music.

"I can read, *sí.*"

"No, I didn't mean it that way, I meant——"

"It's okay." He shrugs again, and starts looking at the framed photos on my windowsill. He stops on one of Ed. Oops. I forgot that one. "Who dat?" he asks in English.

"Nobody."

"Ah, then it must be somebody," he says in Spanish, with a wink.

"You're good," I say.

He scans my CDs. "Too many Puerto Ricans," he comments.

"What?"

"No Dominicans here. All Puerto Ricans." Then, in a mocking voice, "Puerto Rico, Puerto Rico, Puerto Rico. I'm *sick* of Puerto Rico, man."

"What about this?" I ask, referring to the Olga. Again with the laugh.

"*Boricua.*"

"Oh. Sorry." I had no idea. I thought she was Dominican. She sings merengue.

"*Nada*, nothing."

I try to follow him, but trip as I get up and land with a thud on the floor.

"Let me guess," he says in slow Spanish, helping me up. "That 'nobody' dumped you and you went to the club with your friend and now you want to get even. So you pick me, use me, right?"

"You're really good."

He examines me with a critical eye. Smart. Really smart, this guy. Then he kisses me, hard. I melt into him, kiss back. We move to the couch, tumble down. I stop.

"Your turn now," I say, or rather I *slur*. "You're a drug dealer and you are smart and handsome and you can get any woman you want and you use women all the time for your own thing and then you leave them like dirt."

He shakes his head. "You *not* good," he says in English. "You no know me at all."

We continue to kiss and fumble with each other's unfamiliar bodies. I start to rip at his clothes. He feels, smells, tastes as good as I thought he might. Salty. I grope at the zipper of his pants.

He stops me.

I try again.

He stops me.

Stops.

Me.

Me!

"What?" I ask. "You don't *like* me?"

"Sí mi amor, sí me gustas tu, muchísimo," he says. He likes me. A lot.

"So what's the problem then?"

"You drunk," he says in English. "I no never take advantage of no drunk womans." Then, in Spanish, "It's an ethical policy."

"I'm not drunk," I say. My wooden tongue and its slobbery rubber words imply otherwise. Oops.

He looks at his beeper again, then stands up, leans over me, and actually picks me up off the couch.

"Don't do that!" I cry into the salty brown of his neck. "I'm too fat, you'll hurt yourself. You'll drop me."

"You no fat," he says. "Who say that? The nobody? Forget him. You beautiful."

He carries me down to the bed, and tucks me in. I start to cry, big humid alcoholic tears. Drops of mascara-water stain the comforter.

"You think I'm ugly, huh?" I ask. "I knew it. You can get all those pretty girls at the club and I'm just stupid and fat."

"No, no, *mi amor,*" he says, sitting next to me on the bed. He wipes my tears with his fingers. In English, he says, "You so beautiful." He looks surprised and concerned.

"No, I'm not. Look at me. I'm disgusting. No one loves me. Ed hates me. I can't believe he was with that stupid little girl."

"Okay," he says. "I go now. I call you later."

"Yeah, *right.*"

"I love you."

"Oh, whatever." I collapse sobbing into my pillow, the

weight of everything that has happened to me crushing me to nothing. I'm so disgusting my fiancé cheated on me, and now I can't even have a one-night stand with a lowlife drug dealer. Even *he's* too good for me, is that it? Life sucks.

"I like your books," he says, standing in the doorway. In Spanish, "That's why I'm leaving now. You get it?"

"What are you talking about? Get out of here." I bury my head under a pillow.

In English, he says, "Woman got bad books, I do you once, maybe twice, you know?" He walks over, lifts the pillow, kisses my cheek, and smiles. "You, me, we got nothing to talk if you got bad books. Or don't got no books."

"What?"

"I like you," he says in Spanish. "You're a good, decent woman, a smart woman. A professional woman. I don't want to ruin this. I could take advantage of you right now, but that would be unacceptable behavior."

"You've got to be *kidding*."

In slow Spanish so I will understand him, he says, "You've been drinking, too much I think. You might make a decision you will regret. And I don't want you to make a mistake with me. I don't want to be the man you take because you're on the rebound. I'm not stupid. I know a good woman when I meet one. I don't meet many. You're a good woman."

I don't believe it. Mr. Danger the Drug Dealer is the *good guy*? He's thinking about *me*? "Okay," I say. I sit up, sniffling. "If you're so smart, if you care so much about good books, what are you doing selling drugs? That's not a smart thing to do."

He moves back to the bed, sits, and leans to one side, fishing a wallet out of his back pocket. He opens it, and starts flipping through the photographs there.

"Here," he says, stopping on a picture of a woman somewhere in her forties with an obvious resemblance to him. "Here's why." He points. I look at his face and I'm surprised yet again to find tears perched in the corners of his dark brown eyes. *"Mami."*

"She's pretty," I offer.

"She beautiful," he corrects me in English. "And she real sick, *que Dios la bendiga*." He continues in Spanish, going very slowly so I can understand him. "She's got cancer. She can't work. And she's raising my aunt's children, and one of them is mentally retarded. She's in Santo Domingo. You know how we brushed our teeth in her house? With a cup of bottled water, out in the yard." He pantomimes this degrading ritual. "We never heard of running water where my mother lives. Things are bad there. So I do what I have to do."

I try, but have a hard time imagining this smooth-talking, intense-eyed, powerful, gorgeous young man living in that kind of squalor. Do people like him actually come from places like that? I mean, my good leftist upbringing tells me that yes, they do, that there are smart, incredible people everywhere. But I guess part of me never really believed it.

"You could go to school, you could get a regular job." I grab a tissue from the box on my nightstand and blow my nose, feeling somewhat better, but still fat and ugly.

He laughs again. In Spanish, "You can't live on what they pay you here. I don't have time to go to school. These people need money *now*. She'll die before I could finish school. I tried. I had regular jobs. I couldn't help myself, let alone anyone else, on what they pay you here. I need enough money to get her here for treatment."

It occurs to me that he could be totally full of it, manipulating me. But there's something to him. He's not lying. He's crying. Unless he's a brilliant actor, this guy is telling the truth.

"I didn't want to do this," he says. "When I came here, I didn't think I'd end up doing this. You think any of us want to do this?"

"How did you start?"

"They find you," he says. "They look for guys like me. I didn't always have these clothes. I came here with sandals and a woman's coat I got from my sister. I didn't know what cold felt like. You know? And I didn't have enough money to buy a hamburger. I was hungry. These guys always come back, you know, they come back to Santo Domingo from New York and Boston and they have nice clothes and cell phones and they get nice things for their mothers, and they tell everyone they got jobs cleaning buildings or whatever, they lie. So when *Mami* got sick, I came. I'm not the first idiot to think it'd be easy here. That's what everyone says back home."

"What about your dad?"

"I got no dad. He lives in Puerto Rico. He's a *boricua*. Bastard."

"I'm sorry."

He shrugs again. In Spanish, "It makes me a citizen and I don't have to deal with Immigration. I was young when I came, and I didn't know. The dealers that found me made it easy, gave me some money and a car, and here I am, selling drugs."

"How old are you?"

"Twenty." I knew he was younger than I am, but I had no idea. He's just a kid.

"How long have you been here?"

"Three years."

"Where'd you learn about Isabel Allende?"

"Around. There's a Spanish bookstore in Cambridge. I would have gone to school more in Santo Domingo, but you know what they do to boys like me who want to study? They shoot at you. The police. They used to shoot at me just to watch me jump when I walked to school. It's not like here, Lauren. It's another world. You wouldn't understand. Everybody's poor in Santo Domingo."

"Can't you just work and make a better life?"

"No. That's what your kind of people do here. Not there. Not my kind of people."

"Jesus."

I don't know what else to say. He's telling the truth, and his truth is ugly. I don't want to hear it. I just wanted a pretty hoodlum to use and discard. Now I can't do that. I still think he's handsome, only now I feel sorry for him, too.

And I like him. What's wrong with me?

"You go to bed now," he says, checking that beeper again. Then, in English: "I got to go. I come tomorrow, okay, baby? I come see you again tomorrow."

Against my better judgment for the second time tonight, I say yes.

He kisses me good night.

And so begins my relationship with Amaury Pimentel, the literate drug dealer.

Just two weeks to go until baseball season starts. All in favor of the Red Sox moving out of Fenway Park, raise your hands. What's that? You all agree with me that there's no better place to catch a ball game than the great green monster in the heart of Back Bay? There are many things I love about spring in this town—the cherry blossoms on Newbury Street, the street festivals—but the thing I love most is April at Fenway Park. I love the crisp scent of spring in the air. I love the hot dogs, smothered in chili and cheese. I love the beer in plastic cups. Most of all, though, I love Nomar Garciaparra's butt in those tight baseball pants. (Nomar, anytime you're free, I'm free, okay?) Three cheers for the Red Sox, Fenway Park, and tight baseball pants! Sometimes, it's best to move on when something has gotten old and tired. But in the case of our wonderful ballpark, it's better to stay put.

—from "My Life," by Lauren Fernández

rebecca

I TWIST MY key in the door, push it open, and call out.
"Brad?"

No answer.

I hang the crimson coat on the brass hook behind the door, drop my briefcase and purse on the wood floor of the entry, check the usual places: dining table, refrigerator, the message pad on my desk. He has not left a note. The pain in my eye disappears. My neck and shoulders relax. I inhale, deeply, smooth my fists into hands again. He's not home. Forgive me, Jesus, I think, but I'm relieved. He hasn't been here in almost a week.

It's almost too good to be true.

The steamy hot shower feels fine. I linger, lean against the white tiles, close my eyes. And breathe, deeply. I shampoo my hair, feeling my fingers on my scalp for the first time in a long while, really feeling them. I wash my body, taking my time. There's an electricity to my skin today. I can't explain it. I feel good, young.

We have to take hold of our own images, because no one is going to do it for us. I go over the words to tonight's speech in my head. *I'm not unique. There are thousands like me. They just need a chance.* I'm prepared. Tonight will be perfect.

Once I'm clean, I turn off the shower, insert the white rubber stopper in the drain, toss a few orange spice-scented bath cubes into the tub, and fill it with hot water. I add a dash of pink watermelon bubble bath to the running water, push PLAY on the bath stereo to start my Toni Braxton CD. I know all the lyrics by heart now. I slip into the bubbles, lean my head against the peach-colored bath pillow, and listen to my thoughts.

Annulment. Annulment. Annulment.

My stomach flutters with anticipation of being finished with Brad.

I close my eyes, slide down, submerge myself completely in the water, and try to drown out all negative thoughts. Is an annulment a negative thought under these circumstances? I don't think so.

Annulment.

I come up for air, look at my hopeful red toenails peeking out of the bubbles, laugh out loud. It feels good. That can't be a negative thought. I have met Marion Wright Edelman, Colin Powell, and Cristina Saralegui. To a person, all of the successful people I admire have one thing in common: positive attitudes. I think positive thoughts, all the ones I can imagine. But there's something coiled in my belly. I can't concentrate.

My hands run along my skin under the water, the fingers seeking out the pleasure parts I've ignored for too long. I touch myself. I feel guilty, but I always feel guilty when I do this.

For some reason, Andre's face keeps appearing on the inside of my eyelids, smiling. Dimples. I move my finger in slow small circles on my secret spot, and feel my legs tense with delicious pressure. Andre, big strong Andre. How would he move a woman on a bed? I almost say his name out loud. He called again at the office today, and left another message with my assistant, this time: "You Will Dance." It's forward, and inappropriate.

It excites me.

I hear Consuelo bumping the vacuum against the door, cleaning the bedroom. I muffle my thoughts, freeze my hands, afraid she might catch me. I squeeze my legs together again, wait without breathing, so quiet I can hear tiny bubbles popping on the surface of the water. When the sound of the motor retreats, I begin again. I wonder if Brad finds Consuelo *"earthy."* Negative thought. Zap, zap.

Submerged again in the orange and watermelon water, and there's Andre. Sexy. Zap. It's no use. My body sings for him. I thrum, faster and faster, until my body bursts into a million stars.

I open my eyes. What have I done? The light seems too bright. The air too still. I am flooded with guilt. As always, I move quickly forward, try to forget.

I change the scenery to the Sandia mountains after a snowstorm, clean and crisp. I breathe in the color of the sky in my hometown, a bright, clear, and soothing blue. I flip the lever that releases the drain and remove myself from the hot, scented water, wrap my body in a thick white cotton towel, and move into my large, meticulously organized walk-in closet.

If I were not scheduled to speak, I would wear something a little bit sparkly, perhaps my long black dress with the velvet embroidered jacket. But tonight I need something that conveys strength, dignity, and the spirit of successful minority entrepreneurship.

Alberto, my personal shopper, chose an elegant flowing pants suit, in black, cut in a style that makes me look taller than I really am. He took it to a tailor and had a few understated Mexican motifs in bright red and yellow sewn along the cuffs. He has also chosen the shoes and handbag, buoyant and not overly sexy. The accessories are small and folkarty. They must come from somewhere south of the border. Nice touches.

The outfits some women choose to wear to the Minority Business Association events amaze me. Unfortunately, many Hispanic women embarrass themselves—and the rest of us—by showing up in prom dresses. The ones with the worst taste are from the Caribbean. They like colors as loud as their voices, and think cleavage is a business asset.

You could take a random sampling of the outfits worn by the women at these Minority Business Association events and I could accurately attach the outfit to the ethnic group without seeing the actual person wearing the clothes. A tight dress with a ruffle around the bottom would be a Latina. Any kind of suit or dress with an elaborate boxy hat or excessively showy brooch would be African-American. The most conservative suits would belong to the Asian-American women. A skintight catsuit with puffy boudoir slippers would belong to a Hispana, sadly. I do not lie when I say I have seen women at our events in this type of costume.

I ARRIVE AT the hotel early and check in with the organizers. I will give the keynote address during the meal, which is a relief because I am often uncomfortable eating in front of others. Few people understand my eating habits, and I am tired of explaining my reasons for avoiding caffeine, sugar, fat, meat, and dairy. The organizer tells me I will sit in the main hall, at a table headed by Andre Cartier, at Andre's request. At the mention of his name my pulse quickens.

I make an appearance at the informal cocktail party in one of the smaller conference rooms down the hall. I work the crowd, shaking hands and memorizing the names, quickly moving on to meet others. I find it amazing how many people seem to misunderstand the purpose of a cocktail party. You do *not* go to a business cocktail party in order to socialize with your friends and other people you already know. You do *not* go to a cocktail party to enjoy the food and drink. You do *not* go in order to shrink in social terror against the wall and watch all the other people talking to one another.

The purpose of a cocktail party is to meet potential business contacts and to have them meet *you*. I can't believe how many people still go to these things with their friends from the office and stand around with their cold drinks in their right hands. You are supposed to hold your drink in your *left* hand, because the right hand is the one you will be using to shake hands with the people you are supposed to be meeting. You do not make a good impression on someone by shaking hands when yours is cold and clammy.

People begin to arrive in the large hall and take their places at the tables. I join them. Many make mistakes regarding the appropriate time to unfold the napkin and put it in their laps or, worse, forget to put the napkin in their laps at all. The proper time to put your napkin in your lap, of course, is after the head of your table has done so—not, as many people seem to think, as soon as you sit down.

Andre arrives right on time. Of course he does. That's one of the reasons he has been so successful, I'm sure. He is punctual. He is a tall man, with a very dark complexion, almost purely black, and strikingly handsome in a classic sort of way. He makes quite an impression in his elegant tuxedo with the terra-cotta bow tie and cummerbund.

I spot him across the room, shaking hands, smiling, and greeting people as he moves. His manners are easy and excellent. As with the most sophisticated of people, he is so comfortable in his graciousness that you are not aware he is being gracious. All his focus is on others, on the people he makes contact with. He is interested in them, makes them feel good about themselves for knowing him. Isn't that the goal? People do not find you appealing because you impress them with who you are; they find you appealing because you make them feel good about themselves for knowing you.

I stand to greet Andre, and he moves our handshake smoothly into a polite embrace and warm kiss on the cheek. He has not done this with anyone else he greeted in the room. "How are you, Rebecca?" he asks, searching my eyes with his. They are exquisite, almond-shaped and dark. He smells of cinnamon. I am excited to be near him.

"I'm fine, Andre, thank you," I say, a slight quiver in my throat. "How are you?"

"Very well, thank you," he says with his English accent. We remain standing and continue talking. He congratulates me on a recent *Boston* magazine profile of me. I congratulate him on an item I saw in the paper about his company acquiring a smaller software firm last week. People approach, and we both socialize with the confidence and grace of true professionals.

Once we sit down and everyone has turned their attention to the introductory speaker, Andre leans over to me and whispers quietly in my ear, "You look stunning tonight, Rebecca. Truly stunning." I am surprised. I consider returning the compliment, as he does indeed look stunning, but I don't think it would be appropriate for me to do so. I smile politely and thank him, aware that my cheeks blaze. He observes me, and stares longer than is appropriate.

After new members are welcomed and everyone is updated on the issues concerning the organization, including hirings, promotions, and other important milestones for members, dinner is announced. Waiters begin running salads to the tables, and people begin to eat, some at the right moment, others not, some with correct forks, others not. One of the organizers approaches to indicate it's time for me to make my way to the stage. I excuse myself and follow her. I am surprised when the lights are dimmed and a five-minute video on the success of *Ella* is shown on a screen at the far end of the room. I did not know this would happen. I choke down the urge to cry. People clap and cheer when the video ends, and I climb the steps to the podium. Standing here before more than one thousand people, I realize once again: This is mine. I have accomplished my goal.

I give my speech. People laugh when I hoped they would, and clap when I expected they would. I mention nothing of my personal life, other than to thank my parents for instilling in me a strong work ethic and commitment to professionalism. With a sincere smile, I tell the incredible story of Andre Cartier and his magical check, and use it as a lesson to those in the room who have succeeded to be fearless in offering a hand up to others. Andre stands when I ask him to, and accepts his applause. In spite of myself, I feel an almost electric shock through my body as I look at him. I compose myself and finish the speech.

I get a standing ovation. I return to the table and a beaming Andre. I eat the parts of the salad that have not been contaminated with gooey dressing.

Andre offers champagne to celebrate our success with the magazine, but I refuse. I don't drink. He sips his single glass alone, watching me with a smile in his eyes. A sexy smile. I realize I am starving.

I look away and fill my stomach with water.

After dinner, an R&B band starts to play Stevie Wonder covers, and people make their way to the dance floor. Andre winks at me. "Are you going to give in this time?"

"No," I say. "I can't dance."

"Everyone can dance," he says.

"It's not that I don't *like* to dance," I say. "I honestly *can't*."

"Nonsense," he says.

Though I never talk about myself, I tell him about how I tried dancing in college only to have the *sucias* laugh at me. As I recall, Lauren used that opportunity to remind me I was "Indian," which I'm *not*. "Your people can't *dance*," she said. I'll never forget that.

"Those aren't friends," he says, simply.

"No, they are. They're just very honest. Two left feet here."

He continues to search my eyes, says nothing. He lifts one eyebrow, and waits.

"I can't dance," I repeat. I'm uncomfortable.

"Nonsense," he says.

"I look like an idiot when I dance."

He stands up and holds out his hand.

"No," I protest.

"Yes," he says. He leans toward me, brushes a finger along my cheek. "You *can*."

And there, bang, there it is. Lust, for the second time today. To think I had almost forgotten what it felt like.

He takes my hand gently. "Come."

I stand up. "I don't know."

"Just relax," he says.

"I'm warning you, it's not my fault if I step on your toes or hurt you."

He moves closer, looks directly into my eyes, and whispers suggestively, "I think I'd *like* it if you hurt me . . . a little." I blush all over my body and say nothing.

The band has switched from Stevie Wonder to something vaguely recognizable. He sweeps me onto the dance floor and smiles. I'm suddenly very nervous. The music is good, the band is good, and I recognize the song from my middle school years, a funky old song with a strong bass line, something about strawberries. Andre is moving smoothly, easily, and, I can't help but notice, sexily. Not like he's trying to, but just because he is one of those people who is full of sexual energy, a powerful, intelligent person, confident and happy. Women all around us stare at him.

"Like this," he says, moving my shoulders with his large hands. "Loosen up. Just feel the music."

I do a step to the side, bring my other foot in, step-together, step-together. Even *I* can tell I am stiff. I might as well be in aerobics class.

"That's it," he says with a winning grin. "That's it."

I feel like I should be marching in a military parade. My

body doesn't move to music, at least not when people are watching. Step-together.

Andre matches my movements, adds a little twist of his own, exhibiting impeccable manners even now. I remember some of the lyrics from long ago, from a time when life was simpler. I mouth the words.

"That's right," Andre shouts over the music. "Let yourself go."

My head feels light. I am enjoying myself. Is that a sin? When you marry a man, before God and your family, you are supposed to purge your heart of the ability to feel what I am feeling now. You are not supposed to become breathless near another man. You are not supposed to wonder what it would be like to be with him instead of your own husband, not supposed to imagine the two of you walking along the Charles River in the spring.

The music changes to a slower song. Andre moves closer to me, and I back away. He allows me to keep my distance, but we continue to dance. The song is melancholy and I start to feel a little bit sad in spite of my efforts not to. I lean over toward his ear.

"Do you think I'm earthy?" I whisper.

He tilts his head to the side like a bird to indicate amused confusion.

"Earthy? No, I can't say that's what comes to mind when I think of you. Why?"

"Well, how would you describe me? I'm curious."

He grins enormously, pulls me closer, holds me tight, and we sway. People stare, I know they do. Andre begins speaking softly into my ear. "Rebecca Baca, to me, is *brilliant*—and knows it. She is *cultured*—and knows it. She is spectacularly beautiful, but does *not* know it, and she is extremely lonely, but she does not *reveal* it."

I want to turn and run away, leave this place. Leave what I am feeling. I step back, but he pulls me in again, gently.

He continues, low, fast, and urgent. "Rebecca Baca is the woman I think about as I am falling asleep, and she is the woman I think of when I first wake up in the morning. She is the most astonishing woman I know."

I cannot control my heart, or my blood, which feels like it has drained out onto the floor. I am weak with joy. I can't think of anything to say, and am not prepared for any of this. We dance until the band stops playing, and I don't want to stop.

"You know," he says as we gather our coats from the coat check and head out to the valet line, "we could keep going. It's Friday night. I know some nice clubs in town."

"It's late," I say.

"Not true, not true," he says with a good-natured laugh, checking his Rolex. "It's only eleven o'clock."

"I don't think it would be *appropriate*," I say. "You should know that."

He looks puzzled, then offended.

"I'm *married*, Andre. And I'm a public person. That's what I meant. Not because, well—"

He fixes me with his eye, and grins so that his dimples show. "You know," he says, "I have yet to meet your husband. He's never been to a single event."

"I know."

"I won't believe you're really married until I meet him." He frowns in a serious mood, and reaches for my hand and plants a gentle kiss on it. "If you were *my* wife, I would be at every function celebrating your success."

"I am, I'm married."

"Happily?"

I swallow hard, caught.

"Yes," I lie. "Happily married." For the first time I can remember, I have a microexpression. My mouth twitches.

Andre notices, and smiles. "You told me you couldn't dance," he says with a raised eyebrow. "*That* was a lie. You're absolutely certain about a husband, are you?"

I hand the valet my ticket, gain control of my face, smile at Andre. "Good night, then," I say. "I'll see you next time."

We stand without speaking until my car comes. Andre

opens the door gently, and I climb in. As he closes it, he says, "Swear to me you're happily married, and I'll stop pursuing you."

I avoid his stare, put the key in the ignition, and pull slowly away without responding.

I don't want God to know the answer.

I don't love to drag up sappy anecdotes for this column. It's a cheap trick of the trade, and I swore back in journalism school that if I ever had my own column, I'd never pull what I like to call "the Paul Harvey" on you. But fury forces me to relay some touching personal moments with you. See, I have this friend whose generosity is unparalleled in the universe of my friends. It first showed itself when we were sophomores in college and she, upon seeing a poor, coatless woman shivering in a snowstorm, gave away not just the coat on her back, but also her hat, gloves, scarf and newly-purchased paper cup of hot tea. And twenty dollars. In keeping with the teachings of The Bible, a book said friend lives by, she donates fifteen percent of every paycheck to charity, sometimes more. Whenever I mock people, which is about every six minutes, if this friend is around she'll likely ask me why I feel the need to be so mean. I know plenty of selfish, angry people. They're easy to find. But I don't know many people like Elizabeth Cruz.

—from "My Life," by Lauren Fernández

elizabeth

"Y OU CRAZY DYKE," the man shouts.

I press 7 to skip the message. I don't need to hear the rest of it. There have been dozens that start the same way. They want me dead. They hate me. Every evangelical minister in the area seems to have ordered them to descend upon me, to save me from the fires of hell.

A few crazies have even trekked to WRUT-TV from places like Montana as if they were going to appear on *Good Morning America*. But instead of holding posters wishing someone a happy birthday, they wave signs proclaiming, ADAM AND EVE, NOT ADAM AND STEVE. Of greater concern to me than these well-intentioned lunatics is the fact that the producer of the national news show who had, until I was outed, begged me to join their team, now will not return my calls. I get the assistant, and from her chilly tone I sense my worst fear, after losing my mother—they don't want me anymore.

My life changed instantly, after the first *Herald* piece came out. I stopped at the Dunkin' Donuts near the WRUT downtown office that morning, for a strong coffee. The cashier, Lorraine, an older Haitian immigrant who is usually very nice to me, dumped my change on the counter instead of putting it in my hand, and clicked her tongue with disapproval. The *Herald* was spread out on the back counter, by the bagel toaster, open to the now-famous picture of me kissing Selwyn. Lorraine didn't wish me a good day, as usual. She did not tell me about her children in college. She didn't say, as she often used to, that she wished I were her child. She muttered "Disgusting," and retreated to the back room.

My mother must know. But she has yet to mention it. I don't know how to bring it up. I know she makes a point of reading the Boston papers online every day, as a way to stay involved in my life. She hasn't changed toward me in any perceptible way. We'll speak of it eventually, I am sure. Just not now.

Maybe I'm paranoid. I used to look forward to spring in Boston, for walks through the greening Common with all its gardens. Now, I avoid public places. I keep the curtains closed. I work. But I hurry home and hide. Selwyn and I have tried to retain some normalcy; we rent DVDs on the Internet, eat microwave popcorn out of the big plastic Ikea bowl, paint each other's toenails on the floor while the pot roast cooks. Selwyn has sprouted gray hairs since this began, and she gulps down Maalox as if it were water. She is like a green plant, and slowly dies without sunlight. She does not complain about the new locks on our doors, or the threats in her mailbox at the college. But I know. I know. If things don't change, I will lose her. "I had to fall in love with a movie star," she jokes. But there is some truth to it.

The notoriously dull *Gazette* joined the witch-hunt, publishing polls and pie charts about public opinion of the fiasco. They ran a pro-gay editorial, but that did not help enough. Lauren has been kind to me in all of this, and wrote a couple of columns in support of me, telling people to mind their own business. With the exception of Sara, all my friends have stuck by me, which I didn't expect. People surprise you.

Lately the crazies have gotten scarier, with news of my sexuality having made it to that right-wing Christian radio show by Dr. Dobson. Now, there's a national E-mail crusade to destroy me. They write to my boss, a form letter from a Web site. On the site is a letter for the national network as well. I am a hunted woman, a hated woman, and *60 Minutes* wants an interview. (I said no.)

My colleagues don't speak of it. They don't ask if I'm okay. They pretend nothing has changed. But they are uncomfortable. I can feel it in the way they avoid looking at me in the elevator. I can feel it in the fact that we are the only news outlet in town that has *not* dealt with my sexuality as a topic.

What can you do with your heart at a time like this? In the darkness and the cold of my solitary early mornings, I always counted on Lorraine's bright smile and conversation to help me start the day. We had a solidarity that comes from living in darkness, from—what is the word?—*eking*. From eking out our existence on the far side of the sun, from hanging our morning eyes on stars, struggling to stay awake. We usually talked for five, ten minutes. It wasn't much. But it's the symbol of the thing. I miss normalcy. Comforting. Sometimes she gave me free coffee. I am not welcome in my own life now.

As I waited in the truck at a stoplight near my house yesterday evening, an unkempt neighbor, white like raw dough, laughed at me from his doorstep, eating grapes out of his fist in a way too brutal for the delicate fruit. He shouted, "What a waste. Look at ya. Good-lookin' nigger, too. What you need is a good man to set you straight." He *cackled*. He cackled long and hard, like a crazy man. The world spun and there was nowhere to hide. Did he really grab himself *there* with his big, bready fingers? Did he really show me his big pink swollen tongue, this man I used to greet over my fence?

I drove to work in a panic this morning, *mi corazón* flapping against my sternum, and now here I am, in the dark underground parking lot, afraid to get out, cleaning my voice mail on my cell phone. Selwyn thinks I am making far too big a deal out of what she calls the "limited, disposable controversy of your lesbianism," but Selwyn is not a journalist. I am. I shiver, and not from the cold. The world frightens me. I have reported the news for five years. Parents strangle their children. Men torture cats. People make slaves of others. I know what evil the world is made of.

"Don't obsess on this," Selwyn says in my head. That's impossible.

I turn on the car stereo, tune it to the AM news station. It takes ten minutes, then there it is. Liz Cruz is a lesbian, favorite topic of the day. I turn the dial to the talk radio call-in station. The host is laughing, then says, "What is it about these Spics, Jack? Are all the good-looking ones gay? First Ricky Martin, then Liz. Ricky, I don't care. My wife wants you, buddy, so screw all the men you want, you know what I mean? It's great. But not Liz! My wife, she's so happy. Now she's getting even. Life sucks. Next thing you know, they'll say Penélope Cruz is gay. I'll have to kill myself."

I hurry from my car to the elevator.

I go through makeup and the morning meeting without anyone saying a word, though I can tell by the sidelong way they examine me now that they all want to see me gone from their midst. Of course they do. Our ratings are slipping. They all pretend it's okay that I'm still here.

I read my way through the newscast, do what I can to steel myself. Make myself a woman of steel. I cannot care right now. Maybe they won't say a word, maybe they won't honor the venom at all. Maybe I will wake up from this dream and all will be as it was. There is nothing in the news-cast about me.

The newscast ends. I head to the dressing room to remove my makeup. I do not change out of my bright blue suit jacket and pearls. I wear jeans because no one ever sees what news-casters wear below the waist. I usually change into sweats or something more comfortable, but not today. Today I do not want to feel the chill of the WRUT air on my body. I do not want to be exposed.

The news director, John Yardly, knocks on my door, then comes in and sighs three distinct times and shuts the door behind him. It is only morning, but already this heavy-footed man with large glasses glistens with sweat and smells of onions. I can't imagine what it is he eats for breakfast.

"You okay?" he asks. His fingers tap nervously across his thighs. He's always flinchy as a sparrow, but today more so than usual. I manage a smile and tell him that I am. "That's good," he says. "Because we're all concerned for you. You know that."

I continue to remove my makeup, and look at him only momentarily in the mirror. His eyes lie. It is the first time he has mentioned the—how do you say?—hoopla about me. I can see it pains him.

"I'm just going to ask you straight out," he says. He looks embarrassed. "I mean, directly."

"It's okay," I say. "The word 'straight' doesn't offend me, John."

He chokes out a laugh.

"Is it true, Liz?"

Anger washes over me. Under me. Washes all around me. I want to float away. I need Selwyn here. She would know what to say. She would not hurt like this. She has been steeled for many years. This city, this life here, so cold. All coldness.

"Why?" I ask. "Would it make a difference?"

John shakes his head vigorously and laughs uncomfort-ably. "No, of course it wouldn't," he says. "I'm your friend.

We're friends, right? I just wanted to talk to you about it and let you know that if it's true all of us here at WRUT will support you and stand behind you. If you need to talk, I'm here."

"Have you all talked about it behind my back then?"

"No, of course not. But as news director I am going to make it clear that everyone is to be supportive. Nothing will change, in other words."

"Change? Like what?"

"I mean, you're still our favorite morning anchor."

"Oh, you mean like demote or fire me?"

"I didn't say that. I said things wouldn't change."

"It wouldn't be legal if they did," I say. "Right?" Massachusetts is one of the states where it is illegal to discriminate against someone for being gay or lesbian.

"No, it wouldn't," he says with a bitter smile. "But that's beside the point. My point is that even though we're getting more and more calls and E-mails every day—hundreds of them, Liz, from around the country and the world—asking us to get rid of you, we're not going to do that."

Hundreds of calls. They've gotten hundreds of calls.

"We could release a statement," he says. "Try to fix things."

"What kind of statement?"

"Denying it. We could discredit O'Donnell. Everyone hates her anyway."

"Is that why you program her on the show every week? Because everyone hates her?"

"Honestly, yes. People want to see what she says just so they can disagree with it. She's ruthless and tacky. You have a great advantage over her, Liz. People think you're pretty and nice. They think Eileen is a bitch."

"Let me think about the statement," I say. I have to admit, it would be nice to go back to the anonymity of before. At the same time, however, there's something liberating about having everyone, even Sara, finally know the truth. Whatever the consequences. And the truth will still be the truth. If we wage war against Eileen O'Donnell and the *Herald*, there will just be more people following me, more hiding, more of the real Elizabeth Cruz sneaking around the edges of my life with a flashlight and a compass, like I don't belong there, like I have no right to be me.

"We don't have a lot of time, if that's what you want to do. I'd like to get something out to the media in the next few hours at the latest. Thing like this, you can't let it go without acting for too long. I think we already waited too much, but I wanted to see where the public would go on it, and now we know. They're not losing interest. We have to protect ourselves. Better to be up front."

"I know. I'll let you know by the end of today, okay?"

"Fine. Nice work this morning, as always."

He gets up and opens the door. I start to walk past him, but he stops me.

"Before you take the elevator down to the garage, I think you should see something. Come with me."

He leads me to his office, which looks down six floors at the street below. It's midmorning. The usual Government Center bustle bustles, office workers rushing to their jobs. But down below, directly in front of the entrance to WRUT, are six people, bundled in their coats and hats, some holding signs, others burning candles, most chanting together. A couple hold children, or crosses. I can't hear exactly what they are saying, but I can guess. I have seen them as I drive in and out of the building for the past eight weeks. The wicked fire in their eyes says it. The signs say it. THINK OF THE CHILDREN, one says. OUR STATION, OUR VALUES, screams another. Parked along the curb are news trucks from the other stations in town. Reporters are interviewing the protesters.

"They've all been asking to come up and interview you," John tells me, jutting his jaw toward the reporters swarming around. "It's just the news they've been waiting for. Fucking lowlifes."

"I know," I say.

"Right."

"Why do they *care*? It's so medieval."

John doesn't answer at first. He stares at the people. I stare at the people. Together we stare for a full minute. Then, he says, "They care because they all wanted you, all the men in town. All the women wanted to be like you."

"That can't be true," I say.

"Sure it is. TV news isn't about news, Liz. It's about *entertainment*. It's about sex appeal. If you're gay, or lesbian, whatever, they can't fantasize the way they used to."

"Is that what you think?"

"It's what I *know*. Look at George Michael. When's the last time you heard one of his songs on the radio? We got to number one because of you, Liz," he says. "Because you're beautiful and charming and sweet. Because you were the perfect woman for this town. A beautiful black woman who talks like a white woman but is actually Hispanic. It was a goddamned coup. We got all the advocates off our asses when we hired you. We'll fight this thing. Right?"

His last statement was so offensive I'm not sure what to do. "I don't know."

"Think about it," he says with a worried sigh. "Just think about it."

"I will. Can I go now?"

He nods. "Be careful out there," he says. "People are crazy. You want security to go with you to your car?"

I nod.

The guard, a fat, masculine woman, gives me a sympathetic look. "Don't let them get to you," she says as I get into the truck. "They don't represent most Americans."

I put on my hat and sunglasses before I press the button to open the garage door and pull out into the bright light of the day.

Flashes pop and I am blinded.

"Jesus, Maria y Jose," I say. I floor the gas and pull away from the cameras, run the first red light just to put some distance between us. The reporters are worse than the protesters, making something out of nothing to boost their own ratings. I have the dizzy sense I'm being cannibalized. I take narrow back streets through the winding hills of the North End, and get on the freeway at an unpredictable entrance far from the station.

I've gotten so good at driving to throw people off I feel like a criminal. Why should I feel like this, just for being who I am? Why should I have to hide and run? I exhale deeply once I'm on the freeway, moving too fast to be caught.

But where am I headed? I don't want to go home or to Selwyn's. I can't call Lauren or Usnavys or Rebecca because they're all at work. That just leaves Sara. I need to talk to someone, get all this out and decide how to handle it. Will she talk to me? I have to figure out what I'm doing.

I use the cell phone to call Selwyn at her office.

"Don't go home," I say. "The reporters are swarming today."

"Jesus."

"Pretty much."

"We have dinner at Ron's tonight anyway," she says. Ron is her co-worker, a soft-spoken professor who teaches a course on the literature of hate. He and his wife have offered their home to us.

"Okay," I say. "But where do I go until then?"

"Somewhere safe, somewhere they've never seen you before."

Sara.

I dial Sara's number, and she answers, sounding tired and groggy.

She doesn't hang up on me, but she doesn't talk.

"Please," I beg her. "I miss you. I need to talk to you."

"I'm sorry, Liz," she says. "I can't. I'm planning my trip next week with Roberto. I'm sorry. I'm busy."

"Sara! They're out to crucify me!" I start to cry. "I don't know what else to do. I know you don't approve of me, but do you honestly hate me enough to see my career ruined by a bunch of jackass reporters?"

After a few moments of silence, she relents. "Okay, you can come here. But only for a little while. Until we figure out what to do. But you can't be here when Roberto gets home. He'd kill me."

sara

*O*YE, CHICA, WHAT have I done? Elizabeth should not be here. *Mira,* I know that. But she sounded like she was desperate. And she needs me right now. You don't turn your back on ten years of friendship because your husband wants you to. I don't. But still, I need time to talk to Roberto about all of this, to make sure he's not going to do anything really stupid. With him, you never know. Now she's here, in my house, and school's letting out. I don't want the boys to see her here when they get home and tell their dad. I'll have to find a new way to bribe their mouths shut. Candy doesn't do it anymore.

Vilma keeps dusting the same spot on the boys' video-game TV, listening to the conversation I'm having with Elizabeth. She's nosy, but won't betray me. I know her. She is loyal to me, not Roberto.

Elizabeth sits on the overstuffed armchair in our media room, sipping the coffee Vilma brought her. When she brings the small white cup to her lips, her once-graceful hand with the long, thin fingers trembles; it makes a racket every time she puts it back in the saucer. She stares at the spotless beige carpet, clears her throat as if to speak, then freezes.

"Liz," I say. She looks at me, her face like a mask. "*Fíjate.* I don't care who you sleep with. I really don't."

"Really?"

"Yes, really. What do you think I am, an idiot? It makes

no difference to me. But Roberto doesn't want me to see you anymore. He thinks—he thinks . . ." I can't finish the thought. I look down and mumble, stir an imaginary drink in the air. "Me and you, you and me. You know."

Across the room, Vilma trips on her own feet, gasps.

"He thinks we're lovers?" Elizabeth asks with a laugh. I can see Vilma's shoulders rise up, tense. She moves to dust the CD rack, letting out a sigh as she goes. Eavesdropper.

"Yes," I say. "That's what he thinks." Vilma shakes her head. Elizabeth keeps laughing. "Hey," I say. "Why is that so funny? You think I'm ugly or something? I'd be an okay lover. I'd be a great lover, *tu sabes*."

"No, no," Elizabeth says. "I don't doubt that. But I've honestly never seen you that way. I've never—" she cuts herself off.

I hear Vilma whisper "Oh, my God" to herself in Spanish. She gives me a look.

"You've never been attracted to me?" I hear the surprise in my voice. I have to admit, I'm a little disappointed, *chica*. I mean, why wouldn't she find me attractive? I'm some kind of monster now? I should tell Vilma to beat it, but it's sort of fun to shock her like this.

"I'm sorry, Sarita," Liz says affectionately. "You're not . . . my type."

I frown, hurt. "Who is?" I ask her, not sure I want to know the answer. She smiles shyly, one eyebrow arched. "One of the *sucias*?" I ask. She nods weakly. "No way!" I shout. "Okay, okay, *déjame ver*, let me guess." I think for a moment. Rebecca has the shortest hair. Lesbians like women with short hair, don't they?

"Rebecca," I say.

"Not in a million years," answers Liz.

"Then who?"

"Lauren."

This time, I laugh. "Lauren? Crazy Lauren? Writing about being a blooming seed in the paper Lauren? *Coño, chica, pero 'tas loca*. I'm way better-looking than Lauren. *Soy la más bellísima de las sucias*."

Liz laughs. "Okay, if you say so."

"*Olvídate, chica.* You know I'm kidding. Lauren's pretty. She's *crazy*, but she's pretty. She's just weird enough that she might—oh," I stop, realizing I've just insulted Elizabeth.

"Don't worry about it," she says.

"How long have you felt this way about her?"

Elizabeth blushes, or what passes for a blush on her. She looks like a schoolgirl, knees pressed together, mouth pouty. "Years."

"*Ay, Dios mío,*" I say, and we share a good chuckle. I notice Vilma looking at me with a warning in her eyes, so I address her, in Spanish. "I know you claim not to speak English, ma'am, but if this is all too much for your delicate constitution, I'm sure there are other rooms you can dust."

Vilma scowls and leaves the room without a word.

"Have you told her?" I ask Elizabeth, feeling like a gossipy girl.

"Vilma?" Liz asks, incredulous.

"No, stupid. *La Lauren.*"

"No no no no no. Never."

"Can I tell her?" God, I'd love to see Lauren's face when she heard this one. The girl feels everything way too much, lets everything eat her up inside. This would throw her for a major loop. It'd be fun.

"I'd appreciate it if you didn't."

"Please? You never know. She might, you know."

"She won't. Don't. I'm serious."

"Fine. Ruin all the fun."

"Oh, sure. This is fun. I'm not going to get the national job because Rupert hates gays. Running for my life from a bunch of insane reporters. So fun."

"Hey," I say, "what goes around comes around. It's poetic justice, don't you think? The famous anchor and reporter all of a sudden the subject of news?"

"Good point," Liz says. "I hadn't thought about it like that."

The smell of the coffee makes me want to throw up. Dr. Fisk says the morning sickness should have subsided by now, the fourth month, but it hasn't. I'm hungry all the time, but nothing looks good except frozen waffles and peanut butter. The nausea has gotten worse. The good thing about it is this means I'm going to have a girl. My eyes want to close. I want to curl up and sleep for a thousand years. I don't have the energy for this situation. Or the patience.

"*Coño, mujer, que lo que tu 'tás pensando, eh?*" I finally shout at Elizabeth. She bucks up, startles, spills coffee on the colorful floral pattern in the chair's fabric. "You should just quit Christians for Kids and get on with your life. Let them have those ladies with all the makeup and the fake eyelashes. I don't know why you haven't quit yet, honestly. Do yourself a favor and find another charity."

"I can't," she says, dabbing at the spill with her sleeve.

"What do you mean you 'can't'? You have to! Get off the crazy Christian radar. Wait for this whole stupid thing to blow over. No big deal."

"If I quit, then they win, Sara. Don't you see? If I quit then it's like I admit that you can't be a good Christian and be a lesbian. And I don't believe that. I don't believe that at all. I believe God makes no mistakes, and that I'm an earthly expression of His perfection."

"Ever considered becoming a Jew?" I ask. "We have lesbian rabbis."

"I was raised with Jesus," she says. "You know that. I can't just go and be a *Jew*."

"Jesus was a Jew."

"Let's not go *there*," Liz says in English.

"Probably shouldn't."

"No. Probably not."

"Vilma," I call. "We've got a spill in here, *mi amor*. Can you help us?"

Vilma returns from her gossipmonger exile with a wet rag, bucket, and cleaning solution, ears ready for more. Elizabeth gets up, sits cross-legged on the floor next to the coffee table.

"You're going to ruin your health obsessing on this stupidity," I tell her, finally lapsing into the Spanish we most often use with each other. She stares at her tennis shoes. Vilma pretends to hear nothing, her face impassive. Nosy woman. I continue, "The best thing you can do is distance yourself from these people who want to hurt you. Remember, they don't know you like your friends do. They're just writing crap because that's all they know how to do. They've all probably been jealous of you for years, and now they're gloating because you probably won't get the big national break they all dream of. Reporters are hateful little people a lot of the time. Don't let it get to you. Worry about your happiness."

Liz looks at me for a moment, frowning, then says, "You're not one to talk, I think."

"*Ella tiene razón*," Vilma says, without looking up from her task. "Listen to her, Sarita."

It hurts. They're right, of course. But this isn't supposed to be about me. It's supposed to be about Liz. "I wish I never told you all that," I say. "It's not as bad as you think."

Vilma glares at me for a split second, then resumes scrubbing.

"Right. You're just . . . clumsy. Right? Isn't that what you tell everyone?"

I curl my feet under me on the sofa, as if that might protect me from the truth in her words. I pull the bottom of my long blue sweater down over me, to cover the growing curve of my belly and any scratches or bruises that might be showing.

"My heart is broken, just broken," I say. "I can't believe you were shtupping women all these years and never told me."

"I don't *shtup*. That's what men do."

"Whatever you do."

"I love them, Sara. I love women. Don't make it crass."

"I'm sorry," I say. "But I really am hurt. Why didn't you trust me enough to tell me?"

"Sara," she says apologetically. "It's not you I didn't trust. It was me. It took me a long time to even be able to admit it to myself, don't you see that? I still haven't, not entirely."

"I just can't believe it's true, not you. I mean, I always thought lesbians were ugly. You're so feminine. So pretty."

She says only one word to this: "*Mitos*." Myths.

Indeed, Liz looks pretty, normal as always, but I can see circles of exhaustion underneath her eyes. She looks so tired, so sad, so alone. I can't believe she's here. I can't believe she is . . . one of *those*. I try to picture her with a woman, and can't.

"What's it feel like?" I ask.

"What?" she says.

"Being with a woman."

"I don't know how to answer that. Every person is different."

"I've always kind of wondered, you know, normal curiosity."

"Uh-huh."

"I bet a woman knows how to please you a lot better than a man, huh?"

"I don't know, Sara. It really depends more on the person."

"Right. That makes sense. I'm sorry. I'm babbling. I don't know what to say. I wish you'd trusted me more. You should have told me."

"I didn't know how you'd take it."

"I'd take it how I take everything else. I'm not some kind of Dr. Laura."

"I'm not saying you are. It's just I had to be cautious, so much at stake."

"I just wish you'd told me. That's the only thing that's changed between us, you know? I don't trust you as much."

"I'm still *me*," Elizabeth says, tapping her chest with one hand. "Nothing has changed."

"No, I think everything has changed. For you. I think you better quit that organization, and maybe even think about quitting your job. People are crazy, Liz. I got two words for you: Matthew Shepard."

Liz shakes her head. "I don't think it's that bad. Come on. Be reasonable. Most people are open-minded, I think."

Vilma dusts the coffee table, makes brief, sympathetic eye contact with me.

"Are you certain you're a lesbian?"

"I think so, yes."

"Then live as one." I can't believe I'm saying this to Liz. "Be proud of who you are, *mi vida*. To hell with everyone else. Enjoy the attention. Think of all the gay and lesbian kids who see you and feel better about themselves."

"I'll make a deal with you," she says.

"What's that?"

"I'll do that, live proud as a lesbian, when you leave Roberto. He's not going to change. You know that, don't you?"

"We're not talking about me, remember?"

"Why not? Let's talk about you."

Vilma brings a plate of cheese and crackers, and the smell of the cheese sends puke signals to my brain. I guess my daughter doesn't like cheese. I push myself up, run to the bathroom off the kitchen. I don't have time to close the door. I don't even have time to make it to the toilet. Pale yellow bile and chunks of waffle splat on the green tile floor, on the white pedestal sink, on the toilet seat.

Liz follows me, worried, and stands in the bathroom door.

"Oh, my God. Sarita. Are you okay?" she asks.

I press my hands onto the toilet seat for support, turn my head to see her. She looks so pretty. How is it possible? If I were that pretty I'd want every man in the world wanting me. I feel my abdomen contract in a heave, and turn to the water. This time, the vomit sloshes into the bowl. I heave long after there is nothing left in me. My mouth tastes bitter and raw, my teeth filmy and thin.

"Do you want to go to the hospital?" she asks.

"Go away," I say, dabbing my mouth with toilet paper. "Get out of here." I don't think I've vomited in front of Elizabeth since we were freshmen in college, too drunk to care. "I like to hurl in private, if you don't mind."

"You're really sick, I'm sorry. I didn't know."

"I'm fine," I say. I pull the chain to flush the mock-antique toilet and stagger to the sink. I use toilet paper to wipe up the mess, rinse my mouth with cold water, wash my face, pat it dry with an Egyptian cotton towel, beige.

"No," I reconsider, looking at her in the mirror. "I'm not fine. I'm sick about all of this. I'm really worried about you."

"You're vomiting because of *me*?" she asks.

"Yes." I push her out of the way and walk back to the TV room. Vilma has been standing like a sentry outside the bathroom door, with the bucket and rag. She does not look at me or Elizabeth as we pass.

Elizabeth follows me down the hall to the media room, walking fast. I hear Vilma running the water in the bathroom, cleaning up after me. Good old Vilma.

"I'm sorry, Sara," Elizabeth says. Her hands fly in front of her face as she speaks. That used to be what made us such good friends, the Latin way we argued. "I should have been honest with you from the start." She continues to talk, smacking the back of one hand into the palm of the other. "I'm sorry you're letting this get to you. Don't. I'm a big girl. I can handle it. The fact that you accept me no matter what is more important to me than what any of those people at the station think."

I look at the digital clock flashing on the cable box. The boys will be home from school any minute now, wanting their soy milk and organic whole grain cookies, ready to show me their homework. I don't want them to find her here.

"You have to go," I say.

"Why?" she asks.

"Roberto," I say. "We can still be friends, but you have to give me some time to work on him about you. He's really angry about it."

"Roberto's angry because I'm a lesbian?" she asks.

"That's what he said. He called you a pervert and whatever. It's stupid. Don't worry about it. I just can't have the boys catch you here. He thinks we're having an affair. You and me. *Que locura, te lo digo.* Why would he think a thing like that?"

"Sara," she says, coming to sit near me. She sighs, looks me hard in the eye.

"What?" I ask her. "Why are you looking at me like that?"

"There's something I should have told you a long time ago."

I get a pit, another wave of nausea. I can sense what she's going to say. "Don't," I say. "I don't think I want to hear it."

"You should know."

We stare at each other for a long minute, then she says, "You should know because I think you could be in real danger from him."

"Go ahead," I say, bracing.

"Back in college, you remember that trip we all took to Cancún for spring break, you, me, Roberto, that guy Gerald I was dating, Lauren, and that one guy, whatever his name was?"

"Alberto. Pimple man."

"Alberto. Zits galore. Him."

"Yes. How could I forget a trip like that?"

"Okay." She takes a deep breath. "There was one day when we went scuba diving, and you had a hard time with the equipment and decided to wait for us on the boat, you remember that?"

"Yes. I said I'd rather 'Cuba dive,' with margaritas on shore."

"Well, we were all over at this coral reef, and Roberto . . ." She stops. Takes a deep breath. "Roberto swam over to me and touched me under the water."

"What do you mean he 'touched you'?" I'm furious.

"He touched me. He ran his hand along my back and left it on my rear end."

"No, he didn't."

"He did."

"He probably just got pushed to you by the current."

"Sara. Please."

"And what did you do?"

"We were in shallow water. I grabbed his hand and pulled him up and asked him what he was doing."

"And?"

"He said he was doing what came naturally to him as a man."

"That's so stupid. Roberto wouldn't say something that stupid."

"That's what he said."

"We were young, it doesn't mean anything." I can't believe I'm saying such words. I sound like an idiot.

"It was long ago, Sarita. But he looks at me. He's looked at me since then."

"So? Looking's a crime now? Everyone looks at you."

"I just think that might be why he's so angry. And from what you're telling me, things just keep getting worse with him. I'm worried about you. He's not a saint or something. You don't need him."

"I hate him sometimes."

"You should. But not for what he did to me. You should hate him for what he does to *you*."

I look at the clock. I can hear our nanny pulling into the driveway with my car. "You have to go, Liz. Now."

"I'm so sorry, Sara." She hugs me. I hug back, shove her away, hug her again.

"Go. We'll talk later."

"Okay." A tear slips from the corner of her eye down her cheek. "I'm scared."

"My boys are coming home and I don't want them around you."

"God, Sara, do you have to be so mean? I love those boys, and they love me."

"I don't want them to tell their father you were here," I correct myself. "He'd kill me, Liz."

"You think he'd go that far?"

"It's an expression, *cariño*."

"It's more than that and you know it. He could very well kill you."

Vilma peeks her head in the door and asks if I need anything.

"Some saltines," I say. "Please. And some 7UP."

"Yes, ma'am."

"Saltines and 7UP?" Liz asks, a smile flashing through her tears as she gathers her purse and keys. "Are you expecting again, Sara? Don't lie to me. I can always tell when you lie."

"You should quit that job," I tell her. "And quit that charity. There are tons of charities out there. You can get another job."

"You are! You're pregnant again!" She hugs me again. I smile.

"Don't tell anyone," I whisper.

"I won't. Congratulations, *mi amor*."

"Don't call me that," I joke, "or I'll think I'm your type." I blow her a dramatic kiss. She laughs.

"Nos vemos, chica," she says.

"I'll call you soon," I say. "Be careful out there."

She takes a quick look around the entry as she shrugs into her men's parka. "And you," she says. "You be careful in *here*."

I walk her to the front door, and open it. She stops on the front step, turns back, and tries to say something, but I hear the children coming in through the garage door to the kitchen, and shut the front door in Liz's face.

I waddle upstairs to my room and collapse on the oversized California king bed. Maybe it's the emotions from the pregnancy, or maybe it's the shock of having to accept that my best friend is *one of those*, or having to admit to myself what I have always instinctually known: Roberto is in love with Elizabeth.

Vilma appears at my side with a tray of crackers and soda.

"Leave it right there," I say, wiping the tears on the back of my hand.

She doesn't move.

"What?" I ask.

"You should eat something. You don't look good."

"I can't eat right now," I sob. "My heart is broken."

Vilma sets the tray on my bedside table, takes the glass of soda in her expert hands, and sits next to me on the bed. "Here," she says softly, motherly. "Drink, Sarita. You need your strength." I part my lips, and sip a little soda. It makes me dizzy.

"No, please, I can't," I tell her.

Vilma holds a cracker to my lips.

"The baby needs her strength, too," she says.

"You know?" I ask.

Vilma nods almost imperceptibly. "Of course, Sarita. Eat."

I nibble at the cracker, thrilled that she has finally called me Sarita again. When I finish, Vilma makes me eat two more. She makes me finish the glass of soda.

"How did you know?" I ask.

"I know things," she says, tapping her breast over her heart. "Now you get some rest. All this stress is bad for the baby."

Vilma kisses me on the head the way she used to when I was a child, and leaves the room.

I sob into my goose down comforter with the pink flannel duvet for five minutes, until Sethy and Jonah come bounding into my room, all boy energy. They climb onto the bed. Jonah smooths my hair from my eyes with his small hand, and asks me what's wrong. Sethy beats his chest like Tarzan and performs wild somersaults off the bed onto the floor. I tell them Mommy fell down and has a boo-boo and she'll be fine.

"Is Daddy home?" Jonah asks. "Did he make the boo-boo? I hate Daddy sometimes."

"No," I say. "Don't say such things."

Then I hug them and ask them about their days.

"Did you know *Tia* Liz is a *thespian*?" Seth asks, his mouth open in mock horror, his hands slapped to the side of his face like Macaulay Culkin in that stupid movie.

"Shh," Jonah says to his brother. "Don't say anything."

"Who told you that?" I ask Seth, shocked at his timing. Did he see her here? God, I hope not. He better not say anything to his father about it.

"Andrew Lipinski."

"Well, Andrew Lipinski's mommy should wash his mouth out with soap, because it's not true. Don't talk about that again in this house."

We talk more about school, and then I send them down to Sharon and Vilma for their afternoon snacks. I am not usually so distant with my boys, but right now I feel like I can't keep it all together. You know how it is, *sabes*, like any little thing might set you off. I don't like to cry in front of my children.

Roberto comes home from work in a good mood. His cheerful voice echoes in the foyer.

"I won my case, *amorcito*," he calls. He whistles the tune "We're in the Money."

"*Felicidades,*" I shout, congratulating him. Thank God. At least there's *some* good news today in this house. I fix my hair, wipe the mascara from underneath my eyes, and stand at the top of the stairs, smiling like the perfect wife. I don't want him to know I know about Cancún. I will never bring it up, God help me. Roberto dances, holds his arms open to me, and I do my best to rush to him with as much false excitement as I can manage, think of Ginger Rogers all the way down the stairs. He lifts me off the floor, swings me around, laughing. He carries me into the kitchen, sets me down, and plants a kiss on my lips. "You look beautiful," he says. "You always look more beautiful when I win a case."

Vilma frowns into the pot on the stove, disapproving. Roberto doesn't notice. He jokes with Vilma as she prepares our dinner, kosher Cuban steak with onions, rice, and beans and plantains.

"Smells incredible," he says, patting Vilma on the back. He dips a fork into the beans and samples them, leaning past her. He brings his fingers to his lips and kisses the tips. "Incredible."

"If you'll excuse me, *cariño*, I have to go pee-pee," I say, smiling. The smell of the steak frying sends me to the bathroom again. I shut the door, and run the water to cover the sounds I make over the toilet.

WHEN I FEEL better, I search for Roberto and the boys and find them in the media room. Roberto crawls on all fours on the plush carpet, with Seth on his back. Jonah sits to the side and watches with serious eyes.

"What are you crazy kids doing?" I say.

"Are you kidding?" Roberto says. "We're cowboys and Indians! My boys are the greatest! *Olvídalo*."

I flop onto the couch, and Jonah climbs into my lap. He sits on his knees, facing me, and puts a finger to my lips, concern creasing his tiny brows.

"Are you okay, Mommy?" he whispers.

"Of course," I lie. I kiss his cheek. "Go play with your father."

"Do I have to?"

"Jonah! Get." I lift him off my lap and push him toward Roberto.

Vilma serves us dinner in the kitchen, instead of the dining room, because Roberto wants to watch the local news to see if they've covered his big win. He works for Fidelity Investments, and the case has been in the news for months.

The boys eat their dinner and tease each other, and our nanny retreats to her room to read and use the Internet to talk to her friends back in Switzerland. I take a few bites of beans, struggle to keep them down. Vilma notices that I'm not feeling well. She offers me some more crackers. Roberto does not notice. He is chewing with his mouth open, one hand on his belly and the other pointing the remote and flipping the channels on the TV on the counter.

There are a few commercials, and then the local nightly news begins. I look at the television, and can't believe my eyes. There, on the screen, is our house.

Our house.

The camera moves and focuses on Elizabeth's truck, in our driveway. The reporter starts to talk about how the recently "outed" newscaster for the rival station had taken a crazy zigzag route to this "luxurious house in Brookline, near the Chestnut Hill Reservoir" after "crowds" of out-of-state religious protesters and reporters scared her this morning.

Roberto drops the remote to the floor with a clatter. His fist lands on the table.

The reporter looks down at her notes, then says that public records show the house registered to Roberto J. Asís, "a prominent local attorney involved in the controversial Fidelity Investments lawsuit that's been in the news recently."

The reporter says the attorney is married to an old college friend of Cruz's, Sara Behar. "The reason for this visit is unknown," the reporter says suggestively, "and Liz Cruz, when we caught up with her here, wasn't talking."

"Just leave people alone," Liz says to the camera as she shields her face. She is crying. "Mind your own business. Leave this poor family alone."

I can't get to the bathroom in time, and throw up on the kitchen floor as I run. Roberto is already up from his seat, spitting bits of steak as he hurls every insult he can think of at me. The boys hug each other and scream. Jonah starts to follow me, screaming *"Mami, Mami,* no!" but Sethy grabs him and drags him under the table with him. "Hide!" he screams.

Roberto catches me by the hair and spins me toward him. The whole kitchen smells of my vomit. "Daddy! Stop it!" one of the boys cries.

"What did I tell you?" he asks, stabbing his finger into my face. "What did I tell you about that lesbian coming to this house?"

"I know," I say weakly, "I tried to stop her, but she came anyway. She was afraid, and said she didn't have anywhere else to go. I'm sorry."

"Oh, you tried to stop her? Is that why she was here in this house? Because you stopped her?" He shoves me into the counter. I cover my belly instinctively with my hands and back away.

"Please, Roberto, don't," I beg. Vilma and Sharon are nowhere to be found. Vilma has tried to help me before, but I asked her to stay out of it. Sharon tried to help once, too, but Roberto told her that if she did not mind her own business he would have her sent back to Switzerland.

"Our *house,*" he roars. "That was *our house.* I can't have our house associated with that woman. Do you know what this could do to my career? Are you *crazy?*"

He grabs me again as I try to run.

"So, are you in love with her?" he asks, his face centimeters from mine. His hand twists my sweater and rips it.

"What? No!" I struggle out of his grip and lunge away, toward the door that leads from the kitchen to the backyard, where the melting snow from the last storm of the season taps a rhythm on the wood of the porch. I've never seen him this angry before.

"You heard me. Do you have something going on with her?"

"You're crazy!" I scream. He whacks me square between the shoulder blades and knocks the wind out of me. I fall to the tile floor and scoot away. He is knocking things from the counters, coffeemaker, blender, a porcelain cookie jar shaped like a cat that shatters near the table where my children hide. He is a monster.

I can hear the boys crying.

"Seth, Jonah," I cry as he grabs my face and squeezes it hard, twisting my head around to the side and yanking me to stand again. The pain is unbearable. I scream. The boys. I have to protect the boys. "Go to Vilma's room, and lock the door. Now!" They obey me, scattering like frightened birds.

"It's nothing like you think," I say. "Besides, I'm not the one who hit on Liz in Cancún, am I? That was you."

"What?" he asks. "What did you say?" His face is centimeters from mine. I can smell the steak and onions on his breath. A drop of his saliva lands in my eye as he speaks.

"You heard me. I know you love her. That's what this is about. You're pathetic."

He slaps me.

I escape his hold once more, open the back door, and run out onto the porch, into the dark cold of the evening, crying. I can see my breath, clouds of steam. My world is falling apart. The temperature feels low enough that the melting snow might have started to freeze again, in thick, clear ice. Roberto follows me, his eyes crazed.

"Who told you this?" he asks.

"Liz," I say, balancing myself against the railing.

He is on top of me, wrangling me into a headlock of some sort. "What did she say?"

"Nothing." I can't move. He pulls me out of the headlock, close to him, in a too-tight hug.

There are tears in Roberto's eyes. "Nothing?" he asks, stabbing a hand between my legs. "She said nothing? Did she tell you she screwed me? Eh? Right there, between the legs? Did she tell you that part? That she did me in the hotel when you were getting a massage?"

"No," I say. "I don't believe it."

"Did she tell you she did me again when we got back? When you were at your mother's?"

"Stop lying, you *sinvergüenza*."

"It's true. She did." He's smiling, the bastard. "In our bed, and she *liked* it." He pumps his hips hard into my body. "She liked it hard, too, because she's a whore just like you. No wonder the two of you lick each other all the time."

This time, I slap him. "*Carajo,*" I scream. "I hate you." He grabs my hands and twists them back until I think they'll snap off the wrists.

"No!" I scream. "Don't! Roberto!"

He is growling, cursing, insulting me in every way he can think of. The wood of the porch is slick, and I am careful not to fall. I hold the banister for dear life.

"Please, Roberto, I'm pregnant," I cry. "I can't afford a fall right now."

He stops and stares.

"You better not be lying," he says.

"No, I swear to you I'm not lying. Why do you think I've been gaining weight? I hardly eat anything anymore! Why do you think I run to the bathroom every ten seconds? It's to throw up, Roberto."

"Nice try," he says. "That's not going to help you now. Lies won't help you anymore with me, you understand what I'm saying to you?"

"I'm not lying. I *am* pregnant. I was waiting for our anniversary to tell you, to surprise you. I was going to tell you next week in Argentina. Please."

The tears come hot and heavy from my eyes, millions of them. The sight of them excites him.

Roberto shakes me. "Tell me the truth, Sara," he demands. "This isn't a game."

"I'm telling the truth. We're going to have a little girl."

"A little girl?" He still holds me in a painful grip, but his eyes are softening a bit, hopeful.

"Let's go inside," I say. "I'll show you the pregnancy test. I've been hiding it in the closet."

"You better not be lying about this," he says again.

"What about you?" I ask. "Are you lying? Did you really sleep with her?"

"Yes," he says.

"Do you love her?"

"I did," he says. "But I'm over it now. I love you, Sarita. And I can't stand the thought of you and her as a couple. It makes me crazy. It's the worst insult a man can think of." He is panting, red-faced, furious.

"I'm not a lesbian," I tell him. "I'm your *wife*. I love you. You're the only man I've ever loved. Why do we do this to each other? To the kids? *Ay*, Roberto. For the love of God. We need professional help."

"Are you really pregnant?" His voice is smooth, his mouth almost curling into the sweet smile that makes my heart melt.

I run my hand along the side of his face, feeling sorry for him the way I do every time he apologizes after hitting me, "I swear I am."

He yanks my arm in what I think is a move to pull me close, but something happens. I slip on the ice, lose his hand, and then time slows, and I feel each step as I hit it, falling first on my tailbone, then my back, and then rolling right onto my stomach. One, two, three, four, five, six, seven, eight. I hit all eight steps, and land on the sharp ice down below. Did he push me? Or did I slip? I don't know.

I can't move. The pain in my back is too intense. My head is bleeding into my eyes, and my mouth is full of hot, salty liquid. Blood. I hope that it is over, but it isn't. He follows me, cursing and screaming in terror. I want to tell him to be careful on the steps, but I can't talk.

"What's wrong with you?" he cries. "What are you doing falling down the stairs if you're pregnant? You better not be lying to me. Is this how you cover your lies? By falling down the stairs?"

The pain in my uterus comes instantly. I feel a pop, the same way you do when your water breaks and you go into labor. Only this time, it's six months too soon, and the pain is in my entire body. I am paralyzed, either by fear or by injury. I don't know. He kneels next to me, and when I don't move or speak, he squeezes my cheeks, hard. "Get up," he hisses. He's lost his mind. He slaps me again. "This is no time to play games with me, woman. Get up. If you're really pregnant, get up." Then he does something unthinkable: He kicks me, again and again, in the side, and I feel the blood come in cramping waves. Not my baby.

"Please, Roberto, for the love of God," I cry inside my head. "Stop, please."

Then he kicks me again, in the head. I hear a crunch inside my face. In a burst of stars and red, I see Vilma rush down the steps and jump on top of him from behind, a kitchen knife flashing in her hand.

She is screaming, "You killed her, you son of a bitch, you killed her this time!" I see her swollen legs in their knee-high hose fly into the air as he lifts her up, and body slams her to the ground next to me. I hear the knife clatter onto the ice.

It's the last thing I remember.

A new study to be published next week, in the March 24 issue of the BOSTON JOURNAL OF MENTAL HEALTH, *shows that the most successful people in our society also happen to be the best liars. The better you are at lying, the study says, the further you go in your career and personal life. I have to admit, I lie a lot—don't you? Boss asks how you're doing, and you say fine. Friend with ugly haircut asks your opinion and you say, Looks great. The more we care about someone, it seems, the more apt we are to lie to that person. Is it any wonder people are always disappointed in love? We evolved to trust liars most of all.*

—from "My Life," by Lauren Fernández

usnavys

"N AVI, I KNOW you're there. Pick up. Please. We need to talk."

No, huh-uh. I don't *think* so. Not until he apologizes for Rome. I pull the throw blanket around me and let him tell it to the machine.

Three months, and he hasn't had the nerve. Then, last week, he starts calling me again, out of the blue, like nothing happened. I'm not falling for it this time, *m'ija*. What does he think I am, a masochist?

Plus, I stopped at the hospital this afternoon, after Rebecca called and told me what happened to Sara, and I just stared at her bruised-up face with all those tubes in and out of her, and I couldn't believe what the doctor told me: She might never wake up. Her husband did that to her. Rebecca was as surprised as I was by the whole thing. You think you know someone, and then something like this happens, and it's obvious, *m'ija*, that you never knew them at all. Who wants to get married after seeing that? I am so disappointed in the male race.

I hate them all.

I lie back on my green leather sofa and press the remote to change the channel on the big-screen TV across the room. The radiator comes on with a comforting hiss, and where the lace curtains have pulled away in the bay window I can see that rain has started to fall again. It's warmed up a lot, *m'ija*, but some nights you just want the heater on anyway, you know what I mean? Comfort. You need some comfort. I arrange the takeout containers on my lap, and dig in. Soupy chicken, rice, red beans, salad. Comfort food. Two orders of everything. They never give you enough when you order it to go.

I need to get a bigger rug for this room. In this damp cold, it isn't enough. I need warm, tonight. It's one of those nights, *m'ija*, where all you want to do is cuddle with someone big and strong, unless you're me and you can't find anyone big and strong worth cuddling with. It's been like that all my life. I'm feeling so sorry for myself right now I could just cry. I need a good cry. I can cry alone, and I can cry in front of my girlfriends. But I can't cry in front of a man.

Men suck.

It all goes back to that man from Baní who got my mom pregnant in Puerto Rico twenty-nine years ago. Four years later, in Boston, he decided fatherhood was too much work. He went back to the Dominican Republic and left us here with nothing. You'd think I wouldn't remember him, I was so little when he left, but I do. I remember him very clearly. He was a large, dark man. Large as in heavy, but not tall. He was short, stocky, black, and had a thick Spanish accent. He used to have to roll up the bottoms of his pants. That must have been hard for him, you know? I don't think Boston was kind to him. He worked hard while he was here, and never got ahead. And that made him angry. I remember sitting there on the floor by his feet and looking up at him and him talking to me in a cartoon voice that he did to make me smile. It made me laugh. He was so thick and his arms were so strong when he picked me up and held me.

You might think I wouldn't remember the way he smelled in his neck area but I do, I remember he smelled like wood. He used to work as a mover on one of those trucks, lifting people's pianos up stairs all day long, and he came home smelling of wood and sweat. I remember all that like it was yesterday. I honestly do. My mom says there's no way I can remember all that about him, but I remember all right.

I remember my brother Carlos, too. He looked like our dad, and he started working for the movers, too, bringing money home. He made sure I did my homework and he sang me to sleep. I remember that those guys his age didn't like him much because he told the police about them robbing a store. The first chance they got they shot him. That first chance happened when I was there, when he was walking me home from the bus that used to take me to seventh grade across town at the white school. They killed him in front of me. I remember what it sounded like and looked like and smelled like, but I don't want to tell you now. I don't want to think about it. I've had to wake up out of that dream so many times, the one where it's happening all over again and I'm screaming so loud I wake myself up.

That's two men who loved me that I lost and I don't think my heart can take it again. You look at me and you think I'm happy and cheerful all the time, and you don't really know. No one can ever really know about loss the way I know about loss, you know what I'm saying? I finally told the *sucias* about it and they couldn't believe it. I waited eight years of knowing them to tell them about my dad and my brother, and they were shocked, *m'ija*, just totally and completely shocked. They thought they knew me, and that's how it is with me. People think they know me. They don't.

From what I've seen in this life, it's the poor men that get shot or leave you. The men with money look happy with their wives and babies. You don't find many men in the projects, you know what I mean? Where I'm from, you find boys, then later you either find them dead, in prison, or they go back to Puerto Rico or the Dominican Republic or wherever and you never hear from them again. Where I come from, the men break your heart.

Sometimes when I get to thinking about it too hard I feel like I can't go on. As crazy as it sounds, days like this— when all the little buds start popping up on the tree branches everywhere, cheerful and hopeful and ready for spring and love, days like this bring me down so low I don't think I'll get up again. But I have to try, if for no other reason than I'm a landlord with responsibilities.

My tenant is making noise upstairs again. Renting out the top floor was the smartest thing I ever did. His rent covers my entire mortgage, minus one hundred dollars. But I have to listen to his life. He moves furniture, I hear it. He flushes the toilet, I hear it. I hear him brush his teeth, wash his clothes. When he accidentally drops a glass and it breaks, I hear it.

The money I save is worth it. The house is an old three-story Victorian that I'm still fixing up. There's a missing step on the way up the back stairs. And I have to fix that leak in my upstairs bathroom. But I'm a home owner, and I get the tax breaks.

I have my part of the house decorated the way I like it, with mirrors in gold frames, Art Deco vases on the floor with big pastel grasses and feathers in them. I've got shiny black sculptures of tall, thin cats in the doorways to some of the rooms, and a canopy bed in my room. I've got a glass dining table with black chairs. I have everything I need here, and I'm going next weekend and buying a whole bedroom set for the guest room even though my mother tells me it's pointless to make such big purchases for the home until I've found a good man. What if I never do? I ask her. She doesn't even answer that. I try to explain to her that I'm happy the way I am, perfectly content living in this house I own all by myself, filling the rooms with things I like, but I think she can tell it's a lie.

I'm not happy here all alone. I need me a man. A good Puerto Rican man.

Don't tell Lauren this, though. She'll get that pissed-off look of hers and she'll start to lecture me about how I have that guy right here and now but I can't get over how poor he is. I know it, okay? I know. But I did poor already. I don't want to do it again. Sue me! Lauren doesn't know the first thing about being poor. I don't mean poor like she thinks of poor, where you may not be able to go to private school or something. I mean poor where your mom has you looking through the cushions on the sofa to scrape up enough change to buy milk for the week after the food stamps run out and you're all hungry and irritable. Poor like that. I don't want to think about those times. I want to think about now.

This block is pretty nice, but I'm close enough to Jackson Square to worry about my car. The only BMWs you see around here are from the chop shop. You can hear guns going off in the night, and I can't tell you how many times a bleeping car alarm has kept me from my beauty rest. You hear the kids roaming around in packs, too, hooting like owls and yelling at their friends. We've got a new coffee bar down the block, and a French café with umbrellas on the tables outside in the summer. We're *gente*-fying the neighborhood, me and all the other Latino yuppies. Almost fast enough.

I flip through the stations, looking for a good romance movie. There has to be something, some cinematic fantasy I can watch where the men are good and decent.

The doctor keeps forgetting to show up for our dates. For two weeks it's like that. He calls to apologize a few times, sends me flowers to make it up, and then I'm shopping for gourmet cheese at that shop over by Symphony Hall after work one night and guess who walks in with some old Celia Cruz–looking witch in a red wig? Him! He was all dressed up like all the other people who had just come out of the symphony, you know? Long black wool coat and that nice cashmere scarf. I took my little shopping cart and went and stood behind them in line—they were buying organic eggs and whole wheat bread and the kind of orange juice that comes in a clear plastic container with a handle—and I bumped into him and cleared my throat all loud. He turned to see me and you could actually see drops of sweat popping up on the tip of his big nose like mushrooms after the rain. "Do I know you?" he asks with that thick Argentine accent of his. Does he *know* me? The woman smiles politely and puts her hand on his shoulder. She has claws like Cruella de Vil and she's wearing a big white rock on her ring finger. It's his damn *wife, m'ija.* He was married. "No," I said, "you *don't* know me. You must have mistaken me for a run-of-the-mill whore."

He had the *nerve* to try to call me at work the next day with a big story about how he doesn't really love his wife anymore. She's dying of cancer, he tells me, so he has to stay with her until she passes away. He says he stays with her out of *pity.* And I tell him that any man who uses the word "pity" to describe how he feels about his dying wife deserves to have someone take him up in a plane and throw him out without a parachute. I went ghetto mad on him, too. I might as well have been La India. *Quién tu te crees, eh? Tu te crees muy hombre, eh, muy macho así, eh, pero tu no sirves pa' na', tu eres un sinvergüenza, un sucio, no tienes corazón, no tienes na', y no te creo na' que tu me dice' ahora, oi'te? No te creo na'.* I hung up. He didn't call again.

The phone rings now, and I let it go one, two, three times. The machine picks up.

"Usnavys." It's Juan again. "Look. Just pick up, okay? I drove by your place and I saw your car and I saw the lights on. I know you're home. Just talk to me. We have to talk about this. We can't just keep pretending we don't have a problem. I love you."

I leave the phone alone and try to concentrate on the movie. My tenant is thumping around upstairs. I know what it is. I wish I didn't. What the hell does he do up there? That boy be ugly and cross-eyed with a damn Jheri curl, and he gets it more than I do. Next time I get a house and renovate it, I'm going to renovate the ground floor, so I don't have to hear someone else's business all night long.

The FBI agent wants me to move to Texas, right? I hate Texas, girl. You ever seen it? It's like someone took a butter knife and smashed that place down flat. It smells like oil everywhere, oil and garbage. I have been there exactly three times to visit him, and there is *nothing* for a woman like me in Texas. I don't mean to discriminate or generalize, *m'ija*, but when he told me there were Latinos everywhere, I thought maybe I could live down in Texas after all, but I'll tell you what, I need to be around Caribbean people. Those Mexicans down there are so quiet, especially the women. It's like a different world. They look at me like I'm crazy every time I open my mouth and the men all think I'm Jamaican. There's no *culture* down there. You can get a whole hell of a lot of house for not very much money, it's true. He told me he wanted to buy me a great big yellow brick house outside of Houston in something called "Sugarland." That's what I mean. I don't want to live somewhere called Sugarland. He sent me these brochures with drawings of the houses they're building over there. They were beautiful, *m'ija*, with big staircases, chandeliers, and three chimneys each. You know what they charge for that? It's less than what I paid for this dump in the middle of the ghetto, okay? He told me he was in the process of buying one of those big dollhouses and he wanted to put the deed in my name to prove how much he loved me, how crazy he was about me. That boy is freaky, too. He likes big women. That's what it is with him, I think. He wants my body. He's the first man who ever bought me sexy underwear. He likes to look at me. It's crazy! He's a skinny American man, really light Italian, and even though he tries as hard as he can, he doesn't understand how important my culture is to me. There's nothing really wrong with him, but he doesn't have what I really need, *m'ija*, which is a Latin man, and even better than that, a Puerto Rican man. I'd even take a Cuban man. A man with *sabor*. Ain't no way you gonna get a Puerto Rican woman like me down there in Texas with an American man like that in some big house in the Sugarland suburbs. I would die. I need some beans with my rice, *tu sabes*. I need subways and museums and urban life, you know what I'm saying? So he's nice and everything, he's got money and he's even told me he wants to go to medical school and get into forensic science, but can you see it? Me an FBI doctor's wife living in Texas? Huh-uh. I don't *think* so. So we ended that.

So, so disappointed. I'm disappointed in everybody. I'm disappointed in Lauren for seeing that drug dealer. What's the girl thinking? She courts self-destruction. I have no idea why, really. She's pretty smart, reasonably good-looking. But with her it's one horrendous fall after another. I'm getting tired of scraping her up. I expect to see her in the hospital next, with bullets in her from a drive-by. I feel so sorry for her sometimes, accomplished woman like that and she thinks she has to be down with a bad boy just to prove that she's as Latina as the rest of us, because her skin is so white and her Spanish sucks. She has this complex about it, you know. That's just plain sad. He's no good. Amaury got so many women around my old neighborhood we used to call him *Arabe*, because he had a harem.

And then there's Sara. *Pobrecita.*

And Elizabeth. What's wrong with people? You don't like who someone sleeps with, don't think about it. It's not your bedroom. It's not your *business.*

There's the damn phone again. "Navi, it's me, Juan, I'm down at the T station on the pay phone. I'm coming over and you better answer the door."

Ay, Dios mío. I don't need this right now. My hair is nappy. I don't have any makeup on. I'm in my robe and slippers. My breath smells like yellow rice and chicken. Why does he do things like this? I want no drama, like Mary J. Blige. All I want to do is veg out with my *arroz con pollo* and my *pasteles* and my *café con leche*. I need somebody here to massage my feet, you know, but not Juan. I need a *man* man, *m'ija*. Why is it so hard? I'm not going to answer the door when he comes. That's all there is to it.

I finally find an old black and white movie on the romance channel, something with Ingrid Bergman. I set the remote on the glass coffee tabletop, held in place by the white base sculpted to look like Roman columns and a big orb. Even this coffee table reminds me of Juan. His mom has one just like it down in Spanish Harlem. Why is it that everything I have done today has reminded me of him? I went to get my hair done, and there was a man waiting to have his hair cut who looked a lot like Juan, glasses and the goatee. At the takeout restaurant they're playing Michael Stuart, his favorite salsa singer. Every little thing. Every little thing today reminded me of the poorest man in the universe.

The doorbell starts ringing. I haven't had the doorbell replaced yet, either, so it makes that dying gazelle sound that makes my skin crawl. He doesn't just ring it once, either, he rings it, like, a thousand times in a row. Over and over and over. The thing with this house is that the doorbell isn't ringing just in my part of the house, but in my tenant's part of the house, too. So you can hear after a while that they stop getting busy upstairs and my tenant starts stomping down his stairs to see who's at the front door.

I wrap the robe around me as tight as I can and open my front door and walk out into the shared stairwell and see my tenant there, naked as a jaybird except for a ratty white towel around his waist, standing in the freezing cold with the door open, cursing at Juan.

"You stupid idiot," he's saying. "Don't you know how late it is around here? You don't have to ring the doorbell so many times, man, just calm down and somebody will come. What the hell is wrong with you?"

Juan looks past him at me and tilts his head to the side, almost in defeat. "Navi," he says in Spanish. "Let me in?"

My tenant sees me and turns and stomps past me back up the stairs. "Tell your friend not to be so annoying," he says. He has a lot of nerve. I think I'll raise his rent.

"What do you want?" I say to Juan.

"I just want to talk, Navi."

"Talk? It's ten o'clock and you come over here uninvited, like Robert Downey Jr. on a crack high. Go home," I say.

"Please, Navi, can I come in and talk to you for one minute?"

He's wearing the same coat he's worn for the past five years, a black jean jacket with a plaid flannel lining. It can't be warm. No gloves, of course. No hat. It's in the forties out there. He's all wet, like a stray. This *cabrón* has lived in New York and Boston his whole life and he still won't splurge on a decent coat. Look at him shivering there like a wet dog. What's wrong with that boy?

I sigh. "Come in, but one minute is all you get."

Even with all of this, though, I have to admit I'm glad to see him. He looks handsome. He looks healthy, his cheeks glowing pink with the cold, and he looks strong, even if he is skinny. I wish he'd get a good coat and a good hat, maybe even a cell phone so I wouldn't feel so scared about wanting him to hug me on the couch on a night like this when all I want is to watch movies together. He hurts me every time I see his poor, sorry behind.

"Why don't you have a decent coat? What's wrong with you?"

"Let's save the criticism, okay?" he says as he walks through my front door into my living room. He reaches out and shuts the door himself, something I've never seen him do.

"I'm not criticizing you."

"Yes, you are. You always are. That's what you do best, Navi." He's smiling in a confident, crazed way I've never seen.

We sit down, me on the couch and he on the matching green leather love seat. He looks at the aluminum and paper food containers all over the coffee table.

"Looks like it was good," he says with a laugh.

Because I was raised properly—even if we *were* poor—I offer him something warm to drink. There's no food left.

"No," he says. "I want to get right to the point here. You

haven't picked up your phone, and that's fine. You don't want to talk to me, fine. But I want you to know one thing, Navi: I *love* you.

"I hate the way you constantly complain about me, and I hate the way you look at me like I'm dog excrement and I hate the way you think you can always find a guy who's better than me, and I hate the way you have another man waiting in the background so you can hurt me. I hate the way you blame me for everyone who's ever hurt you in your damn life. I'm not your dad. I'm not your brother. I'm me. And you know what? I'm sick of all your other men hanging around all the time. Just admit that you love me. You honestly do. Don't you? Tell the truth. That's what it is."

I don't know what to say. He's right. I know he's right. But I don't want to give him the pleasure of knowing he's right. "Maybe," I say. "Maybe."

"Ha!" He stands up and starts striding around the room like a crazy man. I have never seen Juan like this. "Don't you understand what we're doing here?" he asks. "You love me so much you don't want to let me love you. You get it? You're so complicated, woman, it took me a decade to figure you out."

I feel tears coming. He just said something I didn't ever want to hear. I don't want to cry in front of him.

"Don't you get it? All these clowns, all these doctors and whatever you're waving around in front of my face, these guys are just a front. You have never loved them the way you love me. Admit it. You pretend to let them in because you know they can't actually hurt you the way your dad hurt you. I'm right, huh? You're crying because I'm right, admit it! I can't believe how stupid I've been all these years thinking you were in love with those idiots, and that you just kept coming back to me because you didn't have anyone else to pound on. And me, being so crazy about your stupid Puerto Rican ass that I just took it and stuck around. You know what? I haven't even kissed another woman in ten years, Navi. I haven't looked at another woman, I haven't thought about anyone but you. It's almost killed me, almost made me crazy. All those times you're just insulting me like I don't have feelings, you know? And I just stand there like a chump and take it. The only reason you ever did any of it is because I'm the only one who really sees you, huh? I'm the only one who knows that you aren't some pampered girl like all your little friends. I'm the only one who gets it that you're like George and Weezy, movin' on up. And you hate me for it and you love me for it because no one else will ever understand you like I do. Tell me I'm lying, Navi, tell me it's not true."

"Yeah. See? You can't."

Oh, my God. He's making me cry.

"Your minute's up," I say.

"My minute just started, Navi. You listen to me. It's me, or it's them. You can't have it all anymore. I'm not going through anything like Rome again because of you. I would die for you, you know that? I actually would. We're almost thirty. I want to have kids with you. I want to spend the rest of my life with you and I want to retire to Puerto Rico with you. So what will it be. Me, or them? Them, or me? It's up to you. I'll give you five minutes to think about it, and then I'm out the door and either I'm coming back here with an engagement ring, or I'm never coming back here again."

"Are you asking me to marry you?"

"Yeah, I guess I am."

"You *guess*?"

"I am, okay? I am. I know I can't get you as nice a ring as you want, and I know I won't wear the right thing to the wedding and you'll make fun of me. I know that. Yes, I'm asking you. Look. I'm getting down on my knees right here, right by this ghetto tacky coffee table you think is so nice, this ugly table that makes me sick to my stomach, and I'm begging you. Usnavys Rivera, will you marry me? Will you marry a nice, honest, badly dressed man like me? I'll never cheat on you, I'll never lie to you, I'll be a good father, I'll do everything for us, and I'll love you now and forever, just like I have for the past ten years. Navi, what do you say? Marry me? Quit screwing around with me and marry me already. You know you want to."

"You're taking up my five minutes running your mouth."

"Fine. Okay? Fine. Here's what I'll do. I'm going to go upstairs and fix that leak in your stupid bathroom 'cause I can't stand it anymore, the drip and the drop, 'cause that drip and that drop is as loud as that stupid new pink fur coat you've been wearing everywhere. Where is it? In this closet right here?"

I start to get up to stop him from opening the closet.

"No, you just stay right there. Ah ha! See?" He laughs. "I love you, you stupid ghetto girl. You don't even take the damn tag off. That is so sad. I know my jacket is sad, and you may not like my JCPenney shoes, but at least it's all *paid* for. Now I'm going upstairs, and when I get back you're going to have an answer for me. Okay? Here I go. I'm going upstairs now. Bye."

I stare at the movie. And I cry. I cry and I cry. I cry the full five minutes until he gets back.

"Well, so what is it?" he asks, grease all over his hands. I don't hear the drip anymore. He's fixed the sink.

"It's not a real proposal without a ring," I say.

"Fine." He holds up his hands, like a police officer telling a crowd to get back. "Fine. Stay right there."

He scrambles away and comes back from the kitchen with a bread twist tie, shaped into a ring. "This will have to do for now," he says, fumbling and dropping it and picking it up again. "And it probably doesn't matter because I know you're going to be as disappointed with any real ring I get you anyway as you are in this, so here. Just take it. Take it and realize that it's never the ring that matters. It's the man and the woman and their love for each other and the fact that they could lose their rings forever and they'd still be devoted to each other. Do you understand that, Navi? Take the damn ring. Now what's my answer?"

"This ring sucks," I say.

He laughs. He lifts his arms above his head and yells at the top of his lungs. "I love you, woman! Isn't that enough?"

I think about his question. He's not going to like the answer. "No," I say. "It's not. It's not enough."

Juan crumbles. He puts his hands over his face and when he looks up, there are tears in his eyes and black oil smudged on his cheeks. He looks at me, and then turns toward the door.

"You made your choice," he says. "Now I'm making mine."

And he leaves.

Ay, m'ija. I didn't think he'd do that.

April Fool's Day is one of the cruelest holidays in our cultural lexicon. When else do we so gleefully dash the hopes of those around us? I usually try to avoid talking to people on April Fool's Day, but this year, I had to make one phone call—to my friend Cuicatl. Remember her? The rock star formerly known as Amber? Yesterday, April Fool's Day, I happened to see a copy of this week's Billboard magazine, brought to my attention by one of the music writers here at the Gazette. And there on the cover was my girl, Cuicatl. The article said pre-sales of her soon-to-be-released album have exceeded expectations, and a couple of important rock critics hailed her as the next big thing in American pop. I couldn't believe it, and called to congratulate her. She assured me it was no April Fool's joke, and I almost choked on my joy—and envy. The lesson here for all of us: Never give up.

—from "My Life," by Lauren Fernández

cuicatl

GATO AND I stare at the *Billboard* magazine. It's open to the Latin charts page, and there I am, Cuicatl, at No. 1 for single *and* album. I flip to the Hot 100 chart, and there I am again, No. 32, with a bullet. That's out of all the albums in the nation, English or Spanish. I sip my tea, turn to Gato, and we kiss.

"You did it," he says flatly. His voice sounds far away, and he's not looking at me the way he usually does. His eyes are on his guitar case in the corner. His arms dangle at his sides.

"What did I do?" I take his chin in my hand and turn his head toward me. His face moves, but his gaze shifts only to the wall behind me.

"You made number one." His brow wrinkles sadly. Why would he be sad?

"Gato," I say. He recoils from my touch. "Gato, look at me."

He stands and walks to his instrument. He sighs.

"What's wrong?" I ask. "Why are you acting like this?"

He picks up the guitar case, sets it down, shuffles toward the door, comes back. "I don't know," he says.

"What don't you know?"

Finally, he stops moving and our eyes connect. His are bloodshot. Last night he twisted sleepless most of the night, thrashed and whimpered, tangled on the edges of nightmares he would not speak of in the morning, no matter how many times I asked.

"Us," he says. His arms cross over his chest as he sighs again. There has never been a problem with "us." Ever. He slouches and I realize that since I found success, his shoulders have slowly crept forward, his chest collapsing in on his heart. He is not strong enough for this, what is happening to me. It makes him small in a way he does not wish to be small.

"Nothing's changed, Gato," I say, trying to sound gentle and nonthreatening. It would be hard for any man, but for a Mexican man it would be hardest of all. I stand and reach for him. He moves away again, this time through the hanging beads painted with the image of the Virgin of Guadalupe, into the dining room, where he sits at the bright, colorful hand-painted rustic table, next to his cold cup of herbal tea from this morning. I follow him, and repeat myself. I try to rub his shoulders, his subservient geisha. In the mirror with the hammered tin frame I look tall, too tall. I stoop, make myself little. Something, anything. I kiss the top of his head as lovingly as a mother. Part of me hates that I'm doing this. Part of me just wants to be alone with my guitar.

"Nothing's changed, has it?" I ask.

"Everything's changed," he says low, without looking at me. He brushes my hand from his skin as if I were diseased.

My mouth hangs open the way my mother's hangs open when she sees a price tag she thinks is too steep.

"You're joking?" I ask.

"No, I'm not." He is up and pacing, moving away from me again. I follow.

"But the only thing that's different is the money, Gato. Everything else is the same."

"Exactly."

"What is that supposed to mean?"

"Haven't you heard what they've been saying about you?" he asks. He looks at me with anger as he leans on his hands over the table between us.

"Who?"

"The movement. The people in the movement."

"No," I say. Adrenaline rushes through me as the weight of what he's just said hits. My people are talking about me behind my back? "What are they saying?"

"You see? They're right. You *have* gone commercial. You've forgotten your roots."

"What? That's crazy!"

"They've been talking about it on the Red Zone and the other radio shows for weeks. You don't listen anymore. You're too busy trying to hear your song on the top forty stations."

"I don't listen because I'm overwhelmed with work! How could they say that about me? What proof do they have?"

Gato shakes his head. "You did songs in English," he says.

"And? How is English different from Spanish, really? They're both European languages. And it's my first language."

Gato laughs in disgust. "You used to swear you'd never record in English."

"But you agreed when I said it would be a compromise!

It's one of the sacrifices I have to make now to reach the biggest audience with our message! You said so yourself. English is the crossover language. It's a global language."

"That was before."

"Before what?"

"Before all this."

"All this what?"

"*La raza* is disappointed in you. You show your belly button all over MTV. They're saying you're no better than Christina Aguilera now."

"What?" Anger floods my body. "I'm nothing like her. You know that!"

"Aren't you? They're playing disco remixes of 'Brother Officer' at Jack in the Box. God, Amber."

"Amber?"

"You should have kept that name. It suits you better."

"I'm Cuicatl. And I have no control over how they edit my videos. That's all marketing."

"They're saying you betrayed Aztlán. Like Shakira. I can't live with that."

"I don't believe what I'm hearing. You can't actually think like this about me? Me?" I thump my chest like a gorilla. "You know me better than that!"

"They're saying you're lapping up this whole 'Latina pop princess' label."

"You know that's not true! That's what reporters call me because they don't know how to do anything else. That's not what I call myself."

"Well, you should educate them."

"You think I don't try?"

"Doesn't look like it."

"I tell them the truth, Gato, but they write what they want to. I can't control what every moron in the world writes about me!"

Gato leaves the room again, this time for our bedroom. I hear him moving things about. When he returns, he has three canvas duffel bags.

"Gato, please," I say. "What is this really about?"

"I'm going to stay with a friend." He holds a familiar handmade paper envelope in one hand, with beautiful dried flowers stamped into the thick clothlike fibers.

"Who?"

"A friend." He looks guilty and stuffs the envelope in his jeans pocket. So that's what this is about.

"A female friend?"

He says nothing. I remember the young groupie, a beautiful Mexica girl with hair down to her butt who always tries to be the first to bring him water at the *danzas*. We used to laugh together about her obsession with him, the way she stands at the lip of the stage for all his shows. She sends him gifts, writes love letters. Sends them in thick, handmade paper envelopes that smell of rainwater. I can't remember her name. I don't want to know. She worships him. She is not herself a musician. Of course he wants to stay with her now.

"You can take a man out of Mexico," I say, "but I guess you can't take Mexico out of the man."

"What do you mean by that?"

"Is your ego really this fragile, Gato? You need to run to a little girl who worships you because I can't be that for you anymore? You never thought I'd be first, did you?"

"That's not what this is about."

"That's *exactly* what this is about," I say.

I'm tired. The pain is so deep I drown in it, feel nothing for the time being. It will hit later, as the silence closes in.

"It's about you turning your back on the movement," he says.

"Go," I say. "If you believe I'm a sellout no better than Christina 'show-my-new-titties' Aguilera, then go. If you can't see what I'm trying to do here, my God. I thought you loved me. I thought you knew me. You don't. Get out. I don't need you."

"Fine," he says.

"It would have come for you, too," I say as he opens the front door.

"What would?"

"A record deal, all this."

He stares me down, cold. "It still will. Only *I* won't go commercial."

"My record is hardly commercial."

"That's why it's number one? No one gets to number one by making art. Everyone in the movement knows that. I know that. You know that."

"That's bullshit," I say. "I haven't changed a thing."

"That's not how we see it," he says, feeling a right to speak for the entire *rock en Español* community.

"Then I suggest you *all* have a massive inferiority complex," I say. "That's why you'd rather praise a bunch of *pendejos* who can barely play a I-IV-V-I over a tired ska loop than me! You can't stand for one of your own to actually make it! Especially not a woman!"

"You're not one of ours anymore, Amber."

"Cuicatl."

"*Amber.*" He says the name as an insult.

He steps across the threshold and shuts the door.

I collapse on the Haitian floor pillows, lie in the encroaching silence, and stare at the *Billboard* magazine splayed across the floor and feel guilty. The drummer brought the *Billboard*s, and a collection of other press featuring articles on me. *Seventeen, YM, Latina*. The *Washington Post*. The *New York Times* calls me "a Latina Zack de la Rocha-meets-Eminem—in Cancún."

I flip through them all, read the made-up quotes that are nothing more than approximations of things I said, written in ways I would never say them by people too lazy to take thorough notes or use a tape recorder. If you didn't know me and didn't listen to my work, you'd think it was true, that I was a conflicted, angry "Latina Alanis," or a "Latina Joplin," or a "Latina Courtney Love." The U.S. media write as if a "Latina" *anything* can't possibly be good enough to just be herself, an artist with no ethnic qualifier, no white (or black) mainstream comparison. Of *course* the moshers in the movement think I've turned my back on them. The woman in these articles is nothing *like* me. So *this* is how history gets made. Reporters do self-therapy with people like me as their backdrop and the world as their witness, and the words, however false, stick permanently, available for harvest by countless generations of historians to come. None of us knows the truth of what came before us, ever, or even of what happens now. It's all filtered through reporters and historians. I feel sick. Furious. In other words, I feel inspired to write.

But first, I want to know if La Raza really think I've turned my back on them. I go to the kitchen and call Curly on his cell phone. I tell him what happened with Gato, what Gato said.

"It's not true," Curly assures me.

"He says everyone is talking bad about me."

"They're not." He sounds uncomfortable.

"What is it, Curly? What aren't you telling me?"

He lets out a whistle.

"Spit it out," I say.

"I didn't want to tell you this before," he says. "But the fact is if there's anyone we're talking bad about, it's Gato."

"Gato? Why?"

Another sigh. "Cuicatl. Be strong."

"Why?"

"Ever since you stopped coming to the *danzas* he's been spending a lot of time before and after the ceremonies talking to Teicuih, that young girl from Diamond Bar."

"How much time?"

"A lot. They come together. They leave together."

Gato has been telling me our friend Leroy takes him and picks him up. One night, he called to say he'd stay at Leroy's house because he was too tired from dancing to bring him home.

"You okay?" Curly asks.

Am I? I don't know. I can't tell. "Yes," I say.

Curly hesitates, then begins to speak again. "You know how Gato wanted me to give him his name?"

"Yes." Gato has been after Curly for a naming ceremony for years.

"I had the name. I just told him I didn't, because I didn't want to hurt you."

"Really?"

"Gato's name is Yoltzin. Do you know what that means?"

"Small heart?" I ask.

"That's right."

"I never saw him that way."

"I know."

He's right. I suddenly know that. I still feel like I've been punched. "Yes," I say. "Okay."

"I'll get Moyolehauni and the kids together now, and we'll come to your house and stay with you tonight," he says. "We'll make dinner for you."

"Sure."

"You should have family around at a time like this."

"Okay."

I look around my beautiful new home. Do I miss Gato? I do. Will I? Yes. But I'll live. There's so much else going on. I can't believe how quickly my life has changed. First the money. Then recognition. And now I've lost the man I love. You hear about people finding overnight success? It happens. I mean, it's not exactly overnight, because I've been playing music nearly all my life, and I've paid a lot of dues in the years, but I never imagined all of this.

The money was incredible enough. In one week, Gato and I went from living in the small apartment above the watch repair shop on Silverlake Boulevard to having our own little house in Venice, three blocks from the ocean, with a basement big enough for both of our bands to rehearse at the same time. It's ordinary, the house, but it was expensive, compared to what we were used to. About a month after I bought it, I realized I could have bought something much bigger. I just wasn't used to spending money and wasn't even sure I should.

The other big change was the way my parents treat me, especially after I went *loca* and bought them a week in Vegas, at that hotel that looks like Venice, Italy. They just about died. That wasn't something they ever expected me to do, and they didn't expect me to pay off my dad's truck, either, or buy him a new mountain bike. I surprised him with that.

They don't look at me like I'm crazy anymore. They are polite to Gato, and ask about him. What can I tell them now? "Sorry, Mom and Dad, Gato decided I was a sellout"? They wouldn't know what a sellout was. Why would anyone question success?

How can he think that about me? How can he? Fucker. Who needs his phony ass?

The last time I saw my family in Oceanside, I couldn't believe what I saw on the coffee table, next to the remote and the flier my mom got from the Home Shopping Network. A book on the history of the Mexica Movement. How strange that they should be the ones to ask the questions about Mexica history now, and Gato should be the one to reject me. Is it true? Have they all been talking about me the way he says? Are they that petty?

We didn't splurge, me and Gato, for ourselves. I paid Frank his fifteen percent, even though he didn't ask for it, because he earned it. I asked him to be my full-time manager and agent. He agreed. We have a good relationship. We donated some money to Olin's Mexica Movement group out in Boyle Heights so that they can hire someone to do some serious copyediting of those press releases he sends everywhere. He's a good man, and he means well, but he needs to be more professional. The Mexica have to be more polished and persuasive in how they present the movement to the media. As it is now, too many people think we're crazy. We? Do I have a right to use that word? They supposedly don't claim me anymore, now that I've been invited to perform at the MTV Awards. I think of all the times I put down women like Shakira and Jennifer Lopez—was I being no better than the people who bash me now? Or Christina Aguilera. I just insulted her and I don't know anything about her other than what the media say. I was hating someone I had never met and didn't know. But they'll see. The people in the movement will see. I'll elevate their philosophy to mainstream consciousness.

Then they will see.

Aztlán is rising. Through me.

With the money we are going to make, we'll produce our own version of *The Road to El Dorado,* and this time we will tell the truth. This time, the Indian women won't be whores who flirt with the rapacious Spaniards. This time, the Indian priest won't be a bucktoothed savage in need of "enlightenment" and rescue. This time, the world will know what the Spaniards did to us. This time, we will speak for the twenty-three million of my people who were slaughtered by the Spaniards; this time, the voices of the ninety-five percent of the indigenous peoples of Mexico and Central America who were slaughtered like animals by the Europeans, will be heard. Our holocaust will rise out of every note I play on every stage and I will tell their stories.

Cuicatl will speak.

I feel songs germinating in my head. All this emotion. I start to hum, sing a few lyrics, roll over and stare at the ceiling. I sing as loud as I can. No one is here to hear me. And maybe that's not a bad thing. Maybe I'll do better alone, not having to worry about the delicate ego of a man like Gato. I won't fall apart the way Lauren does. I won't cling beyond reason like Sara. I won't waste my life pining for something I can't find, the way Usnavys does. I will remain here, in this space where the words and melodies find me. I will make music. Nothing changed in my heart when the money came. I need the strength to stand alone. It was men who sold women in the Aztec past, wasn't it? There are nearly five hundred male names in the sixteenth-century Aztec censuses, and less than fifty for women. Men had great names, descriptive of life's possibilities. Women got named by where they appeared in relation to their siblings—first, second—or names that meant things like "small woman." I feel lighter somehow, like I can finally breathe.

I'm happy with the way my album turned out. It slices the way I want it to slice. It rocks. You don't realize how much it costs to do an album right. I could have used even more money, a lot more money, but that will come for the next record.

The record label came through on their promises. They've

been working my project in the media in the U.S. and Latin America—I hate calling it that—and Europe. I've been doing interviews for the past two months, and now they're all starting to hit. I was actually invited to play on the *Live with Regis and Kelly* show, and did that last week, too. Next week I'm doing the *Tonight Show* and *Saturday Night Live*.

I'm going to be on the road most of the rest of the next twelve months, and I want the show to be tight. I won't have the time or energy to miss Gato. I'll put the feelings of loss in a song or two and be done with it.

The English version of my first single (at first I didn't want to record in English, but Gato talked me into it, saying it would be the best way for me to get the word out) is getting play on KISS FM in Los Angeles and all the other big FM stations. They're playing my song on MTV, and kids are starting to call in and request it on *TRL*. I made the video a while back. I can't believe how much the finished version focuses on my stomach muscles and my body, and my tits and eyes, but that's okay. At first I was pissed off, but Gato calmed me down and reminded me that everything is compromise, this is the price I pay now for complete control later, this is the price I pay to get the world to hear the warrior cry of my people. Ironic.

I can't go to the grocery store anymore without someone stopping me to ask for my autograph, without someone telling me I look smaller in real life than I do on TV. I guess TV makes you look big, and that's why my mom likes it so much—she thinks everything she sees there is better than what she has in her own real life. And that's why she likes *me* more now, because she finally saw me on TV. It made me and my ideas real to her for the first time.

The only place I can really go in public without being bothered anymore is the West Side, where pretty much everyone is a celebrity and no one thinks much about it. If I go anywhere east of the Los Angeles River, forget it. I guess most of the Mexican kids aren't listening to the Mexica radio rock shows Gato claims are trashing me. The kids are falling out of their Chryslers, pointing and screaming, so they must like me, eh? It's the price you pay, I guess. I stopped going to the *danzas* at Whittier Narrows, because I kept getting swarmed, and it took away from the ceremony. That probably made the movement people think I was selling out, now that I think about it.

I gave my first big concert in Los Angeles last week, and my brother showed up. I sang the first English single, "Brother Officer," and he stared at me from the front row. He was still uptight, but I thought I saw something sacred in his eye, the eagle power rising in him. I don't think he realized until that moment what I really am. Now he knows. I think he's starting to realize who he is, too. He is an Indian. A proud Mexica man. Maybe that's what this is all about for me. I'm preaching to those who need to hear my message. The converted can reject me, but I'll increase their numbers. They'll see.

I turn on the computer in my office and check my E-mail. There's a message from Frank, outlining the dates of my world tour. It's all set up. I scan the dates and names of the cities. I'll be traveling to more than thirty nations with my message. Goose bumps.

I write back to Frank: "This looks good, all except for May 30 in Managua. I can't be there for that."

That night, the *sucias* are meeting.

I should be depressed. Why? Well, for one I had a birthday last week, and I'm only a year away from thirty now. I'm not married, engaged or divorced. I have no kids.

So there it is. Oh, and then there are all those new articles about how women actually start to lose fertility at the age of twenty-seven, which means I've had two years of declining egg quality and am nowhere near to being a mommy.

But none of this has me down, incredibly. On the contrary, I'm happy. For the first time in my life—I think—I'm happy. Now, for those of you out there who regularly read my column—enthusiastically or reluctantly, I don't care as long as you're reading—you might think I'm happy because of my beau. And it's true, he's made my life a good place to be. But the main reason I'm happy is that I finally realized I already have what I've been looking for all these years. And I've had it for a decade.

I'm talking about family. We know the one I was born into wasn't very good. And we know I've had bad luck finding the right man to create a new one with. But what I've been too blind to see is that the women who have been my friends for the last ten years are my family. In all the ways that count, they are the loving, crazy, creative, animated, vivacious family I always wanted.

Whenever I begin to doubt my own self worth, whenever the pain of my past comes back tugging at the legs of my pants, it's my girlfriends—not my mom, not my dad, not my boyfriends, not my employers—who have my back. They're the ones who remind me I'm beautiful. They're the ones who put things in perspective.

Whenever I start to feel old and despair that I will never have a family, it's my girls who step up and remind me loud and clear: I already have one.

               —from "My Life," by Lauren Fernández

usnavys

THIS IS WHAT you call a *sucias* powwow.

    All of us are here, except for Sara, who's still in the hospital, and Amber, who's on tour in Tennessee somewhere, promoting her album. Album, *m'ija*. She called me a few weeks ago to play one of her finished songs for me from the studio. It gave me chills. Or maybe it was the *batido de guayaba* I was drinking, extra cream, extra ice. We teased her, but that's what we do. I am so proud of her.

    Sara's the reason we came to dinner tonight. Rebecca thought it would be a good idea for us to pool our resources and figure out a plan to keep her from putting herself in danger again. After visiting Sara myself and seeing the way she defends that man—she thinks he was trying to hug her when she fell down the stairs, and says we don't understand what a hard life he's had—I'm all for the idea.

    We meet at Caffé Umbra, one of the city's most fashionable new restaurants. It's a long, narrow room, with high ceilings. The food is sort of European gourmet, and paints the air with intense garlic and cream streaks. Lauren turned us on to the place, ragging in one of her columns about how few women chefs get to be stars the way Umbra's has. I could not care less what kind of genitals my cook has, okay? I want to know one thing: Is the food good? Each table comes with a large green bottle of Italian sparkling water sitting in a champagne bucket. Not once while I was in Rome did I get a bottle of water this nice. I had to come back to Boston to get gourmet Italian water. See what I'm saying? That's just not right.

Rebecca is already seated at a table near the bar when I arrive with Lauren, whom I picked up at her office on my way. I don't know why that girl doesn't get herself a car. She must think we *like* driving her curly head all over town, listening to her constantly complain about her boss. If she hates him so much, why doesn't she quit, or do what I did—shut her mouth long enough to end *up* the boss?

Rebecca wears a chocolate brown double-breasted blazer I saw in the Anne Klein boutique at Saks, over a taffy blue silk sweater. She picked my favorite table, with a view of the Holy Cross Cathedral across Washington Street. To sit and look out at that beautiful gray stone structure while drinking that sparkling water and eating this food, you'd think you were in Europe, only better because everyone *here* speaks English and Spanish the *right* way. The crowd is mostly professionals in their twenties and thirties, I'd guess, with good manners and stylish yet casual clothes. I'm glad I splurged on the Carolina Herrera herringbone suit for this get-together, and these "Oprah Winfrey"–type Stuart Weitzman ankle boots with the spiked heels. I left work a couple of hours early, too, and stopped at the Giuliano Day Spa on Newbury Street for a Swiss Goat Butter body wrap—my favorite. My skin is so soft now, I could melt. Because I'm a regular, they threw in an eyelash tint, royal black. I like it. They have a full salon at Giuliano, and even though everyone raves about it, I look at the little thin-haired white women who work there and I'm pretty sure they don't know how to do hair like mine. I'll leave that to my girls in Roxbury. I know I look good, and so do those guys at the bar looking at me. I wonder what this kind of real estate costs, on a square-foot basis? I look like I own the place.

Rebecca reads the latest *InStyle* magazine, with one of those older women stars on the front, the kind who's still sexy at forty-five. Next to her, in a stack on the table, are half a dozen pamphlets on battered women's syndrome, violence against women, and effective intervention/communication skills. See what I mean? Rebecca thinks of everything. I should have thought to bring things like that. I'm the one who works for a non-profit. There aren't many people I feel like I can learn a lot from, but Rebecca is one I admire. Her hair looks slightly different tonight.

"Did you get highlights?" I ask.

Rebecca's hand lands on her head and she laughs. "I did just a little red. What do you think?"

"It suits you, *m'ija*. I like it."

Our waiter is fashionable, swishy, and arrogant, and he does not need a pen or pad to remember even the largest orders. Sometimes, *m'ija*, I feel bad for all the really talented people out there who waste their gifts. I mean, couldn't he find something better to do with a memory like that?

Hugs all around. We've seen each other at the hospital a few times, and talked on the phone, but this is the first time we've all gotten together since Sara was hurt.

"It's so terrible," I say.

"It was a total shock," Rebecca says. "I had no idea."

"Poor Sara," Lauren says. "I can't believe it."

We all shake our heads.

"All those tubes," I say.

"She's in a lot of pain," Rebecca says.

"That's why we need to have Roberto offed," Lauren says. We stare at her in disbelief. "You're joking, I hope?" I ask.

"No, not really," she says.

Rebecca looks at me and sighs.

"That's a pretty color on you," she tells Lauren, referring to the olive green suede shirt-jacket Lauren wears over a scrumptious Devon cream-colored turtleneck. She also wears tight jeans tucked into butterscotch riding boots, and small gold hoops in her ears. She's thin lately. She looks good.

"Where'd you get the shirt, *m'ija?*" I ask, feeling it with my fingertips. It's good quality.

"The usual, Ann Taylor," she says. "I'm not very imaginative with my shopping, sorry to say."

"It's really pretty with your hair," Rebecca says. I'm surprised because she rarely compliments Lauren. "It would look great with that silver necklace you have."

Rebecca smells like crisp, fresh apples; I take a guess that it's Green Tea perfume by Elizabeth Arden. Lauren wears a perfume I can't recognize, citrusy, with dark spicy top notes.

"What perfume is that?" I ask her. *"Qué rico!"*

"Oh, this?" She sniffs her wrist. "It's something called 'Bergamot,' from the Body Shop. I fell in love with it. You like it?"

"It's really nice. What's it called again?"

"Bergamot." Lauren digs through her roomy Dooney & Bourke shoulder sack and pulls out the bottle of fragrance. She hands it to me. "Take it," she says.

"No, I couldn't," I say.

"Don't be silly. I can get more. I go to that store almost every week. I *love* their stuff. Go on. It's practically new. I just got it."

"But it's yours."

"I want you to have it." She plants a kiss on my cheek.

Lauren is so Caribbean sometimes. I wonder if she realizes it. "Thanks, *mi vida*," I say, knowing it's useless to argue. I open the bottle, dab a couple of drops behind my ears. "I love it. Smell this, Rebecca."

Rebecca sniffs the open bottle and nods approvingly. "Very nice. I'm glad you both could make it," Rebecca says, motioning to the table. "Please, have a seat."

"Me too, sweetie." I give her hand a squeeze. "It was such a good idea to do this. Wasn't it a good idea?" I elbow Lauren, who seems tense. She's definitely got something against Rebecca, and I'm definitely getting sick of it.

"It's a good idea, yes," Lauren says.

We all sit. I take my cue from Rebecca and put the white cloth napkin in my lap. Lauren doesn't follow suit, even though she's begun to happily gnaw on a hot roll from the basket. As carefully as I can, I reach over and put her napkin in her lap for her. She looks embarrassed, and smiles.

"Little bites, sweetheart," I whisper. "Break off little pieces with your fingers, don't take bites with your teeth."

"What can I bring you ladies to drink?" the waiter asks.

"I'd like a Coke," I say, "with lemon."

"Diet or regular?" he asks.

"Do I look like I'm on a diet?" I ask. I push back from the table and gesture to my belly. His nostrils flare. He blushes and doesn't seem to know what to say. The *sucias* laugh.

"One regular Coke," the waiter says. "And for you, ma'am?"

"When did I become a ma'am?" Lauren asks us. Her eye makeup looks great, too. Purples. She finally did purples. I've been after her to try them for years.

"*Miss*, then," the waiter says, pleasantly bitchy. "Is that better?"

"Much," says Lauren. "I'm fine with just the Pellegrino."

Rebecca already has a glass of iced tea. When the waiter leaves, she hands us both a set of pamphlets. "You guys might already know everything in these," she says, "but I found them very informative."

"I bet you did," Lauren says. I have no idea why the girl always has to be so rude.

"Elizabeth should be here any second," I say, trying to change the subject. I feel like when I'm around Lauren I'm always running behind her, cleaning up her messes. She's like my mother, always speaking before thinking.

"Yes," Rebecca says. "I think we should wait until she gets here."

"Poor Sara," I say. I remember her bruised face, and I want to cry. "Why didn't she tell us?" Lauren and Rebecca both shake their heads. No one speaks for a few minutes and we look over our menus.

Elizabeth comes through the door, and walks toward us quickly. She's wearing her usual jeans, sweatshirt, and sneakers, with a men's parka. No makeup. Hugs all around again. Elizabeth smells like Dove bar soap.

"I think they followed me here," she says. She looks frightened.

"Who?" I ask.

"The reporters."

Lauren walks to the window, swaggers really, as if she carried a baseball bat. That girl is ready for a fight anytime, anyplace.

"They have no lives," I say. "Don't worry about it."

Lauren is out on the sidewalk now, up in someone's face, yelling. The man she's attacking wears a camera on a strap around his neck, and as with most people who come into conflict with Lauren, he quickly backs down and walks away. She searches for other hostile forces, and starts toward a car double-parked across the street.

"She's going to get herself killed one of these days," Rebecca says.

"She's fine," I say. "She can handle herself."

Rebecca passes Elizabeth a set of pamphlets. The waiter returns. He recognizes her instantly, his face lights up.

"Oh, my God," he says. "It's you! I can't believe it's you."

Elizabeth braces, not sure what to expect. I do too.

"I, like, so *love* you," the waiter says. "You're my hero! I have your picture on my wall at home. You are so courageous. You're a real inspiration to all of us."

"Thanks," Elizabeth answers, but she looks uncomfortable. She looks out at Lauren arguing with a couple of middle-aged men in a minivan, and the waiter's eyes follow.

"If any of them tries to come in here, trust me, we'll defend you," he says. "I may look like a queen, but I fight like a man."

Elizabeth laughs. "Thanks."

"You know," the waiter gushes, "you're even prettier in real life than you are on TV. I didn't think that was possible!"

"Thanks."

"No problem. What can I get you to drink, Liz? It's on the house." At the bus station, the other waiters are whispering and pointing at us.

"Just water."

"C'mon! It's on the house. How about some wine? We have a fantastic, exotic wine list."

"I don't drink, thanks. Water's fine."

"Tea? Coffee? Nothing?"

"Uhm, you have hot chocolate?" Elizabeth flinches, like she's afraid she's asked a stupid question.

"I can whip you up a mocha cappuccino. How's that?" He puts his hand on her shoulder as if they were old chums.

"Fine."

"Be right back."

Elizabeth seems relieved when the waiter leaves.

"You okay?" I ask her. She nods.

"Celebrity for all the wrong reasons," she says. "It's weird."

"I bet," Rebecca says, still suspiciously eyeing the waiter.

Lauren comes back in, cursing under her breath, cheeks flushed from the cold air.

"You own a gun?" she asks Elizabeth.

"No."

"You should consider getting one."

Rebecca looks up from her menu. "Lauren, please. Don't be ridiculous."

"She needs a gun," Lauren repeats. "Ridiculous is letting these people ruin your life. I am ashamed of our business."

"Let's figure out what we're going to eat," I say brightly.

"I'm just trying to help," Lauren says.

"Of course you are, *m'ija*," I say. "Now sit down and find something you like on this wonderful menu." I hand her the menu. It's like having a child, hanging out with Lauren.

The waiter returns with our drinks and rattles off the day's specials. "For an appetizer we have mussels on basil ratatouille, which is fabulous. Our soup today is a cream lettuce with lobster butter, too good to be true. For entrees we have a lean pork roulade—to die for, I promise you—and a potato and salt cod soufflé you have to see to believe."

My mouth is watering so much I have to swallow.

"You gals ready to order?"

Rebecca nods and looks at each of us; we nod.

"Liz, let's start with you," says the waiter.

"I'll have the lettuce soup. Can you tell me more about the skate wings?"

"Excellent choice," says the waiter. "The skate wings come as four boneless triangles of fried fish, served on a bed of cauliflower and potato, trimmed with peas and crumbles of smoked bacon."

"That sounds good," Elizabeth says. "I'll take that."

"And for you?" He's looking at me.

"I'll have the brisket appetizer, and the shrimp salad appetizer."

"Both?"

"Yes." What does he expect? The portions here are so small you can hardly see them. "And the *goujonettes* of sole."

"Fine choice." He looks at Lauren. "Miss?"

I interrupt. "I wasn't *finished*."

"I'm sorry. Go on."

"I'd also like to try the lettuce soup."

"Fine. Anything else?"

"Make sure you keep the bread coming."

"Of course. Anything else?"

I put a finger to my lips, think for a moment, then say, "No, I think that's all."

"Miss?" He addressed Lauren.

Lauren scowls into her menu. "I'll have the pasta sampler."

"Anything to start with? Perhaps the vegetable aioli?"

"Is it heavy?"

"Not at all. Very light."

"Fine."

"Wonderful. Anything else?"

"That's enough for me." She stares at me.

"And you, miss?"

Rebecca smiles at the waiter. "I'll have the *saucisson*."

"Anything else?"

"No."

"It's a small serving, miss."

"It will be fine."

"Oh, come on," I say. "You're going to starve yourself."

Rebecca shakes her head and hands the waiter her menu. He's written nothing down, but repeats our entire order without a mistake, then heads to the kitchen.

"So," Rebecca says.

"Yes, so," I echo.

"As you know, I thought we ought to put our heads together to come up with a strategy to help Sara recover in
such a way that she'll never have to go through this again."

Lauren, whose elbows are on the table, rolls her eyes.

"It's a great idea," I say. "Let's put our heads together."

"She probably still loves him," Rebecca says. "It's hard
for us to understand why. But she does. And I don't think it
would be productive to criticize her for that. But I think we
need to confront her, in a productive way, and let her know
that we think she's worth more than this. We need to let Sara
know that we're here for her."

Elizabeth sits forward and clears her throat. "I think it's a
good idea," she says. "But I think there's a certain way to
communicate with Sara that works best."

"What's that?" Lauren asks.

"She's got a good B.S. detector," says Elizabeth. "The doctors say she's not in a coma, just sleeping a lot and drugged
because of the pain. Soon, though, she'll be able to have a co-
herent conversation with us, and we have to make sure it
doesn't seem too contrived or like we feel sorry for her."

"That's good to know," says Rebecca. "How do you think
we should handle this?"

Just then my cell phone rings. I answer it. It's Juan. He
wants to know where I am. I tell him I'm at Umbra, just to
remind him I am a lady of style and grace, and then I ask
him not to call me anymore. He's still trying to talk when I
press END. By the time I hang up, I've missed a lot of what's
been said.

"Sorry," I say. "Fill me in?"

Rebecca says, "Well, Liz was saying Sara doesn't want to
be treated like a victim, so we're thinking the best way to
handle this is for all of us to do an intervention with Sara,
but to let Liz do most of the talking. They're close friends,
and Liz knows how to communicate with her best."

"Great."

"I think we should just pool together some money and
have Roberto put out of his misery," says Lauren.

Elizabeth laughs. "Not a bad idea, actually."

"That's very funny, Lauren," Rebecca says. "But we need to be serious here. This is a serious issue."

"Hey, she was just trying to lighten the mood," Elizabeth says. "Why are you always coming down on Lauren?"

"Me?" Rebecca asks. "She doesn't take anything seriously. Excuse me, but I feel like she's always coming down on *me*."

I gasp. I never thought I'd live to see Rebecca confront this situation directly.

"*I* don't attack *you*," Lauren says, eyes flashing.

"Yes, you do. You always roll your eyes at everything I say, and you're always pouting and sighing. What did I ever do to you?"

I've never heard Rebecca's voice so angry.

"Oh, boy," I say. There's no way out of this one. They seem to think they're the only two people in the room.

"You're so uptight, it makes me sick," Lauren says. "Okay, there, I said it. You come in here with your pamphlets, like you know everything, and you try to control the whole conversation and 'strategize.' You can't even compliment me without criticizing me for not wearing the right necklace. You act like you're in a business meeting, I swear to God. You don't even know how to relax enough to hang out with friends."

"Uptight?"

"You heard me."

"At least I'm not crazy and out of control. At least I don't feel the need to tell the whole world about every single problem in my life."

"What's that supposed to mean?"

"Hey, hey, hey, that's enough," Elizabeth says. *"No se pelean."*

"No," says Lauren. "This has been a long time coming, and I'm finally going to tell her what I think."

Lauren lays in to Rebecca with a laundry list of faults.

"Stop it," I say. "Lauren, just stop it." For the first time, I realize Lauren is supremely jealous of Rebecca. How could I have not seen it before?

I look at Rebecca, and am shocked to see she is crying, in a dignified way—but still. She's crying.

Crying, *m'ija.*

I get up and hug her. Lauren looks as surprised as I am.

"I'm sorry," Rebecca says to Lauren. "I'm sorry I'm not perfect. You're right. You're right about a lot of it. I *am* scared. I *am* stiff. I *am* uptight. I *don't* dance. I *am* married to a *'freak.'* But why do you feel like you have to tell me all of this? You think I don't already *know* it?"

Lauren is flabbergasted. "I—I," she stutters.

"You went too far," Elizabeth tells her. "Rebecca's human, Lauren."

"There's something you don't know, too," Rebecca says.

I speak up. "Sweetie, Rebecca. You don't have to say anything. We didn't come here for you to get beat up."

"No, I want to," she says. "Okay, Lauren? Just so you know I'm as messed up as you. I'm in love with Andre, the man who helped me start my company. I want a divorce from Brad, but I don't know how my family will take it. I'm lonely. My dad bosses my mom around, and she's smarter than he is and I hate him for it. I haven't had sex with anything but my own hand in ten months. I want to be with Andre so much I can't focus on my job. There. I think that's all."

She's crying hard now.

"Wow," Lauren says. She looks ashamed.

"I hope you're happy now," I tell Lauren. "Really, *m'ija,* what's wrong with you? I've tried to be patient with you, but it's hard. You hurt your friends, you hurt yourself. I'm sick of watching it."

"No, wait, there's more," Rebecca says. "I envy you, Lauren. I know that surprises you. But I do. You're much freer than I am. You speak your mind. You live with passion. There, I've said it."

Elizabeth has her head in her hands, and we're all sort of staring at the table in silence when the waiter comes back with our appetizers.

"I'm sorry, Rebecca," Lauren says, finally. "I had no idea."

"Here, look at this," Rebecca says. She pulls a pink and white striped Victoria's Secret bag from under the table. "Look what I bought today." She pulls out a racy red garter set, with hose and a bustier, dumps them in a heap on the table.

"No you didn't," I gasp.

"I did."

"Who's that for?" Elizabeth asks.

"No one. That's what's so sad. It will just sit in my drawer. Along with the rest of them."

I laugh. "The secret life of Rebecca Baca, unveiled!"

"Very funny," she says.

"You've got to have someone to wear that for," Elizabeth says. "Otherwise, what's the point?"

"Andre sounds like a great guy," Lauren says. "Wear it for him. Who cares? Not for Brad, though."

"He told me he loves me," Rebecca says. Her smile reveals she's not talking about Brad.

"Andre?" I ask. She nods. "So what's the problem, *chica?*"

"Catholics don't look fondly on divorce."

Elizabeth says, "Look, I've been thinking a lot about God, too, lately. I think he's okay with whatever is clean and pure in our hearts."

"Yeah," Rebecca says. "Maybe."

Lauren hugs Rebecca. They both are crying. Apologies all around.

"Are you all PMS too?" I ask.

"Hell yeah," Lauren says.

"Come to think of it, yes," Rebecca says with a laugh.

"Ay, Dios mío," Elizabeth murmurs.

Then the rest of our meal arrives.

After he serves us, the waiter leans in close to the table. "I didn't want to interrupt before, but there's a guy here who says he knows you ladies. He has a box and says he has something in it for one of you. I thought it might be one of those crazies, so I wanted to check. Do you want me to call the cops?"

We all turn at the same time to look at the front door. And there, with his hair wet and parted down the middle like Alfalfa, is Juan, wearing his best suit (which isn't saying much) and holding a little gold box in his unsteady hands. He smiles and nods my way, awkward as always. My heart flutters in spite of itself.

"*Ay, Dios mío,*" I say.

"Juan!" Lauren cries. "Come on over, buddy."

"No!" I scream. I don't know what to do. I want to run away.

The *sucias* are smiling.

"You know," Rebecca says. "There's another intervention I was thinking of proposing today, involving you and that sweet man standing over there."

"Don't you *love* him, you guys?" Elizabeth asks. "He's got such a clean spirit to him."

"He's a good man," Lauren says. "And he adores you."

I see that Juan has a bouquet of flowers behind his back, still wrapped in clear plastic. He's sweating.

"Thank God you're still here," he says, out of breath, when he reaches our table. "Hello, everyone." He tips an invisible cap to the ladies. "Now, if you'll excuse me, I have some business to take care of."

He crashes to one knee on the floor in front of me, almost falling to the side, and holds the flowers up. He probably bought them in the subway station. "These are for you." I take them. He clears his throat several times, appears to have lost his voice. He starts to speak, but just squeaks. That is so sad. I'm embarrassed to love this man so much.

"Come on, Juan," Lauren coaches him. "You can do it."

He gulps. Opens the box.

Inside, I swear to you, is the most beautiful ring I've ever seen. It's a platinum band, with a three-stone diamond setting. I pointed it out to him months ago, when we were walking through the Copley Mall. I'm amazed he remembered. The ring cost about $6,000—not a lot, really, but for Juan it's a fortune.

"I finally figured out why you hated Rome," he says. "I'm

sorry it took me so long. I should have asked you what *you* wanted to do there, instead of just dragging you where I wanted to go. I thought you'd appreciate the planning, having nothing to think about, being able to just relax, but I was wrong. I should have taken you somewhere nicer to eat. I'm sorry for that, too."

My heart feels like it's going to explode.

"And I figured out why you said no the first time I asked you to marry me," he says. "I thought it was because I wasn't good enough, but that's not it. It's because you don't think *you're* good enough. You're afraid I'll leave you like everyone else did. Navi, I won't. I'll never leave you. I may be short, and I may be broke, but I love you with all my heart, and I have a big heart."

Tears start to slide down my cheeks. Juan's about to cry, too.

"So, I'm going to try again, before it's too late," he says.

I can't breathe.

"Usnavys, *mi amor*, will you marry me?"

I look up at the *sucias*. They're all smiling. I can't talk. I don't know what to do. Everyone in the restaurant is staring at us.

"Say yes, *estúpida*," Lauren says, tactful as always. "What's your problem?"

"Please, Navi, say *something*. My knee hurts," Juan says. "I think I broke it."

I reach my hand out for the box.

"It's perfect," I say. "But you were perfect without it. Of course I'll marry you."

The *sucias* break into applause, and the whole restaurant joins them. Juan drops his head into my lap, finds my hand with his, and plants kisses all over it.

"Thank you," he says. "I promise you I'll make you the happiest woman in the world."

He slips the ring onto my finger, then he kisses me.

"Girls," I say to my friends when we come up for air. "I hope you don't mind, but I'll be leaving a little early today."

"Go," says Rebecca.

"Get out of here," says Lauren.

"Congratulations," says Elizabeth.

I pick Juan up and swing him once around. Then, arm in arm, we rush out the door of Umbra out into the clear, beautiful evening.

Tax time everyone! Why does that make me cringe? I mean, I've never owed anything. I've never cheated or lied on my taxes. I'm a good girl, and always get something back. It's poverty, I think. I'm not poor now, but I used to be. And once you've been poor, money stuff makes you uncomfortable for the rest of your life. It shouldn't. I should leap for joy at tax time, just like I should be able to rationally choose upstanding, gentle men who are good for me, instead of accidentally stumbling into them when I mistakenly pick good guys thinking they're bad. But in matters of the heart, and taxes, "should" is meaningless. Thank God for mistakes like my new man.

—from "My Life," by Lauren Fernández

rebecca

RAD MOVES OUT on a sunny, fresh spring Monday. Birds sing from trees, and flowers dance in the breeze along Commonwealth Avenue. I'm not home when he does it. I'm busy all day with meetings, getting the magazine to bed, attending to tax issues with my accountant, and visiting Sara in the hospital again. I've organized her family and friends so we keep a constant vigil at her side. I don't want her alone. I've never prayed harder for anything in my life than her recovery.

After work, I meet my real estate agent Carol at a trendy yellow-walled café in the South End for a quick artichoke salad and then we're off, looking at brownstones. I have been looking for months, and haven't found anything I really like. I think Carol has just about given up on me. That's why I send her a gift now and then, to let her know that I value her efforts, and that I am serious about finding a home. It must be incredibly difficult to work on commission when you spend months with someone and don't earn a dime. I want her to know I appreciate her. She has assured me that she is taking me to see all of the available brownstones in the South End, but that the housing market is just plain tight right now. I understand. I am nothing if not patient. If there's one thing I've learned from this illusion of a marriage with Brad, it's to wait for the right thing and to trust your instincts. Not to settle, never again.

As usual, the first is an unacceptable rental unit, dirty and abused. The second is a possibility. But the third, I adore. Finally! Months of looking, and here it is, my dream house. I believe this is a sign from God that my life is finally going to turn around.

The brownstone stands on a quiet, tree-lined side street with a grassy median and cobblestones. It is five stories high, with just a couple of elegant, spacious rooms on each floor, and with a large and well-appointed island kitchen on the garden level. As we inspect the cool, dark-toned library, I whisper to Carol that I want to prepare an offer; I do this even though the ancient blonde who is selling the house hints once or twice that it is out of my price range. As I examine the master bath, for instance, the owner points out the bidet, and explains to me in a loud, slow voice that this is what Europeans use to rinse themselves after using the toilet. As I admire the sconces in the foyer, she says, "Yes, they're Minka, that's a very *expensive* kind of lighting." And the first words out of her mouth when we arrived were that she was not interested in "renting the place out."

I let the comments go, and do not dignify them with a reaction. However, Carol's lips curl in on themselves and she gives the seller covert dirty looks all through our tour of the beautiful house. As Carol and I walk down the steps to the cobblestone street with the happily bubbling fountain on the median, she lets out a huff of disgust and apologizes to me, as if it's her fault. She is furious.

"These people," she says. "I'm *so* sorry."

I touch her shoulder and say, "Let the money speak for itself, Carol. That's the best policy. Let's offer an even one point two." It's slightly above the asking price.

I come home, and his things are gone. I should say, his clothes, his toiletries, his computer, and his books are gone. Those are the only things he ever contributed to this apartment, and they're the only things he cared enough about to take.

Finally, there's a note, scribbled in pencil on the back of a used envelope, left on the dining-room table. He's found someone else, he tells me, a woman of integrity and passion and ideas. Her name is Juanita Gonzalez, and he met her on the bus to Harvard Square. He underlines Juanita Gonzalez twice, as if I will care. I guess he's found his earth mother, his immigrant cause, the woman who will finally meet his parents' low expectations for women with Spanish surnames.

Good for him.

The rest of the note informs me he will be filing for divorce. "Fine," I say out loud. I don't really care anymore. This wasn't a real marriage anyway; it was an anthropological experiment.

I stare out the window into the dark for a good half hour, without moving, watching people stroll down the broad median on Commonwealth Avenue in sweaters or button-down shirts, the winter coats packed away for a while. I am happy, almost deliriously so. Yet I feel so guilty I can't stand it. I try to summarize the marriage in my mind. I create file folders in my brain, and outlines, and I organize the entire mess until it seems manageable. I could cry, of course, but I don't see the point. It was like being weaned of Brad, these past few months, slowly getting used to being without him. His disappearance does not surprise me now, and I am not injured by it as much as concerned about how to explain it to my parents and how to arrange for an annulment so that I might one day be married again in the eyes of God.

I fold the note neatly and stash it in the top drawer of the oak desk in my study. I sit down in the leather desk chair and start to go over the bills, writing checks for everything. I seal the envelopes and take stamps out of the gold dispenser for each one. I leave them in a neat stack on the outgoing mail tray. I pick up the phone and consider calling my mother, but hang up. I'm not ready for her comments right now. She will probably think we can work it out. We cannot. I don't want to hear her say it. I think the *sucias* would call each other or me to talk about what was happening to them, were they in my shoes. But I don't feel comfortable talking to any of them about it right now. I don't want the "I told you so" and so on. I imagine they'll come up with suggestions that make no sense, such as going out for a drink. I'll be better off just dealing with this on my own for a few days, sorting out my feelings by myself. Part of me wants to call Andre. He's the only person I think might have a good suggestion for me. But I don't think calling him would be appropriate. What would I say, anyway? *Hi, Andre, I'm getting divorced. I think I love you?*

I walk down the hall to the kitchen for a snack. It's too small, a galley kitchen with hardly any counter space. I really hope my offer on the brownstone is accepted. I wash an apple in the kitchen sink, then stand at the counter and eat it with a graham cracker and a glass of water from the BRITA pitcher. My hands tremble, in part from hunger and in part from the shock—or is it the thrill?—of finally being alone. The apartment is so quiet without Brad's incessant typing and nose blowing, without his philosophical rants to professors on the phone.

I'm not sure what to do next. I think I'll go to the gym, then to the bookstore. When a personal crisis strikes, it is very important to continue with your routines to the best of your ability, to surround yourself with familiar rituals and activities. It is important to remain active, not to spend too much idle time thinking about your problems. Brad never understood that philosophy is like psychotherapy, as far as I can tell; it's the domain of selfish people who are not willing to buckle down and do the hard work necessary to get on in life. It's important to be smart, but it's also important to be active with your intelligence. The more you sit around over-thinking things, the more trouble you get into. I'll get some magazines, new ones I've never heard of, and look for good ideas in them. It's important to keep abreast of the trends in the business and to see what's out there. You wouldn't believe how many new magazines pop up every week.

A MESSENGER DELIVERS the divorce papers before the week is up. Brad has not asked for a single penny of my money. He allows me to keep everything except the money from his trust fund. My magazine is estimated to be worth ten million dollars. He has not asked for any of that. He doesn't want it. And why should he? His parents will be so thrilled we're divorcing that they'll probably reinstate his trust—at least until they hear about Juanita Gonzalez. It is none of my business anymore. I sign the papers without consulting a lawyer, put them in an envelope addressed to Brad's family lawyer in Michigan, and attach postage.

It's done.

I dial New Mexico first, reaching my mother at home. As I expected, she sounds disappointed.

"You aren't getting a *divorce*, are you?" she asks with that teardrop in her voice. I hear opera playing in the background.

"Yes, Mom, I am. I have to."

"God have mercy," she says. "You know what this will do to your father."

"My *father*?" I ask. "What about me?"

"God have mercy," she repeats.

"Sometimes people make mistakes, Mom. I think God will understand."

"If God understood this kind of mistake, He wouldn't make it a sin to get divorced."

"Maybe people made it a sin," I say.

"Blasphemy!"

"Brad only married me because he thought it would upset his parents, Mom. Do you realize that? He thought I was some kind of exotic immigrant or something."

"He was a good man, Rebecca. Marriage is never easy. You have to earn your marriage sometimes."

"Is that what you've been doing all these years?"

I have never before stood up to my mother or disrespected her opinion.

"What are you saying?"

"I'm sorry to disappoint you."

"Lord have mercy on your soul," she says. "I suggest you pray on this one."

"No, I'm not going to pray on this one," I say. "And I'm not working it out. Brad and I are getting divorced. I signed the papers today. And you know what? I'm happy about it."

"I don't believe what I'm hearing. You stood there before Jesus Christ and made your vows. Do you think every day of my marriage to your father has been like a fairy tale? It hasn't. But do you think I just gave up? I did not. We worked hard at this marriage, and this family."

"I respect what you and Dad have, Mom. I do. But you don't know Brad the way I do. He was so wrong for me, Mother."

"Don't be ridiculous. I liked him."

"You didn't know him. I did. I made the right decision. I think God will be fine with that."

"Blasphemy."

"I'm going now, Mother."

"What's next, Rebecca? Next thing we know, you'll come home with a Jew or a colored boy." *Colored boy?*

"Good-bye, Mom."

Click.

I decide to wait until the next meeting of my college friends to tell any of them. And I realize, sadly, that I don't have many close friends other than the *sucias* that I want to bother with the details of my personal life.

I dial Andre's home number, but hang up before the line starts to ring. I will wait until next week.

MONDAY PASSES, AND I resist the urge to call Andre. I don't want to do anything stupid. There is plenty of time. I want to make sure I know what I'm feeling before I make any more mistakes. On Tuesday, my assistant interrupts my call with a writer who's pitching me some new ideas, to tell me that Andre is on the other line. I wrap up the call quickly and take a breath.

"Hello, Andre," I say after I press the button. "How are you today?"

"Hello, Rebecca. Fine, thanks. And you?"

"Fine."

"I'm just calling to check in with you."

"Thank you."

"Actually, I'm mostly calling to apologize for the way I behaved at the function last month. I shouldn't have tried to take the relationship to another level. It was quite disrespectful. I hope it doesn't impinge upon our working relationship."

"Everything is fine, Andre. Don't worry. I wasn't offended."

"You weren't?"

I smile. "No. I wasn't. I appreciated your honesty."

"You appreciated my *honesty*. That's good. That's interesting."

"And . . . I wasn't entirely honest with you in return."

"You weren't?"

"No."

"How so?"

"Well, do you remember when you asked me if I was happily married?"

"Of course. How could I forget? I suspected you were dishonest about that."

"I was. I mean, I am *not* happily married. Not anymore. I'm not sure I ever was."

"I know you won't believe this, Rebecca, not after the

way I behaved with you, but I am genuinely sorry to hear that. For your sake."

"I do believe it. You're a good person, Andre."

"Thank you. So are you. You deserve to be happy."

"I know. I'm working on that now." And then, just like that, I spit it out. The truth. "Brad left me last week, and he already filed for divorce. It's over. I signed the papers."

A long pause. "I'm sorry to hear that. How are you holding up?"

"I'm fine. It was coming for a long time."

"Rebecca, I'm honored that you feel I'm a good enough friend to tell me this."

"I'm sorry to dump all of my troubles on you, Andre."

"You're not dumping. Trust me, I am happier today than I have been in a long time."

"You know, in a strange way, so am I."

"What does your calendar look like for dinner tonight?" *Tonight?*

"Tonight, Andre?"

He laughs softly. "Just dinner, and a couple of friends talking. I thought you might need someone to talk to."

"I don't. I have plans. I'm filling out paperwork for my new house."

"Oh, congratulations. That's great."

"Thank you."

"Where is it?"

"In the South End, a brownstone. It's really spectacular."

"Terrific. I'm happy for you."

"Thanks."

"You deserve it."

"It's just what I was looking for."

"I know the feeling. Listen, if you can't make dinner tonight, how about tomorrow?"

I should say no, shouldn't I? "That would be fine."

"Shall we meet in the South End, then? In honor of your new home?"

"That's a lovely idea, Andre."

"How about Hamersley's Bistro, on Tremont?"

"Hamersley's Bistro is fine. How is seven-thirty?"

"That's fine. I'll see you then. Keep your chin up."

"Oh, I will. Don't worry. I'm not as upset as you might think," I say.

"That doesn't surprise me," he says. "I suspected your husband was a bit of an anorak."

"A what?"

"Anorak. It's British. You might say loser here."

"He's a good person, I think. Just not for me."

"I can't wait to see you."

"I'll see you tomorrow then, Andre. Good-bye."

"Until then."

I continue working at a good clip until the time comes to drive to Carol's Columbus Avenue office to finish up the paperwork on the house. I find a meter directly in front of the office. I don't mean to be superstitious, but I've noticed that when things are going well in my life, when I am making the right decisions and doing the things that God intends for me to be doing, everything falls into place, even parking spaces, or the types of conversations I overhear in public. I told the *sucias* about this once, and Amber told me it was called "synchronicity." Once you are truly on the proper path for your life, she said, the universe drops hints so you know you are doing the right thing. These kinds of things have been happening to me all day.

The seller has accepted my offering amount, Carol tells me, but has counteroffered with a request for a longer escrow period, almost two months. We counteroffer back with an offer to extend the original month-long escrow period by only one week. We fax the offer to the seller's agent, and within minutes get the phone call saying the seller has accepted our terms.

The house is mine.

I stop at the florist and buy a large, tasteful arrangement to be delivered to Carol tomorrow as a thank you, and then return to the apartment and begin to organize myself for the move. I tag the things I will keep, and those I will throw away. I decide that anything that reminds me of my marriage,

Brad, or my former life will go to charity. I will get new furniture to go with my new life.

I take a bath infused with ten drops of marjoram extract—a scent my herbalist assures me clears your mind—and look over some new magazines. When I finally settle into the warmth of my thick flannel sheets, scented with just a touch of grapefruit extract (battles apathy, even sexual) I feel good. Really good. And really tired. I sleep soundly and better than I have in years, and dream of Andre.

THE NEXT DAY, I wake up early and go to my aerobics class. I run the usual errands at the dry cleaners and the florist. Then I return home and call a reliable moving company and schedule a move for the day after closing on the new house. I shower and dress in a black pantsuit with a red sweater underneath, something that I think will transfer nicely from office to evening. I remind myself not to get too excited. This will not be an evening in the date sense of the word, not exactly. I will not allow for such a thing until the divorce is finalized. It will be a casual evening out with a friend, something I have not done in a long time, and I want to be comfortable.

I arrive at Hamersley's right on time, as does Andre. In fact, we both pull up to the valet at the same time, and almost crash into each other. Andre, always a gentleman, allows me to go first. He is wearing a suit, but manages to look young and energetic in it, rather than stuffy. He is a classy man. That is all there is to say about it. Classy and smart and handsome and, yes, wealthy. With good manners. I don't see what's wrong with him, even if he *is* black. I don't care what my mother thinks. She is no better than Brad's parents.

Then, together, with Andre holding the door for me, we enter the restaurant. In a move that makes us both laugh, we instinctively take out our cell phones and set them to "vibrate"—the proper etiquette for dining in public. "It's like looking in a mirror, almost," he jokes. "It's a little scary." I smile.

Hamersley's Bistro is the perfect choice, considering the circumstances. This is not a date. But not entirely innocent, either. I know it, and Andre knows it. It shows in the way he puts his hand on the small of my back to guide me along, and it shows in the way my cheeks flame with emotion, in spite of my efforts to control how I feel.

Hamersley's is elegant, but not pretentious; it is endearing, but not overly romantic, a bright, open, tasteful restaurant high on the list of any stylish Bostonian. Andre has made reservations. The staff knows him by name. We are seated in a corner booth, with a nice view of the open kitchen where the head chef prepares his magic wearing a baseball cap.

We order drinks—he a bottle of red wine, and I sparkling water with a twist of lime. He orders a goat cheese tart appetizer and an oyster appetizer. He gives a toast to my new life, and I clink his glass so hard his wine sloshes onto the table. We both laugh. "I'm sorry," I say. "Nonsense," he says. "It's the first of many moves I hope to see you make with power and joy."

The food is exquisite, and in spite of myself, I eat. This does not slip Andre's notice. He seems pleased.

"Brilliant!" He grins broadly. "This is the first time I've ever seen you eat more than a spoonful of broth or a sprig of salad."

Even though I tell him I don't drink, Andre has a glass of wine poured for me. "A little bit won't kill you," he says. "In fact, I read in *Ella*, that wonderful magazine, that a little bit of red wine is good for the heart. I don't suppose you saw that article? Here, just taste it. This is some of the best. Live a little, Rebecca Baca. It won't hurt a bit, I promise."

I taste it, and he is right. In spite of myself, I sip at the glass until it is empty.

I order the salmon, Andre orders the duck confit, and we begin to talk. He does not ask about the marriage, and I don't offer to talk about it. There's nothing to say. Rather, we get to know each other. He tells me about his parents, Nigerian immigrants who moved to England and found success in the tailoring business.

"That explains your impeccable grooming," I say.

"You could say it runs in the family," he says. "My father always looks put together. Mum too."

"Do you have any siblings?" I ask. I'm surprised I've known him this long and don't actually know the answer to that question already.

"Yes," he says with a fond smile. "I have six brothers and sisters. I am the oldest."

"Wow."

"Yes, wow. And you?"

"No, none," I say. "I'm the only one. That's why they're so disappointed in me."

"I can't honestly believe anyone would be disappointed in you, Rebecca. You've accomplished so much."

"My mom is Catholic. She thinks I should stay married. She's sure I am on my way to roasting in hell for eternity now."

"Ah," he says. "And how do you feel about that?"

"Terrible."

"Yes, I can understand that. Do you believe you're on your way to hell?"

"No."

"I don't think so, either. God has been good to you. You're a good person."

"Yes," I say. "I think so. Thank you."

"Certainly. You know, parents say things they don't mean at times. Most would bite their arms off for their kids. They almost always come around in the end. That's what parents do."

"I know. I'll get over it. I have to live my life for me now."

"That sounds like a healthy attitude."

He tells me of his upbringing in London. His family sounds stable, easygoing and supportive. I tell him of my family, of New Mexico and my love for the desert, of my family's business successes and of my mother's prejudices.

"Like my being here with you," I say. "My mother would not approve."

"And why is that?" He bristles slightly, as if preparing for a blow he has received before.

"Because you're black."

He laughs long and hard but winces a little. "Yes, well I suppose I am. And how do you feel about that?"

"Me?" I shift in my seat, uncomfortable. I did not expect him to ask such a direct question.

"Yes, you." He clears his throat and grins to himself.

"Me? I don't care. It doesn't make a difference to me. I mean, I was raised a certain way, and all of that crosses my mind, but I believe what Martin Luther King said about men being judged by the content of their character rather than the color of their skin."

"Ah, yes. Good old Dr. King. Americans never tire of talking to me about him. Did you know he was not the first man to say this?"

"Oh?"

"José Martí, the great Cuban poet, said it first, a century before."

"Really?" I should know something like that, shouldn't I? Why didn't I ever learn about this Martí person in college?

"Yes, really."

He sips his wine and takes a few bites of his meal. He looks distracted, and seems slightly tense.

"I'm sorry," I say. "I can't help the way my parents are."

"Not a problem. It just always amazes me," he says, "how obsessed Americans are with race. It has been an adjustment for me. Of course, growing up in Nigeria, my parents never had that sort of indoctrination. They had larger problems, problems of institutional corruption and poverty and violence. Issues of caste and rank and an almost complete lack of access to education and other resources. We had a large, bloody civil war in the late sixties, Rebecca, and it led to problems larger than any most people in America can begin to comprehend."

"Of course." I know nothing of a Nigerian civil war, but don't say so.

He continues, "So they didn't raise us with a racial identity, not in the way Americans think of it. We have our own ethnic identities—mine is Yoruba—that appear irrelevant to most Americans but that mean everything to us. To you, we're all 'black.' It's dehumanizing, actually. It's always shocking for me when people here bring up race. I don't perceive race as you do here. It's a foreign paradigm, completely."

I catch myself straightening out the silverware.

Andre's watching me. "In fact, I am generally disturbed by the attitude I have found among many American 'blacks' with regards to race and the way they blame it for everything that's wrong with them. I can't understand that at all."

This I relate to. "I know! I know exactly what you mean. Hispanics do it too. All the time. You should hear my friend Amber. Amber thinks she's a victim of genocide. I try to explain to her that the true victims of genocide are all dead. You can't be a living victim of genocide."

"The culture of blame, America."

"There's a lot of anger out there."

"Yes, there is, but it's directed the wrong way, as far as I see it. I speak at schools, and I see some of these young American blacks skipping school or not studying hard, or dressing improperly, and then blaming 'the system' for their problems. They want to know how I got where I am and how I fought all the prejudice. I tell them the bloody truth, that I didn't run into any prejudice. I worked hard, I was good at what I do, and that was all there was to it. American blacks don't want to hear that. Neither, frankly, do whites, who seem amazed by me for the same reasons."

"Same with Hispanics. Not all of them, but plenty of them. Enough of them."

Andre shakes his head. "In Nigeria, public school was never even an option. It simply did not exist. These kids don't know how good they have it here. That is one of the many reasons my parents left Africa. The blacks here try to get me to join them in their crusades, as if I have the same life experiences they do, and I simply have no interest in it. They call themselves African-American, and they don't know anything about Africa. I ask them sometimes to name just two rivers on the entire continent, and they can't. This is a wonderful country, and if people work hard, they succeed. It's that simple. Look at us."

"I know, look at us."

He stares at me and smiles. "I enjoy looking at you. Absolutely."

The blush, again. "You're pretty easy on the eyes, too, Andre."

He leans across the table and kisses me. It is a small, soft, elegant kiss on the lips. "Your husband is crazy."

"Ex-husband." Soon to be. In my heart, already an ex.

"Ah, I like the sound of that. You know, I could look at you forever, Rebecca," he says. I pull back, ashamed. I'm not sure why, but I worry that people are staring at us. I worry that people might not know I am already divorced, or that they will care that we have different skin tones.

"How about an after? That's 'dessert' to you," he asks, exhibiting his good manners once more by changing the subject in the face of my discomfort.

"I don't eat desserts."

"Yes, I know. That's why you are so thin, isn't it? But one won't kill you. Just one."

He summons the waiter with a subtly raised hand, and asks for suggestions. "What's the best dessert here tonight?" he asks. The waiter recommends the warm chocolate cake. "All right," Andre says. "We'll take one of those, and one of something else delicious. You choose. That, and two coffees. You do drink coffee, don't you, Rebecca?"

"No, actually. I don't. I'll have herbal tea."

The waiter nods once, and disappears. "I'm sorry for ordering for you," Andre says. "I should have asked first. When I first moved to the States, people thought I was crazy for ordering tea instead of coffee. I've gotten used to coffee. I'm delighted you want tea, I assure you. I'll never order for you again."

"That's okay," I say. "It's nice to have someone else take charge."

The waiter returns with the chocolate cake and a slice of blueberry cheesecake. I allow myself a bite of each. They taste so delicious I almost want to cry. Andre pours another glass of wine for each of us and raises his glass in another toast.

"To this weekend," he says with a wink.

"To this weekend," I parrot. Then, realizing I don't know what he's referring to, I ask, "What's happening this weekend?"

"We're going to Maine."

"Who is?"

"We are, you and I."

"We *are*?"

"I thought you knew." He smiles impishly, and the dimples appear.

"No one told me," I say. I am acting sillier than I generally find acceptable, thanks to the alcohol.

He puts one warm, soft hand over mine. "I just told you," he says. "So what do you say? Me and you and a bed and breakfast I know of in Freeport? There's great shopping in Freeport. My treat. If it was earlier in the year, we could even do a little skiing, but the hiking is nice in the spring."

I take another bite of the cheesecake, thicker and sweeter than anything I can remember. I forget to swallow before speaking. "I have never skied."

Andre looks surprised. "You grew up in the Rocky Mountains, and you have never skied? That's shameful."

"You know Albuquerque is in the mountains?"

"Of course."

I laugh out loud. "Andre, you wouldn't believe how many people don't know that. You wouldn't believe how many people around here don't even know New Mexico is a state, much less that its largest city is more than five thousand feet above sea level. Everyone thinks I'm from a hot desert."

"I know more about you than you think. So let's go skiing. We can go to South America. My treat. Skiing is one of my passions. Cross-country? It's not dangerous."

"I don't know."

"Then shopping, for now. You *do* know how to shop?"

"That I can do."

"I'll pick you up Friday after work. Does that sound right?"

"What if I don't want to hike?"

"Then we'll stay inside, or take long non-hike walks in the woods and talk about your magazine."

"Oooh. That I can *definitely* do."

"It's a date then?"

My mother would absolutely die if she knew what I was about to do. I am a married woman in the eyes of my mother's God, a Catholic woman, a Spanish woman from a long line of European royalty. And I'm about to agree to a weekend away with an African Brit who is not my husband. I might even wear the new red lingerie.

"Yes, Andre. I'd like that very much."

I'm not sure why it feels so right, but it does.

I know God would approve.

I don't usually solicit donations in this column, but I just got a terrible phone call. The homeless shelter Trinity House in Roxbury has run out of formula because so many babies were born this spring, and unless they can get more donations of the stuff, babies will go hungry. It appears this is the most fertile spring in Boston's history, thanks to a colder than normal early fall last year. So I'm begging: Forgo the Starbucks today and buy a bottle of Similac.

—from "My Life," by Lauren Fernández

sara

I WAKE UP. The walls are baby blue, the curtains the pink and gray check of a cheap hotel. I hear beeping, smell antiseptic and brown gravy. I turn toward the white shadow at my side, and see a woman adjusting the levels on two IV bags. She sees my open eyes and smiles.

"You're up," she says. She sounds surprised.

Up? I try to repeat the word, but my mouth is dry, my throat filled with pain and plastic tubes. She senses the question in my expression. "You've been asleep for more than two weeks, on and off," she says. "You're in the hospital, Sara."

I'm hooked up to beeping crazy machines left and right. I vaguely remember waking up here before, am disappointed it wasn't a bad dream. The tubes in my nose and throat make it impossible to talk. I just blink and blink and try to feel my feet and arms and hands and legs and everything. I can't. I can't feel any of it. The nurse says she's going to let "everyone" know I'm "up" and she leaves. Then they all come to touch my face with their hands. They smile at me and take their seats.

I look around the room as much as I can without moving my head, which is held in place with a brace of some sort. Two of my brothers are here, and a few of the *sucias*. Rebecca is here, Lauren is here, Usnavys is here. They look tired, like they haven't slept. Amber is not here, though Rebecca soon tells me the huge bouquet of flowers at the foot of the bed comes from her. It does not look cheap. I wonder where that girl got that kind of money. Everyone is here except the people I want the most: My children, and Elizabeth. Where are they?

The people here must all think I'm going to die. I, for one, am surprised I didn't. Did my baby survive? I wonder. I start to blink, harder and harder, trying to get them to understand the question in my brain. I think they do. That's when the stranger in the blue-jean overalls and the purple turtleneck leans over the bed with that look of pity and understanding in her blue eyes. She wears long, dangly feather earrings.

"Sara, my name is Allison," she says. "I'm a case worker for the state, and a licensed counselor with the Boston police's domestic violence unit. Your doctor asked that I be here to help you through your recovery."

My eyes dart from *sucia* to *sucia* and they all avoid eye contact with me. Usnavys cries. Lauren looks out the window at the rain, or snow, I can't tell which. Rebecca flips through a magazine. I conjure all the strength I can to gurgle up a word. "Baby."

Allison's eyebrows express sympathy and I want to scream. "I'm sorry, Sara. You lost the baby."

No. This can't be happening. It can't. My throat tightens around the tubes and I begin to cry. The act of crying feels like swallowing crumbs of glass.

Allison strokes my hair, and I see Lauren put her hands over her own mouth as if to stop herself from saying something.

"The good news is, you're going to make it through this," Allison says. "You're very lucky to be alive, Sara. Your husband might have killed you, I want to be very clear about that."

"No," I say. "You have that part wrong. It was an accident. I fell." My voice is a croak.

Usnavys rolls her eyes at Rebecca, who rolls her eyes back before looking down at her feet. "There she goes again," Usnavys whispers. I don't hear her, but I can read her lips.

"There were witnesses, Sara, including your own children. This was no accident."

"We fought. But then we made up. I slipped on the ice. He'd never push me. I knew everyone would overreact to him. You don't know him like I do."

Allison, whoever she is, looks into my eyes and smiles benevolently. I want to slug her. Why is she here? "You have a broken rib, a broken jaw, a fractured skull, and a broken foot," she says. "And with the blood you lost in the miscarriage, there was some question of whether you'd pull through at all."

I can't believe what I'm hearing. Roberto did this to me? Is it possible it went this far? I work to get another word out. "Boys."

"Your boys are safe," she says. "Your mother flew up from Miami and they're staying with her at Rebecca's right now. Your husband is still in the house and he refuses to let the boys in because they were the ones to call the police. Your father will be coming in this week."

The boys are fine, I repeat to myself. Thank God, I think. The boys are fine. But why aren't they home with Roberto? Why is he alone in the house? They don't understand. It wasn't his fault. Was it? Oh, God. It was. I remember now. He kicked me. I was flat on the ground and the son of a bitch kicked me. Why would he do something like that?

"I tell you all of this because I want you to be clear in

your mind about the seriousness of what has happened to you," Allison says. "Your friends here all told me they had no idea you were being battered, and I know from experience that this kind of injury does not just happen overnight. This has been happening to you for a long time, Sara, and I want you to know that you can't go back, that you have to move on. He's not going to change. They never change. The recovery rates for batterers are very, very low."

My baby. I remember the fall down the stairs, and Vilma, brave Vilma. The knife. I try to say her name, to ask about her. Allison nods.

"I'm sorry," she says. "Wilma is not well."

"Vilma," I correct her, but my tongue doesn't work right.

"Your husband beat Wilma as well, and the stress of it gave her a massive heart attack. She's in intensive care."

Oh, my God.

"Your son Jonah dialed 911. He saved your life. Your husband was arrested for battery, but he's out on bail."

Lauren finally speaks. "That idiot said your son betrayed him by calling the police."

"Not now," Usnavys says. *"Por el amor de Dios, mujer, cállate la boca."*

Is that an engagement ring on Usnavys's finger? I don't believe it.

"Who, the ring?" I ask Usnavys, croaking, momentarily distracted.

"We'll talk about that later," she tells me in Spanish.

"Juan," Lauren blurts, in English. "She finally came to her senses."

Allison, who probably doesn't understand Spanish, smiles. "Your mother asked your dad to come. The state has removed the boys from Roberto's custody and he is not to go near them."

Lauren comes to the bedside, crying. "I'll kill the bastard," she says. "I swear I will, Sara. My brother knows people in New Orleans. I could arrange it. I'm not joking." Rebecca comes and leads Lauren away, saying, "Come on, sweetie. Let's let Sara rest right now."

"We need to know if you'll be willing to press charges," Allison says. I think of poor Vilma, of how this poorly dressed social worker botched her name, of how much I love her. Of how Vilma called me Sarita again. How she is like a mother to me. There has to be a limit, a point at which you don't forgive someone, no matter how much you love them, how long you've known them. This, I think, is that point. I will press charges. If not for me, for Sethy and Jonah, for Vilma.

I feel sick, and the room is growing dim. I'm so tired. I close my eyes and go to sleep.

WHEN I WAKE again, I am alone. It is night, and the tubes are gone from my nose and throat. The head brace is gone, too. How long have I been asleep? I wonder. I am able to lift my head a little, and see I'm not alone, that my father sits near the window in the dark. I grunt to get his attention. He comes over and stands next to the bed. He wears the classic Dad outfit: khaki pants, a Ralph Lauren polo shirt, and brown tassel loafers. I look at the marker board on the wall opposite my bed and see that it is three days since I last woke up. Three days. I'm still tired, all the way through my bones I'm tired.

"Ay, Dios, Sarita," he says. His eyes are red from crying. Then, in Spanish he says, "Why didn't you tell us? Why didn't you tell me?"

"I'm sorry, Daddy," I say. My voice is hoarse and my throat hurts.

"No, I'm sorry. It's our fault, your mom and me, for hitting each other. You thought it was normal."

He's crying.

"No," I say. "I'm sorry. It's my fault."

"You? Sorry? For what? He's the bastard that almost killed you. He's the bastard that killed my granddaughter."

Granddaughter.

"It was a girl?" I ask. My father nods. "They could tell?"

"They could tell."

I begin to sob. The convulsions hurt my ribs so much I almost pass out. "No," I cry. "No, Daddy. Please. No. Dear God."

"Hush now," he says. He stands beside me and strokes my hair, something he hasn't done since I was a very, very little girl. He clicks his tongue to comfort me. "You just rest now. You'll never have to see that man again."

"Find that social worker," I say. "I want to tell her I'll press charges."

He looks confused for a moment, then says, "Oh, you don't know, do you?"

"Know what?"

"They can't find Roberto, *mi vida*."

"What? Why not?"

Dad sighs. "He killed Vilma, Sarita, she passed away yesterday. When the police went to pick Roberto up, he didn't answer the door. They broke down the door and he was gone. He took his clothes, some paperwork. They found his car parked at the airport, with the keys on the seat."

"What?"

"He ran away, *el cobarde*."

"No!" I cry. He stares at me, bewildered.

"You can't possibly still love him after what he's done to you!"

I say nothing, and he takes my hand, plants a small, shaky kiss on it.

"I always wondered if it was him, the bruises. Your mother pointed out that they started when you met him, but she thought it was because you had become a young lady and weren't comfortable in your body yet. Like a horse, she used to say, you were like a horse learning to use its long legs."

"He hurt me, Daddy," I weep. "All the time. For years. I wanted to tell you, but I didn't want you to think I was stupid. I hurt him, too."

"*Ya, ya*, it's over now. Daddy's here. I'd never think you're stupid."

I need to ask him how he could do this. "Where did he go?"

Dad drops my hand. "He killed Vilma, Sara." He is counting his points on his fingers, one at a time, calm and collected.

"He killed your unborn child. He almost killed you." I watch my father, waiting. Dad continues, "Now he's hiding so he doesn't have to face justice for what he's done. You must not talk to him anymore. He's a coward. You have to move on and be strong, for the boys. He would have killed *you* if she didn't stop him. You know that."

"Why is it like this, Daddy? I don't want this to be happening. I want everything the way it was."

"Ay, mi hijita," he says as he collapses in the chair next to my bed. "What am I going to do with you?"

It's too much. I have lost everything. Vilma, my daughter, my husband, nearly my life. I want Liz. I need to talk to her. Where is she? Why hasn't she come yet? Has she left me, too?

"I want Elizabeth," I tell my father.

"She came earlier, while you were sleeping."

"Please call her, make her come again."

"Okay, I will. Now, shh. Close your eyes, *mi vida*, get some rest."

THE NEXT TIME I wake up, she is there, Elizabeth, brilliant in a turquoise sweatshirt and dark blue jeans. I always envied this about her, the easy way she has with clothes, the way she so effortlessly looks beautiful.

The obnoxious social worker, Allison, is here, too, and it appears they've been talking. I can see by the fake smile on Liz's face that she finds Allison as annoying as I do. I want to laugh out loud, but don't. That must be a good sign.

I feel well enough to sit up. Elizabeth apologizes for being there, and says she needed to see me, to apologize. "It's all my fault," she says. "I should never have gone there. I'm sorry."

Allison interrupts. "Liz was just telling me the whole story of what happened. It's not her fault. And it's not your fault. None of this was anyone's fault but the man who beat you. I want you both to understand that."

Yeah, okay, but who asked you?

Elizabeth holds a bouquet of mylar helium balloons, with GET WELL SOON messages on them. She looks at me and smiles shyly. "Pretty tacky, huh?" she asks. "I saw the flowers Amber sent, and I knew I couldn't top those. So I got these instead."

I laugh a little. "Thank you," I say. "Speaking of Amber, where'd she get the money for all that?"

"You don't know?"

"I don't know anything."

"Her record is number one in the country."

"Are you kidding?"

"Not kidding. I thought you knew. She's the next Janis Joplin, in Spanish."

"I didn't. Wow. Good for her."

"Guess you two didn't talk much?"

"Not beyond the *sucia* gatherings. I don't have much in common with Aztec vampires, you know."

We both laugh. It's mean. That's why we're friends, me and Liz. Same sense of humor.

"She's about to be the most famous vampire you know," Liz says. "Be careful what you say."

"Get out of here. Amber? Famous?"

"Would I lie to you at a time like this?"

"No, probably not."

"I always told you she'd make it. You didn't believe it."

"Yeah, you did, didn't you? You've always been nicer than I am, Liz. You've always looked for the best in people. Not me."

We look at each other for a moment, and Liz looks down first, at her feet.

Then I ask her the burning question, in Spanish so Allison can't understand what we're saying.

"Liz?"

"Yes, Sarita?"

"Roberto said something to me that night, the night we fought. I need to know if it was true."

She looks nervous. "Sure, what is it?"

"He . . . he said you guys slept together in Cancún."

"What? No! Never!" She looks like she wants to spit.

"You swear?"

"I have only slept with three males in my entire life, and he wasn't one of them. I don't exactly enjoy men."

"But he was in love with you. I know it."

"Maybe. If he was, he's an idiot."

I laugh. "What kind of women have a conversation like this in a hospital at a time like this?"

"Ones who belong on *Jerry Springer*?"

I laugh in spite of myself. I'm not angry, exactly. I don't know. I'm numb. Her grin is electric. It's like in those movies, where everything turns out to be a bad dream. I'm hoping I'll wake up and everything will be different.

I stare out the window for a few minutes. I think about things, wonder if she's being honest with me. I mean, she lied to me about being a lesbian all these years so she's a good liar. I don't really care anymore. Truth is, I'd rather he slept with her than any other woman on earth. Served him right, didn't it, falling in love with a lesbian? It's almost funny. Isn't that crazy? And I'm not as angry as you might think. Maybe it's the pain meds, but I actually find it pretty funny.

"You know what?" I ask her, finally, trying to lighten the mood, get us back on track toward some kind of normal life.

"What?"

"You know what hurts most of all?"

"What?"

I smile. "That you were never even remotely attracted to *me*. I mean, what's not to want here? Look at me. I'm perfect. You never found me attractive, you said."

"What?"

I laugh. "Isn't that stupid? That's what I'm feeling right now. Seriously rejected."

"I didn't say never," Liz says with a cautious grin. "There were . . . times. A few times, actually."

"When?"

"Just times. Sometimes."

"Like when? Tell me."

"At Gillian's, that first night."

"At Gillian's?"

"Yes. I remember staring at you in the orange light. You wore a long black leather coat and had one of those big preppy bows in your hair. You looked like a reject from the Brat Pack. I wanted to kiss you then."

"Why didn't you?"

"Are you crazy?"

"Why didn't you?"

"I knew you were straight. I didn't want Rebecca to have a seizure."

"When else?"

"Graduation night. When we had that party at Usnavys's mom's apartment with all that disgusting fried food. When we sat out on the fire escape to get away from all the grease and cigarette smoke, to sit in the breeze, do you remember that?"

"I do."

"I can tell you what you were wearing that night, too. Plaid shorts and a pink sweater set, with your pearls. You took the cardigan off because it was so hot that night, and I loved the way your shoulders looked in the night air, soft and white."

"Oh, yeah. I remember that night."

"I wanted to kiss you so badly."

"Why didn't you?"

"You were engaged to Roberto. You were straight. I didn't want to be a lesbian, I wanted to be straight. I fought it all the time. I went home and cried."

"Why didn't you tell me about all this?"

"I didn't want to lose you."

"Well, I'm a normal, curious girl. I wouldn't have minded, you know, trying it out. College and everything. That's what people do."

"No." Liz shakes her head. "Those are the meanest words you can speak to someone like me. I've had my fill of curious straight women, Sara. No one screws you over quite so well as a curious straight woman."

"What about now?"

"Now?"

"Are you attracted to me now? I look like I've been run over by a truck, and no one will bring me any makeup. But still, I'm not hideous or something, am I? I mean, I'm a pretty good-looking woman for a woman with twins who just lost her baby and her husband, don't you think?"

"Sara, please, I think you need to sleep."

"Do you think I'm sexy?"

Liz stares at me with pity. "I love you," she says. "You're my best friend. And you're either really doped up or really tired, or both."

"But would you do me? That's what I want to know." I crack a sarcastic smile. Finally, she sees that I'm joking.

"You're one crazy Cubana, you know that?" she asks.

"Tell me. Would you, right now, *do* me? With all the bruises, and with that stupid social worker watching? It might be an adventure."

"No," she says. "You look like shit right now, Sara. And I prefer my women butch. There's nothing butch about getting the crap beat out of you by a man. And you need to brush your teeth."

We laugh.

Allison sees us laughing, and chimes in. "I'll leave you two ladies to talk," she says. "It's good you've got someone here to lift your spirits. That's what friends are for."

"Great," I say in English, "see you later, Allison." Then, in Spanish, I add, "Get out, you ill-dressed bitch." Liz stares at me in disbelief. I rarely curse. Then she climbs onto the hospital bed. She's so thin it's like she's hardly there. She sits next to me the rest of the night, and there is nothing remotely sexual about the way we cuddle, tell jokes, and watch terrible late-night television, though I do admit I want to kiss her a couple of times during the *Tonight Show* with Jay Leno, just to see what it's like. Must be the morphine.

Liz stays with me until dawn.

Should I be concerned that my boyfriend seems to like my new summer season Victoria's Secret catalog more than I do? I found it in the bathroom the other day, all rumpled and dog-eared, and it's only May! Why are men and women both so conditioned to look at the female body? I'm getting sick of boobs and booty.

—from "My Life," by Lauren Fernández

rebecca

ANDRE PICKS ME up at my new brownstone. I've spent the weekend moving in, and at the last minute took three days off from work to take this trip with him. It was impulsive, and something I would not have done a year ago. I would have panicked because I would have thought no one could run the magazine without me. But Andre convinced me *Ella* could survive a few hours without me. He assured me he could not.

He drives a Lexus SUV this time, white and beige. He wears jeans. I've never seen him in jeans. They fit very well, so well my heart wants to stop. He wears stylish black loafers, a thin beige sweater, and a black leather jacket. All of it seems appropriate for a drive to Maine. I wear khaki pants with black flats, a pale pink sweater, and a black wool blazer. Like looking in a mirror. Again. I've packed several long flannel nightgowns, along with some racier lingerie I've never used; I haven't decided yet what sort of trip this will be, though I have my hopes.

"You look smashing," he tells me. He hugs me, plants a friendly kiss on my cheek. Cinnamon gum? He smells so good. That smile! I want to pull him into my home, lock the doors, rip off his clothes. But I don't. I give him a polite squeeze, and take the arm he's offered to help me down the steep steps to the curb. He carries my suitcase. He opens the passenger side door and helps me in, then loads my bag in the back. The inside of the automobile smells like Andre, faintly spicy and clean. I haven't felt this charged with anticipation since I was a kid on Christmas Eve.

Because it's a weekday, early in the afternoon, the traffic through town is light. Soon, we're on 95, zooming north in the smooth comfort of the Lexus as a funky, sensual CD plays. The lyrics are in a language I've never heard.

"What is this?" I ask him.

"She's a Nigerian singer called Onyeka Onwenu," he says. "She's very good."

"Yes. And she's courageous. She went on a hunger strike a while back to protest not getting paid her royalties."

"That's admirable. Can you understand the words?"

"Of course."

"Is this Yoruba?" I ask.

"Yes." He smiles, pleased. "You're full of questions today." I've been doing a little research on Nigeria, ashamed after our last date that I knew so little about the place, but he doesn't have to know that.

"What are the other languages there?" I ask, but it's rhetorical. "Ibo and Hausa?"

He laughs and corrects my pronunciation of both. "You've been studying then?"

"A little."

The landscape zips by, green and lush. And we talk, easily and about a variety of topics, all the way past Salem and Topsfield. We talk all the way to Amesbury, and pause only briefly as we cross a large bridge, to marvel at the beauty of the place. It seems as if no time has elapsed at all, and suddenly we're at the 495 fork, and minutes from the Red Maple Inn, a bed and breakfast in Freeport, owned by friends of Andre's from England.

"They're quite wonderful people, Terry and Lynne," he says as he drives the Lexus up the gravel driveway, into a clearing in the woods. "They were both in computers but just burned out on it, really. They took their money and retired. This was Lynne's dream, to have a little place like this in the New England woods."

The inn is actually a compound of pale yellow Victorian houses with red and blue trim, arranged around a central garden. Here and there along paths in the garden comfortable lawn chairs have been placed. A few people sit in them now, some reading, others talking quietly over cups of tea.

"It's lovely," I say, realizing as I say it that Andre's speech patterns are already wearing off on me. I rarely use the word "lovely." That's a Brit thing.

"They do all the work themselves on the garden," he says as he pulls the SUV to a stop near a red barn. "Lynne has a real way with plants."

A friendly looking golden retriever lopes toward the car with a big smile on its face. Andre opens his door and calls the dog.

"Precious! Here, Precious!"

I open my door and step out. The air is slightly cooler than it was in Boston, clean. I take a deep breath. Overhead, the sky is a shocking blue. Andre and Precious join me. Brad was never kind to animals. He hated them, actually. Andre puts an arm over my shoulders, and Precious sniffs my shoes. I hear a snap, and look up to see a smiling couple emerge from a screen door in what appears to be the main house.

"Andre!" the man calls out. He's young for a retiree. I was picturing someone at least sixty-five; Terry and Lynne are my age, physically fit and attractive, in a pale, British sort of way.

"Terry, all right?"

"All right?" the man replies. It appears this is a greeting.

Precious is so excited by the commotion she's begun to bark.

"Hush now, Precious," the woman says, clapping once. "Go, in the house now." The dog obeys reluctantly. She wipes a hand on her jeans, and extends it toward me, smiling broadly.

"I'm Lynne," she says.

"Rebecca. It's a pleasure to meet you."

"Welcome to the Red Maple," she says.

"Thanks."

"I'm Terry," the man says. "Glad you could make it. How was your drive?"

"Fine," I say.

"With that guy at the wheel?" he jokes. "Come on in."

"You know, this is the first time Andre's been here with a girl," Lynne teases, elbowing Andre as the four of us walk toward the house.

"Yeah, he's usually here with boys," Terry deadpans.

"Don't mind these two," Andre says. "They think they're funny."

I smile and step into the front hall. The house is lovingly decorated in a country style that makes me instantly happy. Fresh flowers rest in simple glasses and jugs on a mishmash of antique tables. Floral patterns abound, and sunlight fills the open spaces. Several cats lounge about.

"It's charming," I say. Again a word I'd never use.

"Thanks," Lynne says, squeezing my arm.

Terry takes our jackets and hangs them in a hall closet, then guides us to a cozy den off the large country kitchen. "I know you'd love to sit and chat the rest of the evening," he says with a sparkle in his eyes, "but Lynne and I have some errands to run." He winks at Andre. "We'll just hand off the keys now, and catch up later, maybe after dinner. You're in the gingham suite, as requested." Then, he adds, "Very private there."

"Thanks."

"I haven't seen Andre so in love with anyone before,"

Lynne tells me in a whisper. "We know when to get out of the way." I don't know what to say.

Then, as quickly as they appeared, Terry and Lynne disappear, leaving me and Andre with a set of keys. "They're something else," he says, shaking his head. "I've never known two people quite like them."

"They're nice," I say. "And direct."

"Yes." Andre takes my hand. "Shall we?" he asks.

"Lead the way," I say.

We walk out a back door and across another splendid garden (there it is again—"splendid"), up a curving path, through a small forest to a modest house alone on a small hill overlooking a pond. The house is perfect, a dollhouse with its burgundy shutters and door.

"It's so cute," I gasp. "It's adorable."

"I thought you might like it."

The Gingham House is a house unto itself, with no other rooms or people around. There's a small living room, a kitchen, a large bedroom with a king-sized bed covered in a red, purple, and blue quilt. The frame is rustic and made of wood. Bright, woven rugs warm the gray painted wood floor. Checkered valences and tiers decorate the windows, with a spiced apple motif. The walls appear to be papered in colorful, cheery replicas of eighteenth-century designs. Cozy and quaint, a dollhouse built to scale by people with money, vision, and a sense of whimsy.

"I'll go get our bags," Andre says. "Make yourself comfortable."

I fall into a rocking chair and feel stress leaving my body, breath by delicious breath. Stealthily, I part the starchy curtains and watch Andre walk down the path to the main house, marvel at the way the denim stretches over his behind. There's such grace to him. I imagine him on top of me, and can scarcely breathe.

Andre returns with the bags, sets them in the bedroom. He sits on the edge of the bed and looks at me in the rocking chair.

"Here we are," he says. There's a hunger in his eyes that makes me uncomfortable. I love it, but I don't know what to do with it. It's been so long since I was intimate with anyone that I'm afraid to move. I think I'd trip, or knock something over. I feel clumsy and scared.

"Here we are," I repeat. "It's really beautifully decorated. They did a nice job with everything."

He stares without saying a word, smiles.

"The wallpaper, the floors, it's perfect," I babble. "Did they do it themselves, or did they hire a decorator? My friend Sara, she's quite a decorator. Now that she's going to have to support herself, she's thinking of opening a design firm. I think that's a great idea for her."

Still staring with that smile. Silent. He laces his fingers together and watches me. Not knowing what else to do, I keep talking.

"I'm going to help her in any way I can. She needs all the support she can get right now. All of us, my group of college friends, we're trying to help her get the business off the ground, we put together a business plan for her while she was in the hospital, surprised her with it, rented her a store-front in Newton. . . ."

He's still quiet, and smiling, only now there's a hint of a laugh.

I stop talking.

"Come here," he says. He pats the bed next to him.

"I don't know," I say. I shrug like a shy little girl and feel stupid.

"You *do* know. That's why you can't stop talking." He puts a finger over his lips. "Shhh," he says. "Just listen to the woods."

I'm quiet. I hear birds, wind in leaves. I hear water lapping softly at the shore of the pond outside the window. Andre motions for me to join him on the bed. I shake my head, cross my arms. I push my knees tightly together, and rock nervously in the chair. This isn't how I imagined I'd behave when I played this moment out in my fantasies a million times. I'd be sultry, catlike. I'd pounce on him, lick him. I'd wear lingerie, not the simple white cotton bra and panties I have on now.

Andre stands, still smiling, and moves toward me.

"Do you hear it?" he asks, coming around behind the chair.

"What?" I ask.

"The wind." He closes all of the open shades and curtains in the house, locks the door.

"Yes."

"It's so quiet here," he says.

"Yes."

"Too quiet," he says. He's in front of me now, holding his hands out to me. "I want to hear your heart beat."

"My heart beat?"

"Come here." He grabs my hands and pulls me to my feet.

"Shouldn't we be shopping or something?" I ask. I follow him, nervous.

"Later." He leads me to the bed, sits me down, sits next to me. I can't look at him. I'm too afraid. He lifts my wrist, places a finger over the veins, checking my pulse.

"Fast," he says. "Racing."

I'm perspiring. I don't do that. But I am. Andre releases my arms, and walks gently to the kitchen, returning with a bottle of champagne and two long, narrow glasses.

"No," I protest. I walk back to the chair and sit, like a girl punished.

"Yes," he says. "You need it."

"I do?"

He laughs, opens the bottle, pours. "So do I, honestly," Andre says as he hands me a glass. "Here's to Maine, and us." We click the glasses together, and I take a small sip. I think of Brad, my parents, of all the things Lauren said about me. I don't want to be that person anymore. I don't.

I guzzle the entire glass and ask for more.

The sun has begun to set, and the room is filled with a warm, orange glow. The alcohol works through me until the sounds of frogs starting to sing on the pond's edge seem like a part of my soul.

"Feeling better?" he asks.

"Yes."

"Good. Can you sit by me yet?"

"Yes." I move to the bed.

Andre sits close, and kisses me, softly, gently, with closed lips. He kisses my lips, then my cheeks, my neck, my lips again. Tender. His lips are full and soft, his face clean-shaved. It is nothing like kissing Brad, whose odor offended me and whose stubble chafed me. I could breathe Andre forever and never get tired. I nibble his lower lip, feel him smile.

"That's more like it," he says.

I pull away. This is almost perfect, but I want things to be the way I have imagined. The alcohol makes me warm, and gives me the confidence I lacked only minutes ago. "In a minute," I say. "I want to change clothes first."

"Why? You look fine."

"I have something I want to wear," I say. As I pull myself away he whimpers a bit, clings. As I extract myself from his grip, he collapses on the bed with an exasperated laugh, kicks his legs like a toddler throwing a tantrum.

"You're tough, you know that?" he calls. "You've got a shell thick as any I've seen."

I find my suitcase and take it with me to the bathroom. A full-length mirror runs down the back of the closed door. I open the suitcase, and remove the red lingerie. There's not much to it. I open the door again, find my champagne glass, and down what's left. I pour more, then down that, too. Andre has propped himself up on gingham pillows and watches me with amusement.

"What are you doing?" he asks.

"What I've always dreamed of," I say. The words sound funny. I'm tipsy. I giggle and walk back to the bathroom, shut the door behind me.

I remove my clothes, use a washcloth to tidy up the parts of me that need tidying, then remember that tidy means something different to Andre than it does to me. This makes me smile. I take the red bustier, and adjust it over my breasts. They're not big, but they're not small, either. I'm a B cup, and the bustier is creatively padded so that the Bs become Cs, without surgery. Next, I put on the red lace thong panties. My mother would have a heart attack if she could see what I see in the mirror. I sit on the edge of the claw-footed tub, and pull on the red thigh-high hose, first the left leg, then the right. I figure out the garter belt, and attach the straps to the hose. Then I find the red spike-heeled shoes at the bottom of the suitcase, and put them on. I stand and look at myself in the mirror. I look good. I look like a model from one of the catalogs, with slightly smaller breasts. There is no fat on my body, but I haven't lost all of my curves. I look like a healthy, sexy woman—it's something of an out-of-body experience for me because I'm not used to seeing myself this way. I like the way I look. But I'm not sure I can face Andre like this, even with the champagne flowing through my veins. I brush my teeth, apply deodorant and perfume, but still lack confidence.

I fish my cell phone out of my purse, sit on the edge of the claw-foot tub, and dial Lauren's number. She answers.

"Lauren!" I whisper. "It's me, Rebecca. I need to talk to you."

"Rebecca?" she asks. She sounds shocked. "Are you okay?"

"I'm in a bathroom in Maine in my red lingerie."

"You're *what*?"

"I'm here with Andre, but I can't do it. I put the underwear on but I'm scared to death. What do I do?"

"Oh, my God. Rebecca? Are you serious?" I can hear her laughing.

"I'm serious."

Still laughing, she says, "That's great."

Outside, in the bedroom, Andre calls my name and asks if I'm all right. "I'm fine," I call. Then to Lauren I whisper, "I want him so much, but I've never done this. I need your help."

"Okay, okay, Rebecca. Listen to me. You're sexy, okay? You are. You're going to do this. You're going to walk out of that bathroom and you're going to amaze him with your sexual prowess. You hear me?"

"Yes. How do I do that?"

"Just be yourself, Becca. That's all you have to do."

"Myself?"

"Let go of your inhibitions. Just let them go, like a bad dream. Live in the moment. Okay?"

"Should I wear lipstick?"

"Yes, red."

"Okay." I fumble through my makeup bag, pull out a red lipstick, apply. "Lauren?" I ask.

"Yes?"

"Am I pretty?"

"Oh, my God. Yes! You're beautiful. Now go. Quit talking to me. Get out there."

"Okay."

"Use a condom."

"Okay."

"Be confident. That's the sexiest thing. Don't wait for him to do everything. Attack him. You get on top."

I hear myself laughing as if I'm far away. "Okay, I will."

"Call me later and tell me everything," Lauren says. "I mean *everything*."

"Only if you promise not to write about it in the paper."

"I promise."

"Okay, bye."

I hang up, check the mirror again. Andre is knocking on the door.

"Are you on the phone in there?" he asks.

"Lauren. I had to talk to Lauren."

"Everything okay?"

"Yes, go back to the bed."

"If you insist."

"Are you on the bed?"

"Yes."

I take three deep breaths, and tell myself I'm sexy and powerful. I reach between my legs and feel moisture. I let my hand linger for a moment, to jump-start my confidence. My head is spinning from the alcohol and the excitement of this moment. I want it to be perfect. I sniff my finger and my own odor excites me.

I open the door. Andre sits on the edge of the bed reading through a takeout menu for a local Chinese restaurant, elbows planted on his knees. He looks up at me, and the menu falls from his hands. His mouth opens. He seems unable to speak.

I'm not sure how you're supposed to walk in these shoes. You never see women walking in them, only lying down in them. But somehow I have to get from the bathroom door to the bed. I walk, and try to move my hips. The alcohol has filled me now, and I am no longer afraid. I truly believe I am sexy, because I am. I am a woman. Like any other woman. I have all the same parts, the same wishes, the same fantasies.

"Jesus," Andre says. "You're beautiful."

This time it is I who puts a finger to my lips. "Shh," I say. "Don't talk. We've done nothing but talk since we met. Shut up."

He grins with one side of his mouth and leans back on his elbows. His legs dangle over the side of the bed. He's still wearing his shoes. Without breaking eye contact with him, I kneel and remove them. His eyelids flutter, his tongue wets his lips. I run my hands slowly along the insides of his calves, his knees, his thighs, and stop just short of his you-know-what. *You-know-what?* I can't believe I can't even bring myself to think the words. *Just short of his balls. And penis. There.*

"Rebecca," he says. "Come here."

"Shh," I say. I straddle him on the bed. He's still fully clothed, lying back. I kneel over him. I like this. It has always been part of the fantasy for me that he be dressed and I not. He tries to sit up, but I push him down.

"Not yet," I say. "Wait."

He looks amused, and excited. I can feel his excitement underneath me.

I use the same finger I touched myself with earlier to trace his lips, nose, the outline of his beautiful eyes. I stick the finger in his mouth, feel his teeth and his tongue. Then I lean over him, and kiss him, passionately. He pulls me in, powerfully, and flips me over so that I'm on the bottom. The bed creaks with the movement.

"Your turn," he says between kisses. He runs his lips lightly over my neck, one hand in my hair and the other on my breast. "I've dreamed of this moment," he says as he begins to unfasten the bustier. "Since I met you I've dreamed of this. I'm mad about you."

As he kisses my breasts, I watch. His skin is so dark against mine. With Brad, it was my skin that was dark. I hated the way Brad commented on it, so I refuse to say anything about Andre. I remember a phrase I learned in art history class: chiaroscuro. Light against dark. Beautiful.

Noises rise up out of me I've never heard before. Andre plays with my nipples in a way no man ever has. He bites, kisses, touches, traces. My back arches.

"Take off your shirt," I say. He stands and pulls the sweater over his head. I stand too, and look at him. I want to feel his chest against mine. I am pleased to see he has very little chest hair, and no hair at all on his arms or back. His muscles are well defined and powerful. He has very little body fat, either.

"You are so handsome," I say. "I can't believe how handsome you are."

"Thank you," he says. I love his accent, his little smile. It makes me crazy.

We stand in an embrace, kissing. He is warm and solid, as I imagined. He pushes his pelvis against me, and to my surprise I push back. I touch him through his trousers, and am overjoyed to discover he is quite wide, large enough to be enjoyable and not too large to hurt.

"God," I say. He lets out a small moan. His hand reaches between my legs, and slides the thong out of the way. He knows what he's doing, unlike Brad. I cry out with pleasure. Andre falls to his knees, and kisses my stomach.

"You're so strong," he says. "So amazing."

He moves my legs wide apart, and kisses me there. His fingers, his mouth, all concentrated in the same place. I can scarcely stand. He's so good at this, I'm afraid I'll explode too soon. I stop him, kneel next to him, repeat the favor for him as he lies on the floor. He kicks his pants all the way off, and there he is, nude. He is remarkable in every way.

"Stay there," I command. I find my purse in the bathroom, take out a condom. When I find Andre again, he is touching himself, moving his hand along his penis. He stops when he sees me.

"No," I say. "Keep going. I want to see you do it."

I've never watched a man masturbate before, though I've wanted to. Andre obliges me, asks me to do the same. I sit, legs spread, close to him, and pull the thong to one side with one hand, work on myself with the other. He watches. I watch. Until we can't watch anymore.

I roll the condom onto Andre, ask him to stay on the floor. Then I straddle him again, lowering myself slowly onto him, letting him fill me up. We look into each other's eyes, and it feels so good I actually cry.

"Are you okay?" he asks.

"Oh, yes," I say. I begin to move. I smile. We hold each other's hands. "More than okay. This is amazing."

"Yes. It is."

We change positions several times, move around the room, and finally finish on the bed, doggie style. It's a position Brad found disagreeable, but one I find intoxicating. By the end, I scream. Years of pent-up frustration comes from my mouth, and I come for an eternity.

Andre holds me. We kiss, softly.

"Unbelievable," he says.

"You think?"

"Yes. I do."

We rest, doze, for a while. Call for takeout.

Then we do it again.

It is two full days before we manage to get any shopping done at all.

The bridesmaid dress is one of the greatest conspiracies against single women ever invented. Mine just came in the mail, ten days before my friend Usnavys is supposed to get married, and I nearly mistook it for a 1970s prom dress. Thanks, Navi. Now you're sure to be the cutest one at the wedding.

—from "My Life," by Lauren Fernández

lauren

AMAURY RUBS HIS rippling six-pack of a belly under the sheet next to me. We have just finished making love to the soundtrack of morning birds. Fatso sits in the windowsill chattering at them as they fly by, as if they'll drop into her mouth because she's asked, like takeout. No one ever accused that cat of being bright. Amaury has stayed here every night for a month, and she's used to him. So am I. I don't want him to leave. Not even for his class.

In our three months together, I have come to love this man.

The bedroom window is open and that dewy, incredible springtime Boston air flows over our naked bodies, warm and salty. I feel free, for the first time in my life, I truly do. And happy. Last night, before we fell asleep, he looked at me with small fear in his eyes and asked, "Would you mind listening to something I wrote?" It was a short story, in the style of Garcia Marquez. I was floored. I know my Spanish is nothing to write home about, but hanging with Amaury has helped polish it. The boy can write. Even if he *is* a drug dealer. His words had music to them. Merengue. And not Puerto Rican merengue, which I can now distinguish from Dominican merengue. Dominican merengue *rocks*. Puerto Rican merengue? Not.

The *sucias* think I'm crazy. They think a guy who looks this pretty, has eyelashes this long, walks with a swagger, smells like CK-1, wears a cheap-looking beeper, wears his shoes laced and unlaced with equal ease, drives down Centre Street slow and *chévere*, and knows every questionable character along the way—heck, we all think a guy like *that* can't be any good. Couldn't possibly be any good. They laugh at men like him. It's not just the *sucias* either. All professional-looking Latinas smirk at us in public, when we walk through the Stop & Shop holding hands. His kind laugh, too. His boys think he's lost his mind, for being with an educated, independent woman like me.

"I love you," I say. He leans over, kisses my eyelids.

"I love you too."

"Don't go to school. Stay here all day. Let's play."

Amaury laughs. "Wish I could. Sorry." He climbs out of bed, and I stare at the Valentine of his back. He is strong, works out. Solid. "I'll take a bath," he says in English. "You come, *Mami?*"

"I want to sleep," I say, drowsy. "Just a few more minutes."

"Okay," he says.

I close my eyes and float in happiness while the water runs upstairs.

I didn't set out to love Amaury Pimentel, drug dealer. I admit when I first started seeing him I was undoubtedly on the furious rebound from that bigheaded Texican cowboy. But it happened. Suddenly, I found myself staring at my blinking green cursor, unable to come up with a decent sentence because Amaury danced on my brain. Then one day Jovan came by the way he always does, with his dreadlocks bouncing, wanting to flirt. And I had *no interest*. Not in Jovan, not in Ed, not in any of them.

All I could think about was the way Amaury folds his clothes lovingly with his rough, scarred hands. I daydream about the fringed penny-shaped bullet scar in his shoulder from the drive-by, and the way he cries when he hears a sad song. I think of the multicolored beads he wears around his neck, how he holds them in his hand like a single, droopy flower when he undresses. He makes the sign of the cross with them, brings them to his lips with his head bowed in a prayer for deliverance and safety on the streets and for the health and well-being of his beloved mother. *Que Dios la bendiga*, he always says. May God bless her.

Amaury surprises me all the time. He figures out math in his head that I can't even do on a pad of paper. He has more common sense about things than I've ever had in all my life, and he isn't afraid to tell me when I'm being illogical. He reads while I watch TV, says life is too short for the "idiot box," as he calls it. All I want to do these days is file my column, and go home, because in a few hours Amaury will come to the door, ring the buzzer, and enter my world like the most beautiful, challenging puzzle ever. And I love the way he moves in bed, the power in his arms, the fearlessness of his explorations. He never thinks I smell bad, even when I do. He never seems bothered when I don't shave. He never thinks I look fat.

Do I still call Ed a few times a day and hang up on him? Yes, I do. Does he call back and tell me he has caller ID and say that if I don't stop stalking him he'll take out a restraining order on me? I'm not proud of it, but yes. I don't care. I hate that man so much I could kill him with my bare hands.

Amaury returns to the bedroom, puts on his designer boxers, his baggy jeans, his T-shirt and button-down, his beads, his boots, his sunglasses. His cologne. Man smell. I love that man smell. He taps me on the shoulder to rouse me from my dozing. "I'm going," he says. He kisses me. I cling, close my eyes, and nibble my way along his cheek and neck with my lips.

"You coming back?"

"Right after class. You want me to pick anything up?"

"Oatmeal," I say. I'm eating better, and for the first time have not gained weight while happy in love. Amaury suggested I eat more frequently, smaller meals, and drink a lot of water. It's working. If I forget, he's there to remind me, with a glass of water and a slice of whole wheat toast. Who would have thought?

Amaury's taking English as a second language and Spanish literature classes at Roxbury Community College in the mornings. When I told the *sucias* they didn't believe me. He's smart. They just don't understand.

Technically, Amaury lives with his sister, here in Jamaica Plain, not too far from me, actually, on the Franklin Park side of Washington Street. She lives in that skinny little patch of neighborhood where all the triple-deckers look like the one she and her family live in—saggy, splintery, and sad, like someone sat on them. The wooden porch crumbles, covered with graffiti. Empty cans and candy wrappers seem to grow from the dark black dirt in the yard. There are a few scrubby shrubs around, but they're not for aesthetic pleasure, they're for hiding in when the cops come looking for hoodlums. He has driven past with me, but I've yet to meet them.

For the record, Amaury does *not* live in the projects, like Usnavys thinks, and he doesn't have any *children*. I asked him about all of that, and he shook his head. "She thinks I'm *El Arabe*," he says. "There's a guy over in the projects who looks like me, and they used to get us confused all the time. We look the same, and it makes big problems for me. He's an idiot. I hate him. People stop me all the time over there and think I owe them money, but it's that guy they want."

LATER IN THE day, Amaury picks me up from work in his black Accord with the green apple air freshener hanging from the rearview mirror.

"I have to stop at my sister's," he says. "You want to go?"

"Sure." He has never invited me to meet his family before. I'm flattered. I check my reflection in the sunvisor mirror, adjust what needs adjusting.

The ride is smooth, the car smells good. I've never seen someone take better care of a car than Amaury takes care of that thing. You'd think it was a living being, the way he talks to it, pets it, feeds it and waters it, cleans it out, vacuums it with that little old DustBuster he keeps in the trunk.

He has a cassette tape in the car stereo, and sings along with a song that always makes him sad. You'd think a big macho Dominican like that, a guy from a country where the men seem to think it is their God-given right to have four different women going all the time, you'd think he wouldn't start tearing up at every little thing. But Amaury is different. He cries all the time.

He drives to his sister's, singing that song and looking dejected, with one hand on the wheel. He whips the other around dramatically, as if he were performing for a crowd of thousands. *Los caminos de la vida, no son como yo pensaba, no son como imaginaba, no son como yo creía.* The roads of life are not how I thought they'd be, are not how I imagined they'd be, are not how I believed they'd be.

"I was so young when I got here," he says when the song is over. "It's not fair." At that moment, we drive past the men's homeless shelter at the Jamaica Plain end of Franklin Park, and Amaury looks at the guys sitting on the cement picnic table out front, smoking their cigarettes and wearing their thin charity-issue zcoats.

"Ay, Dios mío," he says, gesturing toward them. *"Eso, sí, me da mucha vergüenza."*

The sight of them makes him so sad he almost starts to cry again. Then, in Spanish, he asks, "Do you see now? You see how it is for people like me? These are the choices we have."

When we pull up to the brown, raggedy triple-decker his sister lives in, I see a young boy standing on the second-floor balcony, watching us. He's wearing just a T-shirt and underwear, and starts to jump up and down when he sees Amaury.

"Hey, Osvaldo," Amaury says as we walk from the car to the front door. "Get inside before you catch cold. What are you doing out here?"

I've only been to apartments like this on assignment, usually when someone was shot or arrested. We walk through the front "door," which can't really even be called that because it's missing the actual door part. It's a rectangular hole in the wall with rusty hinges where the door used to be attached. The communal stairwell smells strongly of bleach and urine, and is dark. Still, I can see that the old wallpaper has peeled off and left patches of what I'm sure is lead paint chipping onto the steps. "That *cabrón* landlord still hasn't fixed the light," Amaury says, punching the wall. "He should be in prison the way he treats the people who live here. He thinks we're animals. I tell my sister not to pay the rent until he fixes things, but she pays him anyway. She's afraid of him."

Amaury's sister lives on the second floor. When we arrive, she is sweeping the landing near her front door. Her ample body is stuffed into a pair of very tight red jeans, and she wears a white sweatshirt with a faded Santo Domingo decal on the front. Her hair is pulled in a tight ponytail, and she looks like the oldest young woman I've ever seen, with dark circles under her pretty hazel eyes.

"*Hola,* Nancy," he says, and gives her a hug. She hugs him back. Then, in Spanish, he says, "I want to introduce you to my girlfriend."

I reach out to shake her hand, and she looks surprised. She takes her hand from behind her back, where she is massaging out a knot, and shakes, uncertainly.

"How are you?" I ask.

"*Allí,*" she answers. *There*. It's a sad answer, from a sad woman.

Osvaldo runs through the splintery door leading from the landing to the balcony where we saw him earlier. He's wearing socks with his shirt and skivvies, and holds a small, mewling kitten in one hand. Its eye is full of pus. I want to cry. In the other hand he holds a plastic robot toy, with both arms missing. He smiles, and I can see that this boy is going to be even more handsome than his uncle someday.

"What did I tell you?" Amaury yells at him, holding one hand up as if he might strike the boy. "Get in the house! You're going to get sick." Then, to his sister, "What are you doing letting him run around like that? It's cold. I bought him clothes, use them. That cat looks diseased. Get rid of it, or take it to a vet. What's wrong with you?"

Nancy ignores him and continues her sweeping. If this woman ever had energy or happiness to her, it's long gone. Amaury and I enter the apartment.

There isn't much to it, just a long, lopsided hallway with a series of rooms opening on either side. There are three bedrooms, a living room, a kitchen, and a bathroom. The floors are wood, dull and old. An older boy, heavy and wheezy, sits on the living-room floor playing with marbles. He drops them on the floor and watches them roll to one side of the room. He doesn't have to push them to make them do this; gravity does it. The whole apartment leans, and gives me the dizzy feeling that I've stepped into a carnival funhouse.

"Jonathan," Amaury scolds the boy. "Get up and go clean your room. You do your homework yet today?"

The boy looks up at him with the flat, wet eyes of a cow. He does not look bright, I'm sorry to say. He breathes with his mouth open, and looks at me. "Who's the pretty lady?" he asks. Amaury raises his hand again, as if he will strike the boy. "Don't be rude," he says. "This is Lauren, my girlfriend. Now you go do your homework."

Jonathan gets up and plods in his tight sweatpants and Bugs Bunny shirt to the kitchen. We follow him there. An older woman with bright red hair with gray roots, black hot pants, and a leopard-print sweater stands at a narrow old stove, stirring a few pots of delicious-smelling food. Her wrinkled cleavage pours over the top of the shirt. She smiles, parting her painted red lips to reveal lipstick decorating her yellow teeth.

"Cuca," Amaury says, leaning toward her with a kiss. "How are you today?"

The woman returns the kiss with a jangle of cheap bracelets and turns her eye toward me.

"This is my girlfriend, Lauren," Amaury says. He's smiling like a kid who brought home an "A" on a math test.

"Nice to meet you," Cuca says in Spanish. She has the gruff voice of a long-time smoker.

"Likewise," I answer, in Spanish.

"You American?" she asks.

"My dad is from Cuba," I say in awkward, accented Spanish. "I'm a Latina." She and Amaury both laugh out loud.

"You're American," Cuca says with a patronizing pat to my arm.

"My little American beauty." He kisses me.

Jonathan is standing in front of the open refrigerator, eating generic American cheese slices out of the flat palm of his hand, chewing with his mouth open. He is a large boy whose lips close over food like a horse's. Amaury pushes him out of the way and slams the door closed. "Give me that," he says, taking the cheese from the boy. "Quit eating so much. You're getting fat. Go do your homework like I told you." The boy laughs, though I can tell from the look in his slow eyes that he is hurt.

"You don't have to say that to him," I say, after the boy has left the room.

"Yes I do," Amaury says. "He's fat. Look at him."

"You'll hurt his self-esteem." *Auto estima.* I learned that phrase watching a Spanish-language talk show on TV.

Amaury ignores my comments. "You want something to drink?" he asks. He opens one of the cabinets, and I'm shocked to see right through to the tender green leaves of a tree outside.

"My God," I say. "There's a hole in the wall."

"Yes," Amaury says with a know-it-all smile. "That's what I was telling you before. The landlord here is no good."

He pours a generic brand of grape soda into a couple of squeaky clean jars that serve as glasses, and we return to the living room. A teenage girl appears, talking on a cordless phone. She is very pretty, too. She's speaking in English,

giggling with a friend. She comes to the black leather sofa
and sits down. She wears baggy jeans, a tight, striped
sweater, and large gold hoop earrings, and something about
her reminds me of Amber when I first met her, back in college. Her long, dark hair is highlighted blond and red in the
front, in large chunks. Her hazel eyes are large and beautiful. She wears no makeup at all. Her skin is smooth and perfect. I don't know what went down in the Dominican
Republic, but some beautiful people come from there.

The furniture in the room is very nice, in that new immigrant kind of way. Leather furniture, glass coffee table—it's
a lot like Usnavys's furniture. Why is it that immigrants, no
matter where they're from, always buy furniture like this and
cover it with clear plastic? They can be from anywhere in
the world, but they always have those curio cabinets with
those cheesy little figurines in them, and those brass floor
lamps that look like flowers on long stalks, opening into a
blossom filled with a light bulb. They always have those bedroom sets made out of lacquered wood, white with gold
trim. The curtains are pink, lace, and everything is spotless
and tidy. An entertainment center holds a TV, which is off,
and a stereo, which Amaury turns on, blasting an Oro Sólido
merengue disc.

"Turn it down, you big stupid," the teenage girl shouts, in
the sort of rough and clumsy English that will help her defend herself on the streets someday, but that will never help
her find a good job or get into a good college—or even finish *high school*. She covers her free ear in an attempt to better hear what is being said through the phone into her other.

"Go to your room," Amaury says. "And get off the phone.
You talk too much on that phone."

He grabs the phone from her and starts talking to the person on the other end of the line. He makes a furious face and
hangs up.

"What you doing?" she cries, reaching out to him with
her thin arms and long manicured fingernails with all those
gold rings and bangles.

"I told you, I don't want you talking to boys. No boys, you hear me? You're too young. Focus on your school." He speaks Spanish, she speaks English.

"I hate you," the girl says, trying to get the phone from him. He holds it up over his head.

"What did I tell you? Go to your room."

The girl obeys, but with the angriest look I've seen in a long time.

"Are you always so rough with them?" I ask in English.

He answers in Spanish. "That's one of the things I hate the most about this country. You raise a hand to a child here, and they throw you in jail. In Santo Domingo, children have respect. Here, they have no respect because you can't discipline them."

"Hitting a child doesn't teach them anything but fear," I say. "And being overly strict with a teenager is inviting rebellion."

"Anyway, this is where I live. You like it?" Another thing that amazes me about Amaury: He never argues, or holds a grudge. He lets things go. Allows us to disagree.

"It's very nice," I say.

"Come here."

He leads me to the front bedroom, a tiny room with three twin beds crammed into it. "This is where I sleep," he says. "I share the room with Osvaldo and Jonathan. You think that's nice?"

I don't. It's dreary, and small. But clean. There are hundreds of Spanish-language books piled in one corner. The whole apartment is lovingly tended to, decorated to the best of this family's ability, filled with the warm smells of good food cooking, and music.

"It could be much worse," I say.

"Why do you think we're here, *tonta*?" he asks. "We come from *much* worse. Those kids out there? They think this is a palace. This is all they know. They have never seen those houses where my customers live, over in Newton. They've never seen an apartment like yours."

We return to the living room, and Nancy reappears, shuffling off to her bedroom. She emerges wearing a polyester security uniform, her hair wet and plastered against her head.

"I'm going," she says to us, sighing in her exhaustion and rattling her keys. Then, she calls to Cuca, "I'm going. *Ya me voy*."

After she leaves, Amaury tells me that she works two jobs, back to back, every day except Sunday. She cleans a building in the mornings, comes home for an hour to do housework, leaves for her evening job watching the door of a building at Northeastern University. She gets home at midnight.

"Her husband does the same thing. And I still had to buy this furniture for them, and some food. I still have to help them make the rent every month. You see what I'm saying? This country is ruthless."

"My God."

"Nancy's studying computers in her free time. And English. But they're gone so much the kids are going bad. That's why I'm hard on them, *mi amor*, because they don't have anyone around to teach them right from wrong, except Cuca." His voice drops to a whisper and he rolls his eyes. "Cuca is Nancy's mother-in-law, and she's a little bit crazy." He points to his ear with a finger, and paints a circle with it.

Osvaldo comes in the room with an empty raisin box. He has ripped the back of it in such a way that he is able to hang it on the waistband of the pants he has just put on. He struts into the room, a little boy no more than eight years old, and stops in front of us with a big smile on his face. He pretends the box is a beeper, and takes it off in the same way I have seen Amaury do many times. "*Que lo que*," he says, pretending to be on the phone. He puts his tiny hand over his tiny crotch.

Amaury grabs the raisin box and throws it across the room. "Don't do that," he says, kneeling down so he is eye level with the child. "That's not funny. I told you before, don't imitate me. You understand? Where's your homework?"

Osvaldo laughs and runs away, shouting English-language

curse words. He slams his bedroom door. Amaury sits down next to me on the couch and plants his elbows on his knees, and rests his head in his hands.

"Do you see how it is now?" he asks me. "What am I supposed to do with all of this? They think I'm cool, you know? I try to hide it from them, but they know what I do." He looks up. "That one, Osvaldo, he got sent home from school the other day for pretending to be a drug dealer at school. The teacher caught him with a plastic Baggie full of laundry soap, and they thought it was cocaine. They thought he was actually selling cocaine to other first-graders. They said it's happened before."

"My God."

"Yeah."

He leans back on the sofa, puts his hands behind his head, and blows a deep breath out through his mouth. "Come here," he says, opening his arms to me. I do as he asks, and we sit like that, on his sister's couch, listening to music, until Cuca calls everyone to dinner.

We sit at a rocky table in the cold little kitchen, and eat off of mismatched plastic plates. Cuca has made *mofongo*, a mash of plantains and bacon with garlic, and some sort of greasy chicken fricassee with white rice and red beans. The meal is delicious, and Amaury seems to have softened a little bit toward the children as soon as he gets some food in him. The boys tell him of their days, the teenage girl tells him about a school play she wants to try out for.

"That's good," he says. "Did you read the book I gave you yet?"

"No," she says.

"Why not?"

"I been busy."

"I *have* been busy," he corrects her.

"Shut up," she says. I know how she feels.

He gives her a doubting look, finishes his meal. When everyone finishes, the teenage girl clears the table and starts to wash the dishes in a trickle of cold water in the sink. When she turns the water on, the wall lets out a groan to wake the dead and the pipes clang to life. I offer to help, but Amaury pulls me away. "Let's go," he says. As we leave, Nancy's husband comes home from his first job, as a mechanic, looking as tired as his wife. He greets me, then staggers up the stairs.

"How old is your sister?" I ask when we get back in the Honda.

"Twenty-eight."

"That's it?" She's my age. She looks forty.

"Yes."

"How old are the kids?"

"The girl is fourteen, the boys are eight and ten."

"She had a baby when she was fourteen?"

"That's not unusual in Santo Domingo," he says. "What? Don't act so impressed."

"My God. With the same guy?"

He imitates me. " 'My God.' No, not the same guy. I don't want to talk about it."

"I had no idea."

"I know. That's why I wanted to bring you here. Do you understand me now? Do you understand why I do what I do?"

"Yes."

"Good."

"But there has to be a way out."

He shrugs. "Maybe. If you figure one out, let me know."

"How much do you earn a week?"

"Five hundred dollars, tax free."

I laugh at the "tax free" part. He makes much, much less than I expected. I get an idea.

"I have a friend who just got a record deal," I tell him.

"Yeah? *Felicidades.*"

We park on the curb near my apartment complex, at a meter. Amaury will have to move his car by 6:00 A.M., or get towed. We walk in silence the rest of the way to my apartment. Once we're inside we sit at the dining table and I continue to talk.

"She called me the other day and asked me if I knew anyone who could help be part of her street team around here."

"What's a street team?"

"It's a thing they do in the record business, you have to ask her about it. I think you have parties and play her record and give copies of her records to your friends and try to start a buzz about her music on the street."

"They pay you to do that?"

"I swear. They do."

He laughs. "I love this country." He seems intrigued.

I call Amber at home. She answers her phone in a language I've never heard before, I'm assuming it's Nahuatl. I'm surprised to hear Shakira playing in the background.

"Hey, Amber, it's me, Lauren."

"Please call me Cuicatl," she says. "That's my new name. I'm not a part-time Indian, so don't treat me like one." Humorless, as always.

"I would if I could pronounce it, okay, girl? But I can't. So you're Amber to me."

She doesn't laugh. Ever since she got caught up in all this Mexica movement stuff she hasn't seemed to have much of a sense of humor. Like that one time I talked to her on the phone and she sneezed, and I said *"Salud,"* you know, the Spanish word for "bless you," that means *health*. She got all uptight and said, "I'm not ill. Don't say that." Ooookaaaay.

"Look, I was calling you about that thing we talked about with the street workers for your record?"

"Did you find someone?"

"How much do you pay?"

"It depends on how much work they do."

I tell her the whole story of Amaury. She listens calmly, says, "I'd be glad to help him out, Lauren. Raza are always being siphoned into crime. It's nothing new. It's part of the master plan of the Europeans to destroy us. How much has he been making?" I figure this is a bad time to point out Amaury is probably not Indian, as the Spaniards wiped out all the Indians in the D.R. and Puerto Rico. Let her think of him as Raza. What do I care?

"Here," I say. "I'll let you talk to him. He's right here."

I give the phone to Amaury, and he talks to Amber in

Spanish for at least fifteen minutes. I can't make out half of what he's saying, because he's talking so fast. But I do hear him give her his address and the spelling of his name before he hands the phone back to me.

"Hi," I say.

"He's on my payroll," she says. "I'll match what he's been making, but I want you to make sure he's doing what he needs to do. I'll send you an E-mail outlining what's expected of a full-time street worker."

"Thanks, Amb-Kweecatel, whatever."

"You're welcome. I'm always happy to help *nuestra gente*. He sounds like a nice guy."

He sounds like a nice guy. I like hearing that. I don't think any other *sucia* would say something like that about Amaury.

We hang up. Amaury is smiling. He has removed his beeper, and he's taking it apart with a pocketknife, smashing the insides.

"What are you doing?" I ask him.

"I'm quitting," he says. He's beaming. He stands up and kisses me. "I'm doing what you're always getting on me to do," he says. "I'm starting a new life."

Happy Cinco de Mayo. I really stopped to think the other day about what it's like to be an immigrant. With so much immigrant-bashing going on lately, many of us forget how much courage it takes to leave your home, your language, your family and friends—and how much fear and desperation you'd have to face to do so in the first place. It's overwhelming, really, to think of the hardships many of those around us face every day in starting their new lives, how many challenges, in accomplishing the sorts of things we take for granted: talking to the cashier at the store, mailing a letter, paying a bill, ordering a margarita at a college bar on Boylston.

—from "My Life," by Lauren Fernández

elizabeth

I QUIT AT last. It took me four months, just enough time to see whether my scandal might have a lasting impact on the ratings. It didn't. People still tune in. But this whole experience has had a lasting impact on *me*. I don't want to be in news anymore. I find news, TV news in particular, to be a shallow waste of time. So I do it. Quit. Without hesitating.

John Yardly waited until I had made it through the morning newscast, paced back and forth like a humid, caged animal, nervous and dripping, and then asked me to join him in his office. I'd told him I needed to talk, soon, and I think he knows what's coming. My heart isn't in this nonsense anymore.

As I tell him my plans to leave the business, he stands at his window, observes the small group of dedicated lunatics who still hold a minor hatefest down below. They are here every morning. Don't they have jobs? It has also become a counter-ritual for a handful of equally nutty people who support me to show up on the opposite side of the street with *their* signs. I have become the subject of a morality war between the extreme far Christian right and the extreme far gay left, right here in downtown Boston. Even the national news has covered the story now, pretending the crowds are larger than they are. What I hate the most is the two drag queens who have decided to show up in full regalia, looking like the biggest, hairiest, ugliest women on earth; this does nothing to help my cause.

I think of Colombia more and more, and have a ferocious wish to return.

I don't know how to protect my heart from the look on John's face. The disappointed news director, small and fat and slippery. What can you do with a man like that?

"The ratings," he says. He has the Nielsens out on his desk. The last four months of them, in a neat little stack. "If you made a graph, Liz, it would go straight up. Who'd have thought all this would boost our ratings? I guess people like lesbians. I know my guy friends do."

"That's not necessary to tell me," I say.

"You know, we aren't prejudiced against you here, Liz, we like you. We're your friends, it was a joke."

"Oh."

"Yes, damnit, it was. I can't believe you're just quitting. We've stuck by you for a very long time, considering. You owe us."

"Considering what, John?"

"The controversy, Liz. That's *all* I'm talking about today. If you want to go home and screw a dog, I don't care, okay? Sleep with whatever you *want*. I run a news operation. All I care about is ratings. And the ratings are good. The people have spoken, you know what I mean? I don't know if it's because of your sexuality or your sanctimonious take on religion—a lot of them love that, too. Liz, this is Boston. Liberalville. But whatever it is, they say that they like you. I don't ask them why, sometimes they tell me and sometimes they don't. Plenty of them dislike you because of your accent or because you color your hair blond. There are a million reasons out there not to like you. But most love you. We need you here. Please."

"I'm sorry."

"So you wanna be a producer or what, babydoll? Tell me what you need to make you stay. Anything."

I don't have to think about it for long. At this point, it would be a relief to never have to show up here again. The muses have been biting at me to do something else, something greater than this, with my life. I want to write poetry. In Colombia. I want to go home.

"No, thanks," I say. "I appreciate it. But no. I need out of this business."

"What?"

"I'm sorry. No."

"Look, Liz, you knew you were going to have to go to the other side of the camera eventually, didn't you? You can't be an anchor forever, right? You get a few wrinkles or a double chin, a few gray hairs, you know how it goes. Unless you're Baba Wawa or Katie Couric, that's just the way it goes."

"I don't think you get it," I say. "I don't want anything to do with news anymore."

"Just take the producer slot? We could really use someone like you on the other side. You'll regret bailing."

"Someone like me?"

"You have a lot of experience and good ideas. You speak Spanish."

"I'm sorry, John. I think it's time for me to do something else with my life. I've been feeling that way ever since we took out those ads with the deep voice saying 'We cover weather like news . . . because weather *is* news.' Thanks anyway."

"So you're leaving, then?"

"I guess so."

He sighs. "I'm really goddamn sorry, Liz. You were a good anchor. People have crap for brains."

"Yes."

"You can check down with Larry in human resources, and he'll work out your final pay. You can count on getting a few months of pay at least. We'll work it out for you."

"Thanks."

I stand and shake John's hand. "Hey," he says. "No hard feelings?"

"None," I say. "I wish you only the best. It's been *interesting.*"

"You ever need a good reference for something, I'm your guy," he says.

I decide to call Larry later. I just want to get out of the building now. The air is thick with the sweet smell of death. I don't even remove my makeup. I just grab my coat and hat, and head to the parking elevator, no security escort. I don't want to be here at all. I pull out of the underground parking lot in the truck and speed away from the crazies and their big open mouths, as has become my custom. Once I'm on the freeway, I call Selwyn at her office.

"You remember that sabbatical you've been telling me you could take if you wanted?" I ask. I'm panting as if I've run a mile at top speed.

"Sure," she says. "What about it?"

"How soon can you leave?"

"Now. Summer classes don't start for another couple of days, and I'm not teaching that much anyway. They've got me mostly doing research type stuff this semester, they just want to see me publish books. That's academia for you. Why?"

"So take the sabbatical, then. We're going to Colombia."

"Colombia?"

"You can write there, right?"

"I can write anywhere there's paper."

I explain it to her, and drive. I'm speeding, flying down the road of my life, free at last. I want out of here, out of this cold, gray wasteland, out of this hateful culture where people don't hug unless they want sex from you, out of this hard, frozen land with its bruises and lacerations, out of American-style journalism with its lies and exagerrated non-stories. I want tropical breezes on my skin again. I want to see the faces of my people again, hear the rhythm of our language. I can't explain it exactly, but I have a need to go back to Colombia. I tell her I quit, and tell her of my dream.

"I need to try it, writing poetry," I tell her. "In Spanish, about my life, in Colombia, for Spanish speakers."

"Okay," she says. "Let's think this through. Let's make sure this is what you want to do."

"It is. I've thought about it. I need to spread my wings and fly, Sel, try to be the poet I have always wanted to be. But not in English. Not in their language. I want to write poetry about me and who I am in my own language. I want to write of being a lesbian in Spanish, a language that has never embraced women like me. I want to take my scythe and carve through the jungle of ignorance. And, crazy as it seems, I want to go back to Colombia."

"You're sure? It's pretty unstable right now."

I am. We'll go for one year, and hopefully Selwyn will come to understand who I am. She will learn to dance to the rhythm of me the way I have learned to dance American for her.

Selwyn, being Selwyn, does what she needs to do, and embraces the opportunity to experience something new in her life. We pack our things and eat pizza and dance to Nelly Furtado, her favorite artist. We rent our houses out to college students whose parents can afford it, and store the truck at Sara's house, in her huge, five-car garage.

We arrange through a Colombian real estate company to rent a furnished vacation house along the coast in Barranquilla for one full year. Sara drives us to the airport in the Land Rover, with the boys. She mentions a few teary, crazed phone calls she's getting, from phone numbers police say are in Madrid, Spain. Roberto has not let go. We haven't heard the final word from his sick mouth yet. I'm concerned for Sara, for her finances, for her safety. I can't move away forever, because of her. Because of her—and Roberto, my fear of him—I must return to Boston sooner rather than later. They all hug us good-bye. We get on the plane.

When we arrive in Barranquilla, the air is blue with sea salt and the flowers bloom their perfume everywhere you go. Selwyn puts on a sarong and sunglasses, tucks the Spanish-English dictionary under her arm, and begins to explore the markets and the coffee shops.

I open the window to my new little room with the small desk and the typewriter. I open the window and welcome the muses who fly in on diaphanous wings, and I begin to write.

At home.

By the time you read this, I'll be in San Juan, suffering great indignity beneath the hideous bridesmaid dress. I don't care if it's Vera Wang. It's still awful. Wish me well. I'll do my best to catch the bouquet.

—from "My Life," by Lauren Fernández

usnavys

MY NEPHEWS, DRESSED in boys' tuxedos, cart the cages of white doves out of my uncle's Blazer onto the front steps of the church. As rehearsed, they set them down on the ground next to me and Juan. The birds coo and cluck just the same as common pigeons, *m'ija*. I punch Juan lightly on the arm and say, "Hey, did you know doves sound just like pigeons? Shouldn't they make a classier noise?"

Juan rolls his eyes and kisses me on the lips, again. "Figures you'd think that," he says with a smile.

"What?"

"Doves *are* pigeons. It's the same bird, better publicists."

"No way, don't lie." I smack his arm and the sleeve of my gown falls over my shoulder. Juan pretends to be injured by the blow just in time for the priest to come out and stare at me in terror. He's my mother's cousin's husband's brother, but hasn't liked me from the start of this thing, when I told him I thought I *deserved* to wear white because married doctors shouldn't count. He needs to loosen up. Look at all our guests! Hundreds of people, *m'ija*. Who knew I had so many friends?

As the bells begin to peal in the tower, my nephews pull up the doors on the wire cages. The doves sit there for a minute, as if they don't know what to do. I kick the cages with the pointy toes of my silk Jimmy Choo slingbacks.

"What are you waiting for, pigeons?" I ask them. "Fly, already. Be free."

One by one, the three dozen birds flap out of the cages and rise into the cobalt sky above San Juan, toward the small puffy white clouds. The guests watch them go, eyes shielded with their hands, and they cheer. Then the idiots begin to toss rice in my hair. I *told* them not to do that. Do they know how long it took me to get this mess straightened and glued just right into the goldilocks extensions? I don't want to spend my honeymoon picking *arroz* out of my princess curls, *m'ija*.

Juan and I run for the limo, and I swear he looks like he's going to trip on those too-long tuxedo pants. Poor shrimpy thing. I tried to get him to do a decent fitting, but he said he was too busy. He holds the door for me, and I roll myself in. Juan stuffs the long train to my dress in after me, jumps in, and then I spread out. I was *born* for limos, girl. All this room, the champagne and the little television. I could live back here. I press the button to lower the window and call out to my friends, "Meet us at the beach. And you *sucias* better be hungry, *entienden?*"

There they are, standing in those fluorescent dresses on the sidewalk waving at us. Rebecca with her gorgeous new man, smiling in that new red dress with the plunging neckline. Can you believe she caught the bouquet? He's good-looking—and rich. Not that this means anything. I can't believe the way that girl rubs up on him, it's like she's a different person. I don't blame her, though; he's charismatic and sexy, especially when he looks at her. Wish I would have gotten to him first. *Just kidding!* He's been good for her. Girl needed some meat on those puny bones.

Sara's here with her mom and dad. She's got those little boys of hers. Look at the way she lifts them into the air and smothers them with hugs. That's love. I'm just sick that Roberto has been located in Spain. I hoped he was dead. But still, she better get some money when this is all over. He left, and that's abandonment, *m'ija*, and in the eyes of the law that don't look good. He's also a fugitive, so she should absolutely get the house, everything. In the meantime, the *sucias* have started a Sara trust fund, plus we're all invested in her new interior design business. I always thought she should be doing something like that.

There's Lauren with Amaury. I can't believe how nice he cleans up, *m'ija*. He almost looks classy, except for that hoody limp. I'm glad she brought him. I owe him an apology. It's incredible, the whole thing with him throwing those huge parties for all his friends and Amber selling all those records in New England because of him. Wow! I'm sorry for everything I said about him. I thought he was *El Arabe*. Then when Lauren told me he got a story published in that literary journal and got himself accepted to the Latin American studies program at UMass Boston, on a scholarship, and that he wants to focus on marketing in Latin America and Latin communities? I could have swallowed my tongue, girl.

Speaking of Amber. That rat man she was dating isn't here. He's history, she said, and that was *all* she said. Guess they had a royal Aztec divorce. Amber doesn't mess around. She looks happy, even though you get the feeling she's living in a tower now, all by herself. You'd think she might get some designer gear and sunglasses, go that route, but she doesn't. The bodyguards follow her around. What kind of a life is that? We need to make sure that girl doesn't get too stuck on herself from that record. Keep her grounded. Maybe when this is all done, I'll have her over for a week and and we'll lose those bodyguards and take us some long walks.

Liz is here with that poet of hers. Turns out they can't stay in Colombia because of the government's new habit of jailing or killing gays and lesbians. Does drama follow that born-again poet or what? They look serene, and Selwyn doesn't look half bad with a tan. I wouldn't do her, but, you know, I'm a married woman now.

Juan covers me with kisses. I always wanted to be married in Puerto Rico, and I did it, just like I wanted to, in the church in Old San Juan. I can't believe I made it up the cathedral steps in these shoes, with my long train, without tripping.

All the *sucias* except Rebecca were my bridesmaids. (She had to work until the last minute and just got here.) I know you're not supposed to have that many. Sometimes a girl has to break with tradition. It was *hard* to pick the right color for dresses for those girls! I mean, what color is going to go with all those different skin tones and hair colors? I had to compromise and go with peach.

I got my dress in Paris, *m'ija.* I'm not one of those women who's going to wait overnight outside of Filene's for that one big sale day on wedding dresses. *Ay, no, m'ija.* Paris for me. I didn't make Juan go with me, either, he *asked* to come. But would he let me pay his way? No. I told him it didn't really matter anymore, because what was mine was going to be his soon enough.

"And what's mine will be yours," he said, goofy and sincere.

I had to laugh. I didn't want to hurt the guy's feelings, but it's not going to make a speck of difference that I can access the twenty-three dollars in his checking account. You know what I'm saying?

He leans into me now, all hot and bothered.

"Down, boy," I say, slapping his wrist softly. "Can't you wait?"

"No, I can't. I *want* you."

"Por Dios," I say, shooting him the stare. "You better chill." He laughs and nibbles my lower lip. I nibble back. I love this man.

After that speech he gave me in my house last year, I don't know exactly, but something in me just snapped. That whole thing with Sara got to me. *Ay, no, m'ija*. I had to realize then, maybe it's not about the money. Rich men leave you too, you know. Maybe rich men come with a whole new set of problems to deal with. Or, worse, maybe rich men and poor men all come with the same set of problems and we *act* like they're different. Pigeons and doves.

The driver waits until all the guests are in their cars, and we drive in a big honking snake to the beach outside the city where I've reserved my spot of sand.

The white tents flap in the breeze, surrounded by lush green palm trees. As we walk from the parking lot across the white sand, the beating of the congas grows louder. I can't believe La India, my favorite singer, was available, or that Rebecca, feeling guilty for not being able to make the ceremony, paid for her to perform at the reception. That girl has gotten very generous since she started dating that man of hers. I have to thank him later.

We get to the dining tent, with the portable wood floor, and I circulate, making sure everyone finds their seat. I stop at one table, silent. My mother and father sit side by side, even though that wasn't the seating arrangement, talking about old times.

Ay, m'ija. That was such a big part of how this all happened. I found my dad's phone number on-line and called him, told him how I felt about everything he did to me, and then I *forgave* him, *m'ija*. It was liberating. He said he was a drunk when he left us, and that he found God and got sober later, but he was too ashamed of himself and what he'd done to look me up. I don't know if I believe that part or not, but it felt good to let it all go, to forgive him and stop punishing Juan for everything that man did to me and my mom.

My father came to my wedding.

Now I just have to tell Lauren to take a lesson from him and stop that drinking nonsense before it gets her in real trouble. She doesn't think she has a problem, and I can't say for sure she does. But all of us talked about it, and we decided we'd do like an intervention or something. She's our *sucia*. I don't want any of us to hurt ourselves anymore.

We take our places at our tables, Juan and I at the one on the small platform with the scalloped skirt around the bottom. One by one, our friends stand and give toasts. I know it's breaking with custom, but when everyone is finished, I stand up and make my own toast, to the *sucias*.

"All y'all know this wedding wouldn't have happened without you," I say. They forked over a lot of the money for this. "And I want to say thank you."

Twenty thousand dollars they gave me, combined! It would have cost twice that much back in the States. No, I know, Puerto Rico is part of the States, I'm not retarded. But if you're Puerto Rican, I mean deep down inside a true Puerto Rican, you call it a nation because that's how it *feels*. Lauren, with all her preaching, doesn't understand that. Puerto Rico is more of a nation than the U.S., at least in raw emotion.

"You a bunch of filthy rich dirty girls, you know that?" I joke. "How'd that *happen*?"

"Hey, *I'm* not rich," Sara calls out. "Remember?" She grins. "Yet."

The crowd laughs.

"Now eat!" I command.

I dig in. I've got caviar, lobster, and the little puff pastries. There's the traditional Puerto Rican food, too, you know me, but at least I got those men with big white hats on to serve it on these china plates. I can't have me a party without some *arroz y habichuela'*, you know what I'm saying?

After dinner, Juan and I cut the cake. He feeds me, I feed him. The flash bulbs pop. Smile! We drink champagne. And then, to my surprise, my father comes to stand by the table.

"It's custom," he mumbles, head hung low like a dog. "To share the first dance with your father."

My eyes flood with tears as I take my father's hand, and we dance. His neck still smells of wood. "Daddy," I say, "I missed you."

"I'm sorry," my father says. "For everything. You turned out great. I'm proud to be your dad."

I look up at Juan as we dance by, and his eyes are damp. He smiles and mouths the words "I love you."

I'm filled with the peace that comes from knowing Juan will never leave me. I don't care if we end up living in my little renovated Victorian house in Mission Hill for the rest of our lives. I love him. And that's all that matters. Please, if those big movie stars can marry the lowly key grips or whatever they are, then I can marry this wonderful *hombre* I've adored for ten long years. That's right. Ten years. Oh, I *had* a heart, *m'ija*, all this time. I had a heart. It was just in pieces.

You heard me. That man right there, that goatee-wearing, baggy, rolled-up-tux–having, able to fix anything in my house, nearsighted, good-hearted fool. I've loved him for ten long, stupid, crazy years.

And now I've gone and done it.

Now I have to love him until I die.

I didn't catch the bouquet. But I blame Usnavys. That Puerto Rican housewife throws like a girl.

     —from "My Life," by Lauren Fernández

lauren

IN HONOR OF her newly announced engagement to software millionaire Andre Cartier, we allow Rebecca to pick the restaurant for the *sucias* meeting this time around. True to her nature, she picks Mistral, in the South End, near her incredible brownstone that Sara has made even *more* incredible by decorating it in this style she calls "Yankee Chic." It's Victorian enough for little Miss Uptight, but truly hip and, I can't explain this kind of thing, you know me, the perpetual mess that I am, but it's really fantastic over there, all modern art and Persian carpets and clean smells.

I am early, as usual, because if you're late, you miss the story. Miss the story, and you risk some white guy . . . well, I think I've told you all about all *that* already. A lot of things have changed this past six months. But that's not one of them, unfortunately.

Just this morning, one of my editors stopped by my office to talk about some protests going on down at the *Boston Herald,* over a columnist there who was so ignorant he wrote that we should stop letting Puerto Rican immigrants enter this country. Puerto Ricans, in case you have forgotten, or never learned, have been U.S. citizens since 1918, and Puerto Rico is a U.S. territory, for better or worse. I guess I told you *that* a few times, too. Sorry.

"What do the Latina people, you know, the Latina community, think of all this?" he asked me. He twittered and chirped with all the brilliance of a little yellow canary.

"I don't know," I told him. "But as soon as we all get on our daily conference call this afternoon, I'll ask them all and get back to you."

He nodded and thanked me. He actually *believed* me. He not only believed that all Latinos think the same, but that we all get on the phone with each other every day to plot our next swarthy, mysterious, and magical move. I may have mentioned that I think we have a long freaking way to go in this country, and that sometimes, just sometimes, it feels to me like we're moving backward. Don't. Think. About. It.

I sit at the bar. I'm not drinking anything tonight. I haven't had a drink since two weeks ago, when Usnavys got married in San Juan and all the *sucias* ganged up on me and told me I was a lush. I'm *not*, okay, I am not a drunk, and they, as usual, were just overreacting. I just wasn't happy back then, when I was drinking a little. And being unhappy can make a girl do stupid things. But I'm happy now.

Know what's amazing? Cuicatl's selling more records in New England and New York than any other region except California and Texas—a first for a Spanish rock album. SoundScan shows the numbers started pumping up as soon as Amaury started working for her. I had no idea. I've never seen a person work as hard as he does. He has parties every night, somewhere new, which exhausts me and makes me not so sure of him as my final man in the long line of men I've had. It's like those millions of Dominicans all know each other. He says it's easy because parties are "part of the Dominican psyche." Did you know that? Did you know Dominicans were the single largest immigrant group to New York City in the 1990s? Millions of them came, and until now no one in the mainstream music industry paid attention.

They still haven't noticed at the *Gazette,* but Dominicans are everywhere. I'm too tired of fighting to care.

I never thought that so much of Amber's Mexica success would come thanks to a bunch of Afro-Dominicans. It's hilarious. Next record, Cuicatl says she wants to put more Dominican influence on it. I like Amaury. I'm just not sure I love him. Is that bad? I mean, am I scared because it's so easy, or am I finally realizing I really ought to admit to what I am—a middle-class American—and stop trying to fit the foreigner stereotype loved by my editors? Amaury's a good guy, but he's not perfect for me. But maybe no one is ever perfect. Maybe Amaury is American too. Hmm?

The head of Latin marketing for Wagner called Amaury yesterday, wants a meeting so he can find out my boy's secret. Seems they want to get his help on a few other projects, not just Cuicatl. They've offered him a salary, $50,000 a year, plus benefits. I told him to hold out for more, and he is. He's already saved some money and he and his sister are moving their mother and other relatives to Boston, to a little apartment in Dorchester, so she can get good health care. He's moved in with me for good now, and when he's not working he's going to school and looking up words in his Spanish-English dictionary. It's crazy, but this man does not lie, does not cheat. We exist peacefully together. He's always around, and I'm invited to all the parties he throws. It's inexplicable, but I trust him. I'm a size ten again. You figure out what that means. Means I'm happy! And you know what? He loves me that big. He says he'd even like to see me a little bigger. "American women are too set on being skinny," he says. "It's not sexy."

Speaking of big girls, Usnavys comes next, as usual. She's outdone herself tonight, with a hat. And I don't mean a winter hat. It's full-on spring now, with all the snow melted and all the little white blossoms popping up on the trees everywhere, a beautiful, alive time in Boston, and that means only one thing for Usnavys's wardrobe: color and hats. This isn't the kind of hat you wear to stay warm. This is the kind of hat with a little net that hangs down in front of it, a pillbox hat. It's purple and matches her suit, which has white piping all down the front, and, of course, her feet are smashed into those little pointy shoes. She's dressed like Jackie O. Or an Easter egg. And she's on that little cell phone. It looks even smaller than the one from last year. And, yeah, she looks a little bigger. We've all noticed that. We expect to see a little baby in a pillbox hat and fur coat coming along any day now. Once *it* gets married, you can bet it's gonna whip that ring around like that, too, just so everybody knows, you know, that *another* Puerto Rican has arrived, y'all.

Next comes Sara, alone. She hasn't dated anyone since her husband left and do you blame her? They still can't find the guy, either. They think they've got him, and he disappears again. Creepy. She made her parents rent out their house in Miami—to some young rap star, people, isn't that hilarious? They moved up here with her to help her with her boys for a while. Her mom watches the kids while Sara runs her new business, "Interiors by Sara." I've talked to her a few times, and she and her parents seem to want to sell the house in Chestnut Hill next, and move back to Miami, to that big old house of theirs, "but only once we get the business nationally known, and we start the TV show."

I'll tell you about the TV show in a minute. Be patient, *damn*.

I told you a long time ago I thought Sara would be a great interior designer, and it's true. She's already scored some big clients—it doesn't hurt when you're running a business in Newton Corners to be Jewish, okay?—and the calls keep coming in. She's able to support herself now, and doesn't have the time or desire to focus on anything else. That's what she tells us, anyway, and we respect that. Sara's never been alone before. I guess she's having fun now.

She seems to like it, a lot.

Sara always looked good, as you might recall, put together and everything, but now she glows. She looks a lot younger this year than she did last year, even if she *does* still look a little too much like Martha Stewart, minus the prison stripes. Guess in that line of business looking like Martha can't hurt. Especially if you're planning to start your own Spanish-language TV show about interior design. Elizabeth, who ran back to the U.S. when Barranquilla cops started questioning her "lifestyle," produced the pilot, and Target is already interested in carrying a line of Sara-designed housewares in Spanish-dominated U.S. cities like Chicago and Houston.

That's the TV show. The biggest Spanish network in the country already wants it, for weekday mornings. Sara wants to call it *Casas Americanas,* American Homes. Sounds good to me.

Maybe all this newfound happiness is why Sara wears brighter colors, too. I'm not saying she's up and made herself look like a peacock or something. But look at her. She's wearing a bright orange blouse, with a white sweater tied around her shoulders, and expensive jeans, with orange pumps. She looks like a different woman. Her makeup is still perfect, and her hair, and she's still telling stories. She's *still* loud as hell. But there's something new to her, a genuine joy. It almost, almost, makes me want to cry. You should have seen her in the hospital, with all those tubes and machines. I didn't think she'd pull through. But she did. And now look at her. My *sucias*.

Here comes Liz. Selwyn dropped her off. They had to throw the college girls out of Selwyn's house, where they live again. I'm glad she's back.

Liz has devoted herself full-time to producing the show. She says she can't wait to move to Miami where they hope to base the show, says maybe there she'll be able to finish writing a book of poems. Miami. It makes me sad because I'm going to miss my girls, you know what I mean? I'm starting to feel the pull back to the South myself. Maybe Miami would be a nice change, if that little newspaper down there would actually ever hire a leftist Cubana such as myself. *Not!* Maybe Amaury will do well enough in marketing that I'll be able to retire from the toxic newspaper business and do something truly important, like raise a couple of kids. I don't want to get ahead of myself here, but, hey, it doesn't hurt to dream.

Now then, Cuicatl—I've finally learned to say her name, okay, because it's impossible not to with every teenager on the street shouting it and wearing it on T-shirts—comes next, in a white stretch limo. She tells us her record label arranged it for her, and that she didn't pick it. But, she says, it's about time a Mexica got to ride in style.

Well, excuse *me*.

Who does that Mexica princess think she is, anyway, huh? *I'm kidding*. We are so happy for her, you have no idea. She's the one we worried about the most. She walks in wearing that halter top and those hip-hugger jeans and those boots and those sunglasses, with her hair wild, in every direction, and Usnavys cries, "*Ay, Dios mío, sucias*, I can't believe she still remembers who we are. I told her, when you finally make the big time, don't forget us. But look at her, she acting like she don't *know* me now."

Cuicatl smiles. She looks good. She looks happy. She got dumped by her man and just kept going like nothing happened. She actually prefers being alone—that's what she says. Why can't I be more like that? And, I have to admit this, but only to you. I *love* that girl's music. With all that money behind her new record, she came up with some songs that blow my mind. Her music is deep, and it's beautiful. And I'm just starting to think maybe she has a really good point with all that Mexica talk I used to call "garbage." It's *not* garbage. It's history.

It's true, most of what she says. And now that she has traveled, she tells me she understands what I was talking about when I used to lecture her about how different all us Latinas can actually be, as diverse as all the world, we are. Now that I hear her music and see what all of us have been through, I think she has a point, too. We may be really different in a lot of ways, but there's something to it, this whole being a Latina—perception becoming reality and all of us finding each other and helping each other and—shoot. I don't even *have* to drink to start sounding like a sentimental fool.

Rebecca comes last. I don't mean to front, but she's looking a little chubby—for her. And that's not saying much. She's still skinnier than any Latina I've ever seen, but she has some meat on those bones now. She still dresses like Margaret Thatcher, though—what are you going to do? She looks happy, too. It's Andre. What a catch. I am *so* glad she dumped that Brad fool. Best thing she's ever done. And even though her parents are being weird about Andre, she doesn't seem to care. I hear she even dances now. Not sure I want to see that. Andre's been a good influence on her. She takes out the latest issue of *Ella,* flashing that big-ass rock of hers, and gives us our requisite copies. And guess who's on the cover, girl?

Cuicatl.

Huh. And I thought it was gonna be *me*. Not.

We move to a bigger table, and talk and order our beers and juices (thank you very much, I'm not about to go off the wagon now) and talk the way only *sucias* can talk.

There's a lot of catching up to do.

READING GROUP GUIDE

1. Lauren spends much of her time feeling inadequate and like an imposter. Where do you think these feelings stem from?

2. How do you think Rebecca's husband was raised to view Latinos? How does this impact their marriage? Is his disappointment in her fair?

3. Elizabeth is the only foreign-born of the sucias and yet she spends the least amount of time thinking about her Latin identity. There are two big reasons for this. What do you think they are?

4. Elizabeth does not seem to think her secret and her religion are at odds with one another. Why not? Do you agree?

5. Sara seems to feel some responsibility for what is happening in her home life. Do you agree that she is partly to blame? Why, or why not?

6. How could it be that Sara's home life and the image her friends have of her could be so different? Why do you think she hid the truth for so long?

7. Why does Gato finally stray in his relationship with Amber? How does Amber react? By contrast, how do you think Lauren might have reacted in the same situation?

8. Why does Usnavys think she needs to find a rich man? What in her past makes her believe this? How does this belief impact her happiness?

9. The sucias, like many groups of friends, seem to end up in sets of two. Who do you think these pairs are? Why do you think they are drawn more to each other than to any of the other friends?

10. The sucias are all Latinas, but they are also of different races, religions, and backgrounds. How does this compare to images of Latinas you see in the U.S. media?

FOR MORE READING GROUP SUGGESTIONS VISIT
WWW.STMARTINS.COM

Read on for an excerpt from the next book
by Alisa Valdes-Rodriguez

Dirty Girls on Top

Coming soon from St. Martin's Press

usnavys

So, you *know* I'm not hoochie, okay? But an unhappy marriage can make a woman do questionable things. Things she's not proud of, things she only tells her closest friends—and even then with the understanding that if they blab about it, they'll get their butts kicked. So it is, *m'ija*, that I am cheating on my husband at a big, adobe resort outside Santa Fe, New Mexico. I have never cheated on him before, and I'm not sure I'll do it again. Alls I knew what I had to do it just this once.

My college friends, the *sucias* who've been my support network for fifteen years, since we met as freshmen at Boston University, will arrive here in a few days for our annual reunion vacation trip, a tradition we started two years ago. Me, though? I flew here from Boston yesterday to take care of some personal *business*. A seven-year-itch kind of thing, only a little early. I am not proud of it. I decided I'd seduce the golf pro after I saw his photo in the brochure for the resort. I learned what I could about him, and I concocted my strategy. It worked.

My husband Juan? He'd looked up at me through his smudgy Clark Kent eyeglasses over the morning paper across the breakfast table before I left yesterday, his curly black hair sticking up all greasy wherever it wasn't receding. "Why are you going early, *mi reina*?" he wanted to know. Reina means queen, and to him, I'm still an empress. He doesn't know about the golf pro, and I don't think you should tell him, either.

Yesterday morning, I'd told Juan I wanted to get to the resort early, to observe some outreach programs having to do with Latinas and AIDS in New Mexico, for my work as an executive with the United Way of Massachusetts Bay. It sounded very official when I said it, and he was duly impressed with his empress. "They've been very successful," I assured him, with a wave of my hand. "It's a model that might be emulated here in New England."

He believed me, *el pobre*. He thinks marriage *changed* me. For a while I did, too, but now I know better. Listen to me. After ten years of juggling no less than two men at a time, a woman does not just up and change, even though God and the world know there's a piece of paper and shared taxes involved now. I am a manizer the same way my daddy was a womanizer. I was to the manor born, as the *Americanos* say, and, even though I'm not proud of it, I seem to have stayed the way he met me.

Juan thinks I'm different because he chooses to see the best in people, even when it isn't there. His heart is an emotional hallucinatory. I know, you think that's a plus, right? Being married to a loving optimist like Juan. But *nena*, that's just *it*. Juan believes *everyone* and he does it indiscriminately. Ain't no backbone in *that*. The boy is naïve. Back when he had him a *job* (ah-hem), he believed all them drug addicts when they told him they were clean and sober as an Osmond now, he believed them when they said they were going to get jobs and stop doing shit like steal cars. Then he acted all surprised when they came crawling back into rehab after getting arrested for crime and crack again. I try telling him: "People don't change that much, *m'ijo*, no matter how bad you want them to." Badly. Yes, I know the difference between good and bad grammar; no, I don't give a rat's ass. Whatever, no?

This resort is supposed to look like a pueblo Indian village, like in those Georgia O'Keeffe paintings, where the pastel flower petals looks all coochie unfurling in their glistening glory. I think this place looks like a big bunch of caramels all stacked on top of each other, or like a dusty old stack of wedding cake. Depends on your attitude. At the moment, I've chosen candy over cake.

Chocolate, to be exact.

His name is Marcus Williams, and he's the golf pro—like an older, darker Tiger Woods in his crisp white polo shirt and khaki shorts, with that salt-and-pepper hair and that little sexy moustache. He's probably forty-five or so, but he's got him some deltoids like cantaloupes. You don't think you're going to find a fine black brother teaching golf up on an Indian reservation near Santa Fe, *nena*, but life is full of delicious surprises, *sí*? From what I read about him, I know that Marcus used to be a professional golfer. He retired and came to work here because he likes the desert and dislikes Arizona's take on black people. I've seen his car, and it's a white Cadillac, so you know he's got at least a little something-something stashed away from the days when he almost won the U.S. Open and Nike came knocking on his door. I learned all this about him on the Internet, following his comments on message boards and things like that. I plan my attacks like an army general, always have.

I should tell you, Juan don't play golf. Doesn't. He doesn't play golf. Dominos, yes; golf, no. Nintendo, yes; skiing, no. I try telling him, you will never get ahead in business inviting CEOs to play dominos, *nene*, but he's like, "I don't want to play anything with CEOs except Revolution, I want to play with my tio and my sobrino and the people I actually like." Whatever.

All my life I'd dreamed that I'd marry the kind of man who played him some golf, and liked to ski and go places like Jackson Hole, okay? I imagined it, and it felt good. So, I'm not saying I'm falling in love with Marcus or any nonsense like that, I'm just saying Marcus plays golf and Juan doesn't. Marcus has a Cadillac and Juan doesn't. Marcus wears polo shirts, Juan does not. I'm just saying that sometimes you have things in your head a certain way and life spins you a different way, and you still wonder about that

road not taken, only my road not taken is more like a little
path for golf carts. I like Marcus, and I wonder, you know, if
I'd married me someone like that would I still be struggling
to pay the Bloomingdale's charge on time. I wonder if I'd
still be choosing to go to fancy dinners for work alone because I can't bear the sight of my husband in his Che Guevara t-shirt and tuxedo jacket sitting next to me. I am a
woman of class and substance, and I'd like to imagine what
it would be like to be married to a man of class and substance, or at least to spend some time with one. So sue me.

Oh, and the best part? Marcus likes me back. I knew he
would, though, and not just because he said my Boston accent was cute. It's because I look good and I smell good and
I'm full of compliments of the type and caliber that make a
man feel important. That's all. Oh, and he likes some big
thighs, know what I'm sayin'? You *know* how black men feel
about curvy women of a generous size and proportions. Uh
huh. He gave me a lesson this morning, wrapping his big old
arms around me to show me how to swing, holding me so
close I could smell the manly spice of his deodorant and the
heat of the sun on his clean cotton clothes. He eased his
hand over mine and whispered in my ear, "Don't swing
carelessly, Usnavys, don't lose focus on your game, girl."

I could have taken him right then, okay, *nena*? I coulda
had him this morning, that's how bad he wanted me. But I
had lunch to attend to in the resort cafe. Some things are better if you have to wait for them—including me. I sat outside,
behind my big sunglasses with the golden DIOR on the
sides, with a view of the kiva-shaped pool and the jagged
plum-colored mountains, with my copy of Oprah's magazine and a *Gourmet* magazine to keep me company. I started
with some baby pork ribs marinated in red chile and hoisin
sauce—with a side of rainbow-striped designer cole slaw
with black seeds in it. To drink, I had sparkling water with a
twist of lemon, and a sweet white Zinfandel. Then, because I
knew I'd need some energy for the afternoon, I had the leg
of lamb, marinated in garlic sage oil. There was polenta on
the side, which is really grits but nobody around here is going

to tell you that, baby, with tomatoes and pine nuts all sprinkled up on it. They say pine nuts are the most expensive nuts in the world to harvest, because it's so damn hard to get them out of the pine cones, the caviar of the nut world. I had a local red wine with the main meal. Even though I am not big on drinking so much in the middle of the day, I knew I might need to drift away a little bit because of what was coming. There was something else I wanted to tell you. What was it? Oh, right, *m'ija*. The rest of the meal. What was the side dish? I remember now. You would have died, girl. It was sautéed *vegetables*, which ordinarily would not sit well with me because I do not *do* vegetables, but they were tossed with a pecan demiglace and mint. It was so good I almost decided not to go for dessert, but when I saw the light, simple strawberry cheesecake, I could not refuse.

Same goes for Marcus. Look at him. *Look* at him. You know what I'm saying?

No, Marcus will not be finding out I'm married. Are you crazy, girl? He *doesn't* need to know. Four *years* married. I'm not trying to hurt Juan, the main man in my life since high school. Seriously. He's good enough at doing that all by himself, okay? He started that masochistic trend by not having him a real job, with real pay. He made it worse by deciding he wanted to quit his job as the director of a rehab center for Latino men to be a "stay-at-home *papi*"—because I, an executive with style and grace, made three times his salary. We agreed we didn't want a nanny raising our Carolina, because I can tell you from personal experience, that whole nanny thing is for people who care more about their dogs than their children. I always thought it would be me at home with the kid, not him. He's all, "Go ahead and stay home, but we'll have to downgrade a few things on my salary." I drive a BMW, *nena*, and I wasn't about to go back to a backfiring Neon with a dragging tailpipe. So here we are.

Pero, Mister Mom, how *joto*, no? I don't care how good he is with her. Watching Juan answer questions from *Dora the Explorer* with our daughter does nothing to make me exactly lustful for him. Dora's all, "Do you see a monkey?", and Juan's like, "Right there, Dora!", pointing his finger and shit. I can't stand that show. That Dora girl, and Diego too, they sound like they been drinking lead paint. I appreciate my husband. I do. Seriously. I just don't want him. He might as well dress his hairy ass up like a French maid, *m'ija*. That's how much he's turning me on lately.

I know kids need their parents to stay together and all that. I mean, I *thought* that was basically true, until I heard some guy on a progressive talk show saying how the Bible actually doesn't say squat about monogamous marriages, and how David in the Bible had him seven hundred wives, and how up until three hundred years ago, polygamy was the damn norm for most of the world. I didn't believe it, and went and looked it up, and saw that it was true. All these "family values" people who thump the Bible around don't even know what they're thumping, that there was lots of humping going on in that book. That made me think. Lots of things do.

God knows I don't want to hurt our daughter (even if she does act like a filthy little tomboy), but I was raised to want a real man, a man's man, and right now I can't believe my stay-at-home *flojón* fits that description. Anyway, he's too tired to seduce me anymore, right? Girls like me? We're raised to be conquered by our men, okay? That's the verb we use for seduction, *m'ija*. It's *conquistar*. To conquer. With his dishpan hands and aching back, Juan doesn't have the strength to *conquistarme*. It's sad.

Don't get all preachy with me about this, either. Listen. Tell me, *nena*, do real men make their grandmama's *sancocho* recipe from memory, cracking the corn cobs in half like a practiced *campesina*, with their favorite daytime talk show playing on the kitchen flat-screen? Do real men call *abuelita* in Bayamón to ask her the best way to mash the *tostones*, all the while licking yellow cupcake batter from the wooden spoon out of the pink Williams-Sonoma bowl I bought myself for Easter last year? Cupcakes he takes to Carolina's exclusive preschool for her snack day, while I'm slaving away at the office in a *pants* suit? *Tell* me. Don't be shy now. I'd like to know. *Do* they? *Bueno.*

Mira, I know it's retro, the way I'm thinking and so on and so forth. But I, like George Washington and *esa animal con pistola* Lolita Lebron, cannot tell a *mentirita*. Okay? It's that simple. It's like this: With the way my family goes on about it, like when my mami clicks her tongue like a chicken and says how disappointed she is I couldn't do better than some masculine moocher, I feel like he's taken my womanhood from me, like he done gone and taken my uterus out with pinking shears.

Marcus, when I invited him up at the end of the golf lesson, lifted his big mirrored aviator sunglasses and watched me walk all the way across the putting green to the clubhouse in the bright white sunshine, a smile of scandal and surprise in his wide-set, honey-colored eyes. I was all, swish-to-the-left, swish-to-the-right, and I wore me a pretty pink golf *skirt*, okay? Not wide-ass khaki shorts like all the other women with their flat butts. Those women look like they're about to wrestle a crocodile down or something, girl. Not me. I wore me a sexy little skirt, and he watched my *nalgas* like they was one of them golden pocket watches German hypnotists pendulum around when they say "You're getting sleepy." My body is mad *hypnotic*, right? Five four, a size twenty curved up in all the right places, thirty-three years old, and men still be *begging* me for a piece, okay? You know I got it like that, girl. You *know* I do. I take good care of myself, that's all.

Five minutes ago, at two in the afternoon on the dot, Marcus knocked on the door to my mountain-view suite and I, wearing only my black lace bodystocking, shiny black dome pumps, a three-strand pearl choker, and the hotel-issue robe, answered. I don't wear a body stocking because I'm embarrassed of my size or anything like that. It's just nice to have something holding me all in place. After having a baby, things jiggle wiggle a little more than a girl is used to, and this way I have the support. Anyway, it took less than twelve seconds of his nervous small talk for the thick white robe to slip off.

Whoops.

So, like, there I was, all curves and soft brown skin. I have to tell you, I have gotten sexually bold in my thirties. If you're a modern Latina, I swear it's like you spend your whole twenties working like *loca* to get over your Catholic guilt at being sexual at *all,* just so you can be a vixen in your thirties. Marcus whispered, "Whoa," and stuttered after that, wanted to ask me what I did for a living, what brought me to the resort, what city I lived in, and all that kind of nonsense, but I shut him up quick. "I don't *know* you, Marcus," I said, handing him a cherry-flavored condom as I draped myself across the big bed with its earth-tones southwestern bedspread, "and you don't know *me.* Let's keep it that way for now, *nene, 'ta bien?"*

When he heard the Spanish, he was all, "What's a fine African American woman doing talking Mexican?", and it was all I could do not to turn him around and drop-kick his ass back to the club house, okay?

"For your information, I am Puerto *Rican,"* I told him, pointing to my luscious neck with my French acrylic tips. "And the language you heard was *Spanish.* Ain't nobody in the world speak no *Mexican,* okay? Mexican? That's not a *language,* now shut your mouth before you start to look ugly to me, and let's do this thing."

I had to pull him to me after that, not because he didn't want none of mama's island papaya pie, but rather because he was all human Popsicle in shock, like he couldn't move. Men dream about women doing this kind of thing to them all the time, but there aren't many *mujeres* who can pull it off, you know what I mean? So, when it happens, they get stiff as uncooked pasta. A practiced *campesina* like my girly husband has become coulda broke that boy in half with her bare hands.

Now, here we are, ten minutes into it, and Marcus has apologized for his ignorance about Spanish. "I am sorry. That was very uncouth of me. You wouldn't know I went to Yale talking like that, I suppose," he said, and I was all "Yale?" and he said, "Yeah, I have a law degree that I don't use anymore," and that's when he told me he was a widower whose wife used to be an attorney, and that he's actually quite well-off and only does the golf pro thing because he loves golf and needs to be around people so he doesn't go crazy.

That last made me have to respect him, *m'ija*, and even though I don't want to, I am now seeing him as more than a piece of ass. Now he looks like a potential friend, which is no good. I mean, my husband Juan? Soon as that boy sees we've got enough money, he quits his job and stays home. But not Marcus. Marcus has enough to retire on and live comfortably, but he would rather work because he takes pride in work and likes it. Why didn't I marry me a man like this, girl? That's what I want to know. Why did I think Juan would shape up just because I bought him some nice shirts? Life doesn't work like that, and now it's too late. Or not. I don't know. You make your own life, and it ain't over until it's over.

I push the possibility of falling for Marcus out of my mind and focus on the task at hand, even though if I'm honest, I'd say he looks a lot better now that I know he's a man of means and substance. He's gotten over his stage fright nicely now, too, and there's a passion to him that pleases me. I was worried he'd be wooden about this, but he isn't. He's all down on his knees at the edge of the bed, his oval face all up in my coco-puff, nosing around like a pig in truffles. And if you were to bottle it, I bet it'd cost like truffles, too. I'm that good.

He's making satisfied sniffles and there's the sloppy wet sound I haven't heard in a while. It has been. *Too* long. Okay? Something happens when you have a baby, *nena*, and it has nothing to do with your body. It's all flat psychological. You and your husband? You get so tired from the whole thing, all the up and down all night with the baby, all the fights over whose turn it is to change the diapers or warm up the bottle, all the arguments about the best way to do this or that, that you just lose interest in each other like that. I didn't lose interest in sex, okay? I just lost interest in sex with *my husband*. It's been three months since Juan and I knocked the booties, and I wouldn't care if we went another three *years*, I really wouldn't.

"A little more to the front," I tell Marcus. He follows instructions and, oh my goodness, girl, gets a bullseye. Juan, though? Please, girl. The *one time* I tried to suggest he do it differently, three months ago on a night when I worked late and got home in need of loving, he sighed and looked all beleaguered, wiped his mouth on the back of his soggy gorilla hand like I made him tired, and whined, "Do I *have* to?"

What is *that* shit, *m'ija*? "Do I have to?" Please, psh. How can you get busy with a man who asks you something nonsensical like that? I was all, "If there's something you'd rather be doing, then by all means, *nene*, go do it." I closed my legs to him then, and I haven't had the urge to open them to him again. It's not entirely my fault that I've wandered down the path to Marcus. It's Juan's fault, too, for not trying harder to keep me interested.

"*Asi, papito*," I call to Marcus as I run my hands over his short, kinky hair.

"I'll assume that means, Yes, Daddy, in Puerto Rican Spanish," he mumbles.

"Yes it does," I say. He smiles up at me as he tweaks my nipple with one hand, and I feel like I'm on fire.

I read one time that some marriages *need* affairs, because they reignite the flames that went out between husband and wife. Honestly? I love my husband because he's the only fool who completely understands where I come from. I don't have to explain anything about being a Puerto Rican New Englander to him, because he's one, too. I'm hoping that's what happens here, okay? That I can take these flames that this golf pro man has fired up in me and keep them lit up like the Olympic torch until I get home.

"I want to be inside you," he mumbles, twisting out of his polo shirt, coming up toward me all sculpted muscle. He's removing the golf-pro shorts, and mama is pleased to see his club's nothing less than a seven-iron.

"What a boy wants, a boy gets." I arrange myself for easy access. "Gimme that putter, baby. Sink it in the hole."

"More like a driver, but who's going to quibble over semantics at a moment like this?" he asks as he slides in with a groan, and tells me how warm and soft it is. Like I didn't *know*. I'm pure melted butter, *nena*. Okay? He begins to rock me, gently, with a sweet smile on his face. I don't mean to, but I start to make some little noises. Before I know it, my eyes have rolled back in my head, and I've begun to suck my own damn finger. For Catholic girls, it's easier to be kinky with a man we don't know.

Don't think less of me, okay? I have never been a one-man woman any more than my daddy was a one-woman man. It's in my genes. I didn't sleep around, exactly. But you know how I did. I had multiple possibilities to get me through my day. My girlfriends can confirm this for you when they get here. Just ask them, any of them. All my adult life, until I got married, I juggled men, at least two at a time, as a form of insurance. If one left me, the way my daddy did, or didn't pay enough attention to me, the way my daddy did, or got his ass shot dead by hoodlums, like my brother did, there was always the other one to step in. I been like that since high school, when I first started dating Juan and realized my love for him was so big it might crush me if he ever lost interest. I kept them all at a distance after understanding that. None of them have been close to my heart except him, and now he's breaking it with his Santa Madre act. I am a sound investor—never put in more than you can afford to lose. The safest bets involve a diversified portfolio. I'm all about biology and financial planning.

The pumping gets faster. Marcus goes to work, okay? Something about athletes. They know their bodies. *Ay, m'ija.* Why does *chingando* have to feel so good? Wouldn't the world's problems be solved if sex felt more like plunging up a clogged toilet? You don't like to think God screwed up, but with the whole sex-drive thing, He just might have. Without pleasurable sex, there'd be no risk of overpopulation, no AIDS, no unwanted pregnancies, and no cheating wives.

"Harder, baby," I tell Marcus as I press my eyes closed and flex my calf muscles. I could get used to this man. Yes, I could. If I weren't married, I mean. Which I am. I am married. Have to remember. That. Oh. God. "I'm almost there."

He says nothing, and, like the husband I wish I had married instead of the one I got, does exactly what I ordered.

When we finish, he leans up on his elbow, all sweet-looking, kisses me gently on the lips, and says, with a tear in his eye, "It has been a long time since I did that, Usnavys Rivera."

"Pssh. You're lying."

"No, no, I'm not lying." He closes his eyes, flops onto his back with a satisfied, melancholy smile, mouthing numbers as he counts on his fingers. His eyes open and he regards me seriously. "Three years. It has been three years since I made love to a woman."

"What? Why? You scared of girls, Marcus?"

The tears brim a little more, and one of them traces a line down his cheek. He wipes it away with a strong, solid hand. I'm sure doesn't do dishes all day. "No, I'm not scared of girls. Three years ago. That's when my wife died. I haven't met anyone who interested me, and, frankly, did not think I ever would. Until now."

I balk. "I'm the first? Since your wife died?"

Marcus nods, and smiles with a hint of sadness that is quickly replaced by something that looks like love. "You remind me of her. You two. You look alike. She was a fire-cracker, just like you."

"A firecracker," I say. I don't know what else to tell him. I remind the man of his dead wife, and he loved her, and I know he's transferring that onto me and I don't deserve it, but still. Transfers can feel real, *m'ija*. They can. You shouldn't be jealous of a dead woman, but for some reason, I am. I imagine the house they lived in, the wine they shared on the terrace, the elegance of her husband a sharp contrast to the ordinariness of mine.

"So, I hope this won't be the last time we see one another," he says. "I'd love to get a number for you in Boston. I travel out that way quite a bit. And now that I've met you, I have more reason to go more often."

I should know better, girl, I should. I realize that. This is the part where a nice person would tell the truth about her husband and child. Denial is a wonderful thing though, when you need it. So it is that I get up and walk to the desk, and I write my cell number down on the little hotel pad of paper. I rip off the sheet, hand it to him, wondering how on earth I'm going to keep Juan from finding this shit out. I'm going to have to start policing my phone like a guard. I'm going to have to sneak and lie my ass off. What is wrong with me, *m'ija*? I shouldn't have opened this door, but what the hell else am I supposed to do?

The man, Marcus, this beautiful man who pleased me, is crying, and he plays golf, and I remind him of a woman he loved. And you know what that all means, don't you? It *means* that even with my size and attitude and my current moral relativism, even with my head all screwed up like this and my heart flying in a thousand different directions, he just might be able to love me the way I have deserved to be loved all my life.